PRAISE FOR
KEITH R.A. DeCANDIDO

"If the *Trek* franchise has a future, it lies with people like Keith DeCandido—writers who can balance continuity and innovation, capturing our imagination with something new while remaining firmly rooted in the shared mythology we've grown up with."

—*TV Zone*

"DeCandido is a writer of some skill, breathing life into characters and a culture when it would be all too easy to rely on the existing mythos created by the television shows. He doesn't just duplicate it; he gives it depth."

—*SFReader.com*

"DeCandido captures the world and characters of the show perfectly, giving fans much to enjoy here."

—*Booklist*

"DeCandido writes these characters exactly as they appear on the screen. DeCandido's Archer IS Scott Bakula's Archer. DeCandido's Spock IS Leonard Nimoy's Spock, etc. . . . DeCandido is like the second coming of Peter David. He knows the characters so well and expands them so perfectly that it will be a shame if he never writes for on-screen *Trek*."

—*Cinescape*

"Many fans wonder about the unfinished portions of the tapestry that is the *Star Trek* universe. There are thousands of unanswered questions. Author and editor Keith R.A. DeCandido obviously loves to play in that big sandbox. He is entirely at home with both the setting and the characters. His writing exhibits an innate curiosity about that universe and the creativity to recognize the stories just waiting to be told within it."

—*TrekNation.com*

W9-COV-706

STAR TREK®

ARTICLES
of the
FEDERATION

Keith R.A. DeCandido

Based on *Star Trek* and *Star Trek: The Next Generation*®
created by Gene Roddenberry,
Star Trek: Deep Space Nine®
created by Rick Berman & Michael Piller,
Star Trek: Voyager®
created by Rick Berman & Michael Piller & Jeri Taylor,
and *Star Trek*®: *Enterprise*™
created by Rick Berman & Brannon Braga

POCKET BOOKS
New York   London   Toronto   Sydney   Outpost 22

An *Original* Publication of POCKET BOOKS

POCKET BOOKS, a division of Simon & Schuster, Inc.
1230 Avenue of the Americas, New York, NY 10020

This book is a work of fiction. Names, characters, places and incidents are products of the author's imagination or are used fictitiously. Any resemblance to actual events or locales or persons, living or dead, is entirely coincidental.

ISBN: 1-4165-0015-4

First Pocket Books paperback edition June 2005

10 9 8 7 6 5 4 3 2 1

POCKET and colophon are registered trademarks of Simon & Schuster, Inc.

Cover art by Mark Gerber, cover design by John Vairo, Jr.

Manufactured in the United States of America

For information regarding special discounts for bulk purchases, please contact Simon & Schuster Special Sales at 1-800-456-6798 or business@simonandschuster.com.

For George, John, Thomas, James, James, John, Andrew, Martin, William, John, James, Zachary, Millard, Franklin, James, Abraham, Andrew, Ulysses, Rutherford, James, Chester, Grover, Benjamin, William, Theodore, William, Woodrow, Warren, Calvin, Herbert, Franklin, Harry, Dwight, John, Lyndon, Richard, Gerald, Jimmy, Ronald, George, Bill, and George, for almost two hundred and thirty years of service.

HISTORIAN'S NOTE

This novel commences shortly after the events of the feature film *Star Trek Nemesis,* as well as the novels *A Time for War, a Time for Peace* by Keith R.A. DeCandido, *Death in Winter* by Michael Jan Friedman, and *Titan: Taking Wing* by Michael A. Martin & Andy Mangels.

JANUARY 2380

"It sure is hell to be president."
—Harry S Truman

CHAPTER ONE

ELE'ER SAT IMPATIENTLY on her stool in the learning room. Mother was late, of course—she always was late for their learning sessions, which meant they ended later, which meant that Ele'er was always late for sky-singing. Ele'er hated being late for sky-singing because it meant she couldn't go through the warm-ups, and when she couldn't go through the warm-ups, she sang poorly, and the songleader gave her that disapproving look. Ele'er would explain that Mother had been late with her lesson and that it had been important, but the songleader never cared.

Mother finally transported into the learning room in a shimmer of light. Ele'er knew she'd used a transporter because she was running late.

"I apologize for my tardiness," Mother said, pulling a padd out of a pocket in her cloak and sitting on the larger stool that faced Ele'er's. While they were both seated, Mother remained on a higher plane by sitting on her taller stool, reinforcing her position as both parent and teacher. Ele'er started to remind her that she'd be late for sky-singing, but Mother didn't give her the chance. "Today's lesson will involve the politics of the Federation."

Ele'er felt the folds of her skin tighten. She *hated* when the lesson involved politics.

"We are going to observe the Federation News Service,

because they have a segment called *Illuminating the City of Light.*"

"That's a stupid name," Ele'er muttered.

"What was that?" Mother asked tersely.

Sighing, Ele'er enunciated the words this time. "It's a stupid name."

"It is not at all a stupid name, Ele'er." Mother folded her hands on her lap, which meant she was going to start quizzing her daughter. "What is the seat of the Federation government?"

Ele'er sighed. "Earth."

"More specifically, please."

"A city called London."

"Wrong, Ele'er." Mother made a note on her padd that Ele'er assumed was a demerit. "It is in Paris, in a building known as the Palais de la Concorde."

Though Ele'er was tempted to point out to Mother that she had no need to know the differences among the many cities of a planet that (its role as the seat of the Federation government notwithstanding) was light-years away from Bre'el IV in terms of both distance and relevance, she knew that it would probably just result in another demerit.

"What is the name of the native population of Earth?"

"Human." That was an easy one.

"And what is the nickname that humans have for Paris?"

Ele'er felt her skin folds tighten again. "I don't know."

"The City of Light."

"Do the other cities on Earth not have light?"

Mother made another note on her padd; Ele'er feared another demerit. "Of course they do, don't be absurd, Ele'er. Now then—"

This time, Ele'er saw where Mother was going with her

questioning. "This FNS segment discusses the goings-on in the Federation government in Paris?"

"That is correct."

"So the presentation's purpose is to provide insight into what happens in the City of Light—which is why it has that name."

At that, Mother put her fists to her chest, with wrists crossed—a gesture of respect and gratitude. "Very good, Ele'er." She made some more notes on her padd. "Now, then, we will watch."

Mother removed a control from her cloak and pressed a button on it. The emitters located in the walls lit up, and five figures seated at a desk appeared in the middle of the learning room. One of them was a Bre'ella like her—Ele'er thought he looked familiar, but she couldn't place his face, though his cloak's red color indicated a high office.

The images were frozen. Mother asked, "Can you identify the species and sexes of the people sitting with Councillor Nitram?"

Councillor Nitram, of course, Ele'er chastised herself. She was grateful that Mother's phrasing of the question— assuming that Ele'er knew Bre'el's representative on the Federation Council—had saved her the embarrassment of admitting that she hadn't recognized him.

Ele'er peered at the images. Such identification quizzes usually were the purview of biology lessons, not political ones, but it was characteristic of Mother to throw in queries from other disciplines to keep Ele'er on her toes.

The one on the far right with the dark skin looked like she was a native of Earth, so Ele'er pointed at her and said, "Human female."

"Correct." Mother made a note on her padd.

Next to the human was Nitram, and next to him was a female with spots encircling her face just under her hairline. Ele'er knew that there were two species with that characteristic, but she couldn't remember either of them. Taking a wild guess, she said, "Betazoid female?"

"No. That is a Kriosian female, though I would have credited you if you had said Trill, since you have never seen this segment and are not aware that its host is from Krios. The next one?"

This was a person with blue skin and no hair. She remembered that Andorians had blue skin. "Andorian *chan.*"

Mother's lips pursed for the first time since she arrived, which meant her displeasure was even worse. She made several notes on the padd, and Ele'er feared she was setting a record for demerits this lesson. "No, that is a Bolian male. Andorians have antennae."

And I was so proud of remembering the Andorian genders. Ele'er tried not to sigh.

"The final one?"

This last one she knew: "An Efrosian male."

"Very good. I will now play the recording of the show, and you will watch it. When it is over, I will quiz you on its contents. If you have a question at any point, I will pause the recording and you may ask."

Ele'er stared intently at the hologram.

The Kriosian woman spoke when Mother started the playback. "Good evening. This is *Illuminating the City of Light,* I'm your host, Velisa. It has been two months since Federation President Nan Bacco took the oath of office, after winning a close election against Ktarian Special Emissary Fel Pagro. Tonight on *ICL,* we'll be examining President Bacco's first eight weeks in office. Is she taking the Federation in a new direction after seven years of Min

Zife? Is she simply treading water? Or is she floundering on the galactic stage?"

Velisa started introducing the panel, starting with the Efrosian and going down the line.

"With me tonight to discuss these issues are Ra-Yalix, a foreign policy advisor for Presidents Amitra and Jaresh-Inyo; Sovan, the chief Earth correspondent for *Bolarus and You;* Federation Councillor Nitram of Bre'el IV; and retired Starfleet Admiral Taela Shanthi. Welcome, all of you."

Each of the panelists made some kind of acknowledgment. Shanthi bobbed her head once, Sovan muttered something Ele'er couldn't make out, and Ra-Yalix smiled. Nitram, naturally, brought his fists to his chests, as was proper.

"Admiral Shanthi, how do you feel Bacco is handling the Romulan crisis?"

The human woman folded her arms on the desk in front of her. "I believe that the solution that was brokered by Captain Riker of the *U.S.S. Titan* was one that will eventually lead to stability in the region."

"And I think you're out of your mind," the Bolian said.

"Sovan—" Velisa started.

"No, Velisa, this is ridiculous. The Romulan Empire's a disaster area. Most of the senate was assassinated by a *Reman,* who later got blown up by Starfleet, and now you've got fifty factions vying for power, and what's Starfleet's brilliant idea? Bring the *Klingons* in."

Ra-Yalix spoke up then. "The Remans wouldn't accept being a Federation protectorate, Sovan. What else were they supposed to do? The Remans engineered a coup d'état on a scale unseen in recent history. With Shinzon and most of his inner circle dead, they don't have the resources to govern themselves, but they were hardly about to go back to being slaves."

"I'll grant you that," Sovan said, "but to give them protectorate status under the Klingons?"

Shanthi scowled. "The Klingons will do what they promise. They will ensure that the Remans are given the opportunity to determine their own fate. They will also focus the warring factions among the Romulans."

Sovan made a snorting noise. "Romulans and Klingons being angry at each other has *always* been a recipe for disaster, not peace."

"I have a question," Ele'er said. Mother stopped the playback. "Who are the Remans?"

Mother made a note on her padd. "Where is the seat of the Romulan Empire?"

"Romulus."

"What is Romulus's sister planet?"

Ele'er's skin folds tightened. "I did not know it had one."

"It does. It's called Remus, and on that planet live a mutated offshoot of the Romulans, who serve as slave labor. Or, rather, they did until a Reman named Shinzon engineered the elimination of the praetor and the ruling senate. Then he was killed, and that left a power vacuum in the empire."

"I understand." Now what everyone was saying made more sense to Ele'er. If the government fell—if, in fact, *two* governments fell in succession—that would leave the Romulan Star Empire in chaos.

Mother resumed the playback.

"We're getting off the subject a bit," Velisa said.

"Not really," Sovan said, "because my problem isn't with the solution that Starfleet came up with, it's that Bacco agreed to it without any hesitation or consultation."

Shanthi shook her head. "That is incorrect. Ambassador Spock spoke before the council in order to—"

Sovan laughed. "Ambassador Spock? First of all, Spock

hasn't been a proper ambassador for ten years. He's been living on Romulus on an unsanctioned mission—"

"Actually, the mission *was* sanctioned," Ra-Yalix said. "The council endorsed Spock's endeavor to achieve unification between the Romulans and Vulcans."

"And never mind the fact that Vulcan is *part* of the Federation." Sovan shook his head. "That doesn't make him the right person to consult on this solution, if you ask me. Plus, what about the fiasco with Tamok?"

Councillor Nitram said, "Ambassador T'Kala was responsible for deceiving the president and the council into believing that Archpriest Tamok was coming to the Federation for an audience with us."

"Yes," Sovan said, "and a consultation with an actual Romulan spiritual leader might've been a bit more useful than one with a rogue ambassador with an agenda."

"Sovan—" Ra-Yalix began, but the Bolian would not stop talking. Ele'er found him to be very rude.

"Instead of listening to other viewpoints, she just trusted Spock and some captain. Bacco is letting Starfleet do all her work for her."

Before anyone could respond to that, Velisa said, "One element of government that Starfleet has no jurisdiction over is that of appointments to the various sub-councils. Councillor Melnis of Benzar will be retiring at the end of the month, which opens up his seat on the judiciary council. Councillor Nitram, whom do you think President Bacco will appoint to that seat?"

Nitram paused before speaking. "I would not presume to speak for the president."

Ele'er thought that was a stupid thing to say. Mother, however, was nodding in approval. *He's being asked his opinion,* Ele'er thought. *Why will he not give it?*

Velisa tried asking a different question. "Do you believe that Councillor Melnis's replacement will simply take the seat?"

Shaking his head, Nitram said, "No. Councillor-Elect Linzner does not have sufficient experience in jurisprudence to hold that seat. If he is selected by President Bacco, he will not be ratified by the council. However, I do not believe that President Bacco will do so. But I cannot say whom she *will* choose."

Sovan smiled. "It'll be Artrin. He's been making his feelings known on that subject for years. Every time the judiciary council hands down a decision, Artrin goes out of his way to comment on it. He had a distinguished career as a magistrate on Triex for ninety years before he was elected councillor."

"I agree with Sovan." Ele'er was surprised to hear those words from Ra-Yalix's mouth after their argument over the Romulan discussion. "The only reason why Artrin wasn't put on judiciary in the first place was because a seat wasn't available when he became a councillor six years ago. Melnis's retirement changes that."

"There are other qualified candidates," Nitram said. "Councillor Eleana has the necessary expertise."

"I actually agree," Sovan said, "but I don't think Bacco will have the courage to make so controversial a choice. Eleana has taken any number of unpopular stands regarding criminal rehabilitation, facilities maintenance, and security protocols. She voted against blood screenings every time it came up prior to the Dominion War. She held minority opinions on most matters before the council, and I just don't see Bacco putting her in so strong a position as one on judiciary—in fact, I don't see the council approving her even if Bacco *does* put her up. Artrin's record is more middle-of-the-road, and he has the public profile. The council won't have any problem with him. Bacco can't afford a difficult appointment. She's going to have a hard enough time."

Velisa stared at the Bolian. "Why do you say that?"

"Bacco was elected in a very swift campaign with very little time for the voters to get a chance to know her, unless they were already familiar with her record as governor of Cestus III—and even then, it's not much. Zife's second term saw one problem after another, from the collapse of the Trill government, to the gateways and Genesis disasters, to the brief war with the Selelvians and the Tholians, to the problems with the Ontailians, to Tezwa—culminating in the first presidential resignation in the Federation's history."

Shanthi spoke for the first time in a while. "While I agree that President Bacco has large shoes to fill, I also believe that she will adequately fill them. I am familiar with her record on Cestus III. She was faced with an immigration crisis when they took in refugees from the Cardassian Demilitarized Zone, and she also weathered a Gorn attack on the planet during the war."

"I don't disagree that she made a good planetary governor, under some unique circumstances, but my point is that she's got to work with the council. Both Zife and Jaresh-Inyo were councillors who were elected president. Amitra was a cabinet member for three presidents before getting elected herself, and all the presidents she served under worked in the Palais in some form or other before being elected. Bacco's the first outsider in a long time to actually win an election."

Ra-Yalix laughed. "It doesn't hurt that nobody from the Palais ran in this election. The only candidates were a Starfleet admiral, a special emissary, and a governor."

"Which is," Velisa added, "the first time that no member of the Federation Council participated in a presidential election in a hundred and fifty years. But then, this was a unique election."

"I have another question," Ele'er said. Again, Mother paused the playback. "Who did you vote for, Mother?"

Mother did not answer for several seconds. Then, finally, she said, "It does not matter."

Ele'er hid a smile. *That means she voted for Pagro.* Ele'er hadn't paid much attention to the election, since she was not old enough to vote, but she did know that the last president resigned. Ele'er wasn't entirely sure why. She supposed she could ask, but she decided she wanted to see more of the conversation first.

Velisa continued when Mother restarted the playback. "One thing that is not unique is the current situation between the Deltans and the Carreon. Ra-Yalix, how do you think President Bacco should be handling the situation?"

"While I confess to admiring the president's stated desire to see the parties work out their differences themselves, I'm afraid that any optimism in this regard is probably . . . shall we say . . . unwarranted."

Nitram asked, "What is wrong with allowing Delta and Carrea to settle their differences internally?"

The Efrosian chuckled. "Because it's unlikely that this time will be different from any other. The animosity between Delta and Carrea dates back to long before Delta joined the Federation—the two nations tried to colonize the same worlds when they first went out into space. The Carreon have been careful to limit their aggression since Delta became part of the Federation, but they've never been willing to give in."

Shanthi added, "I was stationed near Delta IV when the

Dominion attacked it. It was that attack that resulted in the poisoning of Delta's water table, which in turn led to the breakdown of their water reclamation system, which was not designed to deal with the impurities that the Jem'Hadar introduced with their attacks. Although they were able to purify the water for a while, those measures broke down when the Dominion poison adapted. Other worlds have supplied water as a stopgap, but sooner or later, Delta must have use of its own water."

"The point is," Ra-Yalix said, "that the president is going to have to step in soon, because these two planets aren't going to talk to each other except to make threats."

Ele'er hated to admit it to herself, but she found the discussion fascinating. In fact, the only thing she didn't like was Councillor Nitram's near-total silence. She felt that the representative of her world to the Federation Council should be more willing to speak. *Maybe he shouldn't be obnoxious the way that reporter is, but still . . .*

Velisa looked around at the panel. "So, to conclude, how do you think President Bacco is doing in her first two months?"

Ra-Yalix said, "I think she's proceeding with caution for the time being, which is prudent. Once she gets the lay of the land, as it were, she'll be fine."

Sovan shook his head. "Caution is the worst approach she can take. The people need a leader who can fill the vacuum left by Zife, and move the Federation past the Dominion War and its aftermath. She won't do that by treading lightly."

Nitram simply said, "I look forward to continuing to cooperate with President Bacco on an agenda that will do as Mr. Sovan says—move the Federation forward."

Shanthi leaned back in her chair. "I think she has done a fine job and will continue to do so."

"Well, thank you Sovan, Ra-Yalix, Councillor Nitram, and Admiral Shanthi. Good night, everyone."

Mother turned the viewer off and looked at her daughter. "Do you have any questions?"

Ele'er smiled. "Yes—can we watch this again the next time it is on?"

◆

CHAPTER TWO

◆   ◆

NANIETTA BACCO, newly elected president of the United Federation of Planets, wondered what quirk of fate had led to her being at once a person who despised meetings with a fiery passion, yet who also wanted more than anything else to go into the world of politics—a profession that was approximately ninety percent meetings.

She sat behind the large desk in the presidential office in the Palais de la Concorde in Paris on Earth. The desk was made out of a hard, lightly patterned material known as *salish,* native to Atrea, which had been brought to the Palais by President Amitra and left behind when she'd declined to run for a second term. Her successors, Jaresh-Inyo and Min Zife, had both used different desks, but Nan had always been fond of the feel of *salish*—it had the sturdiness of metal and the romance of wood—and so she had

had that desk put in when she'd taken office. The desk had a rotating holographic image of her daughter, Annabella, as a girl, of Annabella as an adult with her husband and children, of just the children, and of Nan's own parents on their wedding day on Cestus III a hundred years ago.

Behind her—in fact, all around her—was a panoramic view of Paris. The office was a half-circle, with the entire curved part of the wall taken up with a window that showed the River Seine, the Tour Eiffel, the Bâtiment Vingt-Troisième Siècle, and of course, the Champs Elysées, which ran under the cylindrical fifteen-story structure that housed the nexus of the Federation government.

"The Deltan ambassador keeps insisting that they can handle it, and Eleana's backing her play. They don't want interference."

Seated on either the large sofa parallel to her desk or the several chairs that formed lines perpendicular to both ends of that sofa were several of Nan's policy advisors, as well as Esperanza Piñiero, her chief of staff. The comment had been made by Ashanté Phiri, one of Esperanza's four deputies. All four deputies were in this meeting, along with Ashanté's husband, Fred MacDougan, the head speechwriter; the secretary of the exterior, a taciturn Rigelian named Safranski; and Admiral William Ross, who served as Starfleet liaison to the president.

Esperanza said, "They've also been going at it for a month, and they haven't gotten anywhere. I think we need to bring them here."

Shrugging, Ashanté said, "Then they'll just yell at each other here."

Z4 Blue, who had, after a great deal of wheedling and convincing by Esperanza, given up a forest quadrant governorship on Nasat to become a deputy COS, spoke from his specially modified chair. "There's a big difference between arguing on some moon in the Delta system and arguing in the Palais. Here they're under the gaze of the council and the president."

"And the press." Another deputy, a hyperactive Zakdorn woman named Myk Bunkrep, leaned forward in her chair, so much that Nan feared she would fall out of it. "I can talk to Jorel," she said, referring to the press liaison for both the president and the council, Kant Jorel, "get him to have some reporters 'accidentally' stumble in on their meeting, or ambush them as they come out of the transporter room."

Ashanté rolled her dark eyes to the ceiling. "Yes, that *guarantees* that they'll be friendly and open to a negotiation."

"They're already disinclined to talk." Myk blew out a breath through her mouth, wedged as it was between the thick folds of cheek skin that was peculiar to Zakdorns. "Why not take advantage?"

"Hold on a moment." Xeldara Trask tugged on one of her oversized earlobes, as she always did before she said something, a habit of the Tiburonian's that Nan found irritating. "Why are we even having this discussion?"

Nan smiled. "I've been asking myself that question for the last five minutes."

Most of those present chuckled—Myk being the exception, as she never quite grasped humor, her one character flaw, as far as Nan was concerned—and then Xeldara said, "I'm serious, Madam President, why don't the Deltans just use another water reclamation system? I can't imagine that the Carreon's is the only one available."

"It's a time factor," Esperanza said. "Traditional systems will work eventually, but their water will be irreversibly contaminated by that time. They've been staving it off, but—"

mains along the Romulan border, the *Enterprise* is investigating reports of Breen incursion in Sector 204-E, and the *Hood*'s found some ancient machinery on Gorak IX."

"What kind of machinery?" Esperanza asked.

"Captain DeSoto's report wasn't specific."

"Well, find out—it's been my experience that ancient machinery tends to activate and turn everyone on your ship into newts if you're not careful."

Nan tapped her fingers on the *salish* desk: "I'm a lot less concerned about a ship full of newts than I am about the Borg."

"The indications are remains, ma'am," Ross said in what the admiral probably thought was a reassuring voice. Then he smiled. "We've found remains like that in several other places—here in the Alpha Quadrant, in the Gamma Quadrant by the *Defiant*, and by *Voyager* when they were in the Delta Quadrant. I don't think it poses an imminent threat."

Nan found herself wholly not reassured by Ross's words. "Yeah, well, keep an eye on it anyhow, just for my peace of mind. The Borg have attacked this solar system twice already, and I don't think the third time will be the charm."

"Yes, ma'am."

"Anything else?"

"Council appointments," Esperanza said.

Nan nodded. "All right. Admiral, Safranski, thank you both. I'll expect to be hearing from both of you by the end of the day."

Ross and Safranski both rose from their chairs and said, "Thank you, Madam President." As they departed through the leftmost of the three doors into the office, which took them to the turbolift area, their footfalls barely registered on the dark green carpet Nan had installed in place of the white carpet that Zife had favored. The other two doors led to the waiting room—which was how people generally came in—and to Nan's private study, respectively.

"Right." Ashanté pulled a padd out of her pocket as soon as the door shut behind Ross and Safranski. "We've got openings on judiciary, government oversight, and interplanetary commerce, and that, in turn, may create more openings."

Esperanza asked, "What've you guys come up with?" Nan knew that Esperanza had assigned Z4 and Ashanté to make a list of recommendations for all three seats among the current crop of councillors.

"Judiciary's Artrin," Z4 said.

"Definitely," Ashanté added. "He'll be ratified in a walk."

"For government oversight, we were thinking of either Sanaht, Jix, or Quintor."

Nan stroked her chin. Those three represented Janus VI, Trill, and Antede III. Sanaht, a Horta, had served in the council for over seventy-five years but had always avoided high-profile sub-councils. The others were comparative newcomers, having joined the council three and seven years earlier, respectively.

Shaking her head, Esperanza said, "Not Jix."

"Why not?" Z4 asked.

"Because she's only been in the council for three years, and the reason she got appointed is because the last one resigned during that parasite mess. I don't think that's the right person to put on government oversight. I don't think Sanaht is, either."

"I disagree," Ashanté said. "Sanaht's perfect. Everyone on the council respects him."

Xeldara smiled. "That's because they're afraid he's going to eat their chairs."

Returning the smile, Ashanté said, "The point is, he'll be ratified easily."

"Easy appointments would be nice," Esperanza said, "but we need a hawk. Quintor's the right one for the job."

Ashanté's smile fell. "Esperanza, we can't afford a floor fight over appointments. Quintor's spent the last seven years pissing off everyone else in the council chamber. Besides, it's not like it's a major sub-council, it's government oversight. What do we need a hawk there for?"

Nan spoke before Esperanza could reply. "Because the last president resigned."

The office grew quiet. Nan exchanged a glance with Esperanza. Unlike everyone else in the room, the two of them knew the real reasons why Min Zife, his chief of staff, and one of his cabinet members resigned, and it had nothing to do with the realities of managing the Federation in the wake of war, as his resignation speech had oh-so-nobly assured. They had secretly armed Tezwa, an independent world on the Klingon border, putting those weapons in the hands of a lunatic prime minister who'd used them on a Klingon task force and a Starfleet vessel. Zife had known of the weapons but hadn't warned the Klingons or his own people about them, and then tried to cover up the crime before he'd been discovered by Starfleet. If the real reasons had gotten out, government oversight would have roasted him for lunch—right before the Klingons declared their right of vengeance and made war on a longtime ally who'd lied to them and whose depraved indifference had led to the dishonorable deaths of thousands of warriors.

"What about interplanetary commerce?" Esperanza asked, signaling that the discussion on government oversight had ended.

"That's easy," Ashanté said. "We promised that seat to

Beltane during the campaign in exchange for her support. That's not the problem."

"Hang on," Xeldara said, tugging her ear. "Is she qualified?"

Z4 made a tinkling noise. "Overqualified. She was the leader among Elaysians for expanding the mandate of the trade agreements on Gemworld. Frankly, she should've been on commerce years ago."

Ashanté sighed. "But that opens up a seat on technology. Z4's about to tell you it should be C29 Green—"

Z4's antennae twirled outward. "It *should* be C29."

Rolling her eyes, Ashanté said, "He can't even operate a padd without three aides giving him a tutorial, and you want to put him on technology?"

"He oversaw half a dozen technology initiatives on Nasat. He's right for the job."

Esperanza asked Ashanté, "Who do you prefer?"

"Almost anybody else."

A warning in her tone, Esperanza started, "Ashanté—"

"Severn-Anyar, Govrin, Gelemingar, or Nitram."

Nan knew that the councillors for Grazer, Pandril, Gnala, and Bre'el IV were all qualified, but she was surprised at one name missing. "What about Jix? We're not giving her judiciary. Why not put her on technology?"

"She's not as qualified as C29," Z4 said.

"*Aside* from C29, all the choices are good ones, ma'am, including Jix," Ashanté said, with a glower at Z4.

Running a hand through her paper-white hair, Nan said, "Give Sivak full reports on all six of them—I'll make a decision by the end of the week."

Fred said, "Ma'am, I don't think we should wait that long. I think we need to have Jorel announcing *all* your appointments in the next day or two, and you should be available to answer press queries soon after that."

Myk leaned forward. "Besides, with Tantalus coming up for review again, we need judiciary—"

Nan held up a hand. She had a shuttle trip to Luna this evening, so she could look over the recommendations then. "Fine, fine, I'll decide by the time I get back from the moon tonight—make sure Sivak gets 'em before the shuttle takes off. Anything else?"

Xeldara tugged on her ear again. "I think we need to talk about the travel office again."

Nan rolled her eyes.

Esperanza quickly said, "I think we've covered that."

"I don't think we have, Esperanza." Xeldara leaned forward. "Jorel told the entire press room that the president was meeting with Archpriest Tamok. Ambassador T'Kala assured us up, down, backwards, and sideways that she'd arranged with the council travel office and with what was left of her government to get Tamok here. And what happened? He never left Romulus—he didn't even plan to come to Federation space to meet. It made us look like idiots when we hadn't been in office for five minutes. There need to be some kind of consequences."

Nan let out a long breath. "We've suffered the consequences. The press laughed at us, T'Kala looked like a devious schemer out to make the Federation look bad—which puts her in company with every other Romulan politician I'm aware of—and we apologized."

"The people in the travel office—" Xeldara started, but Nan refused to let her repeat herself. Xeldara had been bringing this up in every meeting since it happened, and it was wearing on Nan's last remaining nerve ending.

"I'm not about to fire people for honest mistakes. This wasn't the fault of anyone in the travel office, and I'm not about to make scapegoats out of them. We screwed up, we said we screwed up, and even if we didn't, lots of other people were standing in line to tell us we did. We try to make some kind of restitution now, it'll look petty. Given a choice between looking stupid for trying to do something right and looking nasty for doing something wrong, I'll go with option number one. What else?"

"Ma'am, I think—"

The nerve ending finally snapped. Nan glowered at the Tiburonian. "I *know* what you think, Xeldara, I've been listening to what you think for the last month. Say it again, and you can explain it to the press when you announce your resignation as deputy COS."

Esperanza stood up. "I think we're done."

"Damn right," Nan muttered.

Fred, Ashanté, Z4, and Myk rose from their chairs. After a moment, Xeldara did, too. Each of them said, "Thank you, Madam President."

"Xeldara," Esperanza said, "wait in my office, all right? We need to go over some things."

She nodded. "Sure."

When they were all gone, Nan fixed Esperanza with a cheeky grin. "Can I assume the 'things' you're going to go over are when to shut the hell up in a meeting with the president?"

"Don't worry about it."

Nan laughed. "I'll take that as a yes." She got up from her chair and looked out at the vista of Paris. "Look at that."

Esperanza moved to stand next to her. "Look at what?"

"That." Nan pointed at the Champs Elysées. "You know, until the seventeenth century, it was just fields. Then

Marie de Medici made a tree-lined path. It was named after the Elysian Fields in Greek mythology, which was where good people went after they died. By the eighteenth century, that path was a fashionable avenue—Marie Antoinette used to stroll it with her friends all the time."

Esperanza smiled. "Was that before or after she ate all the cake and got her head cut off?"

"Not sure, but I'm guessing before."

"Right, because she wasn't doing much walking after the decapitation."

"The point is—"

"There's a point?" Esperanza grinned. "Trying something new, are we, ma'am?"

"Hush, you. The point is that the Champs Elysées has remained Paris's main thoroughfare for seven hundred years. The Louvre, the Hôtel de Ville, the Arc de Triomphe, the Bâtiment Vingt-Troisième Siècle, the Place de Cochrane, they're all here. The Tour de France has been run here for centuries, every parade in Paris comes down here, and it's on this very spot that the Traité d'Unification was signed by all the governments on this planet two hundred and fifty years ago."

Esperanza was still grinning. "Ma'am, I could've sworn you mentioned a *point.*"

"Try a little patience, Esperanza, they keep telling me it's a virtue."

"We're politicians, ma'am—both patience and virtue tend to get in the way of the work."

Nan chuckled. "The *point* is—it's all because some rich woman who lived in a monarchy decided she wanted a place to walk. From that came this."

"It's my hope, ma'am, that we'll do a little better than the Medicis. Or Marie Antoinette."

"We can learn a lot from Marie Antoinette. For one thing, I'm coming around to the idea of bringing beheadings back. Did you know that during the French Revolution almost three thousand people were executed via guillotine on the very spot this building was constructed on? You think if we put Artrin on judiciary, he'll support that?"

"Probably not, ma'am."

"Too bad—still, it'd make the meetings go faster."

"No doubt, ma'am. Is there anything else?"

Nan stared at her chief of staff. Though she saw a woman in her early fifties with olive skin and raven hair tied back in a severe ponytail, Nan couldn't help but see her as an infant, born to Nan's two best friends back on Cestus III, Victor and Nereida Piñiero. Their daughter, named with the Spanish word meaning "hope," had gone to Starfleet Academy, had had a distinguished career until the end of the Dominion War, then had resigned her commission and returned home. While there, she'd convinced Nan—who had been planetary governor for seven years and had had no ambition to be anything more than that—to run for president. That opportunity had come sooner than expected with Zife's resignation, and Nan knew that she wouldn't have stood a chance of even being seriously considered as a candidate, much less a winner, without Esperanza.

"Nah, that'll do for now. Oh, I want Jorel to tell the press what we're doing with Delta and Carrea. In fact, have him do it before we tell the ambassadors."

"They'll be pissed that we didn't talk to them first."

Nan shrugged. "They're already pissed. Besides, I've found that if you eliminate the talking-to-them-first stage, the whole thing goes a lot faster."

"Which explains some of your loopier decisions back on Cestus."

Grinning, Nan said, "Yeah."

"Thank you, Madam President."

Esperanza left, and Nan hit the intercom that put her in touch with Sivak. The elderly Vulcan—he was over two hundred—had organized Nan's affairs for the past three years on Cestus, and she often wondered how she'd managed to survive without him prior to that. *Not as often,* she thought with amusement, *as Sivak himself wonders it.*

"Sivak, what's next?"

"As I informed you before your senior staff meeting, the next item on the agenda is your security briefing. Admiral Abrik, Captain Hostetler Richman, and Secretary Shostakova are waiting. Madam President, I once again would like to make my offer of several Vulcan techniques that enhance the memory—"

Nan let out a long sigh. "Shut up and send them in, in that order."

"Very well, Madam President."

Sometimes Nan also wondered how she managed not to kill Sivak.

The door opened to reveal an elderly Trill man in severe civilian clothing, an elegant young human woman wearing a Starfleet uniform—four gold pips and a gold collar indicating a captain in security—and a short, stout human woman from the high-gravity colony of Pangea dressed in the bulky one-piece outfit favored on that world. They were, respectively, Jas Abrik, a retired admiral who served as her security advisor; Captain Holly Hostetler Richman, the liaison to Starfleet Intelligence; and Raisa Shostakova, the secretary of defense.

Raisa and Holly approached the sofa, while Jas made a

beeline for the chair next to the one modified for Z4's use. Since this was a smaller gathering, Nan moved out from behind her desk, intending to sit in the chair opposite Jas.

As they came in, she said, "I'm an old woman with a weak heart, folks, so *please* don't tell me that *another* major power in the quadrant has fallen."

Holly smirked. "Not since the last one, ma'am."

"That's a relief."

The two women sat on the sofa. Holly, who was tall with long legs, sat ramrod straight, her feet planted comfortably on the floor. By contrast, Raisa had awful posture, even though she was in a lighter gravity than she was accustomed to, and she sat hunched on the sofa; her lesser height meant that her feet were dangling over the edge of the couch, looking just like Nan's youngest granddaughter, an image that Nan hoped she would one day cease to find amusing. Besides, it wasn't especially fair to Raisa, who may have looked like a little kid sitting in a high chair, but who in fact had coordinated the planetary defenses on Pangea during the Dominion War and had been responsible for the upgrades to those defenses that had kept that planet from suffering the same fate as Betazed and several other Federation worlds that had fallen to the Jem'Hadar.

As for Jas, he sat on the edge of his chair, as if expecting to bolt any minute.

Regarding the retired admiral, Nan gave him a smirk of her own. "Expecting to run a race, Admiral?"

"No, ma'am," Jas said in a subdued voice.

"Then relax, will you please? You look like you're about to jump on a grenade."

"Yes, ma'am." Jas moved back slightly in his chair.

Nan sighed. Dealing with Jas Abrik had been awkward from the beginning, as he had been the campaign manager for Nan's opponent during the election. However, Jas *also* knew the real reason why Zife had resigned, and in exchange for not revealing that information—thus plunging the Bacco administration into a war with the Klingons before they'd had a chance to change the color of the carpet—Esperanza had offered Jas the position of security advisor.

In that, at least, he had proven to be competent. He'd been in Starfleet for decades, and that experience was now being put to good use.

Leaning back in her chair in the vain hope that it would inspire Jas to do likewise, Nan said, "I'm gonna go out on a limb here and assume that we're starting with the Romulans."

"Good guess, ma'am." Holly held up a padd and started reading from its display. "Outpost 22 along the Romulan Neutral Zone picked up a ship heading straight for it from the Miridian system in Romulan space."

"Military?"

Holly hesitated. "In a manner of speaking."

Nan rolled her eyes. "What the hell is—?"

"The outpost's sensors read it as a *Shirekral*-class vessel."

That got Jas's attention. "What?"

"My history of Romulan ship registry's a bit rusty," Nan said dryly.

Jas was back to the edge of his chair again. "Madam President, the *Shirekral*-class vessels haven't been in operation since the late twenty-third century."

"Earlier than that, actually—this one still has an ion drive." Holly gave Nan a firm look. "Ma'am, vessels of this type were common during the Earth-Romulan wars of the twenty-second century, but all the ones that were still in active service in the late twenty-third century had their ion drives replaced with the singularity drives that they still use."

"All right," Nan said, "so we've got a bunch of Romulan soldiers on a ship that was obsolete a hundred years ago."

"Actually, ma'am, that's not what we have. First of all, no Romulan soldier would be caught dead on a ship that old—even with the military in the mess it's in right now. Also, we've been able to make a general lifesign reading on long-range, and every indication so far is that the ship is full of Remans."

Nan blinked.

Raisa shot a look at Holly next to her. In a voice that had a trace of a Russian accent, she said, "Repeat that, please, Captain."

"The outpost's long-range sensors are picking up Reman lifesigns—and *only* Reman lifesigns."

"Hell." Nan let out a long breath. "What do you think, Holly?"

"I think they're refugees."

"That's a stretch," Jas said.

Holly glared at the security advisor. "They're heading *straight* for Outpost 22, Jas, and they're doing it at warp three-point-one-two, which is faster than those ships are supposed to be able to go. Twenty-two is in the middle of nowhere, but it's also the closest Federation station to the Miridian system. No way that it's not their intended destination. The chances that they're heading toward it by coincidence are infinitesimal." She turned back to Nan. "Madam President, it is my opinion that these are Remans who will be requesting asylum in the Federation."

"I believe that Captain Hostetler Richman is correct, Madam President." Raisa leaned forward, her feet now touching the floor. "I believe these are Reman refugees."

"Based on what?" Jas sounded annoyed. So was Nan, but for different reasons.

"Because Remans have never operated in Miridian. They have not had to. It is a system that was taken by the Romulans approximately fifteen years ago."

"Okay, I'm missing a step here," Nan said. "What does that time frame have to do with anything?"

"It is not the time frame, Madam President, my apologies—it is that the Miridian system has an indigenous lifeform that has provided the slave labor that, in other parts of the empire, has traditionally been performed by the Remans. Since Shinzon's coup, the Miridians have also risen up, and with their infrastructure in tatters, the Romulans have been unable to quell the uprising."

Holly picked the ball back up. "We've been getting reports of the Miridians creating a kind of underground railroad—supplying ships and methods of getting out of Romulan space."

Nan nodded. "That explains the clapped-out ship." She thought for a moment, then looked at her secretary of defense. "Raisa, what do you think?"

"We must turn them back."

All three of the other people in the room looked at Raisa with shock. Nan snapped, *"Excuse* me?"

Before Raisa could answer, Jas added, "Assuming these *are* refugees—and I'm not a hundred percent sold that they are—we *can't* turn them back."

"We *have* to turn them back," Raisa said in a hard voice.

"How the hell can I justify that?" Nan asked incredulously. "How the hell can I tell people fleeing Romulan oppression—"

"They are *not* fleeing Romulan oppression, Madam President."

Nan frowned. "Don't be ridiculous, of course they—"

Holly's eyes widened. "She's right, ma'am, they aren't."

Looking over at Jas, Nan asked, "*You* want to interrupt me, too?"

Jas pursed his lips. "Ma'am, they're right. All Remans residing in Romulan space currently live under the protection of the Klingon Empire."

"What do you—" Then Nan put it together. "Oh, dammit."

Raisa put her hands together in front of her chest. "If we grant the Remans' request for asylum—"

"Assuming that's what it is," Jas added.

Knew he'd get his interruption in there somewhere, Nan thought irritably.

Nodding to Jas, Raisa said, "Assuming that, yes, then we will be violating our treaty with the Klingons."

"Unless we clear it with the Klingons first," Holly added.

Nan snorted. "Want to lay odds what they'll say if we ask?"

"No, ma'am."

"Yeah, me either." She shook her head. "How long do we have?"

Holly frowned. "Ma'am?"

"How long until that ship reaches the Federation border?"

"Eight weeks, ma'am."

Nan opened her mouth, then closed it, then opened it again. "Eight *weeks?*"

"Yes, ma'am. They'll be in communications range in six weeks." Holly's lips curled up a bit. "Those old ships are *very* slow, ma'am—and the outpost sensors are *very* good."

"Apparently." Nan sighed. "All right, fine, keep an eye on it, maybe get a Starfleet ship over there just in case."

"Yes, ma'am."

Raisa put her hands down on her lap. "Madam President, I believe you should speak with our ambassador to Qo'noS."

Jas rolled his eyes. "What the hell good would *that* do?"

"To take the High Council's temperature, so to speak. It is possible that they will be willing to let us take some of the Remans off their hands."

"They won't." Jas folded his arms. "And the new ambassador won't have any clue what—"

Nan took some pleasure in being the interrupter this time. "Ambassador Rozhenko has lived *in* the empire for the last six years. It's worth talking to him, anyhow."

Shaking his head, Jas said, "It's a waste of time."

"You've made your feelings abundantly clear, Jas," Nan said witheringly. "What else?"

They went over security concerns regarding various other governments. Nan was distressed to learn that Orion Syndicate and Ferengi pirates were still harassing the relief ships to Cardassia Prime. She had thought that problem was solved, and that Starfleet had driven off the privateers. *Apparently not,* she thought with a sigh.

Holly's last report from outside the Federation involved the Tzenkethi. "Our listening posts along the border have picked up some chatter about one of the *Tzelnira's* children being sick."

Jas added, "The *Tzelnira* are—"

"The appointed ministers of the Tzenkethi government serving under the autarch, yes, I *know,* Jas." Nan glowered at her security advisor. "My son-in-law was a relief worker during the Tzenkethi War."

"I'm sorry, ma'am, I didn't—"

"It's not like you see me every day or anything," Nan said dryly, "but I would think you'd have figured out by now that, if I don't know something, I'll ask."

Jas didn't sound in the least bit contrite when he said, "I *did* say I was sorry, ma'am."

Nan stared at the old Trill for several seconds before turning back to Holly. "Sick with what?"

"We don't know, ma'am. We're not even sure it's true, but there's been a lot of similar chatter."

"All right." She smiled. "If that's the worst we're hearing out of Tzenketh these days, I'm just gonna count my blessings. What else?"

◆

CHAPTER THREE

◆　　◆

ASHANTÉ PHIRI WAITED for Z4 to explode.

It didn't happen in the turbolift down one flight to the fourteenth floor, where a third of the offices of the presidential staff were located, including those of the chief of staff and her four deputies. It didn't happen while she gave Fred a quick kiss before she, Z4, and Xeldara got off. Fred was heading down to thirteen, where he and the rest of the speechwriting staff were headquartered; Myk was proceeding to the second floor, where Kant Jorel's office, as well as the press holocom, were.

Xeldara tugged on her left earlobe as the three of them moved away from the turbolift doors. "I'm off for my scolding. What do you figure, Esperanza has five more minutes with the president before she comes down and hits me over the head with a rock?"

Ashanté glowered as the three of them exited into the office area. "If she doesn't, I will. How many times did I tell you not to bring up the travel office again on fifteen?"

"I think it's an issue, and I think it'll bite us on the ankle if we're not careful."

Z4 made a tinkling noise. "Softs have the most peculiar metaphors."

Snorting, Ashanté said, "You're only just noticing this now? The point is, Xeldara, it's not an issue on fifteen anymore. You want to bring it up again, bring it up with Esperanza."

"Who then won't tell the president about it. I wanted to—"

"Get yelled at by the leader of the biggest political entity in the Alpha Quadrant?"

Z4 made a different noise. "You certainly don't aim low."

"I said my piece, and I'm happy with that." Xeldara sounded both stubborn and petulant.

"Hope you're happy with the job market," Ashanté muttered.

Xeldara bore right toward the chief of staff's office, which was smaller than the president's and only had about half the view but was still pretty spectacular. Ashanté and Z4 moved straight ahead toward their own offices, which had no windows, located as they were in the center of the circle that each floor in the Palais formed. Aside from the chief of staff, members of the cabinet got the other offices that lined the outer walls of the fourteenth floor. The four deputies and their staffs worked in what was generally referred to as the warp core, because it was the center and where all the work that kept the government going got done.

To his credit, Z4 waited until they were in Ashanté's office and the door closed behind both of them before exploding.

"Why did you shoot C29 down?"

"Because he's a crappy candidate, Ziff."

Z4's antennae curled up. "How many times have I told you not to call me that?"

"About the same number of times I told you that C29 Green was a bad choice for the seat on technology."

"Very funny."

Ashanté sat down on her chair and activated the workstation at her desk. Fourteen messages were waiting for her. *And it's not even midmorning yet. I love my job.* She looked up at Z4. "We shouldn't have him on the list."

"I want the president to make that call."

"She's not gonna take him."

Z4 threw out four of his arms. "You keep *saying* that, but you don't *know* him."

"I met him once or twice when I was with Councillor Djinian, I've read his record of voting, and I know how he's perceived on the first floor."

"What is *that* supposed to mean?"

Leaning back in her chair, Ashanté said, "It means that the other councillors perceive him as someone with no thoughts of his own. He votes with the majority every time. He's never had an unpopular vote, and he always swings the way the wind is blowing. He just does what other people tell him to do, and that's not someone we can afford to have on technology. They're building new toys *every day,* and we have to have people on technology who can keep up."

Z4 made a noise similar to what wind chimes sounded

like when they got tangled up. "You don't know *him*. He's a good man, Ashanté, and he has very far-reaching ideas about the uses of technology."

"They're not evident in his voting record, and that's what we have to give the president, and what the rest of the council will look at."

Z4 stared at Ashanté for several seconds. Then he said, "C29 used to be a forest quadrant governor, just like me."

Ashanté knew that already. "Yeah, so?"

"About forty seasons ago, a scientist named V1 Red came up with a method of transporting among the forests. For the longest time we had bridges—and we still do—but they took a long time, and vehicles aren't really practical in the depths of the forests on Nasat."

Frowning, Ashanté asked, "How'd you guys—?"

"We built vehicles that could take us into the sky, and those were used for transport, too, but what V1 Red wanted to find was something that wouldn't require a sub-orbital flight to just go across to the next forest but wouldn't take more than a day. So he came up with a series of pneumatic tubes that would send Nasats at high speeds through to the other side, complete with inertial dumpers at each end to slow them down when they got there."

Ashanté was about to ask how that was practical, but then she looked at the chitinous shell that covered most of Z4's body and remembered that most Nasats could curl up into their shells, which would probably protect them, especially with that inertial dumper thing.

Z4 continued. "He was a relative of the governor of his own forest, V5 Red, but in order to properly test and construct this, he needed the cooperation of at least one other forest quadrant governor. So he went to every one adjacent to his own—including mine, by the way—and we all turned him down. The idea was impractical, it was dangerous, and it wouldn't do any good. We all said that.

"With one exception." A tinkle of amusement, then: "C29 Green. He didn't even need convincing—he heard V1 out, liked what he heard, and gave approval to try it. A number of us took him to task for it, telling him it was insane to even try it. You know what he said?"

Ashanté shook her head.

"'If it doesn't work, what do we lose? But if it *does* work, we win a lot.'"

Chuckling, Ashanté said, "Down-home wisdom."

"Something like that, yes. So they built it, even though every other governor on Nasat thought it was insane and that even if it worked, nobody would use it. And you know what? It *did* work, perfectly, and those tubes are all over Nasat now. You can read all about it in pretty much every history of Nasat that's been written in the last forty seasons, but you know whose name will be left out of it? C29 Green."

That surprised Ashanté. "Why?"

"He didn't want credit. He said that it was V1 Red and V5 Red who got it going, he just agreed to be the other end. I asked him about it later, and his exact words to me were, 'Who cares who gets credit, as long as the right thing is done?'"

Ashanté stared at Z4 for several more seconds. Then she sighed. "You know why the president made me deputy COS?"

"Because you worked for her since she first ran for public office?"

"Not quite—I spent five years as the chief aide to Councillor Djinian, before I decided that spending most of my time several dozen light-years away from my husband wasn't any fun and I went back to Cestus III. But in that time, I got to know the first floor very well, and I gotta tell you, Z4—I never would've even *guessed* that about C29." She sighed again. "Put him on the list."

"The list?" Z4 let out the tangled-wind-chime noise again. "What about—?"

"What about Severn-Anyar, Govrin, Gelemingar, Nitram, and Jix? They're *all* qualified to some degree or other."

Grudgingly, Z4 said, "I suppose."

"But when you write up C29's recommendation? Include that story. In fact, *only* include that story."

"Why?"

Ashanté grinned. "The other reason why I got this job is because I know how Nan Bacco's mind works. And that story you just told me is the kind of thing that's right in her wheelhouse. If you'd told it on fifteen half an hour ago, we might not even be having this discussion."

"I'll make a note of that."

"Good. Now, since we need to get these together today—"

"Right." Z4 turned to leave. The door opened at his approach, but then he stopped. "Ashanté? What's a wheelhouse?"

She laughed. "It's a baseball term."

"That's that sport the president likes?"

Ashanté nodded.

"Do you think my job would be easier if I understood the sport?"

"Ziff, I've been to a hundred baseball games, both with and without the president, I've been listening to her stories about Babe Ruth and Satchel Paige and Willie Mays and Barry Bonds and José Ramirez and Buck Bokai and Aloysius McSweeney and Kornelius Yates for over twenty years, and I still don't understand the sport. Just nod a lot and pretend you understand all the references, and for God's sake don't actually *use* any of them in her presence, and you'll do fine."

"All right, thanks."

"I'll do Severn-Anyar, Govrin, and Jix. Can you do Gelemingar and Nitram?"

"You do Nitram—I don't think I'll be able to recommend him with a straight face after the way he voted on disaster relief last year."

Ashanté sighed. "He voted with his conscience, Z4."

"That's great, but I still don't want to—"

"Fine, I'll do Nitram, you do Govrin. See you at noon."

Ozla Graniv nearly leapt out of her chair when the beeping started.

It took her a moment to orient herself and remember where she was. Finally it hit: She was in the Earth bureau offices of *Seeker,* one of the leading newsmagazines on Trill. She was *Seeker*'s Palais de la Concorde correspondent, and the alarm that just went off was there to remind her that the morning briefing was about to start and she should activate her holocom, which she did. Then she simply had to wait for the other side to activate, and, from her perspective, she would no longer be in her tiny office in Chartres but in a room full of reporters from all over the Federation and beyond.

Part of her missed the old days, when the press would roam the Palais and get their briefings in person. That had ended when the Breen had attacked Earth during the Dominion War. The Palais had become a fortress after that, with no one who hadn't been there on official government business allowed in or out. However, President Zife hadn't been able to justify cutting the press out altogether, but he'd benefited from the recent advances in marrying holographic technology to communications technology. Now the press could be briefed without having to leave the comfort of their offices, homes, or, in some cases, homeworlds. Also, if reporters were offworld for whatever reason, they could still participate in the briefing.

And they can also do it when they're up all night crashing on a deadline. Ozla had toured the Palais in the company of Kant Jorel and Myk Bunkrep in order to write a story on how the Bacco administration had made over the top three floors of the Palais in their own image, as each administration was wont to do. The story wasn't due for another few days, but tomorrow morning Ozla was getting on a transport to take her to Tezwa, a story she had been begging her editor to let her do for ages.

"You're our Palais correspondent," Farik had said on the screen on her workstation, his enviable view of the Tenaran ice cliffs behind him, *"you don't do this sort of thing."*

"I used to. Remember that exposé I did on the Orion Syndicate? The one I—"

"Won the Gavlin for, yes, I know, and that's why you got the Palais gig. You deserved it."

"And I'm grateful, Farik, I really am. But I feel like I'm trapped on Earth. I want to get out some more. Besides, you've been wanting to do a follow-up on Tezwa, and with Vara gone and Baleeza retired, you don't have anyone who—"

"All right, all right!" Farik had laughed, then, and held up his hands in surrender. *"I'll get Gora to cover the Palais for a month or two while you go to Tezwa."*

Tezwa had almost been the flash point of a war between the Federation and the Klingons. The Tezwan prime minister, a lunatic named Kinchawn, had acquired Federation nadion-pulse cannons from the Orion Syndicate and had threatened a Klingon colony. The Klingons had responded, along with a Starfleet ship, and they'd been decimated by the cannons until the Starfleet crew had managed to disable them. The commanding officer of that ship—a rather infamous captain named Jean-Luc Picard—had then claimed the right of *batyay'a*, which meant that he took credit for conquering the world, thus keeping it out of Klingon hands.

Unfortunately, Kinchawn hadn't yet finished. Though he'd been deposed after the cannons' destruction, he'd gone into exile and made dozens of guerrilla attacks on the capital city, which, combined with the damage done by the Klingons in their initial attack, had led to a body count on Tezwa that had been at Dominion War levels.

However, in the last few weeks, the Romulans had crowded Tezwa off the newsfeeds.

Vara deserves better than that.

Vara Tal was the reporter from *Seeker* who'd been sent to cover Tezwa. She'd been killed when a runabout had been blown up by Kinchawn's forces—an explosion that had also claimed the lives of several civilians and Starfleet personnel. Farik had sent *Seeker*'s seniormost reporter, Baleeza Gral—who also reported for *Seeker* when he was Renna Gral and Tristor Gral—to replace Vara. What he'd seen had been sufficiently awful to convince him to retire from reporting, after doing it for two hundred and fifty years as three different people.

Nobody's reporting this story anymore. Somebody has to do it for Vara.

A moment later, her holocom beeped, and she found herself sitting, as usual, between Edmund Atkinson of the *Times*—who would no doubt claim to be in his office in London but who she knew was really on a beach in Mexico—and Regia Maldonado of the Federation News Service, who was, she was sure, in FNS's Tokyo office. Several other reporters were scattered around the room, most legitimate, a few not so much, in Ozla's estimation. She was amused to see that Annalisa Armitage of the *Free Vulcan Gazette*—probably the most laughable publication in a Federation that, thanks to the total freedom of the press, had its share of laughable publications—was still coming to the briefings, despite being mocked at every turn. *Then again, the FVG's probably used to that, since they've been advocating Vulcan superiority since the twenty-first century. Hell, the only reason the Vulcans themselves don't mock the FVG is because they don't do that kind of thing. . . .*

At the podium stood the only two people who were physically in the room: Kant Jorel, the liaison between the press and the Federation Council, and his assistant, an Andorian named Thanatazhres th'Vroth. Zhres had actually lasted in the job for more than two months, which, Ozla thought, was probably a record. Kant had been the press liaison since shortly after his native world of Bajor had joined the Federation three years earlier, and he had gone through over half a dozen assistants in that time.

"First of all," Kant said, and his words quieted the room down, "President Bacco has said that she's looking forward to the negotiators on both sides of the current dispute between Delta and Carrea coming to Earth to resolve their differences here in the Palais. She also knows she has the support of the ambassadors from both worlds, as well as Councillor Eleana, who has said several times that she looks forward to a peaceful solution to the dispute."

Edmund raised his hand. "So you're saying that they've agreed to come?"

"I've said they *are* coming, Edmund. Please listen to what I say, not what I imply."

Smiling, Edmund asked, "Where would the fun in *that* be?"

"You want fun, stay on that beach in Mexico."

Ozla had to cover a smile at the wounded look on Edmund's holographic face.

On the other side of Ozla, Regia spoke up. "Jorel, I have a source that says that a shipload of Reman refugees is heading for Outpost 22 along the Romulan Neutral Zone."

"Bully for your source," Kant said with an insincere smile. "I can't comment on that."

Another reporter was about to say something, but Regia didn't give him a chance to speak. "I'm sorry, Jorel, but what does that mean?"

Kant fixed Regia with a withering gaze. "I should think that'd be obvious, Regia. Either I know all about it but am not allowed to say anything yet, or I know nothing about it and am saying I can't comment by way of covering, or some third possibility that I can't say out loud. You people use words for a living, I would think you'd be able to recognize my own choice of words for precisely what it is. Maria?"

Maria Olifante, the reporter from Pangea's news service, asked, "Has there been any word from ex-President Zife since his resignation?"

Frowning, Kant said, "I'm not sure what you mean."

"Has he had anything to say about President Bacco's victory, or about her policies?"

"We haven't heard from President Zife since his resignation. I'm sure he's enjoying his retirement."

Ozla smiled. She'd only met Zife two or three times— press access to the president had been at an all-time low during his administration, mostly due to security concerns—but he'd struck her as the type who would enjoy retirement. Some politicians were born to be in politics, but Zife had always seemed like someone who'd simply been doing a job. That wasn't necessarily an indicator of poor performance, but it didn't indicate an overriding passion, either.

Bacco, on the other hand, came across as the type who would continue to be involved in governing until the day she keeled over from exhaustion. Ozla generally found that she preferred that kind of politician, though Zife's type tended to live longer.

Maria wouldn't let the point go. "C'mon, Jorel, you expect us to believe that Zife doesn't have an opinion about Bacco?"

"I long ago stopped expecting you people to believe a thing I say. T'Nira?"

The briefing continued for several minutes. Ozla noticed that Kant never once called on Sovan, even though the Bolian had his hand up several times. *Looks like Kant's still angry about Sovan's performance on ICL. I did warn him. . . .*

Ozla always turned down invitations to do talk shows like that. She never felt like she was accomplishing anything except self-promotion, and she didn't feel comfortable doing that. She reported news; the fact that it was her reporting it was comparatively irrelevant.

Besides, she was terrible at speaking extemporaneously. That was why she liked writing.

When the briefing ended, the holocom room faded and she was back to seeing where she really was: in Chartres at her desk.

As she went over the draft of the article on the changing

face of the top three floors of the Palais, she made a bet with herself as to how long it would be before Sovan called her.

Five seconds later, her comm beeped. "Hi, Sovan," she said without even checking to make sure it was his blue face on the screen.

"Can you believe him?"

"I rarely do." Ozla still hadn't looked up.

"He cannot keep treating me like this."

"Actually, he can. He's under no obligation to call on you when you raise your hand." Then she did look at him. "And you're under no obligation to stay quiet on the subject, either."

"If I write about him snubbing me, it'll just annoy him. I don't want to get on Kant's bad side."

"Oh come on, Sovan, you've been doing this longer than I have—you know he doesn't *have* a good side. He's not gonna like you anyhow, so run with it."

"Look, you'll be talking to him, right? About your trip?"

Ozla was, in fact, planning to let Kant know that she'd be out of the room for a few months while she did her Tezwa story. "Yeah, why?"

"Any chance of putting in a good word?"

Rolling her eyes, Ozla said, "There is in fact *no* chance of that."

"Ozla—"

"Sovan, you went on *ICL* and talked about how incompetent Kant's boss is."

"Yes, but he respects you. I think he may even like you."

Kant had, in fact, treated Ozla with less disdain than he did most of the press, which, she supposed, could be construed as liking her by his lights. "Doesn't matter—see, my editor respects me, too, and if he found out that I sang the praises of a competitor—"

"Never mind, then."

Ozla sighed. "Look, Sovan, you're a good reporter, and you'll still get the good stories. Why are you worried about this stuff?"

Sovan's face widened into a huge grin. *"I'm not, really, I just wanted an excuse to talk to you before you went to that disaster area. Why are you going there, anyhow? It's a pit."*

"Because it's a story—and it's one nobody's talking about anymore."

"It's all anybody was talking about for a month."

"One month is nothing. This needs more attention."

"If you say so."

"I do. Now that you've contrived your excuse to talk to me—"

"Listen, Ozla—be careful, all right? We already lost Vara."

Ozla hesitated. "I know—that's why I'm going."

"All right." Sovan moved as if to cut the connection, but Ozla stopped him.

"Sovan, listen—Zife. Did he retire to Bolarus?"

"No."

"You're sure? He didn't maybe come in discreetly?"

Sovan chuckled. *"Zife doesn't know how to be discreet. No, he's not here. Trust me, someone at BY would've found him. He was never able to keep his movements secret, not when he was a district representative, not when he was planetary minister, not when he was a councillor, and* certainly *not when he was president. He's nowhere near Bolarus."*

"All right." She tapped her finger on her desk. "Thanks, Sovan—and thanks for the well wishes. I'll see you in a few months."

"I hope so. Good luck, Ozla."

Sovan signed off.

Ozla tapped her finger for a few more minutes. Then she com'd her assistant. "Traya, can you get me President Zife's speech to the council of governors on Pacifica from three years ago?"

"Sure."

Then she put a call through to Zhres.

"It's Ozla."

"I am sorry," the Andorian's soft voice said over the speaker—Ozla was talking into his ear unit, so there was no visual feed. *"Mr. Kant's in a meeting with Ms. Piñiero right now."*

"That's fine, Zhres—could you just let him know that Gora Yed is going to be taking my place in the room for a few months?"

"I can't imagine he'll care all that much."

Ozla laughed. "No, he probably won't, but I want to let him know as a courtesy."

"I'll pass that on—then I'll remind him what that word means."

"Good luck. How've you managed to last so long in the job?"

"There is a human saying that applies: Mr. Kant's bark is worse than his bite."

Frowning, Ozla said, "I don't know what that means."

"It means he sounds worse than he actually is."

"Thanks, Zhres."

She was about to cut the connection when Zhres asked, *"If you do not mind my asking, Ms. Graniv—where will you be? A well-deserved vacation, I hope?"*

Ozla chuckled. "No such luck. I'm going to Tezwa."

A pause. *"Why in Thori's name would you go there?"*

Wondering if *everyone* was going to ask that question

and resigning herself to the fact that they were, she said, "Because someone needs to."

"That does not strike me as a good enough reason."

"It's good enough for me. Take care, Zhres."

"Good-bye, Ms. Graniv—and good luck."

✦

CHAPTER FOUR

✦   ✦

FRED MACDOUGAN struggled over adjectives.

It was always the most difficult part of the speechwriting process for him. He had no trouble with metaphors, with imagery, with references, with alliteration, with cadence—but adjectives nailed him every time. Were the people being honored "noble" or "upright" or "steadfast"? Was the location of the speech "verdant" or "pretty" or "beautiful"?

If it wasn't for adjectives, I could write twice as fast.

Right now he was working his way through the speech that President Bacco would be giving in two weeks' time when he went to Andor to meet with their genetics council. The trip was opening with an address to a gathering of Andorian scientists who were struggling with the Andorians' population issues, and Fred wanted to get it just right. True, it didn't need to be finished until the trip—of which Andor was but one stop—started the next Monday, but he wanted to nail it and at least get a draft into Esperanza's hands by the end of the day. Andor was a founding member of the Federation, and three years earlier their genetic crisis had finally been made public. The president had to support their research, and it was important to show that every effort was being made—not just on Andor but throughout the Federation—to help them along. Zife had done absolutely nothing in this regard; he hadn't visited Andor once in the past three years. Fred was glad that the president had taken the initiative to rectify that oversight of her predecessor.

The intercom beeped. Sighing, he activated it. That sigh was leavened by the sight of a beautiful dark face framed by intricately braided waist-length hair. "Hey there, babe," he said to his wife before he realized that Z4 was standing next to her at her desk.

"Fred, c'mon, we're on the job."

"Right, sorry." He grinned. "Hey there, Deputy Babe."

"Much better." Ashanté shook her head. *"What're the president's next few speeches?"*

"Tomorrow at 2000—1100 local time—she's dedicating the Dominion War memorial museum on the Golden Gate Bridge."

Z4 made a tinkling noise. *"I thought that was at noon."*

Fred frowned. "Hang on, let me check." He called up the president's schedule for the following day on another screen. "Yeah, sorry—the event's at noon local, which is 2100 our time, but she's leaving the Palais at 2000."

"Why is she leaving the Palais an hour early? Is there another stop?"

"No."

"Then why—?"

Fred rolled his eyes. His wife was a lovely woman and a

world-class political mind, but sometimes she missed the obvious stuff. "Because that's how long it takes to get to San Francisco from Paris by shuttle."

"It takes five seconds by transporter, and she's got one right next to her office."

"Uh—" Fred blinked. *She's not the only one who misses obvious stuff, I guess.* "Yeah, good point."

"I'll get on that," Z4 said. *"It's probably the travel office again."*

Ashanté chuckled. *"That'll give Xeldara something new to complain about, at least. In any case, that won't work for what we want. What's next?"*

"It'd help if I knew what you wanted."

"We need to have the president show her support for her nominees—starting with Artrin."

"Ah."

She pointed at the screen. *"What about the trip next week?"*

Fred didn't need to consult the schedule for this one. "She's going to Vulcan for the annual FTC meeting on Monday." The Federation Trade Council had its annual meeting on a different planet every year. The previous three years, it had been Bajor, Betazed, and Pacifica—all garden spots. *So, of course, my first year going, and they hold it on a desert.* "Then we go to Rigel to talk to the couriers, then to Andor for—"

"Hang on, why is she talking to couriers at Rigel?"

"They won't upgrade their warp drives."

"So?"

"About ten years ago, a couple of Hekarans discovered that existing warp engines were damaging the fabric of space. All vessels had to stay at warp five or lower until they found a solution—which Starfleet did, inside of about six months, and within a year, all Starfleet ships were up-graded. Within three years, so were most civilian ships."

Z4 made another of his noises. *"What does—"*

Ashanté put a hand on one of Z4's legs. *"Let him work through it—it always takes my darling husband three times as long as is absolutely necessary to explain himself. It's part of his charm."* She grinned. *"At least that's what I keep telling myself."*

"I love you too, dear." He frowned. "Where was I?"

"Warp five."

"Right. There's a whole mess of couriers in the Rigel system that have ships of their own design that were about fifty years old when this new regulation got handed down. They haven't made the upgrades because they would take too long with the design they've got. Since most of their work is within the Rigel system, they don't go to warp that often, and they almost never reach warp five when they do, so it isn't really much of an issue."

"So why're we—?"

"Their ships are now *sixty* years old. They need maintenance, and it has to be done with parts that don't exist anymore because their engine type is against the law. They need to upgrade, and they need to do it now before their crappy, ill-maintained engines suffer a warp-core breach."

"So the president is going to Rigel to convince them to do it?"

"Yeah."

Ashanté looked baffled and angry at the same time, a look that always worried Fred when he was on the receiving end of it, though the consequences usually didn't manifest until they got home and she announced that he only *thought* he was sleeping in the bedroom.

"Fred, this is off the president's sensor screen. Send the technology secretary."

"That's a great idea!" Fred hit his forehead with the heel of his palm. "Of course, why didn't I think of that? Send Secretary Forzrat! What a brilliant notion!"

Ashanté knew him well enough to sense the sarcasm. Indeed, Fred was laying it on sufficiently thick that one need never have met Fred to be aware of it. *"She already went?"*

"Twice. No soap. The next step is to forbid them from flying with their ships, which will grind stellar commerce throughout the Rigel colonies to a screeching halt. The couriers are saying that the short-term falloff in usable ships while they upgrade will ruin them, but that's nothing compared to what'll happen if we shut them down."

"But shutting them down makes us look bad—especially since they don't actually go warp five, so what's the big deal?"

"The president needs to convince them that it's better to take the short-term problem for long-term gain, instead of getting short-term gain and the long-term problem of a ship exploding when it's full of people because they couldn't—"

"All right, all right, I got it. You sound like you swallowed a position paper."

"Didn't need to." He grinned. "I wrote it."

"Of course you did." Ashanté groaned, then held up her hand before Fred could say anything else. *"Never mind, we'll talk about that later."*

Fred didn't like the sound of that.

"What else is on that trip?"

"Andor—the genetics council—and Sirius and Kharzh'ulla. She's—"

"No, that's it—Andor. Can you work in something about the judiciary council and Artrin's record into the opening remarks?"

"Uh—" Fred thought about it a moment. Judiciary did oversee some of the allocations for the research being done on Andor—mostly to make sure it conformed to ethical and legal research guidelines. "Yeah, I can probably swing that. I'm working on that speech right now, actually."

"Trying to find the right adjectives?"

"Not at all." Fred tried to sound wounded at the very notion and knew he was failing miserably.

Z4 said, *"Thanks, Fred. Meanwhile, I'm going to have a conversation with the travel office."*

"Have fun," Fred said.

After Z4 left Ashanté's office, the latter gave her husband a penetrating stare.

"Don't give me that look, darling," he said in return.

"Don't 'darling' me, cupcake—why the hell do you have the president—"

"She wanted to do it, Ashanté. *She* came to *me* after Forzrat came back the second time and said she wanted to put in an appearance. It's not like she's going out of her way—Rigel's between Vulcan and Andor, and it fits into the schedule, since FTC ends four days before the genetics council meeting begins."

Ashanté let out a long breath. *"Fine. Add in some stuff about Artrin."*

"Will do," he said as she reached for the control to terminate the call. Before she could, he said, "Hey!"

She hesitated. *"What?"*

"I love you, you know that?"

"I heard a rumor, yeah." She shook her head. *"I love you too. Go find some adjectives."*

After she cut the connection, Fred opened a new one to his research assistant, an eager young Dorset named Rol Yarvik Rol. "Rol, get me everything you can find about Councillor Artrin na Yel."

"*Sure thing, Boss.*"

Z4 Blue was writing up his recommendation for C29 Green when his door buzzed. "Come in," he said without looking up from his work.

The door to Z4's office slid open to reveal Ne'al G'ullho from the travel office. "Uh, hi," it said. "You wanted to see me?"

Z4 looked up at it. The Damiani was young, with teal skin, all-white eyes, and horns protruding upward from each temple. "Not especially, but it's really the best way to talk to you."

"You guys are still angry about Tamok, aren't you? Look—"

Expressing his irritation, Z4 said, "I don't care about Tamok."

"It was Ambassador T'Kala, she—"

"We *know* whose fault it was, Ne'al, that's not what this is about."

Ne'al threw up its hands. "Come on, Mr. Blue, you guys have—"

"Us guys haven't been doing anything. It's all been Xeldara Trask—the rest of us know it was Ambassador T'Kala's fault."

Putting its hands back down, Ne'al said, "Oh. So what is this about?" It took a seat in Z4's guest chair.

"The president's itinerary tomorrow has her leaving for San Francisco for the dedication of the new museum at 2000."

Ne'al nodded. "True."

"That event starts at 2100."

"Also true."

Z4's antennae curled in annoyance. "Any particular reason for that one-hour gap?"

Shrugging, Ne'al said, "Because that's how long it takes to get to San Francisco from Paris by shuttle."

"It takes five seconds by transporter, and she's got one right next to her office."

Ne'al nodded again. "I know, but the president's transporter'll be down at that time. Regular maintenance cycle."

Z4's antennae were now about to curl into his head. "You *do* know that there's this big transporter bay down on the second floor, right? That hasn't been removed by Breen saboteurs or anything, has it?"

Now Ne'al started to shift uncomfortably in its seat. Z4 had sat in regular humanoid chairs before, and he could understand the urge. *I don't know how softs function in those things. . . .*

"The thing is—" Ne'al started, then hesitated.

Z4 simply stared at it.

Letting out a breath, Ne'al then said, "See, that one will also be down. For, uh, for the same reason."

"Regular maintenance cycle?" Z4 asked incredulously.

Ne'al nodded a third time.

Right at the moment, Z4 was grateful that his fourteenth-floor office didn't have a window, because he felt a great urge to jump out of it. "Ne'al, do you know why we have two transporter bays?"

"My guess is so we can avoid this kind of problem."

Dryly, Z4 said, "That would be an accurate guess."

"And in theory, that works fine," Ne'al said, folding its hands together, "but there's only one problem."

"That being?"

"We didn't avoid this kind of problem."

The urge switched to wanting to throw the Damiani out the window. "Ne'al—"

"See, the two bays are on separate maintenance cycles, maintained by two different staffs," Ne'al said quickly. "All the technical support on fifteen and in the basements is completely separate from the first through fourteenth floors—they need extra security."

Much as Z4 hated to admit it, that made sense. And there were no transporters in the basement because the ground around the Palais was transporter proof—it was impossible to beam in or out of the area benath the Palais for necessary security reasons. "That's fine, but I still don't see—"

"Ninety percent of the time, the maintenance schedules of the two staffs don't overlap. Ninety-five, even."

"So what happened?" Z4 asked in a low voice.

Ne'al shrugged. "We fell into the wrong five percent."

"Right. So you want me to go to President Bacco and explain to her that she has to waste an hour of her life on a shuttle because we fell into the wrong five percent."

"It'll have the definite ring of truth to it," Ne'al said with a smile.

Z4 glared at Ne'al, and its smile fell. "Do you know where we are, Ne'al?"

"Your office."

"More generally."

"Paris."

"Exactly. City of Light, famed in song and story, seat of the Federation Council, and location with the second-heaviest amount of shuttle traffic anywhere in the entire sector. Do you know what gets the heaviest?"

Ne'al shook its head.

"San Francisco."

Now Ne'al nodded again. Z4 suspected that it was intimidated into silence by Z4's demeanor, which was fine, as it meant his demeanor was having precisely the desired effect.

"Shuttle trips for the president are security nightmares. Do you know what Starfleet Security's code word is for when the president takes a shuttle trip?"

Ne'al shook its head again.

"'Golden Gate.' Know why?"

A third head-shake.

"It refers to when the Breen invaded Earth and, among other things, destroyed the Golden Gate Bridge. It's a tidy way of summing up what a security nightmare it is when the president flies out in the open, a nightmare which is compounded by being in the two highest-traffic zones in the sector." Z4 stood up and walked around his desk so he could loom over the still-seated Ne'al—something he couldn't do once the much-taller Ne'al got up, so he wanted to take advantage. "Now, I want you to change the itinerary so that President Bacco leaves for the noon event at 2050. She will be taking one of the transporters. I don't care if you have to drag Montgomery Scott over from the S.C.E. office in San Francisco, I don't care if you have to animate the statue of Zefram Cochrane in Montana, but make sure *one* of those damn transporters is working at 2050, clear?"

"Zefram Cochrane invented warp drive."

Z4 was thrown off-kilter by Ne'al actually speaking, then again by what it said. "What?"

"The transporter didn't exist when Cochrane created warp drive. In fact, I don't think it existed until after he retired to Alpha Centauri. If we animated his statue, I don't think he'd know what to—"

"Just get it done, Ne'al." Z4 touched the control on his desk that opened the door.

Ne'al took the hint and ran out of the office.

As Z4 sat back down at his desk, his assistant, a fellow Nasat named Q2 Brown, commed him. *"You've got a call from the Tzenkethi embassy."*

That got Z4's attention. "Is it Emra?"

"Yes."

Emra had served as Tzenkethi ambassador to the Federation for years. Once, he'd tried to open up trade relations with Nasat, but the talks had fallen through when the Tzenkethi had refused to agree to terms that had been in any way favorable to the Federation as a whole. The Tzenkethi only traded with outsiders if they had to, and the situation had been sufficiently desperate that they'd made the overtures to Nasat in the first place, but nothing had come of it.

Still, Emra had always been an unusually reasonable person for a Tzenkethi politician—which was probably why he'd gotten the job, but also probably why he wasn't able to be effective at it—and they had stayed in periodic touch, both while Z4 was a forest quadrant governor on Nasat and now that he was in the Palais.

Activating his comm, he said, "Mr. Ambassador, how are you?" There was no visual image—Tzenkethi never used visual communication.

"I am fine, Mr. Blue my old friend, but I am afraid that I will need to speak with your president as soon as possible."

"Why not just request to speak before the council? They'll be in session tomorrow, and—"

"No, no, no, my friend, it cannot be the entire council. I have too many enemies on the first floor of the Palais—but President Bacco may see reason."

Z4's antennae curled up again. "Emra, what's this about?"

"I cannot say over an open channel, Z4. Suffice it to say that it is urgent and it involves the Tzelnira. *Can you do this for me?"*

Z4 hesitated. "Let me talk to Esperanza Piñiero and get back to you."

"Do so quickly, please."

"I'll be in touch." Z4 cut the communication, then asked Q2 to get the first free moment Esperanza had.

When she was done going over the amendments to the allocation bill for Betazed, Esperanza Piñiero checked her schedule and saw that she was supposed to meet with Jas Abrik. *This ought to be fun.*

She commed her assistant, Zachary Manzanillo, who'd been with her ever since she left Starfleet and started working for Nan Bacco on Cestus III. "Is he here?"

"Not yet. Should I page him?"

Letting out a sigh, she said, "Yes, please."

During his years in Starfleet, Jas Abrik had cultivated a reputation for punctuality. That reputation had gone out the window pretty much the microsecond that he started working as President Bacco's security advisor.

Of course, he always showed up on time for his briefings on fifteen. He had enough respect for the office to do that. But anywhere else in the Palais, he took his sweet time getting there—unless he was the one calling the meeting, in which case anyone who had the temerity to be late got an earful.

Zachary came back on. *"I've got Admiral Abrik in his office."*

"What the hell is he doing in his office?"

"I could ask him."

"Very funny," Esperanza muttered. "Put him through."

Jas Abrik's face appeared on her viewer. *"What do you want, Esperanza?"*

"You to be in my office for the meeting we scheduled yesterday. You were going to brief me on the Reman refugee situation."

"I'll have a briefing for the president in an hour."

"In an hour, the president's going to be on a shuttle bound for Luna."

"I think this is a little too important to handle through intermediaries. I can brief her on the—"

Clenching her hands into fists that were so tight that she feared she'd draw blood, Esperanza said, "It doesn't matter what you *think,* Jas. You know how this works. It all comes through me. Just like when I was first officer on the *Gorkon*—you didn't get in to see Admiral Nechayev until I cleared it. And you *don't* get to go to fifteen when you're not scheduled to unless you do it through me."

Jas glared at her for several seconds. *"When you sold me on this job, you said it was so I could help make policy. That means I get the president's ear."*

Esperanza rolled her eyes. "Oh please, Jas—you *do* have the president's ear. You talk to her every morning. Outside of that, you talk to me whenever you need to, and when I think it's appropriate, then you get to see her. I should think you of *all* people would appreciate the concept of chain of command." She opened her fists and put them down on her desk. "Now, then—what is the latest on the Reman situation?"

"The ship isn't moving any faster—in fact, the latest report from the outpost is that it's slowed down a bit. Meanwhile, Starfleet is sending the Intrepid *to do border patrol for the next two months, and they'll be at 22 when the*

ship's in range—but that's not the problem, which is why I'm not indulging your power games right now."

In a tight voice, Esperanza said, "Be very careful how you speak to me, Admiral Abrik. What the chief of staff giveth, the chief of staff taketh away, and it wouldn't take me more than six and a half seconds to convince the president to fire you."

Jas glared at her. *"You know what'll happen if you do that."*

Esperanza simply glared back, not giving a millimeter. Jas had taken the job in return for not revealing the truth behind Zife's resignation.

"Anyhow, it doesn't much matter, because we may have a bigger problem. Outpost 13 is picking up weapons fire in the T'Met system."

Based on the way Jas started that sentence, Esperanza had a feeling that this wasn't just the exchange of weapons fire between Romulans that had become common in the months since the senate's fall. "Klingons?"

"And Romulans."

"Are we sure?"

"No, which is why I need another hour."

Esperanza hesitated. "Would you recommend canceling the Luna trip?" Normally she'd phrase this more directly—along the lines of, Should she cancel the Luna trip?—but she felt the need to put the retired admiral in his place.

"When is she back?"

"Tonight."

"Then no, assuming you can get me a secured channel to the shuttle."

"That's the only kind of channel any of the shuttles have." The president had three shuttles—the *al-Rashid,* the *T'Maran,* and the *sh'Rothress,* named after three twenty-second-century Federation presidents. "Keep me posted, Jas. I need to be in the loop on this, especially if the press gets ahold of it. I'll need to know what to tell Jorel."

"Don't tell him anything. The press doesn't need to know about this."

"And don't tell me how to do my job," she snapped. "It's not a question of what they need to know, it's a question of what they *do* know and might hit him with in the briefing room."

"Fine. I need to get back to work now, if that's all right with you."

Sighing, Esperanza cut off the comm without a word. *Arrogant, self-righteous jackass!*

"Esperanza," Zachary said a moment later, *"Z4 just called—he needs to see you as soon as you're available."*

"Well, my meeting just ended prematurely. Send him over."

◆

CHAPTER FIVE

◆ ◆

ESPERANZA WALKED UP TO Sivak's desk, located just outside the president's office. Two members of Starfleet security stood by the door, with two more at the other door, and two more at the turbolift entrance.

"Is she free?"

Sivak didn't even look up from his workstation. "President Bacco is reading over several important papers before her trip to Luna."

Esperanza smiled sweetly, which nicely hid her instinct to haul off and belt the supercilious Vulcan. For years, Esperanza had been begging Nan Bacco to fire him, but she insisted that he was the only one who kept her life organized. Esperanza could think of several people off the top of her head who could have done as good a job or better—starting with Zachary—but the president insisted.

"That doesn't actually answer my question, Sivak."

Now he did look up. "One could, I suppose, argue that, as president of the United Federation of Planets, surrounded as she is by half a dozen armed guards, she is never truly free, is she?"

I can't believe I'm debating philosophy with a Vulcan when I just want to see the president. Then Esperanza thought about all the times she'd had to deal with Sivak and realized that she in truth had no trouble believing it.

Sivak opened the intercom. "Madam President, Ms. Piñiero wishes to meet with you."

"Good. Send her in."

Esperanza blinked. *I don't like the sound of that.* She'd known Nan Bacco since birth, and she recognized that tone in her old friend's voice: The president of the Federation was angry about something.

Sure enough, just as Esperanza walked past the two guards into the president's office, the occupant of that office was screaming while holding up a padd. "Esperanza, what the hell is this?"

"It looks like a padd, ma'am."

"It's what's *on* the padd that I'm asking about."

Moving toward the desk, Esperanza said, "Well, ma'am, since I left my psychic powers in my other pants—"

"Nobody likes a wiseass, Esperanza."

Smiling, Esperanza said, "Given how well-liked you are, ma'am, I'm not sure I believe that."

"Fair point. Anyhow, this is the schedule for tomorrow's council session."

Esperanza moved to sit in the guest chair closest to the desk. "What about it?"

"One of the things we're voting on is renewing the trade agreement with Aligar."

Shrugging, Esperanza said, "Yeah, we've been trading with them for kellinite. We had to, during the war—the way we were losing, replacing, and rebuilding ships, we had to—"

President Bacco sat down and let the padd clatter onto the *salish* desk. "That's nice, but the war's over. You know how they mine the kellinite?"

Esperanza shook her head. "I assume with the usual equipment, they—"

"Slaves, Esperanza. They use slaves."

That caught the chief of staff off guard. "I-I didn't know."

"Well, I did know—you know how I knew? Those jackasses tried to peddle their kellinite to us on Cestus right after I became governor. I was all set to do it, too—we needed to upgrade our planetary defenses—but we did a little research and found out that they oppressed ninety percent of their society. That's not a typo—*ninety* percent. Nine out of every ten people on Aligar is owned by one-tenth of the population. What the hell is the Federation doing getting involved with these people?"

Esperanza let out a breath through her teeth. This wasn't going to be easy to explain. "It was war, ma'am, we—"

The president rolled her eyes. "Oh, for the love of everything, Esperanza, do *not* drag out the 'It was war, you civilians can't *possibly* understand' Starfleet *crap*. I know there was a war on. I was there when it happened, and on top of that, I had a bunch of Gorns decide to blow my capital city into tiny pieces, so kindly don't lecture me about the sacrifices you need to make during wartime."

Esperanza closed her eyes for a moment. "I'm sorry, ma'am, I didn't mean—"

"Yeah, you did, and you know you did—and I don't mind the perspective, it's the attitude I have a problem with. Like you know better than anyone 'cause you were in Starfleet. I think you and I are both pretty cognizant of the fact that there are plenty of screwups we can lay at Starfleet's doorstep."

"Yes, ma'am." Esperanza saw no reason to argue—besides, there were bigger fish to fry. "If we can—"

But the president hadn't let this out of her teeth yet. "I understand why we had to deal with the Aligar during the war—desperate times, desperate measures, strange bedfellows, and whatever other damn wartime cliché you want to throw at me—but the war's been over for four years. Is there any compellingly good reason why we should be setting aside our principles now? Or has it just become second nature?"

"No, ma'am," Esperanza said after a brief pause, "and I think you should make that argument tomorrow. But, ma'am, there's something else—something more important. Actually, several somethings."

The president sighed. "I don't suppose this can wait until after I get back from the moon."

"No, ma'am."

President Bacco leaned back in her chair. "No, of course

not, because if it could, you wouldn't have come in here. What is it?"

"Well, first of all, Jas will be giving you a briefing in about half an hour—probably while you're on the shuttle. They've picked up weapons fire in Romulan space, and they think it's a dustup with some Klingons."

President Bacco put her head in her hands. "Hell and damnation. Do we know anything for sure yet?"

"No, ma'am—that's what Jas is supposed to tell us in half an hour."

"Does it have to do with those refugees we think are heading for Outpost 22?"

"No, ma'am—it's in a completely different sector."

"Small favors." The president leaned forward. "Have someone get in touch with Ambassador Rozhenko on Qo'noS, and have someone else get me a location on Ambassador K'mtok, in case we need to get him here in a hurry. And keep T'Latrek, Mazibuko, and Molmaan around."

Esperanza understood the need to talk to both Rozhenko and K'mtok—the Federation ambassador to the Klingons and the Klingon ambassador to the Federation, respectively—as well as Councillors T'Latrek and Mazibuko, who represented Vulcan and Earth and were the chair and second chair of the external affairs council. The third councillor the president listed, though, didn't seem to fit. "Why Molmaan?"

"Zalda's got the unlucky position of being right near the Klingon border *and* the Romulan border. It's one of the reasons why they were fast-tracked into Federation membership a hundred years ago—they kept having wrecked ships from both sides crash-land on their planet. So Zalda in general's always kept an eye on both empires, for their own self-interest. And I know that Molmaan has serious opinions on the subject."

Esperanza smiled. If there was one thing Nan Bacco respected and admired—and liked to make use of—it was people with serious opinons. Then again, Zaldans were never shy with their opinions, serious or otherwise. They had a cultural bias against politeness, which generally meant that Zaldans produced very entertaining politicians. Molmaan fit that mold. *It's gonna be an interesting meeting when we all get together. . . .*

Then the president looked down at the desk. "Coffee, black, unsweetened." A steaming mug materialized on the center of the desk. As she picked it up by the handle, she said, "Bring Ross in, too."

"I've already talked to Ross—he's bringing Akaar over from San Francisco."

"Who?"

"Fleet Admiral Leonard Akaar. He was on site for the arrangement with the Klingons, and he just reported back after the *Titan*'s little trip outside the galaxy."

"All right, good."

Esperanza braced herself before saying, "Also—"

"There's more?" The president sounded pained.

"You knew the job was dangerous when you took it, ma'am."

"Remember what I said before about wiseasses?"

"Yes, ma'am." Esperanza waited until the president took another sip of her coffee. "I'm not sure about this one. Z4 got a call from Ambassador Emra."

The president frowned. "Which one's Emra?"

"The ambassador from Tzenketh."

At that, President Bacco almost sputtered her coffee. "*From* Tzenketh?"

"Yes, ma'am."

"We *have* an ambassador from Tzenketh?"

"Yes, ma'am."

She set her mug down. "Correct me if I'm wrong, Esperanza, but don't the Tzenkethi hate the Federation and everything it stands for? Didn't they react to our attempts to open trade agreements with them by starting a war? And hasn't every peace overture with them been treated with contempt and loathing on their part toward us?"

"Yes, ma'am."

"And yet they sent an ambassador." The president rose, still holding her coffee mug, and started to pace behind the desk, staring out at the view of Paris. "The things people do baffle the hell out of me sometimes. All right, what did this Emra tell Ziff?"

Esperanza smirked. "You know he hates being called that, right?"

"Wouldn't call him that otherwise," the president said with a like smirk.

Getting back on track, Esperanza said, "Well, Emra and Ziff—" She shook her head. "He and Z4 have a history from an abortive attempt at opening up trade between Tzenketh and Nasat."

The president swallowed her coffee before saying derisively, "I'm sure that went resoundingly well."

"The thing is—he says that he needs to talk with you. Not with the council, but with you."

"What about?"

"All the ambassador would say is that it has to do with the *Tzelnira.*"

That got the president's attention. She whirled around and looked right at Esperanza. "The *Tzelnira?*"

This surprised Esperanza. She knew that Alberto had

been a relief worker during the war before he married Annabella, but simple recognition didn't explain the president's reaction. "Yeah—why?"

"This morning, during the security briefing, Holly mentioned some chatter about one of the *Tzelnira*'s children being sick."

Esperanza frowned. "You think this is related?"

The president shrugged. "Who the hell knows?" She stared out the window again. "Why not just go to the council? He can request an audience when we're in session, same as any diplomat."

"Z4 asked that. He said he has enemies on the first floor."

"Oh, please." The president turned back around. "*I* have enemies on the first floor. What, does he think having that in common will unite us in a bond?" She moved back to her chair. "Still, set up an appointment for you to meet with him tomorrow and let me know."

Nodding, Esperanza said, "Fine. And if he insists on seeing you?"

The president smiled. "Remind him of the fact that I wasn't even aware of his existence until today, which should give him a fairly good idea of what level he's at on the food chain around here. He wants to see me, and he wants to go around the council, he's gotta do better than cryptic messages to my senior staff."

Esperanza stood up. "Will do, ma'am."

"Anything else?"

"Jorel made the announcement at the briefing about Delta and Carrea. I'm counting the microseconds before their ambassadors and Eleana are crawling up my ass."

"Thank you for that lovely image. Ashanté and Z4 have their recommendations?"

Esperanza nodded. "Almost. They'll be waiting for you on the *al-Rashid*."

"Okay, then."

"Thank you, Madam President."

◆

CHAPTER SIX

◆　　◆

JAS ABRIK STARED AT the framed painting in the center of the wall opposite where he sat at the round table that took up most of the space. The painting—Claude Monet's *Bridge over a Pool of Water Lilies*—was a treasure from Earth's pre-unification period. According to one of Abrik's aides, the style of painting was known as impressionism, so called because it conveyed the impression of something without rendering it slavishly. One could see the brushstrokes easily—in fact, they drew attention to themselves. And yet, combine them, and it looked just like a footbridge over a lily-laden stream. There was no mistaking it for anything else.

Also seated at the table were Admirals Ross and Akaar, Captain Hostetler Richman, and Secretary Shostakova. Akaar sat ramrod straight in a chair that barely fit his massive form, huge arms folded over barrel chest. Abrik knew that the Capellan was some kind of royalty in exile or other, and he certainly had the attitude for it; Abrik had always found the admiral to be a pompous ass.

Ross was engaged in a whispered conversation with Hostetler Richman. *Probably comparing intelligence notes.* Ross did a great deal of work with Starfleet Intelligence as a junior officer, and in fact had been Hostetler Richman's mentor.

What the hell is taking so long? Abrik thought as he gazed at the wall chronometer. *Piñiero and the councillors should have been here by now. At this rate, we may as well wait until Bacco's back on-planet.*

Originally, the Monet Room was one of a dozen secure meeting rooms on one of the basement levels of the Palais. During the Dominion War, many offices and operations were moved to the belowground spaces, making it necessary to convert several of the other meeting rooms to office space. This particular room had become Zife's "war room," where much of the top-level strategizing had been done. After the war's end, the Monet Room remained where the Federation government's security operations were conducted—or, at least, discussed.

"I have a question."

Abrik looked over at Shostakova, who was sitting quietly three chairs down from him. He pointed at his own chest. "Me?"

"Yes. Your spots—do they go all the way down?"

Abrik couldn't help it. He burst out laughing.

At the secretary of defense's nonplussed expression, he quickly said, "I'm sorry, Madam Secretary, but I haven't been asked that question since I was an ensign. Yes, they go all the way down."

She nodded. "Interesting. I wonder why that is."

Frowning, Abrik said, "Excuse me?"

"I simply wonder what quirk of evolution led to—"

Before Shostakova could continue her musings, the door opened to reveal Piñiero, along with Councillors T'Latrek, Mazibuko, and Molmaan. They went for four of the empty seats, Piñiero looking like a coiled spring, two of the councillors looking somewhat more calm, and the third looking angry. From T'Latrek, a Vulcan who had a reputation for grace under pressure, the calm was to be expected. Abrik didn't know Matthew Mazibuko all that well, so for all he knew, he had a reputation similar to T'Latrek's. As for Molmaan, the look of anger was to be expected from a member of a species who, as a rule, didn't hide their feelings.

"Sorry," Piñiero said, "but the president only just took off from Luna—the function ran late."

"Someone could've told us that half an hour ago," Abrik muttered.

As she sat in her chair, Piñiero smiled sweetly. "A half hour ago, we didn't know it was running late, and we were concerned that we'd lost contact with the president. It was just solar flares, though, and she's on her way back." She touched the intercom in front of her. "Zachary, we're here—put the president and the ambassador through."

The wall opposite the Monet painting had a large viewscreen, which lit up with a split-screen image, Bacco on the left, Ambassador Alexander Rozhenko on the right. Rozhenko was the son of two previous Federation ambassadors to the Klingon Empire. One-quarter human and three-quarters Klingon, Rozhenko's parents were Worf, son of Mogh, and K'Ehleyr. Abrik wasn't entirely sanguine about his qualifications to replace his father, who had served with distinction for four years before declining to continue in the post, citing a desire to return to Starfleet. That was, to Abrik's mind, Starfleet's gain, but the Diplomatic Corps' loss. Worf was one of the few people who could navigate the treacherous waters of the Klingon-Federation alliance; K'Ehleyr, who served for only two years before she was brutally murdered during the transfer of power from Chancellor K'mpec to Chancellor Gowron over a decade earlier, was another of those few. They had to hope like hell that Rozhenko had inherited at least some of his parents' skills.

"Do we have anything new?" Bacco asked, not wasting any time.

"A bit, ma'am," Hostetler Richman said. "Outpost 13 detected disruptor fire of both Klingon and Romulan design in the T'Met system, as well as at least three Klingon *Karas*-class strike ships and one Romulan *D'Deridex*-class warbird."

"So the Romulan military's getting into it with the Klingons. Who fired first?"

Hostetler Richman hesitated. Abrik did not. "We don't know, Madam President."

"Why the hell not?"

Abrik managed to restrain himself from saying, *Because sensors aren't magical detectors that read everything at all ranges, and if you had any hard experience of anything outside Cestus III, you'd know that.* "The outpost's sensors have gaps, and one of those gaps is when the exchange of fire started. When the gap ends, both sides are going at it."

Hostetler Richman added, "Thirteen is the closest outpost to T'Met, but that doesn't mean it's exactly *close*, ma'am. There are limits to what we can detect."

Piñiero asked Rozhenko, "Mr. Ambassador, what's the High Council saying?"

"Nothing yet—they're waiting for a report from Captain J'kral—he's the one who led the strike ships—but General Khegh is pretty sure that the Romulans fired first."

"Right." Abrik snorted. "It's not like they'd say anything else."

T'Latrek was sitting serenely with her hands together, her index fingers steepled. "The Romulans would not fire first unless they were provoked."

Shostakova leaned forward. "Some in the Romulan military would view the Klingons' very presence as a provocation."

Bacco said, *"Didn't that ship pretty much sail when this whole shebang started? They agreed to this arrangement."*

"They agreed reluctantly," Hostetler Richman said. "And some fleet commanders might not have liked the arrangement all that much."

Akaar's voice was surprisingly subdued. "I believe the problem may be more fundamental than that. Since Shinzon's coup, the Romulan military is in disarray. Where once they were united under the political guidance of the praetor and the senate and the spiritual leadership of the emperor, they now have neither. Emperor Shiarkiek was assassinated during the Dominion War and never replaced, which created a crisis within the Romulan hierarchy that was made all the worse by the Watraii affair. Shinzon had some of the Romulan military on his side—and plenty of it against him. With their fleet already sundered, they have splintered even further with this new arrangement. There are at least five different factions vying for power—six if you count the Remans. Any action taken by a Romulan ship cannot be taken as sanctioned by the Romulan government as a whole because right now the Romulan government's authority is limited."

Bacco let out a breath. *"This is just going to get worse when those Remans hit Outpost 22, isn't it?"*

"Probably," Piñiero said.

"Definitely." Councillor Molmaan spoke with more finality than the chief of staff. "President Bacco, I think that we should send ships into Romulan space. It's the only way to guarantee peace in the region."

"I must disagree with the councillor from Zaldan," Mazibuko said in a quiet voice. "Adding more armed ships to the equation is unlikely to guarantee anything resembling peace."

Molmaan glowered at Mazibuko. "I'd expect *you* to say that. But the only thing that will keep Klingon and Romulan passions in check is the presence of the Federation. Otherwise I guarantee there will be a war."

"War's never a guarantee, Councillor," Bacco said, *"and it's a last resort, not a first one."*

"For us, maybe. Not for the Klingons, nor the Romulans."

"I disagree," T'Latrek said. "Where Klingons seek battle for its own sake, Romulans do not—they only seek battles they can win."

Abrik was about to point out that they were getting offtopic when Bacco did it for him. *"Much as I'd love to dive into these philosophical waters, let's save it for when people aren't shooting at each other. Mr. Ambassador, I need to know what the High Council's response to this is, and I need it yesterday."*

"Yes, ma'am."

Bacco then looked around the rest of the Monet Room. *"As for the rest of you, keep on this. Admiral Ross, I want whatever ships you can divert to the Romulan border to head there now. Make it clear that we're keeping an eye on things."*

Ross nodded. "The *Intrepid*'s already on the way. I can also send the *Bellerophon,* the *T'Kumbra,* the *Malinche,* and the *Prometheus.*"

"The Prometheus *is the one that can split in three, right?"*

"Yes, ma'am. The *Prometheus*-class is our best quick-response combat vessel."

Abrik said, "We should put ships near the Klingon border, as well."

"What for?" Piñiero asked.

"To make it clear that we're keeping an eye on *them,* too."

Shostakova shook her head. "They are our allies."

"For now."

"They will view this as hostile," T'Latrek said calmly.

Again, Abrik snorted. "They view *everything* as hostile!"

"And they've been itchy since Tezwa," Bacco said.

Rozhenko spoke up. *"I'm with Secretary Shostakova. Putting ships on the Romulan border is a show of support for the empire. Putting ships on the Klingon border'll just isolate us from both of them."*

"If they fired first, we *don't* support them." Abrik was wondering why someone with only two months of diplomatic experience was doing anything in this conversation other than take instructions from the president.

"We'll stay off the border for now," Bacco said, *"but meanwhile, I want K'mtok's ass in a chair in my office first thing in the morning."*

"He'll be there, ma'am," Piñiero said. "We can slot him in at 0900."

"Make it later—I want you there, too."

"No need, ma'am. I can be there at 0900. Emra canceled. Said it was nothing, just a mistake on his part."

"Uh-huh." Bacco sounded dubious. *"Maybe you should have Z4—"* Then she waved her hand in front of her face. *"Oh, forget it—the whole damn thing was his idea in the*

first place. He wants to cancel, that's one less thing I have to think about."

Piñiero smiled. "Down to only six billion, ma'am?"

Several of those around the table chuckled. Abrik was not one of them.

Neither was Shostakova. "The difficulty here is that we do not know if this is an isolated incident. Until we know who was commanding that warbird—"

"Everything that happens in Romulan space right now is almost by definition an isolated incident, Madam Secretary." Akaar made the pronouncement in his usual pompous tone.

"Hang on a second," Bacco said, *"we've got the Federation's leading expert on Romulans right there in Romulan space. Esperanza, tell Ambassador T'Kala to get Spock for us."*

Piñiero shifted in her seat. Abrik wondered what that meant. Piñiero was fairly comfortable with the president, so for her to react like that was telling.

Abrik wasn't the only one to notice; Bacco picked up on it right away. *"What is it, Esperanza?"*

"They found T'Kala in her apartments, dead. Suicide."

Now why don't I like the sound of that? Abrik thought glumly.

"We sure it was a suicide?" Bacco asked.

Hostetler Richman nodded. "We're sure, ma'am. T'Kala did it in full view of the security cameras at the embassy. Used her honor blade and everything."

"In that case," Akaar said, "it was an honorable suicide. To be expected given that the government that assigned T'Kala no longer truly exists."

Sighing, Bacco said, *"I'll bet anything that the first question Jorel gets tomorrow is if she killed herself in embarrassment over what happened with the travel office. Look,*

I don't care how we get Spock here, but get him here. Right now we're talking through our hats. I want someone who actually knows what he's talking about, which pretty much rules out everybody in this meeting." Several people chuckled at that also. Abrik was assuredly not one of them. "*All right, I'll be back in the Palais in two hours. I don't care if you know anything or not, I want a report every two hours from each of you.*"

"You'll have it, ma'am," Piñiero said.

"*Good. See you all soon.*"

Everyone in the room, with the notable exception of Molmaan, said, "Thank you, Madam President."

Abrik himself only said it because it was proper and it was expected. It certainly wasn't a sign of respect. He had a feeling that President Bacco was going to lead the Federation to ruin.

MARCH 2380

"Success is the ability to go from one failure to another with no loss of enthusiasm."
—Winston Churchill

CHAPTER SEVEN

◆   ◆

COME ON, ALREADY! Sephara directed the thought at her roommate. *It's going to start!*

Using her voice, Gira said, "I'm coming, I'm coming," from the other room.

Sephara sighed. For some reason, Gira always preferred to use clunky vocal communication instead of speaking telepathically like any sensible Betazoid. It wasn't as if they were dealing with weird flatbrain aliens who could only communicate verbally.

But then, ever since Enaren University's housing department had seen fit to put Gira and Sephara together, the latter had spent most of her time wondering about the eccentricities of the former.

Gira came in holding a bowl full of *hilrep* fruit in her right hand. "Okay, I'm ready."

Sephara's face scrunched up in annoyance. *I'm allergic to hilrep!*

"Ow!" Gira put her left hand to her forehead. "You don't have to broadcast so loud."

You could have brought a fruit that I can eat.

"You said you weren't hungry." Gira fell, more than sat, on the couch, her body language echoing her thoughts, which indicated irritation with her roommate.

Well, Sephara had plenty of irritation to throw back at her. Giving up on speaking telepathically—honestly, it was like talking to a child—she said, "I said I didn't want a meal. There's a big difference between eating a meal and munching on fruit while we watch *ICL*."

"I'm *sorry*, but *hilrep* is all we have in the pantry."

"I thought you were going shopping."

Sephara read guilt in Gira's thoughts as she said, "I never said that."

Aghast at so bald-faced a lie, Sephara sat down in the easy chair, as far from Gira as possible. Since the war, replicators on Betazed were at a premium, and university dorm rooms didn't have them as a power-saving endeavor. Sephara had always found that ridiculous, but nobody had asked her.

Fine. I'll just sit here and eat nothing while you munch on your filthy hilrep. Sephara then picked up the remote unit and activated the holo unit that would show them the discussion program they needed to see as a requirement for their political studies class.

The image in the center of the room lit up with four people sitting at a desk: the Kriosian host, Velisa, along with a female human in a Starfleet uniform, a male human wearing a suit that Sephara found hideous, and an Antedean of indeterminate gender who looked just like Sephara's seafood dinner last night. Behind them, a viewscreen was visible, showing a Vulcan woman.

"Good evening. This is *Illuminating the City of Light*, I'm your host, Velisa. Originally, we were going to be spending our time talking about the war between President Bacco and the rest of the Federation Council that has been going on for the past six weeks—however, this morning, FNS broke the story that a ship full of Reman refugees is heading for Federation Neutral Zone Outpost 22 at low warp and will be in Federation space within a few days. We'll be getting to the president's problems with the council soon enough, but we'll be discussing the Remans first. With me tonight to do that are Admiral Kathryn Janeway of Starfleet; Edmund Atkinson, a political reporter for the *Times;* Councillor Selora Quintor of Antede III; and, remotely from the Palais de la Concorde in Paris, we have Sorlak, associate counsel in the Palais legal office. Welcome, all of you."

The panelists all made indications of acknowledgment, except for the Antedean, who seemed to just wiggle. Sephara found it gross.

"Sorlak, I'd like to start with you," Velisa said, looking back at the viewscreen. "What are the legal ramifications of these Remans asking for asylum?"

"It is premature to speak of such things, Velisa, until such a time as the Remans actually do so."

Adopting a supercilious tone that Sephara found rather enticing, Atkinson said, "So you haven't talked to them yet?"

"I am not in a position to speak to them, Mr. Atkinson, as those communications are being made by the personnel at Outpost 22. However, since you are no doubt speaking figuratively, I can only say that several attempts have been made to contact the vessel that is approaching the outpost, but they have yet to respond. Sensor scans indicate that their communications systems are only operating at a low power level, and it is possible that they are using their minimal power only for internal communications."

Velisa said, "Well, let's assume that they *do* ask for asylum. What happens then?"

"The petition will be reviewed by the legal office and a decision will be made."

"And what would that decision be?"

Sephara thought that while Velisa was being a bit too aggressive in her question, the Vulcan lawyer was being ridiculously obtuse.

"Until the actual petition is reviewed, it would be the height of illogic to speculate as to what the legal office's decision would be."

The Antedean spoke in a high, squeaky voice. "It should be added that the legal office's decision is only a decision for the legal office. It will then take the form of a recommendation to the council, and the *council* will make a decision."

"Councillor Quintor, do *you* think that the Federation will grant an asylum request—*if* that's what the occupants of this ship are after?"

"I'm not entirely convinced that that *is* what they're after, but a lot of it would depend on the reasons for the asylum request."

Atkinson chuckled without mirth. "I should think that would be obvious, Councillor—they've lived as slaves for centuries, and violence between Klingon vessels protecting Remus and Romulan military vessels has been escalating since the incident in the T'Met system two months ago, and the settling of the Remans in the Ehrie'fvil colony has not gone especially smoothly. Just yesterday a dozen Remans were attacked in their homes by supposedly unidentified attackers."

"It should be pointed out that the Remans are not slaves now, so if that is their only reason, they would not be granted asylum."

"That's ridiculous!" Atkinson said. "They're being attacked in space, they're being attacked on Romulus. What other reason do they need?"

"One which actually applies, Mr. Atkinson."

Velisa spoke up before Atkinson had a chance to respond to that. "Admiral Janeway, you look like you want to say something."

Janeway hesitated for a moment. "I'm sure, of course, that certain legalities need to be worked out, and I can understand Ms. Sorlak's reluctance to commit to any course of action—but the Federation was founded on the principles of freedom, of self-determination, of equal rights for every sentient being. I can't imagine that the Federation would turn away refugees who have suffered oppression in an enemy nation for so long. When I commanded the *U.S.S. Voyager,* and we were trapped in the Delta Quadrant, we took in several people who had separated themselves from the Borg collective. One of them is at Starfleet Academy now. They were in the same situation as these Remans, and if they want to seek a better life in the Federation, who are we to turn them down?"

The Antedean councillor wiggled again. "You make a very compelling argument, Admiral, but there are several flaws in it. One is that the Romulan Star Empire is not an enemy nation. They have not been our enemies since they joined forces with us and the Klingons during the Dominion War six years ago. And, indeed, the Romulan Star Empire barely exists as a political entity right now."

"The kind of chaos that results in the fall of a government," Janeway said in a tight voice, "is exactly the sort of situation into which the Federation must provide humanitarian aid."

"What an ethnocentric term," the Antedean said.

Atkinson joined the conversation again. "The word's root may come from the word *human,* Councillor, but the meaning has evolved. Are you and Ms. Sorlak really going to sit here and tell us that the Federation is going to turn away refugees from its border?"

"I have said no such thing," the Vulcan woman said archly. Sephara decided she didn't like her. *"And the Fed-*

eration has, in fact, been providing aid to many parts of the Romulan Empire for the past three months. But there are several factors at stake, not the least of which is that the presence and/or status of the Romulan Star Empire is wholly irrelevant to this discussion."

"How is *that*, exactly?" Atkinson sounded annoyed, not that Sephara could blame him. *How could the Romulans be irrelevant to a discussion about Reman refugees?*

"Because the Remans are a protectorate of the Klingon Empire. If we grant them asylum, we risk endangering the Khitomer Accords."

Janeway said, "These Remans may view the Klingons as simply exchanging one oppressor for the other."

"They may, yes. That is why I cannot speculate as to what the legal office's decision—or, rather," she added with a look at Quintor, *"recommendation will be."*

There was a very brief pause, which Velisa filled in quickly. "Obviously this is a more difficult issue than one might think. We could probably go on for some time, but I would like to cover what we originally invited you all to discuss."

"That's *it?*" Gira asked, and Sephara could read her roommate's irritation. "They barely *started* covering the issue."

"What else were they supposed to say?" Sephara asked verbally. "All they did was say 'I don't know' fifteen different ways. Honestly, if they were telepaths, the conversation would've been over five minutes sooner and wasted a lot less of everyone's time and energy."

Velisa was still talking. "Six weeks ago, President Bacco railed into the rest of the Federation Council over the Federation's trade agreement with Aligar for kellinite. She urged the council to vote to discontinue the agreement, which is up for renewal. Here's an excerpt from the speech, made in an open session of the full council."

The image switched to that of the Federation Council Chambers, which Sephara knew was in a city called Paris, though she couldn't remember what the name of the building was. *I hope that isn't on a quiz.*

"It probably will be," Gira said snidely.

Sephara stuck her tongue out at her roommate.

At the center of the image was a white-haired human woman, who was standing at a podium emblazoned with the symbol of the Federation. Some of the councillors were visible on either side—Sephara picked out a Bajoran, an Andorian, a Tellarite, and a Zakdorn—though most of the council seats were not visible.

"Over ninety percent of Aligar's population work for no compensation of any kind, are given no freedoms of any kind, have no liberties of any kind. They have no choice in their lives, no say in their government, no voice to be heard. And the work they do is backbreaking and humiliating. They don't have any proper medical care—workers who are injured are discarded and left to die, with new people sent in to take their place. All of Aligar's wealth is concentrated in the ten percent of their population that does the least to earn it. Now that's how they run their world, and if they won't change their ways, there's not a lot we can do about it. But we can—we must—cease our support of it. During the Dominion War, we had trade agreements with several nations that we found distasteful, that we found repugnant: the Son'a, Aligar, Mordaliia. But the war's long over, and it is far past time that we allowed ourselves to support this sort of vicious oppression of almost an entire species. We cannot continue to call ourselves a society that values freedom for all sentient life, and then hap-

pily take kellinite from a world that doesn't consider its sentient life to even be sentient."

Velisa resumed, "Although her argument was enough to sway several swing votes on the council toward non-renewal, the effects of her speech to the council have been tremendous. The council has ground to a proverbial halt, as several orders of business proposed by the president's office have been slowed down. Councillor Quintor, is it true that President Bacco's—there's no other word for it—chiding of the council has resulted in this slowdown?"

"First of all," Quintor said in her annoying voice, "I would like to say that I voted against the initial trade agreement with Aligar and have voted against it every time the agreement came up for renewal. Antede has never had any kind of ownership of people in its history—in fact, our world was first introduced to the concept when we made contact with other worlds, and we always found it to be repugnant. Lack of any kind of slavery is a basic requirement for any world to be even considered for Federation membership, so the notion that we should trade with a nation that has a population that is ninety percent slaves is abhorrent."

"And yet, we continue to be allied with the Klingons," Atkinson said snidely, though Sephara had to concede that the reporter had a point.

"Yes, we do," Quintor said, "and I find that equally abhorrent. When the Klingons withdrew from the Khitomer Accords six years ago, there was a resolution for the Federation to remain signatories to the agreement, so that if the empire wanted to re-ally themselves with us, they could simply re-sign the treaty—as, in fact, they did a year and a half later. I voted against that, as well. I have always been against the Federation-Klingon alliance."

Before Atkinson could say anything else, Velisa said, "We're getting off-track, Councillor."

"Yes, of course, my apologies, Velisa. In any case, I disagree with your assertion that there's been any kind of 'slowdown.' We are carefully considering any legislation or appointments made by the president's office, as we always do. Such decisions do have far-reaching consequences."

Atkinson laughed. "Oh, come off it. Councillor Artrin was nominated for the judiciary council two months ago, as were Councillor Beltane for commerce and yourself for government oversight—with no movement in sight for the council to ratify any of them."

Quintor wiggled again. "I was honored to even be nominated for government oversight—but it is a position that requires careful consideration. As does judiciary."

"I would disagree with the councillor on the second point," the Vulcan woman said. *"Councillor Artrin has an impeccable record, and has long been qualified for the judiciary council."*

"So you *do* think the council is stonewalling President Bacco as a punishment?" Velisa asked.

"I would never presume to ascribe such motives to esteemed members of the Federation Council."

Sephara laughed at that. If this conversation had been telepathic, Sorlak would never have been able to get away with such a bald-faced lie. That reminded Sephara that Vulcans weren't supposed to lie—she wondered if that held true for Vulcan lawyers.

"Turn it off," Gira said.

"What?" Sephara asked, though she, of course, heard both Gira's words and the thoughts of disgust that prompted them.

"They're not saying anything interesting. I can't believe that we're required to watch this idiotic program."

Not wanting to get into an argument, Sephara turned it off, just as Atkinson started raving about something. It was easier to do that than to argue with Gira when she was being unreasonable—which was pretty much any time she was awake.

So what do you want to do now? Sephara asked.

To her shock, Gira also responded telepathically. *Anything else, as long as it doesn't have to do with school.*

Why don't we do that food shopping you never did?

Gira liked that idea, and the roommates got up to get food, the world of Federation politics forgotten until they would need it for class.

✦

CHAPTER EIGHT

✦   ✦

ESPERANZA PIÑIERO got off the turbolift on the fifteenth floor to see Sivak seated at his desk and none of the security guards present—which meant that Bacco wasn't in the office.

"Oh hell, are they *still* in session?"

Sivak didn't look up from his workstation. "Were I to answer that in the negative, it would be a lie."

Sighing, Esperanza looked at the chronometer. The session had gone on for eight hours, four hours longer than expected. She knew that the new business had taken up three and three-quarters of those hours—most of that being the Reman situation, now that it had gone public—to be followed by voting. If it was taking this long, there was obviously some contentious discussion going on before the votes could actually be taken. They had hopes that the council would *finally* vote on Artrin, Quintor, and Beltane, but Esperanza was starting to think that that was a forlorn hope.

"Call me the instant she walks out of that turbolift, all right?"

"That is unlikely."

Esperanza frowned. "Why the hell is that?"

Sivak looked up at her, an eyebrow raised. "There is no need to yell, Ms. Piñiero. I merely consider it to be highly unlikely that you will be in your office to receive a call when the president comes off the turbolift."

Her mood already crappy, Esperanza found that Sivak's usual nonsense was fraying her last existing nerve ending. "And why is *that?*" she asked in a tight voice.

"Because seventeen-point-nine seconds ago, the session *did* end. President Bacco is on her way up now."

Esperanza counted to ten in English, Spanish, and Bajoran, then said, "Why didn't you just say that?"

As the turbolift doors opened to reveal four of the six bodyguards, who then went through the side doors to take up their positions at the other two entrances to the president's office, Sivak said, "I believe I just did."

"You do know that I can order the security guards to kill you and then just make up a reason, right?"

The eyebrow shot up again. "That is also unlikely."

A second turbolift door opened to reveal the other two guards and Nan Bacco. Esperanza could almost see the cloud over the president's head, which she did not take as a good sign.

"Sivak, find out what the score in the game was."

"Madam President, it was an exhibition game, I don't see the relevance—"

"Right now, Sivak, I couldn't give a tinker's damn whether or not you see the nose in front of your face, much less the relevance of my request. I just spent eight hours with the council, which is about seven hours and fifty-nine minutes more than I was interested in spending, during which we accomplished about as much as a one-legged person at an ass-kicking contest. I swear, there was more governing on Chalna today than there was here, and the Chalnoth are anarchists." She looked at Esperanza. "What do *you* want?"

"I wanted to know how the session went, but you pretty well answered that one, ma'am, thanks."

President Bacco snorted. "How the hell did FNS find out about the Reman ship?"

"They're a news-gathering organization, ma'am. Honestly, the surprise is that nobody picked it up before now. And this is better, really—it'll be at 22 in a few days, so there'll only be a few days of speculating about what we'll do in response, instead of two months of it if it'd gone public right off the bat. Besides, the Remans' comm lines are still down, so we can honestly say we don't know what to expect."

"The hallmark of my presidency," Bacco muttered.

Sivak spoke up. "The Pike City Pioneers A-squad defeated their B-squad by a final result of eleven runs to ten."

The president looked disappointed. "It was an intrasquad game today?"

"Yes, ma'am. They will encounter the Palombo Sehlats

tomorrow, and the Prairieview Green Sox the day follow-ing." Sivak looked up from his screen. "I was unaware that there was any legislation on Cestus III that required all municipalities to begin with the letter P."

"Keep reading the schedule, you'll find Lakeside, John-son City, New Chicago, Os—Oh, hell, why am I arguing with you?"

"A question that torments us all, Madam President."

Esperanza smiled. The sport of baseball had been re-vived on Cestus III after falling out of favor on Earth in the twenty-first century. A league had been incorporated during Nan Bacco's first term as planetary governor, and she had been an avid follower of the Cestus Baseball League ever since. When the presidential campaign started, Bacco joked that she was considering dropping out when she realized that she'd be away from Cestus for the entire baseball season for at least four years. Exhibition season had just begun—games that actually mattered would commence in a month's time, when the president would be traveling home to throw out the ceremonial first pitch at Opening Day. It was one stop on a goodwill tour to various Federation worlds, which had been deliberately timed to allow her to throw out the first pitch, something she'd done every year since the CBL started.

The president ignored Sivak's rebuke and asked, "You postponed the afternoon's meetings?"

"Yes, ma'am. The secretary of agriculture will return at 1800, the secretary of defense at 1815, the secretary of housing at 1830, and Mr. MacDougan at 1845."

Frowning, the president asked, "Why'm I meeting with Fred again?"

Sivak tapped a command onto his screen. "To discuss the address to the Titan Shipbuilder's Guild tomorrow."

"Aligar's gonna be an issue there," Esperanza put in quickly before the president could object.

She objected anyhow. "We locked that speech two days ago."

"And then this morning, the guild officially denounced your suspension of trade with Aligar. I told Fred to rework the speech, and then I put him on your calendar—for 1400, originally."

"Dammit, is Aligar gonna bite me on my ass for the rest of my term?" Before Esperanza could answer, the president waved toward the entrance to her office. "C'mon inside, I've been standing for eight hours and my feet are about ready to sue for separate maintenance. I need to sit and I need to abuse someone, and you've always been my favorite target for that."

"Ma'am, you know I serve at your pleasure, but I think sitting on me is taking that a bit too far. Or did you mean the abuse?"

They moved toward the door. "That abuse is gonna get physical if you don't watch it." She sighed. "Right now my pleasure is to yell at someone, and if I do it to the staff, it'll be on FNS by midnight. Every other damn thing we do winds up there. Did you see *ICL* yesterday?"

"I thought Sorlak did well. And Quintor—"

"Quintor made an ass of herself." President Bacco went around to the other side of her desk but didn't sit down. "And where the hell does Admiral Wrongway, or whatever the hell her name is, get off pontificating like that?"

"It's Janeway, ma'am," Esperanza said as she took up a position on the opposite side of the desk, "and everything she said was completely right. But all of it is conditional on what the Remans actually *want*, and we still don't know what that is."

"Speaking of that, has Spock made it out alive yet?"

Esperanza nodded. "He'll be here tomorrow."

"About damn time—what took so long?"

"Flying around in Romulan space is dangerous these days; the relief ships were late arriving because they had to take more circuitous routes. Since that dustup two months ago, we've had, what, six different firefights erupt?"

"Seven. I started reading over Abrik's reports again to keep myself from falling asleep during the council session."

That got Esperanza nervous. "Ma'am—"

"It was during Gleer's diatribe."

Esperanza's concerns abated. Bera chim Gleer, the councillor from Tellar, had a capacity for long-windedness that had to be heard to be believed. The shortest he'd ever held the floor during a council session was forty-five minutes, and that particular one was only abbreviated because the councillor had an illness. Usually he went on for an hour and a half at least. "What was he on about this time?"

"Well, it started out about the need for the council to carefully consider all appointments, then it went on to how the council has to carefully consider refugee requests, and then he went on and on and on about Artrin's fine accomplishments on Triex—which I thought was hilarious given that he's doing as much as anyone to hold up the man's appointment—and then I stopped paying attention, to be honest, though he ended with something about Vulcans."

"Well, Tellar, Kharzh'ulla, and Brantik have been making the most use of the trade agreement with Aligar, so his constituents are getting hit the hardest."

"Yeah? What's his excuse for being an ass the rest of the time?" The president sat down. "There was one bit of good news: Beltane got in, eighty-seven to sixty-seven."

A wave of relief washed over Esperanza. "About time."

"Yeah, well, she was only the most qualified person avail-able, so I can see why the council wanted to drag their heels on ratifying her." The president slammed a hand into the *salish* desk. "Dammit, Esperanza, what the hell are these jackasses playing at? Are they *that* pissed about Aligar?"

"About Aligar? No. About the way you phrased your displeasure about Aligar? Absolutely."

The president frowned. "What the hell's *that* mean? All I did was argue as to why trading with Aligar wasn't tenable anymore."

"No, ma'am, due respect, you didn't." Esperanza hesi-tated. "If you had phrased your speech as a request to not renew the agreement—which, I might add, is how you told me you were going to play it when you insisted that we didn't need Fred to draft some notes for you to use—it would have been okay, but you phrased it as a rebuke. You chastised them, ma'am. You told one hundred and fifty-four councillors that they were immoral, that they were wrong, that they stood against what made the Federation great. You questioned their patriotism right there in the chamber. Honestly, I'm amazed they reacted as calmly as they did."

The president snorted. "Your definition of calm differs from mine."

Esperanza sat down in the nearest guest chair. "Ma'am—this isn't the governor's office on Cestus III."

"Really?" The president rolled her eyes. "What was your first clue, the view out the window? For crying out loud, Esperanza, I'm not *that* feeble, I—"

"My point is, Madam President, that you're not the leader of the Federation the way you were leader of Ces-tus. Intellectually, of *course* you know that, but instinc-tively? On Cestus, you were the final authority. Here, you aren't—you're just the most important cog in a very big wheel. You work *with* the council, they don't work *for* you."

President Bacco was silent for several seconds, staring off at a corner of the office with her hand at her chin.

Esperanza finally felt the need to prompt her. "Ma'am?"

The president shook her head. "Sorry, I was thinking about creative ways of killing Gleer."

"Ma'am—"

"Fine, fine, you're right, Esperanza. You're almost always right—it's probably your most annoying quality."

"Thank you, ma'am."

"Don't hold me to that, though—you have plenty of other annoying qualities, too."

Esperanza nodded. "Of course, ma'am."

"Any ideas on how to fix this?"

That caught Esperanza off guard. She had twelve other things on her mind at the moment. "I think we can just ride this out, and—"

"We can't *afford* to ride this out. The government's grinding to a damn halt." Bacco thought a moment, then said, "I'm gonna apologize."

Her eyes widening in surprise, Esperanza said, "Really?"

"What, I'm not allowed to apologize?"

"Well, it's not typical, ma'am. Of the president of the Federation or—well, of you."

"Then it's time I started being atypical, 'cause typical ain't gettin' the job done. I'll take the floor at the next session and fall on my sword." She sighed. "I assume Raisa's gonna talk to me about the Remans?"

Grateful for the change of subject, Esperanza said, "Yes, ma'am. No new news yet, obviously, since they're still running silent."

Shaking her head, the president said, "This damn thing's been hanging over us for two months now. I'll be glad when it's over. Anything new from the Klingons?"

"No. They still say they haven't made any aggressive moves, that the Romulans have always fired first."

"And the Romulans?"

Smirking, Esperanza said, "Depends who you ask, and what time of day."

"Yeah." The president let out a long breath. "Oh, and I think Artrin'll be ratified soon. Honestly, they were ready to take a vote, finally, but Severn-Anyar said she hadn't finished reading through all of Artrin's magisterial decisions."

Esperanza frowned. "She's had months to do that."

"Yeah, that's why I think it'll be over soon—the delaying tactics are getting particularly feeble. One other thing that was introduced was a resolution to continue the water supplies to Delta until they hammer out their nonsense with Carrea. Speaking of which, should I take it as read that the Wescott Room continues to be a source of contention?"

This time it was Esperanza who rolled her eyes. In addition to the president's office, the fifteenth floor of the Palais included two large meeting rooms—the Raghoratreii Room and the Wescott Room, both named after past Federation presidents. These two in particular were the ones who'd signed the Khitomer Accords and the Organian Peace Treaty, respectively, and their portraits hung on the respective walls. The latter room had been the site of the regular meetings between the Deltan and Carreon delegations for two months now.

"Yeah, they're still going at it. The latest is that the Carreon are asking for exclusive trading rights to *eeriak*."

Frowning, the president said, "Isn't *eeriak* their biggest export?"

"Yeah, and it's not replicable. Delta's economy will collapse if they only trade to Carrea, since they can't possibly import enough to make it worth Delta's while to go exclusive."

"Talk about feeble delaying tactics. When do you think I should get into it?"

"Another couple of days, I think the Deltans are gonna walk out, so I'd say within a couple of days."

"All right. Well, at least Delta will have water for another month, thanks to a handy one hundred and fifty-one to one vote."

"I assume Delta was one of the two who abstained?"

"Yeah—the other was Ontail who, once again, didn't show up."

Esperanza blew out a breath between her teeth. After the incident at the Rashanar Battle Site, the Zife administration had managed to keep the Ontailians from leaving the Federation altogether. However, Councillor Lo had only been at two council sessions in the year and a half since Rashanar.

That, however, was a discussion for another time. "Who was the one negative vote?"

Glowering, the president said, "Who do you think?"

"Quintor?" Esperanza asked with a wince.

"I tell you, Esperanza, I'm starting to relax my enthusiasm for appointing her to government oversight."

"If it was anything other than government oversight, I'd agree."

The words hung between them for a moment.

"You realize," the president finally said, "that it probably won't matter. What Zife did probably won't even come out during my presidency—and even if it does, that won't matter to the *current* council. Honestly, do you really think I'd do something as depraved as what Zife did on Tezwa?"

"If you'd asked me the same question about Min Zife two years ago, I'd have said the same thing I'd say about you now. But who the hell knows? And the point is, we have a responsibility to make sure that sort of abuse of power can't—"

Waving her hand in front of her face, the president said, "All right, all right, I know—*I'm* the one who gave *you* that speech after we found out about Zife, remember? And I know that Quintor will question *everything*, which is what you want in that position, but—" She let out another breath. "I'm just hoping that particular council gets very little work."

"I'll do everything I can to make sure that happens, ma'am."

President Bacco nodded. "Good. Anything else?"

Esperanza smiled. "Eleven to ten, huh? Real pitchers' joust, wasn't it?"

"It's pitchers' *duel*, you heathen." But the president returned the smile. "All right, it's 1815, so I'd better start seeing my 1800 appointment. What was it again?"

"Sivak said it was Secretary Kolrami."

The president leaned back in her chair. "Oh joy, I get to be lectured at by the agriculture secretary. Why did we appoint her again?"

Esperanza got up from her seat. "Because she's the Federation's leading expert on agriculture, and she's been criticizing the Federation's position on several issues for ten years now, and you thought her arguments were cogent."

The president shook her head. "Yeah, well, that was before she was directing them at me. Now I just think they're tiresome. I'm starting to question our methods of choosing a cabinet. Next time around, let's just pick people who don't know a damn thing about the subject—this way I can have fewer meetings."

"I'll look into that, ma'am," Esperanza deadpanned. "You want me or one of the guys here when you talk to Fred about the speech?" Esperanza had taken to referring to her four deputies as "the guys."

"Send Ashanté—she's better at keeping Fred focused. Besides, they make a cute couple, and after eight hours with the council, I need all the cute I can get."

Chuckling, Esperanza turned to leave. "Thank you, Madam President."

◆

CHAPTER NINE

◆   ◆

BEY TOH'S STOMACH was growling and his head was pounding as he entered Sisko's Creole Kitchen in New Orleans. As he walked in, the smell of cayenne peppers and Cajun spices and tomato sauce managed to at once alleviate the headache and make the stomach growl more.

When Fred MacDougan had offered him the job as a member of President Bacco's speechwriting staff, he had done so in this restaurant. Toh had been serving as the speechwriter for the Federation ambassador to the Klingon Empire, but when Fred had made the job offer, he'd found it irresistible.

It hadn't hurt that Fred had made the offer in this

restaurant. Until that interview, Toh, a Bajoran by birth, had never set foot on Earth, and had had no idea that they had such magnificent cuisine.

Sisko's was therapy for Toh, and right now he needed it. ·

"Toh! How's it going?" The always-happy voice of the restaurant's owner, Joseph Sisko, cut through the chatter of the early lunch crowd, though it was dinnertime for Toh, still on Paris time as he was. He turned to see Joseph's ever-smiling visage, white teeth shining in his dark face. As ever, he wore a brightly colored shirt and dark pants, greeting the guests as they walked in as if he'd been waiting all day for them.

"It's been better. Did you know that tomorrow's the assistant technology secretary's hundredth birthday?"

Joseph's grin widened as he put his hand on Toh's shoulder. "Toh, I hate to tell you this—but I didn't even know there *was* an assistant technology secretary."

Toh laughed. "Yeah, well, the president's supposed to give a short birthday greeting to him tomorrow."

"So?"

Grimacing, Toh said, "Guess who gets to write it?"

Leading him to a table in the corner, Joseph said, "So what's the problem? You can do this sort of thing in your sleep."

"That is the problem—I *am* doing it in my sleep, because the assistant technology secretary is quite possibly the single most boring individual in the entire galaxy. To make matters worse, I have to write this for the president."

"Isn't that what you do?"

Toh sat down in a chair that faced the giant alligator that hung from the ceiling. Joseph said it guarded the restaurant at night, and that it always was a pain to wrestle it back to the ceiling before he opened, a story that everyone accepted without question. Toh had thought it odd at first, until he'd spent some time in New Orleans; something about the city fostered the absurd, the paranormal, and the ridiculous, so that you accepted even the most outlandish notions as fact.

"It is what I do, yeah, but—" He sighed. "For three years, I wrote speeches for Ambassador Worf. It was the easiest work of my life—the man is the most taciturn Klingon in existence. Verbose for him is six words. Now I'm writing for Nan Bacco. Did you see her speech about the Aligar a couple months back?"

"Saw bits of it on FNS," Joseph said. "My grandson wrote for them, you know."

Toh plowed on, having heard Joseph talk about his son, his daughter, his two grandchildren, and his daughter-in-law plenty of times over the four months that he'd been coming here. "Well, *nobody* wrote that speech for her. She did that on her own, off the cuff. I don't know why she even bothers with a speechwriting staff. She's one of the most eloquent people in modern politics, and *I* have to make her sound interesting when wishing a hundredth birthday to the most spectacularly uninteresting person in the cosmos." He looked up at Joseph plaintively. "*Please* tell me the jambalaya's good tonight."

Joseph's expression grew grave. "I'm afraid I can't tell you that." Then the grin came back. "The jambalaya's *great* tonight."

Toh laughed, an action he wouldn't have thought himself capable of an hour ago. "Sold. Bring me the biggest bowl you have—and some *kava* juice."

"Coming right up." Joseph again put his hand on Toh's shoulder. "And don't worry—you'll do fine. Everybody's got a story—even the boring ones. It's just a matter of diggin' around a little."

With that pearl of wisdom, Joseph went off to place Toh's order.

Heartened by the prospect of imminent jambalaya, Toh took the padd out of his jacket pocket and started making notes. *Maybe there's something to what Joseph said. There's got to be something. And if not—I don't know, I'll riff on the number one hundred. Can probably get five minutes just on that, especially with the famed Bacco Proclivity for Unnecessary Adjectives and Adverbs.*

Shortly after he finished the jambalaya—and three *kava* juices, as the spices were particularly inflammable today—and was starting to almost approach the possibility of feeling vaguely confident about small portions of the speech, someone walked up to the table.

"Excuse me—you work at the Palais de la Concorde, don't you?"

Toh looked up to see a Triexian—or maybe an Edoan, he always got those two species confused. "Uh—"

"Actually, I know you do. You're Bey Toh, and you work for Fred MacDougan, right?"

Thinking it best to neither confirm nor deny, Toh said, "Look, I don't mean to be rude, but I'm—"

"I have something I need to tell you." The stranger sat in the chair opposite Toh, which he found unconscionably rude. "It is something that you need to tell Mr. MacDougan, and that he needs to tell Ms. Piñiero, and that she needs to tell the president."

Wryly, Toh said, "Your grasp of the chain of command at the Palais is nice to see, Mister—?"

"My name isn't important."

"It is if you don't want me to call Joseph over here and have him throw you out." Toh smiled sweetly as he said it.

Reluctantly, the stranger said, "I'm Kralis na Then."

Triexian, then. "And what do you do when you're not in-terrupting meals and sitting at people's table without per-mission?"

"I did wait until you were done eating, Mr. Bey."

"Fine, but you're still on the hook for the second one, and I'm giving you ten seconds before I call Joseph over."

Kralis was wearing a coat with a flared bottom under-neath his middle arm. With that arm, he reached into a pocket and pulled out a padd. "This is a judgment that was rendered by the Supreme Magisterial Authority on Triex eight years ago."

Toh frowned. "The SMA on Triex eight years ago was Councillor Artrin, wasn't it?" Fred had been going on at great length about how he'd had to put endorsements of Artrin, and President Bacco's other appointments, into sev-eral speeches, not all of which were natural fits. *At least Beltane finally got ratified. . . .*

"Yes, it was. Trust me, I don't want to do this—but I don't have a choice. Someone gave this information to Councillor Severn-Anyar. I don't know who did—but it doesn't matter now."

Toh shook his head. "I don't understand—we have all of Artrin's decisions. They're public record."

"Not all of them."

With that, Kralis rose from his chair and left Sisko's without another word.

The padd remained on the table.

Sighing, Toh picked it up. For a moment, he feared ac-tivating it, but then he dismissed the notion. *Nobody would want to blow up someone on my level. Which, was why he came to me. Anyone else, he'd never get near, so shove it under the nose of the junior staff person.*

Not knowing whether to be flattered or insulted, Toh

activated the padd and read the only file that was on it: A decision rendered by Supreme Magisterial Authority Artrin na Yel on the fifth day of Torus in the year of the Fortil. To his surprise, it was an emergency session, called when the magisterial office was usually in recess.

Toh read the decision.

Then he read it again.

Then he read it a third time.

"You okay, Toh?"

Toh looked up in surprise at Joseph, who looked concerned. "Huh?"

"You've gotten mighty pale, son. Do you need—"

"It's nothing," Toh said quickly. "Or, rather, it is something, but it's not you." He got up from his chair. "I've got to get back to the office. Sorry. Talk to you later!"

Toh didn't hear what Joseph said as he ran out the door toward the nearest transporter station.

Within twenty minutes—there was a line at the station, and his government ID didn't do anything to expedite matters, which rather annoyed him—he was back in his office. The first thing he did was contact Rol Yarvik Rol, who was working late on a project for Fred.

"Whatever you need, Toh, can it wait? Fred is—"

"Just a quick question, Yarvik. You've read over all of Artrin's decisions, right?"

"Yeah, why?"

"Was there a decision on 5 Torus Fortil?"

"There aren't any decisions in Torus, that's when they're in—"

Toh snarled. "I know that, I mean an emergency session."

"Artrin didn't preside over any emergency sessions."

"You sure?" Toh had been afraid Yarvik would say the very words he was saying now.

"Completely sure. Why?"

"Nothing." This was too big for a researcher. *This is too big for me,* he thought. "Is Fred still in his office?"

"He's with Ashanté down at that café they like. He said he'd be back in an hour."

"Okay, thanks." Toh cut off the connection, took a moment to pray to the Prophets for guidance, then put a call through to Fred. *He's gonna hate being interrupted like this, but he's with Ashanté, and that'll save some time. And better to tell them sooner than later, especially if the council already has this.*

The last time Esperanza Piñiero felt this ragged was after the *U.S.S. Gorkon* was told to hold the Delavi system for three weeks during the Dominion War. They were at red alert the entire time, and by the end of the second week, Esperanza felt like she had run six marathons in the space of two hours. Her muscles ached, her mouth tasted like engine coolant, and a phaser drill was on overload behind her right eye.

Four months in the Palais gave her a tremendous sense of déjà vu for those days in the Delavi system.

Still, another day seemed to finally be at an end. The president's speech on Titan had gone well. The shipbuilder's guild seemed mollified about Aligar—though they were expressing concern about the Rigel colonies following the directive to change over their warp drives.

She opened an intercom channel to her assistant. "Please, Zachary, by all that is holy on thirty worlds, tell me that we're done for the day."

Her office door slid open to reveal Zachary holding a padd. "Not quite. Sorry, this just came in from the travel office." He walked it over to her at her desk.

"Let me guess," Esperanza said as she took it. "They felt bad for not having screwed anything up in a few months?"

"Sort of. They had to change the president's itinerary for the goodwill trip."

Esperanza glowered at Zachary. "We spent six weeks hammering out the details of the trip. It was vetted by half the people in this building. What could they possibly want to change now?"

Zachary smiled. "It's kind of funny, actually."

At Esperanza's look, his smile fell. "Right now, Zachary, you could get the entire Luna-See Troupe up here and have them perform their whole repetoire from *Again, the Ears* to *Zakdorn's Sun Is Going Nova Tomorrow,* and it wouldn't be funny."

"Okay, well, in any case, it turns out that the original itinerary had one problem—we would be arriving on Lembatta Prime on the day before an eclipse."

The phaser drill now moved to her left eye. "What, they don't have lights on Lembatta?"

"Oh, they have lights, but, uh—" Zachary took a breath. "Whenever there's an eclipse, and also the day before and after, it's a major religious holiday. Essential work is still done, but anyone not actually doing that is obligated to stay at home and meditate."

Esperanza leaned her head back and looked to the ceiling in supplication. To her annoyance, the ceiling was wholly bereft of aid or comfort.

She looked back at her assistant. "So if we hold a town hall meeting on the day before an eclipse—"

"No one will show up."

"Wonderful. They rearranged the itinerary?"

Zachary nodded. "And that should be it."

"Good," Esperanza said with more enthusiasm than was probably politic. Knowing it was wholly futile, she still said to Zachary, "You can go home, I'm just gonna read this and then head out."

As always, he said, "I go home when you go home." Then he went back to his desk, the door sliding shut behind him.

Esperanza's eyes were glazing over as she read over the itinerary. None of it seemed untoward. Lembatta had been moved to a week later, so Ventax II would be a week earlier, Kessik IV would be at the end of the trip instead of the beginning, and Cestus III—

Oh hell.

The phaser drill was now working on both eyes.

Slamming her hand on the intercom, she said, "Zachary, who put this together?"

"The travel offi—"

"I mean who in the travel office?"

"I'm not sure."

"Are any of them in now?"

"I think Ne'al G'ullho is still—"

"Get it up here *now.*"

Esperanza got up and went over to the replicator that was inset in her office wall. She was about to ask it for an herbal iced tea, then she decided to throw caution to the wind. Putting her hand on the activator, she said, "Jack Daniel's Single Barrel, neat, alcoholic."

If this were regular business hours, the computer would point out that Federation law prevented members of the government from drinking alcoholic beverages during working hours. *Whoever passed that law didn't realize that every hour is a working hour in the Palais.*

She slugged down the amber liquid; it burned as it went down her throat, then formed a warm spot in the upper part of her chest.

Her intercom beeped. *"Ne'al is here."*

"Get it in here." The thick-bottom glass made a resounding thunk as she placed it on her metal desk with a bit more force than was necessary.

A young Damiani entered, its goatee untrimmed. "Yes, Ms. Piñiero, what can I do for you?"

She held up the padd. "Do you know about this?"

"I don't know what this is," Ne'al said slowly.

Great, now I'm *doing it*, Esperanza thought with a sigh. "This is the president's updated travel itinerary for the goodwill tour."

"Oh, right. I think Mantor handled that one himself."

"Good, I know who to fire tomorrow, then."

Ne'al's teal skin started to lighten. "Uh, Ms. Piñiero, I don't understand what—"

"All right," she said with a sigh, "I probably can't fire him for this. But the only way to keep him from being in the president's doghouse for the rest of his natural life is to either get him in here tonight or fix this yourself."

Now looking confused, Ne'al said, "Ms. Piñiero, I'm afraid I still don't understand. The itinerary had to be changed to accommodate—"

"I know all about the Lembattans. What I have a small problem with, and what the president will have a *huge* problem with, is that you moved the Cestus III leg of the trip."

"Oh, that. Well, we figured since it was the president's home, it didn't matter when it was. Good thing, too, because if we kept that on the same date, it would make the rest of it damn near impossible."

"Well, you get to do the impossible, Ne'al, because the way this itinerary runs now, the president is going to miss Opening Day."

A blank look. "Opening Day of what?"

"The baseball season on Cestus III. And before you ask another stupid question with your mouth hanging open the way it has been for this entire conversation, let me explain the basics. Baseball is a sport. It's been played professionally on Cestus III since the president was first elected governor. It's the president's favorite sport, and watching it is one of her primary leisure activities. She has also, every year since the incorporation of the CBL, thrown out the ceremonial first pitch on Opening Day at Ruth Field in Pike City. Now you are going to go back to your office, and you are going to move solar systems if you have to, but you are going to keep Cestus right where it was on the itinerary and rearrange everything else. If we have to extend the trip an extra week—"

"We can't do that." Ne'al said those words with more assuredness than it had said anything else since walking into Esperanza's office. "She has to get back on the first, because that's when the Trinni/ek delegation is arriving."

Damn. Esperanza had forgotten about the *Io*'s first contact, which had been followed by conversations over subspace with a diplomatic team led by a bright young ambassador named Colton Morrow. A Trinni/ek team was going to visit the Palais at the beginning of May, right when the president came back from the goodwill tour.

"Fine, then do what you have to do to make it work."

Ne'al let out a long breath. "We can probably get someone from Starfleet to rig up a hologram that can do the job."

Esperanza stared in open-mouthed stupefaction. "Please tell me you were kidding."

"No, those Starfleet Corps of Engineers guys can do pretty much anything. They—"

"I don't mean kidding about being able to do it, I meant kidding about taking that seriously as a legitimate alternative to being there."

"Why not? You know how good holograms are these days—nobody'll know the difference."

Putting her head in her hands, Esperanza sat back down at her desk. "It doesn't matter what the audience thinks. This is something that is very important for the president to do herself. I suggest a hologram to her, I guarantee that I'll be fired inside of six seconds, and the president's known me my entire life, so I think you can figure out how fast your ass'll be out the door if you ever say that out loud again."

Sounding surprised, Ne'al asked, "It's really that important?"

"It's really that important." Esperanza picked up the glass of Jack Daniel's. "A lot of this job is larger than life, Ne'al. And the president can handle that—she can handle the council snits and the press laughing at your office and Remans who approach the border without saying why—but every once in a while she needs something that's real."

"So she planned this entire goodwill tour as an excuse to go home and throw off a pitch?"

"Throw *out* a pitch." Esperanza made the correction without even thinking. "And don't be an idiot, of course not." She took a sip of her drink. "We did a study right after we came in here and discovered that in seven years, President Zife never once—not a single time—went and talked to ordinary citizens. He visited starbases and Starfleet outposts. He met with other politicians and other people connected to or in his government and similar people in other governments. But he never talked to the people who voted for him."

She set the drink back down, more gently this time. "When she was governor, once a month, for one whole day, the president always made sure she had town meetings. She'd just let anybody who lived on Cestus who wanted to talk to the planetary governor come in and say their peace. She'd answer questions, tell stories, share anecdotes, and *listen.*" Esperanza shook her head. "The president's one of the best talkers I know, but on those days, she also listened better than anyone I know, and she always made sure that whoever she was listening to had her rapt attention." She looked up at Ne'al. "I asked her about it, wondered if it was maybe a waste of time to spend twelve days a year listening to this nonsense, and you know what she said? 'I spend three hundred and sixty-five days a year listening to this nonsense; on twelve of those days, I just eliminate the middle party. This is how government's *supposed* to work.'" Esperanza smiled. "I think that's when I decided that I had to convince her to run for president."

Ne'al stood staring at Esperanza for several seconds. Then it picked up the padd. "We'll make this work, Ms. Piñiero. First thing in the morning, you'll have an itinerary."

"Thanks, Ne'al."

It nodded and departed.

Esperanza picked up the glass again and drank down the rest of her Jack Daniel's. Then she hit the intercom. "And with that, Zachary, I'm going—"

"Esperanza, Ashanté and Fred are here to see you, along with Toh. They need to talk to you right away."

Closing her eyes, Esperanza said in a voice that made it sound like her throat was coated in Klingon bloodwine, "Can't this wait until morning?"

Fred answered, *"It really really can't, Esperanza."*

Opening her eyes back up, Esperanza said, "Fine, come in." She stared at the empty glass. *I get the feeling I'm gonna need another one of these. Or three.*

President Nan Bacco stood alone in the Ra-ghoratreii Room, just down the hall from her office on the fifteenth floor of the Palais. She looked up at the painting of President Ra-ghoratreii. The Efrosian was known to most Federation citizens as the president who signed the Khitomer Accords on the Federation's behalf. Previously, the room had been simply called the Red Room, after the color scheme of the walls, provided by President al-Rashid in the early days of the Federation. After Ra-ghoratreii served out his third and final term, his portrait was hung in the Red Room, and the space was renamed (and repainted).

During the administration of President Amitra, she had converted this room to her office. She'd felt the presidential office was too ostentatious, a feeling shared by Jaresh-Inyo. However, Min Zife had felt the president should have the grandeur of the larger room, and so he'd converted this room back to a meeting room and returned to the larger room with the panoramic view.

There weren't a lot of things on which Nan agreed with her predecessor, but that larger office was one of them.

This room now had a large replicated wooden table in the center, rectangular in shape, and able to seat up to fifty people if needed. Nan had arranged for there to be only seven chairs—one at the head, three on either side. The wood on the table was meant to simulate oak, and the only thing that broke its elegance was the padd sitting in front of the head chair.

A few moments later, one of the doors opened. Nan

turned away from Ra-ghoratreii's image to see Councillors T'Latrek of Vulcan, Matthew Mazibuko of Earth, and Kellerasana zh'Faila of Andor enter. They each nodded to Nan and took their seats. Soon they were followed by the last of the permanent members of the security council— Bera chim Gleer of Tellar, who did not nod, but simply took his seat, and Huang Chaoying from Alpha Centauri, who gave Nan a small bow before taking her seat.

Finally the subject of their meeting entered: Artrin na Yel of Triex. He also served on the security council. Along with the ones from the five founding worlds of the Federation, the security council also included councillors from eight other worlds. The present configuration had Cait, Damiano, Gnala, Huanni, Rigel, Sulamid, Triex, and Zakdorn as the "back eight," as it was called around the Palais.

Nan feared that Triex would be off that list by the time this meeting ended.

When Artrin took a seat between Gleer and Mazibuko, Nan sat at the head of the table. "Thank you all for coming at this late hour. I apologize for being cryptic, but it was necessary."

"Madam President," T'Latrek said, "should this meeting not be held in council chambers?"

Somehow, Nan managed to control her reaction. After the previous day's eight-hour marathon, she was in no rush to go back there, especially since she was the only one who had to stand the entire time. "It may come to that, but I want to keep the meeting informal—and off the record— for the time being. I want to tell you all something that my staff informed me of tonight, and then I want Artrin to tell his side of the story just to the six of us."

With an understandable undertone of indignance, Artrin asked, "My side of *what* story, exactly, ma'am?"

Nan picked up the padd. "On 5 Torus in the year of the Fortil on Triex, in an emergency session, you rendered a judgment in your capacity as SMA to imprison a Federation citizen by the name of Wusekl without a trial."

Most of the councillors looked at Artrin at that. T'Latrek, however, looked at Nan. "There is no record of Councillor Artrin rendering any judgments in emergency sessions during his time as Supreme Magisterial Authority."

"*Public* record, no," Nan said.

Artrin spoke up more readily than Nan had been expecting. "The emergency session was classified. The year of the Fortil was eight years ago. It was shortly after the explosion at the Antwerp Conference and the declaration of martial law on Earth."

"During the height of paranoia over changeling infiltration," Matthew said.

"Yes."

Kell looked at Nan. "Ma'am, what was this Wusekl person accused of?"

"Funny you should ask." She looked directly at Artrin. "Being a changeling infiltrator."

"Was he?" Gleer asked Artrin.

"Witnesses saw him altering his shape," Artrin said matter-of-factly.

Nan rolled her eyes. "Yeah, well, that's hardly surprising, since Wusekl is a chameloid. See, the Founders aren't the only shape-shifters in the galaxy by a long shot."

Artrin shrugged, an odd gesture from a three-armed being. "We couldn't be sure that it wasn't a Founder posing as a chameloid, and using that species' own shape-changing ability to divert suspicion."

"Right." Nan leaned back in her chair. "So of course you opened up an investigation, did a full medical workup, got testimony from Wusekl's friends and family, right?" Her question was laced with sarcasm; she knew full well that hadn't been done.

"That would not have been prudent," Artrin said.

Chaoying stroked her chin. "You feared a public outcry."

"Exactly." Artrin seemed relieved that Chaoying, at least, understood his position. Certainly Nan was having a hard time with it. The Triexian looked at her. "Madam President, I do not see what the issue is. It was a time of war—"

Before Nan could explode at Artrin, T'Latrek came to the rescue. "That is incorrect, Councillor. War with the Dominion was not officially declared by this council for one year and seven-point-three months after 5 Torus Fortil, shortly after Dominion forces took Deep Space 9."

"That isn't the point. The Triexian people needed to be protected."

This time, Nan wasn't letting T'Latrek's cooler head prevail. "Really? I'm a little befuddled, Councillor, as to how people in a free society are being protected when innocent people are imprisoned without any kind of due process. Those are the actions of a totalitarian state, and I will *not* tolerate them in this government for as long as I am president."

Kell asked, "That poor man isn't still imprisoned, is he?"

Shaking her head, Nan said, "No, when our friend here got elected to the council, his replacement as SMA reversed the decision within about six seconds. Wusekl's a free chameloid today—although, Artrin's replacement being a politically savvy type, Wusekl's freedom was contingent on keeping quiet about his imprisonment. Well, that particular gag is going to come off."

Artrin stood up. "Madam President, you cannot use

your access to classified Triexian documents to let loose with a vendetta against—"

Nan smiled at that. "Oh, you think I got this from Triex by waving around my executive privilege? No, no, no. You see, Councillor, I got this from a member of my staff."

"How can someone on your staff give you such information?" Artrin sounded justifiably confused once again.

"Someone gave it to him in a public restaurant."

Now Artrin's voice sounded dangerous. "Who?"

Nan snorted. "Don't get your bowels in an uproar, Councillor. We don't know who. He gave a name, but it belongs to a Triexian who's been dead for seventy years. The reason why he gave it to one of my junior staff is because someone *else* already gave it to Councillor Severn-Anyar."

Gleer slammed his furry fist on the table. *"That* is why she requested a further delay on his ratification vote?"

Nodding, Nan said, "That's right. And if they can give it to a councillor and a presidential staffer, you can bet all the ale on Romulus that they can give it to someone in Jorel's press room. I can tell you one thing, Councillor, we are *not* going to let the story break there."

Artrin was still standing. "My actions were wholly within the purview of Triexian law."

Matthew set his hands gently down on the table. "Your actions were wholly in conflict with Federation law—more to the point, sir, they were wholly in conflict with *natural* law."

Nan held up the padd. "Do I take it, Councillor, that you do not regret this particular decision?"

Artrin said nothing for several seconds. "Our people were scared. When Wusekl changed shape, he was almost *lynched.* Yes, we could have done a medical exam to reveal that he was not a changeling—the Founders are a liquid life-form, and chameloids are basically humanoid. But it wouldn't have mattered. The people would have called for his blood. I did what I had to do to keep him safe—and to keep Triex safe."

Nan then looked at the other councillors in turn. Each of them nodded affirmatively. Taking a breath, Nan then said, "For the safety of your political career—not to mention mine—you're going to go into the press room tomorrow morning, and you're going to announce your resignation from the Federation Council, and you're going to tell them why. I want the Palais to control the story for as long as we possibly can. But I also want the word to go out far and wide that we are not this. We were manipulated by an awful foe who did everything they could to break us, to tear us asunder, and to bring about our ruination. We have come dangerously close to sacrificing our ideals, but we will *not* go over that precipice. And the first sign that this is so will be your resignation tomorrow. Is that understood, Councillor?"

Artrin shook his head. "What I did *needed* to be done for the safety of Triex."

Matthew shook his head and chuckled. "There is a saying among my people, Councillor Artrin. It was said six hundred years ago by a great man. He said, 'They that can give up essential liberty to obtain a little temporary safety deserve neither liberty nor safety.'"

Artrin simply stared at the other councillors. Kell looked aghast, Gleer annoyed (which wasn't much different from how he normally looked), Matt pitying, Chaoying thoughtful. T'Latrek, of course, was the soul of equanimity.

Finally, the Triexian said, "Very well, Madam President. I will resign first thing in the morning."

"Wrong. You'll come to my office first thing in the

morning, at 0500, where we'll go over your resignation speech, then you'll go with Jorel to the press room."

"As you wish."

"That'll be all."

Artrin stood at attention. "Thank you, Madam President."

Then he departed.

Nan let out a long breath. "Nice job with the Franklin quote, Matthew—I'm just sorry I didn't get to use it."

"It was not my intention to steal your thunder, ma'am."

"S'all right. I had plenty of thunder left over." She looked around the table. "Thank you all for your support."

"We could hardly do otherwise," Gleer said. "His actions were appalling. I cannot believe he said nothing."

"*He* could hardly have done otherwise," T'Latrek said with a withering look at Gleer. "By Triexian law, he was not permitted to speak of a classified judicial session in the presence of anyone who did not participate in it."

Chaoying added, "And he was doing what he felt was right for his people."

Before anyone else could say anything, Nan said, "Maybe he thought it was necessary eight years ago." She sighed. "I don't know, maybe it was—maybe it did keep that chameloid protected. But his resignation is just as necessary, if not more so."

"Agreed," Kell said emphatically.

Nan stood. "Thank you, everyone. I'll see you all tomorrow."

Everyone also rose, except for T'Latrek. "May I stay a moment, Madam President?"

"Of course," Nan said. T'Latrek had served on the council for over eighty years. She hadn't run for president only because she herself had never felt the need to. Hers was one of the wisest and most respected voices on the council, and Nan was not about to turn down a request for a private meeting.

After the others departed, Nan took her seat again. "What can I do for you, T'Latrek?"

The Vulcan councillor folded her arms on the table, her fingers interlocked. "It was not necessary for you to have the five of us participate in this meeting, Madam President. I am, however, gratified to see it."

Not expecting a Vulcan to express gratitude, Nan smiled. "It was necessary—for a lot of reasons."

"Perhaps, but you could have simply spoken to Councillor Artrin in your office and demanded his resignation. But you gave him the opportunity to speak his peace. For that, you are to be commended. It is my hope that this spirit of cooperation will become more typical of your administration than it was of the previous one."

Nan smiled. "Or of my first few months?"

"The first few months of any presidency are fraught with precisely the sort of difficulties you have been suffering. They are exacerbated by your predecessor, who, during the war, took a much more autonomous role than is usual for a Federation president. In the years following the war, that autonomy remained, despite the best efforts of the council. It caused a certain amount of resentment among the more emotional councillors."

Chuckling, Nan said, "Everyone but you?"

"Not quite everyone."

Was that a smile she almost started? Nan wondered.

T'Latrek continued. "Your statements regarding the Aligar trade agreement were interpreted by many on the council as what you humans sometimes call 'more of the same.'"

Nan sighed. "Yeah, you're right, I haven't exactly been playing well with others."

"Perhaps the most important lesson in your job, Madam President, is to learn that one cannot do what one thinks is best, but rather what will do the job best." T'Latrek looked up at the painting of Ra-ghoratreii. "I served in President Ra-ghoratreii's administration, as a junior policy advisor on external matters. I was one of his advisors during the Khitomer conference. One evening, at Khitomer, after the final negotiating session with Chancellor Azetbur and her staff, he met with myself and several others." T'Latrek paused to take a breath. "The president informed us that he thought the Khitomer Accords—which he was preparing to sign the following morning—were a terrible idea. That the Klingon Empire was only suing for peace because they were crippled by the destruction of Praxis, and that they would use the treaty to use us to build up their resources, and then—when they were truly a superpower in the quadrant again—they would wage war on us. He was convinced that this would be the case—but he also knew that he could not turn his back on Azetbur, and that the treaty was necessary for the short term, even if it would be disastrous in the long term."

"But he was wrong," Nan said. "Aside from that one blip eight years ago, the empire's been our staunchest ally."

"Yes, he was incorrect in his prediction. People in your position often make mistakes, Madam President. What matters is how those mistakes are dealt with afterward. In President Ra-ghoratreii's case, it did not matter, because he did not truly commit the mistake. In yours—" T'Latrek unfolded her hands. "—it remains to be seen. But I have faith in your ability to learn from those mistakes and not repeat them."

"I appreciate the confidence, Councillor," Nan said, then added with a smirk, "Though I suspect that learning from my mistakes will just result in newer, more interesting mistakes down the line."

"That too is in the nature of the position you occupy." Then that almost-the-beginning-of-a-smile came back. "It is one of several reasons why I have avoided running for your office, Madam President."

Nan laughed. "Well, Councillor, you're a much smarter person than I am."

"That, Madam President, goes without saying," T'Latrek said archly. "One other item, if I may?"

"Of course," Nan said with a "go-ahead" gesture.

"I understand you are meeting with Ambassador Spock tomorrow morning."

"Assuming the travel office didn't send him to the Badlands by mistake, yeah." Nan figured out where T'Latrek was going before the councillor had the chance to articulate it. "You want to be in on the meeting?"

"I believe my inclusion would only be logical."

Not only could Nan not argue with that but she was also kicking herself for not thinking of that sooner. T'Latrek was the councillor in charge of external affairs; she supervised most of the Federation's foreign diplomats, including Spock. When Spock had spoken before the council after Captain Riker had brokered the agreement with the Klingons to make them the Remans' protectors, T'Latrek had been one of those who had argued against him—but who had eventually been persuaded by his arguments for the council to support Riker's solution. "More than logical—sensible. I apologize, T'Latrek, you should have been part of the meeting from the git-go."

"Apology accepted, Madam President. May I ask who else will be participating?"

"Jas Abrik, Raisa Shostakova, and Starfleet's sending Admiral Akaar over."

"I would recommend that Starfleet send a different admiral, Madam President." T'Latrek spoke with as much disapproval as the president was ever likely to hear from the councillor.

"Why is that?"

"Admiral Akaar has a personal relationship with Ambassador Spock. The ambassador was instrumental in saving the admiral's mother when the latter was pregnant with him. I do not believe he will serve as an objective judge of Spock's words."

"Maybe not, but that's not what I want from him. He's been Starfleet's point man on this from the beginning, and I want him in there. However, if you want a blunt assessment, why don't we bring Molmaan into it?"

"A reasonable compromise. Thank you, Madam President."

Standing up, Nan held up her hand and parted her two middle fingers in the Vulcan salute. "Thank you, Councillor. Peace and long life."

T'Latrek rose and returned the salute. "Live long and prosper, Madam President."

◆

CHAPTER TEN

◆   ◆

KANT JOREL TRIED not to grind his teeth while Artrin made his resignation speech. He said all the right things and apologized for what he'd done—though, to Jorel's surprise, Artrin limited his apology to the victim of his decision. The councillor was forthright and eloquent.

Jorel knew it would go badly once he was done.

Reluctantly, he had to give credit to President Bacco for doing it this way—and for letting Jorel see the resignation first. He had made a couple of changes, softening some of the language to make Artrin look more contrite, which he'd accepted. By doing it in the room, by preempting the story before somebody could break it, Jorel got to control the story, at least initially.

The apology, however, had been ad-libbed. Jorel worried about the reaction to that.

Not nearly as much as he worried about the subsequent press questions that he would get when Artrin was done.

When the councillor finished, he opened the floor for questions. Earlier, Jorel had told him to call on Regradnischrak from *Sebrotnizskeapoierf* first. A lightweight from Antares, he wouldn't ask a substantive question, and it would give Artrin a chance to get his bearings.

To Jorel's surprise, Regradnischrak asked a better question than Jorel would have credited him with. "Councillor, why did you limit your apology to this chameloid you wrongly imprisoned?"

"Because he is the only one to whom I owe an apology." He pointed to Regia Maldonado of FNS.

"I'm surprised you feel that way, Councillor," Regia said. "Don't other people deserve an apology? The people of Triex, the people of the Federation, your fellow councillors and the president—don't they deserve an apology?"

"No. Triexian law states that classified judicial sessions may not be spoken of in the presence of anyone who did not participate in the session, unless one is instructed to by a superior. If I had told them, I would have violated the law. I have nothing to apologize for on that front."

"So why talk about it now?"

"I am—or was—a Federation councillor. My superior—the president of the Federation—ordered me to speak of it. Let me repeat that I deeply regret the decision that I made and the damage it did to Wusekl's life. What I do today is all I can offer him in recompense. But he is the damaged party, not the people of Triex, not the people of the Federation, not my fellow councillors, and not President Bacco." He then pointed to the new reporter from *Seeker*, whose name Jorel couldn't remember. Idly, he wondered when Ozla would be coming back from Tezwa—and why she thought going to that hellhole was such a good idea.

The young Trill asked, "Where is Wusekl now?"

"I honestly don't know. He was granted his freedom six years ago and left Triex."

"So you never kept up with him? Checked to see how he was faring?"

"To have done so—particularly from Earth once I became councillor—would have risked violating the very law that prevented me from discussing it." He then pointed at Sovan, whom Jorel had told the councillor to call on last.

"Do you know who'll be replacing you as Triex's councillor?"

"The Triexian Curia will vote on a replacement to serve out my term. Thank you, that is all for now."

Artrin left the room with all the speed that a three-legged person could muster—which was considerable—and Jorel then approached the podium.

"Before you pester me with questions, I have some announcements. As you've probably all heard, Ambassador Spock is meeting with the president today to discuss the ongoing Romulan problem."

"Jorel," Maria Olifante said, "I've gotten reports of more violence in the Revelok system and a double murder in Ehrie'fvil. Can you confirm that?"

"I've gotten the same reports, but nothing more than that—there'll be a Starfleet briefing today at 1500, so you can ask them then, since they're the ones who told us. Now, if I can go on without further interruptions—Ambassador Spock will be meeting with the president this morning, and Spock may also speak before the council when it is in session this afternoon. During that session, President Bacco will also introduce her new nominee for the judiciary council to replace former Councillor Artrin."

Edmund Atkinson asked, "Do we know who that is yet?"

Jorel smiled. "Depends on your definition of 'we,' doesn't it, Edmund?"

Rolling his eyes, Edmund spoke more slowly. "Can you tell us?"

"You know, I've never understood the whole idea of announcing when you're going to announce something. If I said, 'President Bacco will be announcing that Councillor Whoever will be her nominee for judiciary at 1330 when council is in session,' then she really won't be announcing it at 1330, because I'll just have done it for her. So, no, I can't tell you, because I really don't want to spoil it for the president."

Of course, it helps that nobody's told me who it is, either, Jorel thought with a sigh. Esperanza was huddled with her deputies, going over candidates so that they'd have a recommendation by 1300.

Jorel continued. "After her morning meetings, the president will be attending a reception in honor of the hundredth birthday of the assistant technology secretary, Toshiro Czierniewski, where she will be giving a toast, and after that will be the council session." He noticed that Kav from the Tellarite News Service was waving his furry hand about. Giving in to the inevitable, Jorel called on him.

"Councillor Artrin—sorry, *former* Councillor Artrin—did not call on me, Jorel, and I had a question of great import."

"Kav, all your questions are of great import—to you."

That got a laugh out of several reporters. Kav, however, was undeterred. "Why now?"

Jorel frowned. "Why what now?"

"Artrin made his judgment several years ago. He was nominated to the judiciary council several months ago. So why is it *now* that he is revealing this and resigning?"

"Because the president only learned of it yesterday, when a member of the Palais staff uncovered it in the course of research on a different topic." What amazed Jorel was that nobody asked that question of Artrin.

"So President Bacco's statements of support of Artrin were done without any knowledge of this incident?"

"Correct. Nofia?" The Deltan reporter had her hand up, and Jorel had had enough of Kav.

"Has there been any progress in the negotiations in the Wescott Room?"

Jorel had been expecting someone to ask about that and wasn't at all surprised that it was Nofia, mainly because there weren't any Carreon in the room, the news media on Carrea apparently not being interested in reporting on the doings of the Palais from up close. "I spoke with both ambassadors last night after the last session. Ambassador Tierra said that progress is being made, and she's hopeful that the Carreon will agree to provide Delta with the water reclamation system they desperately need. Ambassador Yorgas said that progress is being made, and he's hopeful that the Deltans will accede to the Carreon's reasonable demands."

Nofia smiled. "I take that to mean that no progress is being made, which is pretty much the same story for the past two months. Is there any chance that President Bacco will intervene?"

"I'd say there's a chance, but whether or not it happens today will depend on several other factors, most of them related to the once and future Romulan Star Empire." He picked up his padds from the podium. "That's all for now. I'll have another briefing this afternoon after the session ends."

The reporters all disappeared as the holocom was deactivated.

"I must say, I do *love* being able to just turn them off like that."

Jorel's assistant, Zhres, was standing nearby. "So you have said on several occasions."

"And I'll probably continue to say it as long as it's true. Has anybody hammered us on Sorlak's appearance yet?"

Zhres's antennae quivered. "I'm sorry?"

Rolling his eyes, Jorel said, "Sorlak was on *ICL* a few days ago, and she went on at great length about the confidence the president had in Artrin. I deflected Kav, but I don't think that's going to slow anyone down. Keep on the feeds, see who pounces on that."

"Right." Zhres moved off to his office. Jorel headed for the turbolift. He needed to talk to Esperanza right away.

"This is a most impressive office, Madam President."

Nan chuckled at the remark from Ambassador Spock. Resplendent as he was in his black robe of office with Vulcan lettering emblazoned down one of the folds, his hair was thinner than Nan thought it would be. *But then even legends get old eventually. Look at me.*

Spock was seated in one of the office's chairs; Esperanza was seated opposite him, with Raisa next to her. T'Latrek, Molmaan, Jas, and Akaar hadn't arrived yet.

"I'm surprised you haven't been here before, Mr. Ambassador," she said, leaning against the front of her desk.

"I have been in the president's office, but not since your election—indeed, the last president I visited was President Amitra. All presidents supply their own unique stamp upon this room."

Nan chuckled. "So it's been three presidents since you've been back here."

"My mission to Romulus was always expected to be a long-term one, Madam President."

"Well, what Romulus has been through hasn't been particularly long-term, Mr. Ambassador."

"I am confused at the use of curtains over the window," he said.

At that, Nan couldn't help but laugh. "Too low-tech for you?"

"My own needs are of no consequence. I simply find it hard to believe that the windows are not capable of being polarized to keep harsh sunlight out of the room, while still affording you the panorama."

Never knew you moonlighted as an interior decorator. Somehow, Nan managed not to say that out loud. "There are times when I don't want the distraction of the view, and I hate the way the window looks when it's opaqued—it's like working in a damn obelisk. Hence, the curtains." As she spoke, the door slid open to reveal the two councillors and the admiral. Still no Jas Abrik. *I swear, I'm going to kill him.*

Akaar walked over to Spock and gave him a Capellan salute. "You honor us all with your presence, Spock."

"The honor is mine, Leonard."

As Akaar took his seat, the door slid open to reveal Jas. "I'm sorry I'm late," the elderly Trill said as he entered, "but I was in the Monet Room. Madam President, the *Shirekral*-class vessel that has been approaching our border has reached Outpost 22. It has identified itself as the Reman Free Vessel *Vkruk*, and its captain has requested asylum in the Federation for himself and his crew, which includes twenty-nine Remans of both sexes."

"Fascinating," Spock muttered. Louder, he said, "Vkruk was the name of Shinzon's viceroy."

Nan sighed. "I just love cheap symbolism."

"These could be some of Shinzon's people," Esperanza said.

Jas took a seat on the sofa. "Speaking of Remus, I'm afraid there's more—there was a cave-in in one of the dilithium mines on Remus, *and* there was an explosion on one of the farms in Ehrie'fvil."

This just gets better and better. Ehrie'fvil was the name of the continent on Romulus where the Remans had relocated. Remus itself was barely habitable, used only for mining dilithium and manufacturing heavy weapons. The

Remans could service the Romulans there but not command their own destiny, as Remus could never be self-sufficient. This news came on the heels of a Reman couple being found brutally murdered yesterday. "How bad?"

"At least a hundred confirmed dead in the mine. As for the farm, nobody was killed, but the damage was extensive."

T'Latrek asked, "One assumes the incident in Ehrie'fvil was deliberate. What of the cave-in? Was it truly an accident, or was it too sabotage?"

"For now, all we know is that something happened. I only have the hundred dead from Ambassador Rozhenko. He was meeting with Chancellor Martok when the news came to the Great Hall. I'm hoping to get another report in fifteen minutes."

Spock turned toward Nan. "If I may, Madam President?"

Nan gestured toward Spock even as she took the chair opposite him, next to Esperanza. "Go on, Mr. Ambassador, you're the reason we're all here right now."

"In coming here, I intended to propose a course of action regarding the Reman problem. The incidents that Admiral Abrik has just described simply make my proposition all the more logical."

Nan regarded Spock. "And what would that proposition be?"

"The Remans require their own world."

Molmaan let out a sharp breath. "The Remans already have a continent."

"While Ehrie'fvil was a tenable solution three months ago, it was contingent on the Remans' being able to make use of the land to create their own economy. The disaster that Admiral Abrik has described is only the latest difficulty. There have been attacks on the Remans' crops—it has been impossible to prove sabotage, but impossible to disprove it as well. In addition, there have been continued instances of violence on Romulus itself that parallels the violence in space."

Nan scratched her chin. "So you think getting them away from the Romulans is the right course of action?"

"Yes. The violence has escalated and is now interfering with the peace process."

Esperanza shook her head. "I'm not sure I like the idea of that—it sounds like we've given up on the notion of them living in peace."

Raisa said, "I do not believe that was ever an option; if it were, the Klingons would not be needed."

"Or even desirable," Jas said. "If your goal's to bring about peaceful coexistence, you don't do it with the Klingons breathing down your necks."

Spock steepled his fingers in front of his face. "I share your misgivings, Ms. Piñiero. I too would prefer that the Remans and Romulans live in peace. However, I no longer believe that goal is viable, much as we had hoped it would be. Between them, the Klingons and Remans have enough ships to transport all the Remans currently living in Ehrie'fvil to a new world."

Molmaan threw up his webbed hands. "Fine, let them! Why are we even having this conversation? The Remans don't want any part of us—they made that very clear when Captain Riker offered them an opportunity to become a Federation protectorate—and neither do the Romulans. Let them all kill each other."

Esperanza said, "The violence is escalating, Councillor. If it keeps up, we won't be able to stay out of it."

"Why not?" Jas asked.

"Why not what?" Esperanza asked right back.

"Why not simply let the Klingons and Romulans fight it out?"

Spock raised an eyebrow. "You would condemn the Remans so callously?"

Jas gave Spock a withering look. "Not to put too fine a point on it, Mr. Ambassador, but they had their chance, and they spit in our faces."

Raisa said, "That is no excuse to simply abandon them."

"What more excuse could we possibly need?"

Nan gave Jas a withering look of her own. "I wasn't aware we were in need of one, Jas—I thought it was what we did naturally."

Jas was silent.

Turning to T'Latrek, Nan asked, "What do you think, Councillor?"

"I think removing the Remans from Romulus would defeat one of the primary goals of having the Klingons act as the Remans' protector—uniting the Romulan factions."

"Since when do we want that?" Jas asked. "A united Romulan front hardly benefits the Federation."

"The benefits to the Federation are irrelevant," T'Latrek said.

"She's right," Nan said before Jas could object. "A united Romulus will benefit the Romulan people—*that's* what I'm concerned about. If what happened on Remus today really was an accident, it happened because there isn't anyone maintaining the machinery down there. Weakened central authority—and Tal'Aura's authority is pretty damn weak—means this sort of thing is gonna keep happening, and the victims won't be the military, they won't be the politicians trying to angle for a senate seat now that the old senate's been turned to pixie dust—they'll be the Romulan people."

Another silence descended upon the room, before Akaar finally spoke. "Although the councillor's theory is sound—indeed, it was one of Captain Riker's selling points of the plan—it has not been working in practice. The parties are not talking, because they are blaming each other for attacks on Klingons, or they are blaming the Klingons, or blaming the Remans. Their attention is focused—but not on what is important."

Nan turned to her chief of staff. "Esperanza?"

"I think Ambassador Spock is right. When slavery ended in the country of the United States here on Earth five hundred years ago, the government didn't just tell them, 'You're free,' and leave it at that. Slave families—who worked on large farms—were given a segment of land and a farm animal from their armed forces that they could call their own. But it didn't work very well in practice, and the law that gave them that land was revoked. It was centuries before the former slaves were able to achieve proper equality with their former masters."

Chuckling, Nan said, "So you're saying the forty acres and a mule in Ehrie'fvil isn't working either?"

"No, ma'am. It was a good idea, truly, but the Romulans and Remans aren't holding up their end. We need new options here."

"This doesn't change the fact that the Remans don't want our help," Jas said. "So we find them a world, so what? How do we get them to it without annoying the Klingons?"

Raisa said, "I believe, Admiral, that you have provided the answer. The Klingons."

Jas blinked. "Actually, that's true. Damn, I didn't—" He turned to Nan. "Ma'am, as you probably know, the Klingons expanded into Sector 798-C a few years back."

T'Latrek put in, "The Klingon Empire refers to that vicinity of space as the Kavrot Sector."

"Whatever." Jas glowered briefly at T'Latrek, then turned back to Nan. "The point is, they did a huge survey of that area and have only actually planted their flag on a few worlds. They shared some of their sensor data with us a year ago—specifically the areas they scanned but didn't explore or didn't think were worth their while."

Nan liked the sound of that. "Check it over, Jas." Then a realization struck. "This may kill two birds with one stone, actually."

"What do you mean?" Esperanza asked.

"Those refugees—this may give us somewhere to send them."

Nan's intercom beeped. *"Madam President,"* Sivak said, *"I have Ms. Huaig in the Monet Room for Admiral Abrik."*

Jas jumped up from his chair and moved toward the door to her private office. "Ma'am?"

Nan sighed. Everyone in this room had the clearance to listen to a conversation between the security advisor and his deputy, but Abrik obviously preferred the security.

The hell with it, she decided. *We all need to hear this.* "Sit down, Admiral. Sivak, pipe it in here."

"Yes, ma'am."

Abrik did not look pleased as he sat down.

The screen on the wall facing Nan's desk lit up with the image of a young Delbian woman. This was Roshenz Huaig, Abrik's deputy. She looked surprised.

"Rosh, this is the president."

"Uh, ma'am, I was trying to reach Admiral Abrik." The young woman sounded flustered.

"He's in here with me, along with a cast of thousands. I assume you have an update on the Reman refugee situation?"

To her credit, Rosh recovered quickly. *"Yes, ma'am. I've spoken with Commander Bowles at Outpost 22. She says that the Remans have specifically requested asylum."*

"So we were right," Esperanza said.

"Not entirely, Ms. Piñiero. Their leader, who is called Jianuk, is requesting asylum from other Remans."

"That's ridiculous," Jas said.

"I do not agree with that assessment, Admiral," Spock said. "Jianuk was one of Shinzon's soldiers. They fought together during the war."

"Ambassador Spock is correct." Her initial surprise having passed, Rosh was now all business. *"The twenty-nine Remans on the* Vkruk *were all loyal to Shinzon—emphasis on* were. *They claim to have been persecuted by their fellow Remans because they condemned Shinzon's actions. They wish to live out their lives in the Federation."*

Jas looked at Nan. "What are your orders, ma'am?"

"Still the admiral, huh, Jas?" Nan realized immediately that her tone was unnecessarily snide, but Jas had it coming. Besides, it gave her a chance to think. "Rosh, tell Commander—Bowles, is it?"

"Yes, ma'am."

"Tell her to render whatever aid and assistance the *Vkruk* requires. Tell them their asylum request is pending, but in the meantime, they'll be guests of the Federation at the outpost."

"Understood, ma'am."

"Get right on that."

"Thank you, Madam President." With that, Rosh signed off.

Nan looked around the room. Jas sat on the sofa, looking slightly petulant, as if Nan had denied him the right to do things his way, or perhaps as if his deputy had stolen his thunder. Next to him were the two councillors, T'Latrek looking placid, Molmaan looking aggravated. Facing Nan were Spock and Akaar; surprisingly, the Capellan was the more stoic of the two. Spock actually looked thoughtful. Turning to her left, she saw Esperanza, her right hand, and Raisa, looking nonplussed.

"All right, we've got us a mess here. Everyone weigh in, I don't care how stupid you think you'll sound. You can rest assured that you can't possibly sound any stupider than I'm going to when I give the inevitable press conference that will result from this incident. Raisa?"

"My feelings have not changed, Madam President. These Remans are, for all intents and purposes, refugees from the Klingon Empire. Accepting their asylum request could damage our relationship with the empire."

T'Latrek said, "I do not believe that will be an issue."

"Why not?" Nan asked.

"Because we *have* a relationship with the empire. This need not be done in secret. Ambassador Rozhenko can plead the Remans' case to the High Council."

"Wait a minute," Jas said, "how do we even know these people are on the level?"

Nan frowned. "What do you mean?"

"These people were loyal to Shinzon—the same Shinzon whose first action upon taking over the Romulan government was to invade the Federation. Are these really people we want to just let in?"

"I agree with Admiral Abrik and with Secretary Shostakova," Molmaan said. "It's lunacy to let them anywhere near us. Sure, we can repair them and give them a hot meal, but after that, let them find a neutral planet, or a nation that doesn't mind getting into interstellar conflicts. Maybe the Tholians'll take them."

"If that was an attempt at humor," Nan said, "it failed."

Molmaan smiled, an action his face was ill-suited for. "I don't have a sense of humor."

"Worked that much out on my own, Councillor. Esperanza, what do you think?"

Esperanza folded her hands on her lap. "We still need to inform the Klingons just of the asylum request—if we're going to be pitching Reman relocation to them anyhow, we may as well do this, too."

Nan nodded.

However, Esperanza wasn't finished. "But I disagree with T'Latrek on one point. It shouldn't be Ambassador Rozhenko who makes the case, it should be Ambassador Spock."

Everyone turned to look at Spock at that. For his part, Spock gazed at Esperanza, one eyebrow raised. "Indeed?"

"You're the best man for the job, Mr. Ambassador. You've spent most of the last decade in Romulan space, and you're also someone the Klingons have always respected. A plea from you will mean a lot more."

"I'm afraid I must respectfully decline. My place is on Romulus."

"Not hardly, Mr. Ambassador," Nan said.

Again the eyebrow-raise, this time at Nan. "Madam President, you yourself sanctioned my mission to Romulus."

"I sanctioned the mission because you made a good argument down on the first floor a couple months ago. But throughout this meeting, everyone's been calling you 'Mr. Ambassador'—except for Molmaan, of course, but Zaldans aren't big on honorifics. You know why we're doing that? Because, to the best of my knowledge, you're still a Federation ambassador. Which means, in real terms, that you work for me—unless you're resigning your post, in which case I'm going to have to have security throw you out, because you will no longer have clearance to be on this floor." Nan leaned forward in her chair, looking Spock directly in his unblinking eyes. "Am I making myself completely clear?"

She and Spock continued to lock eyes. Neither of them blinked. Finally, Spock said, "Very well—I will go to Qo'noS and speak to the High Council."

Nan turned toward the sofa. "T'Latrek, if you'd be so kind as to work out the travel arrangements and the itinerary with Ambassador Rozhenko."

T'Latrek bowed. "Of course, Madam President."

"All right," she said as she got up from her chair, "that's it. Thank you all."

Most of those in the room said, "Thank you, Madam President" before they left. The exceptions were Molmaan, naturally, and Spock, who simply inclined his head toward Nan and departed with T'Latrek.

Esperanza stayed behind. "What do you think?"

"I think Spock's pissed at me."

Grinning, Esperanza said, "I thought Vulcans didn't get pissed."

"He's half-human." She shook her head and walked around to the other side of her desk. "You know, Esperanza, when you sold me on the notion of running for president, you never mentioned the part about having living legends in my office and irritating the hell out of them."

"I wanted it to be a surprise."

Nan chuckled. "Seriously, though, I don't like any of this. We're making preparations, we're making recommendations—but we're not *doing* anything."

"We're not empowered to do anything," Esperanza said. "It's the Klingons' call."

"Yeah, and it always goes well when they're left to their own judgment." She sighed. "Anything else?"

"You did good here. It may not seem like we're doing anything yet, but we're putting the pieces in place so we can."

"Yeah." President Bacco sighed. "We're gonna get our asses kicked on Artrin, aren't we?"

Esperanza nodded. "Yeah, but we'll weather it. Don't forget, you wanted to drop in on the Wescott Room before Toshiro's birthday thing."

Nan brightened. "Right! I forgot about that. Good, maybe I can accomplish something there—'cause I gotta tell you, Esperanza, right now I don't feel like we're accomplishing a damn thing."

✦

CHAPTER ELEVEN

✦   ✦

ALFEAR YORGAS was bored.

This entire negotiation was a waste of time. He had been given very simple instructions by his superiors on Carrea: "Don't give the Deltans anything." An easy enough instruction to follow; it only required that he be creative in coming up with ever more ridiculous demands on the Deltans in exchange for their water reclamation system.

However, the negotiations had dragged on for months, including eight weeks trapped on this madhouse of a planet in this hideous room, sitting across from the beautiful face and bald head of Ambassador Tierra, a face he would gladly cave in with a jagged rock at this point.

He stared up at the portrait of the human who had served as this tiresome Federation's president over a hundred years earlier, and after whom this Wescott Room was named. According to Yorgas's researches, this human was the youngest person to attain the office of the presidency in the Federation, a distinction he retained to this day, apparently. Yorgas didn't care that much; he had only investigated out of a morbid curiosity. He found the entire concept of the Federation to be loathsome, as much because they had the Deltans as part of it as anything. Carrea would never be part of a nation that had Delta as a member.

Yorgas's latest demand to Tierra had been for the right to put a scientific base on Brannik IV. He'd been saving that one for when he was really desperate, because that had been a bone of contention between their two worlds for years. Delta laid claim to Brannik IV—but did nothing with it.

Tierra sat calmly in her chair and said, "Brannik IV is an important strategic—"

Slamming his hand on the large wooden table, Yorgas bellowed, "Enough! You have been spinning that lie for centuries!"

"It is no lie!" Tierra's calm quickly evaporated. "Our military base there—"

"Can just as easily be put *anywhere*. But Brannik is the only other planet we have found where the animal life matches the fossils on our homeworld from the *Oida* age. Studying Brannik might provide some answers regarding that period. Yet you continue to prevent us—"

"Oh, *please*," Tierra said with a dismissive wave. "You

only wish to gain a foothold in the solar system that is most proximate to ours so you can spy on us."

Rolling his eyes, Yorgas said, "Trust me, we have little interest in watching your deviant planet all have sex with each other constantly."

To Yorgas's surprise, Tierra laughed at that.

"What amuses you, Ambassador?"

Instead of answering his question, Tierra turned to one of her aides. "Kedda, I owe you dinner."

Yorgas didn't like the sudden jocular tone. "What are you talking about?"

Now Tierra looked right at Yorgas and fixed him with a smile that six months ago might have charmed him. Deltan pheromones were well known throughout the galaxy, and their effect on Carreons was nauseating. One risked turning into a quivering mass of sexual idiocy in the presence of a Deltan, which was why Yorgas found them so despicable. Still, even Yorgas had to admit that Tierra, at least, had a certain charm. However, the long months of negotiation had bled all the charm out of her from his perspective, and so now the urge to cave her face in with a rock simply increased to a desire to light her boots on fire and watch her slowly burn to death.

"What I'm talking about," she said, "is that Kedda bet me a dinner that today would be the day that you would finally resort to name-calling. I'm actually impressed, Ambassador, that it took this long for your prudish idiocy to come to the fore."

That simpering bitch. "The fact that we don't flaunt our base instincts for all to see doesn't make us idiots, Ambassador, it simply makes us moral."

As Yorgas was speaking, one of the doors to the Wescott Room opened to reveal President Nan Bacco, who said,

"Because of course, Ambassador Yorgas, morality is an absolute throughout the galaxy."

Yorgas felt his face grow colder with embarrassment. This president was also human, but unlike the one in the picture—who was unusually tall for a human, with broad shoulders and a hard face—this one was female, short, and frail-looking. Bacco had come across as more formidable in the footage he had viewed before coming here, and he now realized that it was a trick of the camera, as it were.

"I would disagree with that, *Yar* Bacco," he said, addressing her formally. "Morality cannot be anything but an absolute."

"Well, that's easy for a person representing a monolithic morality to say—assuming you *do* have a monolithic morality. Does every Carreon behave with the same morals?"

"Of course," Yorgas said, even though he knew it to be false. But he would not show weakness before this woman.

She took a seat that was halfway between Yorgas and Tierra on the side of the table. "Well, I envy you that, Mr. Ambassador, I really do. If everyone shared the same morals, we'd probably have a much easier time of it."

"Time of what, *Yar* Bacco?"

Bacco hesitated. "I was about to say government, but honestly, the answer to that would be 'everything.' It must simplify things for you so much, to come at everything with such great moral certitude."

"I suppose it does," Yorgas said after a moment's thought. "I had not considered it that way before."

"In any case, I didn't come in here to discuss moral relativism. I came here to talk to you all about how these negotiations are coming."

Tierra started to say, "They are—" but Bacco held up her hand.

"Spare me the platitudes and the false promises, Ambassadors. If I want the public face, I'll talk to our press liaison, who has been shoveling your manure for two months now. The fact is, these negotiations are nowhere."

Yorgas said, "The Carreon have made several generous requests for items to be traded for our water reclamation system. The Deltans have refused every one of them."

"Because none of them *are* generous," Tierra snapped. "They are insults to the Deltan people. They have not been answered in kind only because we are desperate."

Turning to Bacco, Yorgas said, "You see, *Yar* Bacco, this is the type of slander I have had to put up with since these negotiations commenced."

"Well, we wouldn't want you to have to suffer slander, Ambassador, so on behalf of the United Federation of Planets, I do apologize for that, and for Ambassador Tierra's behavior."

To Yorgas's great amusement, Tierra looked furious. "Thank you, *Yar* Bacco."

"Madam President—" Tierra started, but again, Bacco cut her off.

"One moment, please, Madam Ambassador." She turned to look at Yorgas. "The thing is, I've been reading over the transcripts of your meetings, Mr. Ambassador, and I've discovered something interesting."

"And what is that?" Yorgas asked with a broad smile. *This is going well. This foolish old woman will give me everything I ask for. She even apologized!*

"That you have stonewalled these negotiations. That, in fact, you have not been acting in good faith but instead doing everything you can to drag out this process."

Yorgas's face went cold again. "*Yar* Bacco, I can assure you that I have done no such—"

"Spare me, Mr. Ambassador. Your offers haven't been generous, they've been outrageous—and what's more, you know they're outrageous. Unless, of course, you're far more incompetent than we've been led to believe. Either way, the Carreon have insulted the United Federation of Planets, and we are not going to stand for it." She stood up. "Quite simply, Mr. Ambassador, we've had enough. You've been harassing the Deltans for a long time, and now you're holding them up over a water reclamation system that will cost you nothing to provide, yet they cannot live without." She pointed an accusatory finger at him. "You, sir, are condemning an entire species to dehydration just so you can derive pleasure from watching Ambassador Tierra and her staff squirm. I gotta say, Mr. Ambassador, how you can do that and still claim *any* kind of moral high ground is a mystery that I will take to my grave."

"*Yar* Bacco—" Yorgas started, but this time it was he the president interrupted.

"Mr. Ambassador, if you do not come to an agreement with Ambassador Tierra within the next thirty minutes, the Federation is going to declare war on the Carreon."

Yorgas felt his breakfast start to rise in his throat. He swallowed it down, but the bitter taste remained in the back of his mouth. He stood up and clenched his fist. "This is outrageous! On what grounds would you declare war?"

Bacco actually smiled—smiled! Yorgas had never been so insulted in his life. Then she said, "Well, for starters, the person in my position is properly addressed as 'ma'am' or 'Madam President.'"

That, Yorgas could not believe. "You would go to war, engage your Starfleet in a military engagement that would result in countless casualties—over an *insult?*"

"I did say 'for starters,' Mr. Ambassador. We'd then go

to the depraved indifference of allowing this situation to continue, and negotiating in bad faith. It's that last one that especially got my dander up—you see, Mr. Ambassador, negotiation is all we have to *prevent* war. But if you're not even going to give us that, then we only have one option left."

Yorgas put his hand to the back of his head. This was disastrous. The Federation was the largest power in the quadrant. They'd successfully beaten back the Dominion after they'd gained a foothold in Cardassia. They were allied with the Klingons, who were experts at warmaking.

Then he calmed down. She had to be bluffing. "Then declare your war, *Yar* Ba—" He hesitated. "Madam President. Send your fleets."

"Oh, I don't have to send any fleets. Right now there's a ship in orbit of Carrea, the *U.S.S. Cheiron.* It's a *Centaur*-class ship, it's got eighteen phaser emplacements and four torpedo launchers. Not sure what its complement of photon and quantum torpedoes is, but you can rest assured that it's enough to pulverize your planet."

"You wouldn't," Yorgas whispered. The *Cheiron* had been investigating solar flares in Carrea's home star system, at the request of the Carreon Science Institute, since Starfleet had better sensors than the Carreon science ships. *I can't believe that they'd—*

"Now you could risk an interstellar incident, Mr. Ambassador. Or you can let the Deltans have the water reclamation system."

Trying to maintain some shred of his mission, Yorgas said, "We must have *something*, Madam President."

"You're right." Bacco turned to Tierra. "Why don't you give them Brannik IV?"

Tierra nodded. "Very well."

Yorgas's mouth fell open. He closed it quickly, then said, "You'll—you'll give us Brannik?"

"No," Tierra said in a soft voice that sounded like honey, "but we will allow you to set up your scientific base. Our satellites will remain in orbit, and they will be watching you to make sure that all you do is watch the animal life."

Yorgas looked back and forth between Tierra and Bacco. "You two planned this."

"That's right," Bacco said. "We got together and decided ahead of time to make you look stupid. Kinda like what you've been doing to her for the past few months."

The Carreon ambassador found that he had nothing he could say in response to that.

Bacco clapped her hands together. "Well, then—I'm glad we had this chat. I'd hate for us to go to war, especially since we'd likely torpedo you back to the *Oida* age. I'll leave you all to work out the details."

Tierra and her staff all said, "Thank you, Madam President."

Yorgas said nothing, but he did remain standing, even after Tierra sat back down. *I have been humiliated. And now I must return to Carrea and tell them that I gave in.*

He sighed. *I can only hope that finally getting the base on Brannik IV will mitigate my punishment.*

Ambassador K'mtok did not like to be kept waiting.

He sat in the waiting area outside President Bacco's office. According to the supercilious Vulcan, the Federation leader was in some kind of meeting. The Vulcan also pointed out that if the ambassador would set up an appointment, there would be a much better chance of his arriving at a time when the president could see him.

Were he on Qo'noS, the Vulcan would have been dead before he could have completed his sentence. Indeed, it had taken much of K'mtok's willpower not to take out his *d'k tahg* and plunge it into the Vulcan's chest. Still, such actions would not only cause an interstellar incident, but they would also provoke the guard standing at the entrance to the president's office into firing her phaser sidearm at K'mtok, disintegrating him in an instant. He had only been ambassador a few months—he wanted to enjoy it for quite some time.

He was *not* enjoying waiting, but he would have enjoyed even less waiting until his official appointment tomorrow. This Bacco woman was toying with the empire, and he would have none of it.

The turbolift doors opened to reveal another guard, as well as President Bacco and a Deltan woman K'mtok didn't know. The ambassador only knew she was Deltan from her distinctive scent—Deltans all smelled of fornication. If they weren't such hideous, hairless creatures, K'mtok might have found it invigorating.

"—right," the Bacco woman was saying as she and the bald-headed woman exited the lift and headed toward the door, "but putting you on judiciary's gonna be tricky."

"I believe, Madam President, that it is the least you can do after costing us Brannik IV."

"No, the least I can do after costing you Brannik IV is getting you a water reclamation system that will actually reclaim your water. Anyhow, the appointment's got nothing to do with the deal with the Carreon, it has to do with Artrin resigning. The fun part's gonna be replacing him on the security—" She finally noticed K'mtok. "Mr. Ambassador—I wasn't expecting you until tomorrow."

"Tomorrow will be too late. I will speak to you now."

Bacco turned to Sivak. "Have I got anything else besides Toshiro's shindig?"

"No, ma'am—however, you are already fifteen minutes late for that."

Turning to K'mtok, Bacco said, "Well, I wouldn't be much of a leader if I showed up any sooner than half an hour late to an official function. You've got fifteen minutes, Mr. Ambassador—I suggest you make it good." She then turned to the Deltan. "Councillor, I'll see you at 1330."

"Thank you, Madam President." The Deltan then looked at K'mtok. "Mr. Ambassador."

"Councillor," K'mtok said, realizing that the woman was Eleana, the representative of Delta IV to the Federation Council.

Bacco moved toward the door, where the second guard had also taken up position. She expected K'mtok to follow her without prompting, a compliment the ambassador hadn't been expecting.

As soon as the door shut behind him, K'mtok said, "You are not considering granting asylum to the Remans at your outpost." He deliberately did not phrase it as a question.

"Really? I wasn't aware that precognition was among your many talents, Mr. Ambassador."

K'mtok frowned. "I assume that was a typical human attempt at humor."

"Actually, my attempts at humor are pretty atypical, but that's neither here nor there."

"That was not a prediction, Madam President, it was a statement."

"Sounded like an order to me."

Shrugging, K'mtok said, "You may interpret it that way if you wish."

"Oh, I don't wish—because, you see, there's only one person who gives orders in this office, and it is most assuredly *not* you." The woman sat down at her desk and indicated the chair opposite it. "Have a seat, sir."

"I prefer to stand."

With more steel in her voice than K'mtok would have expected from an elderly human woman, she asked, "Remember what I said about giving orders, Mr. Ambassador?"

Under his gray beard, K'mtok smiled as he took the proffered chair. He had dealt with Bacco's predecessor only a few times before his resignation, but K'mtok had had little congress with Bacco herself since her election. *Perhaps she will be a more worthy opponent than I expected. She certainly is more invigorating than that spineless Bolian.*

"Now then, why don't we start this conversation over again. I believe you had a concern about the Reman refugees at Outpost 22."

"They are not Reman refugees, Madam President. They are Klingon protégés. Under the terms of the Khitomer Accords, you are obliged to turn them over to the empire at our request."

Bacco stared at him for a moment. "I take it that your presence here is that request?"

"Correct."

The president rubbed her chin. "You are aware of the Remans' situation, aren't you?"

"No, nor do I need to be. Madam President, the treaty is clear. The 'situation,' as you put it, is of no consequence. A Defense Force vessel, the *I.K.S. Ditagh*, is on its way to Outpost 22 right now. It will arrive in four days. At that time, you will turn over all seventy-nine Remans to Captain Vikagh, who will remand them to Klingon custody."

"Oh, will I?" Bacco said with a wholly inappropriate smile.

K'mtok realized that he had once again phrased his statements incorrectly. Most Federation citizens—even ones in positions of power—were intimidated by a Klingon giving orders. This one was made of sterner stuff, her appearance notwithstanding. "Perhaps I phrased that badly, Madam President."

"Drop the 'perhaps,' and I'll agree with you. Look, you want to send the *Ditagh* to the outpost, that's your right. See, I'm pretty familiar with the Khitomer Accords. For reasons that should be pretty obvious, my staff and I've been reading them over. There are lots of terms to them, some involving trade, some involving weapons bans, some involving extradition—and part of it states that Federation and Klingon ships are allowed to travel freely in the other nation's space." She leaned forward and placed her hands on the desk, which was of a substance K'mtok was unfamiliar with. "Because I've been familiarizing myself, I happen to know the paragraph you're referring to when you say that if the empire requests that Klingon nationals requesting asylum must be turned over to the empire, they will be. And your situation isn't as cut and dried as you're making it out."

K'mtok was less impressed with this woman now. "Do not be absurd, Madam President. It is, in fact, completely 'cut and dried,' as you so colorfully put it. The treaty is very clear."

"Yeah, it is. It refers to Klingon *nationals.* That means Klingons who are citizens of the empire, as well as the various subject species. However, it does *not* apply to the Remans."

"That is ridiculous, the Remans—"

"Are *not* Klingon nationals. They're not citizens, they're not *jeghpu'wI'*, they're just under your protection."

K'mtok stood up. "This is outrageous! You would deny us our rights because of a semantic difficulty in the treaty?"

Bacco also stood up, which denied K'mtok his ability to look down on the human. "Semantic difficulties in treaties start wars, Mr. Ambassador. Maybe it does apply to the Remans—and maybe it doesn't. It's something that needs to be worked out. Now, if you want to be part of those discussions as a representative of the Klingon Empire, that's just fine. We'd welcome your input—in fact, we encourage it. You're our allies, and we're supposed to work together on this kind of thing. But if you're gonna stick to your guns and insist on the most rigid stance on this without *any* kind of negotiation, then I am going to be very much inclined to go for the interpretation of the treaty language that serves your purposes the least well, am I understood?" Again, she leaned forward, this time her fists balled on the desk. "Those Remans have been persecuted, Mr. Ambassador, not just by the Romulans, but by their fellow Remans. Their asylum request isn't from you or from Romulus, it's from their brothers and sisters. I think there's a little room to maneuver, don't you?"

Every instinct in K'mtok's body screamed out to tell Bacco that the Remans must be remanded to the empire, and that was that. But Bacco's offer made that difficult. He could, of course, take that position and simply not report Bacco's offer to the High Council—but no, that was too risky. Bacco would inform their ambassador, and that infant that had replaced the *toDSaH* Worf had Martok's ear. Martok would learn of it one way or the other and then ask why K'mtok had not conveyed it to the council.

"I will consult with my government and inform you of our decision."

Bacco nodded. "Glad to hear it. By the end of the day, if you please."

K'mtok refused to give that ground, having already given so much. "I promise nothing, Madam President. I will inform you of our decision when that decision is made—*whenever* that may be."

He then turned on his heel and left the president's office. *This battlefield will be more difficult than I expected.*

Edmund Atkinson had yet to grow tired of the council chambers.

No matter how old and cynical he became—and he was more of both than he liked—he always felt a mild thrill whenever he entered the huge chamber that took up most of the first floor of the Palais de la Concorde. Below the floor ran the Champs Elysées, which the Palais straddled, supported by duranium beams at the four corners. In one of those beams was the turbolift that led to the basement levels.

But, though many classified activities went on in the basements, it was in this room that much of the Federation's government work got done. Though the building was cylindrical, the chambers were rectangular. In front of the south wall was the podium emblazoned with the symbol of the United Federation of Planets, which matched that of the flag hanging from the pole behind it. That podium was where the leader of the session stood. During full council sessions, that was the president's place. On the south wall itself was a viewscreen that could be used for a variety of purposes, the most common being the display of vote tallies.

On the east wall were four rows of twenty seats each, with a matching set on the west wall. These one hundred and sixty seats were for the councillors, which currently numbered one hundred and fifty-four. Edmund knew that when the chambers had first been constructed, there had been only one row on either side. When the one hundred and sixty-first planet joined the Federation, two more rows would be added to keep the room's balance, and allow for the next twoscore worlds to be added to the Federation's numbers.

The north wall gallery was where spectators were allowed to observe open sessions. Most sessions of the full council were open to the public, and even the ones that weren't were recorded. Occasionally—regularly, during the Dominion War—sessions were sealed for security reasons. However, this session most assuredly wasn't, which meant that Edmund could watch the session directly. He found that preferable to waiting for Jorel's interpretation of the session after the fact in the press room. Edmund wanted to see who was going to be nominated in Artrin's stead on judiciary—and, of much greater interest, who was going to be nominated to take Artrin's place on security. If someone from the "back eight" of security resigned or was replaced, their seat on that council was always given to another world rather than their replacement.

Edmund's favorite part of the council chamber was the center. That was the speaker's floor. With the exception of the president, no one could speak to the council except from that floor. Councillors could speak to each other or via the workstations in front of them to people outside the chamber, but, in full council sessions, any official council statements for the record had to come either from the podium or the floor. Whoever designed the room had arranged the slant of the roof so that the space was almost perfect acoustically. One could clearly hear every word from the floor no matter where you sat.

However, more than one person could have the floor, and it didn't have to be a councillor. Some of the greatest debates in Federation history had happened on that floor: President al-Rashid and Councillor (later President) sh'Rothress arguing over what constituted the proper criteria to admit new members into the then-still-nascent Federation; Ambassador Sarek debating Ambassador Kamarag over the Genesis Device; Sarek again, this time debating his own son Spock about Cardassia; Councillors Gleer of Tellar and T'Latrek of Vulcan arguing over the level of security necessary to prevent changeling infiltration on Earth in the wake of the attack on the Antwerp Conference; and most recently a barely civilized discussion between Ambassador Lwaxana Troi of Betazed and Elim Garak of Cardassia over the allocation of postwar relief efforts.

Edmund wondered what he'd see today. *Maybe another T'Latrek-Gleer dogfight. I can get an entire column out of that. . . .*

They began with the usual tedious business, including taking a roll call. One hundred and thirty-two of the councillors were present. Edmund knew that several of the ones proximate to the Romulan or Klingon borders had returned to investigate matters on their homeworlds. Also conspicuous by her continued absence was Councillor Eftheria Lo of Ontail. *Given all the trouble the Federation went to to keep them in, you'd think they'd at least show up once or twice.*

Once the preliminaries were out of the way, Bacco paused for a moment before speaking. "Before we continue, I'd like to offer an apology to the entirety of the Federation Council. Two months ago, I did something incredibly stupid. I neglected to treat all of you—and those of you who are part of this august body but not actually present—with respect. When I expressed my displeasure over our trade agreement with Aligar, I did so in a manner that was unfair to you—indeed, that was insulting to you. I let my own feelings get in the way of my responsibilities to this council and to the Federation. It has led to an unconscionable breakdown in communication between this council and the president's office, and it stops here, now. So let me just say that I am sorry—and let's get to work."

Edmund blinked several times, then made a note in his padd. He'd been covering politics for the *Times* for thirty years, and he'd never heard a politician make so *honest* an apology.

"As you all know," Bacco said, "Councillor Artrin resigned this morning. The Triexian Curia will appoint a new councillor within the next week to serve out his term. For obvious reasons, the president's office hereby withdraws his nomination for appointment to the judiciary council. In addition, Triex is now removed from the security council. I hereby nominate for appointment to the judiciary council Councillor Eleana of Delta, and I hereby nominate for appointment to the security council Councillor Krim Aldos of Bajor."

This time, Edmund almost fell out of his chair. Like many people, he believed that Eleana would make a most interesting addition to judiciary, but she had made enough enemies in this room to make her ratification difficult.

Krim, however, was an even bigger risk. He'd been a last-minute replacement as Bajor's first councillor when the original choice had died unexpectedly, almost three and a half years ago.

Edmund made a bet with himself that he quickly won as the light in front of Bera chim Gleer's seat went on, indicating that he wished to speak on the floor. *May as well get comfortable,* he thought, *Gleer doesn't do short speeches.*

Was it Edmund's imagination, or did Bacco sound pained when she said, "The podium recognizes the councillor from Tellar"?

The Tellarite councillor stalked down the length of his row and stomped toward the center of the chamber. With his furry hands, he clutched the lapels of the silvery jacket he wore over an embroidered shirt. His pants matched the jacket, making it look like he was glowing. He stared at Bacco with his sunken eyes—which put his back to Edmund—and began to speak.

"With all due respect, Madam President—are you mad? Bajor has only been in the Federation for three years. To put them on the security council is the height of irresponsibility. In addition, I point you to Councillor Krim's record. He was a rebel on Bajor, then supported a coup d'état that was disgraced. He has spent most of the last decade out of the public eye and had not participated in the least in the realm of politics until he was placed on this council by his wife, the first minister of Bajor. Is it wise to trust the delicate matters handled on the security council to such a person?"

T'Latrek's light went on, and Edmund thought he was going to burst with excitement. *I was hoping she would get into it.*

Sounding much more cheered—the president knew the entertainment value of a good floor fight, after all—Bacco said, "The podium recognizes the councillor from Vulcan."

The Vulcan woman glided out from her seat and joined Gleer. Her own arms were not visible in her long, black cloak of office. Her gray-flecked black hair extended past her shoulders and was swept back in a simple, practical style that required no grooming beyond running a brush through it. T'Latrek's eyebrows were severe, her eyes pitiless, her mouth a perfect line perpendicular to a nose that would have been called aristocratic on a human. She fixed those pitiless eyes on Gleer.

"Anyone who lived as an adult on Bajor prior to their liberation from Cardassia twelve years ago and who is in any way politically astute probably was part of their resistance movement. Either that or they collaborated with the Cardassians, and I assume my colleague would not want such a person to serve on the security council—or on the council at all."

"That goes without saying. I would never support such a person and would be against his being placed on the council."

"For something that goes without saying, you do feel the need to describe it at length," T'Latrek said witheringly.

Score one for the Vulcan, Edmund thought as he made more notes. Gleer looked like someone had urinated in his soup.

"In addition," T'Latrek said, "First Minister Asarem is not Councillor Krim's wife, but rather his ex-wife."

"An irrelevant distinction," Gleer said dismissively.

"To Tellarites, perhaps." Before Gleer could respond to that, T'Latrek said, "However, the reasons why we should ratify Councillor Krim's appointment to the security council have very little to do with Councillor Krim."

"They have everything to do with him!"

T'Latrek continued as if Gleer hadn't interrupted. "They have to do with the planet he represents. In the past decade, Bajor has been a very important planet in quadrant politics. It houses the gateway to the Gamma Quadrant. It was the staging ground for the Dominion War. And it is the Federation planet that is closest to Cardassian territory. Its proximity to the wormhole, to Cardassia, to Tzenketh, and to the Badlands makes its strategic value as great as that of any world in the Federation."

"I do not deny that," Gleer said irritably. "Bajor's importance is obvious even to the meanest intelligence."

Edmund half expected a comment about Gleer's own cranial capacity at that, but T'Latrek wasn't going for cheap shots today, apparently.

"It is for that reason that Bajor's presence on the security council is a necessity. We cannot expect Bajor to accept its role in the security of the Federation without giving it a concomitant voice in that security. To do otherwise would weaken their position at a time when their strength is of paramount importance to the Federation."

Gleer huffed. "I believe that what is of paramount importance to the Federation is not having someone on its security council who opposes the very notion of Bajoran membership *in* the Federation." He turned to look at Krim, seated on the end of the fourth row closest to the president, then he looked at T'Latrek. "Do you deny that that is so?"

While T'Latrek and Gleer spoke, Edmund looked out over the council. After all these years covering the Palais, he had gotten fairly good at interpreting the body language of the different species that were represented on the council. Matthew Mazibuko of Earth was inscrutable as ever, though he did seem to shift uncomfortably when Gleer spoke. Lari Beltane of light-gravity Gemworld, in her specially modified chair, gripped the arms of that chair more tightly when T'Latrek spoke, indicating that she was on Gleer's side of the debate. Gnalish councillor Gorus Gelemingar's tail waved back and forth impatiently during the entire talk, so Edmund assumed he didn't care all that much. Linzner, the new councillor from Benzar, blinked a great deal when T'Latrek spoke, and leaned into her breathing apparatus when Gleer spoke, so she was probably on the Vulcan's side. C29 Green of Nasat was having an animated conversation with someone on his comm unit, and he was not the only one who was tuning out this latest in a series of debates between these two.

Then, as Gleer looked at Krim, Edmund did likewise. To the reporter's amusement, Krim was smiling.

In response to Gleer's question, T'Latrek raised an eyebrow. "It would be the height of folly to deny that which is on the public record. However, my colleague neglects to mention that the Circle Commission, which studied the coup d'état in question, exonerated Councillor Krim of any wrongdoing."

Gleer snorted, a most unpleasant noise. "That was simply politics."

"There was no political gain to be had by exonerating Councillor Krim," T'Latrek said in a withering voice. "He was, at the time, out of the sociopolitical arena completely, nor did he use his exoneration as an excuse to reenter that realm."

Before Gleer could respond, Krim started laughing. Then, belatedly, he activated the light in front of him. The law did not specify an upper limit to the number of people who could hold the floor, but few presidents had ever allowed the number to exceed three. At that point discussions generally devolved into shouting matches.

Bacco did not look pleased at the laugh, but at the light, she nodded and said, "The podium recognizes the councillor from Bajor."

Krim had one of those faces that looked like it had seen everything the galaxy had to offer and wasn't especially happy about it. As soon as he reached the floor, T'Latrek inclined her head and said, "I yield the floor." She returned to her seat.

Gleer, naturally, stood his ground.

"You wished, Councillor Gleer," Krim said in a voice tinged with amusement, but also with a weariness that Edmund hadn't been expecting, "to question me regarding my position on Bajor's membership in the Federation. Frankly, sir, I do not see how it is germane to this discussion. Whether or not I approve of Bajor's being in the Federation does not matter, because Bajor *is* in the Federation. What's more, even if I were still against it, it would continue not to matter, because my function here is not to represent the Federation to Bajor—but rather to represent Bajor to the Federation. I am a patriot, sir. I always have been. It is why I fought the Cardassians. It is also why I accepted the post as head of the Bajoran Militia after the Cardassians withdrew. I was responsible for Bajor's security at a time when it was at its most insecure. And now I stand before you as the representative of a world that has played quite an important role in galactic politics while having comparatively little voice in those selfsame politics. We joined the Federation in part to change that."

"Yet you opposed the notion." Edmund wondered if Gleer would keep hammering that point into the ground.

"Yes, I did. But the time for that opposition has passed. When this council votes on bills and motions and such, do the councillors who voted against it refuse to participate in their implementation? Of course not." He turned his back on Gleer, which caused the Tellarite to huff. "Councillor T'Latrek has ably described the importance of the Bajoran sector to the security of the Federation. I know the Bajoran sector better than anyone else in this room. I do not believe there is anyone else who is not already on the security council who is better qualified to replace Councillor Artrin."

"Bah. Perhaps you are qualified to judge the security of the Bajoran sector, but that is but a few star systems—a tiny percentage of the amount of space that falls under the purview of the Federation and its allies. Do you truly claim to be able to handle the duties of forming policy on areas of space about which you know nothing?" Before Krim could respond, Gleer looked to Bacco. "I hereby propose that the vote be postponed so that there can be more consideration and debate." Gleer then looked right at Beltane.

Beltane suddenly became very preoccupied with her workstation.

Edmund smiled as Gleer looked at several councillors, including Jix, Djinian, Enaren, and Tomorok, no doubt hoping that one of them would second the proposition, which was the only way for it to be considered.

No one spoke up.

Again Krim smiled, then he spoke to the podium with far more respect than his colleague. "Madam President, I hereby propose that the vote be taken at the end of this session."

T'Latrek quickly seconded the motion.

Well, that's over, Edmund thought. T'Latrek's support meant a great deal in this room, and Krim speaking for himself so eloquently—and making Gleer look like an even bigger fool—won the day. Edmund seriously doubted that there would be more than token opposition to Krim's appointment. Bacco had won too many people over with her apology for them to start stonewalling appointments again.

However, Gleer was not a councillor to be trifled with. Edmund suspected that those councillors he'd turned to to second his proposition would find themselves regretting not having done so down the line.

✦

CHAPTER TWELVE

✦   ✦

ESPERANZA PIÑIERO looked up at *Bridge over a Pool of Water Lilies* in the vain hope that its tranquil setting would ease her worry.

At that, it failed, which made her wonder why they bothered to hang the damn thing in this meeting room.

That, she knew, wasn't fair. It had been the Monet Room before it had become the war room for the Zife administration, and at this point that function was too entrenched in the Palais structure for it to be changed.

Also present were Raisa Shostakova, Safranski, Jas Abrik, Roshenz Huaig, Holly Hostetler Richman, William Ross, and Leonard Akaar. They were waiting for a comm line to get through to the Federation embassy on Qo'noS. Nan Bacco was in a security council session, the first since Krim Aldos had been ratified by a ninety-seven to thirty-five vote three days earlier. They were going over various bits of business and also standing by for Esperanza's call in case the security council would need to deal with the situation.

Finally, the screen lit up with the faces of Alexander Rozhenko and Spock. As soon as Esperanza saw the expression on the former's face—Spock was too stoic to give anything away—she knew it wasn't good news.

"Ambassadors, this is Esperanza Piñiero—the council's in session, so the president is busy. What's the good word?" She was trying to sound optimistic, but she wondered if the attempt sounded as pathetic to everyone else in the room as it did to her.

"*I wish we had a good word to give you, Ms. Piñiero.*"

Spock added, "*In fact, there is some good news. The High Council agreed with our notion of providing the Remans with their own homeworld. The worlds that I suggested in the Kavrot Sector were all deemed acceptable, and the council has chosen Klorgat IV.*"

"I assume the bad news relates to Outpost 22."

"*Indeed,*" Spock said. "*The empire's acceptance of the relocation of the Remans is contingent upon our delivering all twenty-nine Remans aboard the* Vkruk *to the* Ditagh *when it arrives tomorrow.*"

"They won't budge on that?"

"*Not a chance,*" Rozhenko said. "*The High Council doesn't care about the internal politics of the Remans— their mandate's to protect all of them.*"

"What about the Khito—"

"*I know what you're gonna say, Ms. Piñiero, but—*" Rozhenko hesitated. "*Councillor Kopek summed up the High Council's feelings on the subject when he said that so literal-minded an interpretation of Paragraph 27 of the Khitomer Accords is, and I quote, 'cowardly.'*"

Abrik barked a laugh. "Klingons sure do know how to cut us to the quick."

Spock said, *"Their resolve is absolute. They have no intention of negotiating."*

"Mr. Ambassador," Ross said, "I can't believe that the Klingons are being this stubborn on so minor an issue. Are you sure there's no room for negotiation? Some concession we can give them in exchange for allowing us to grant the refugees asylum?"

"I proposed that very notion, Admiral, and it was rejected without reason."

Rozhenko then said, *"I think I can take a guess why, though."*

"Really?" Abrik asked, his voice laced with sarcasm.

Esperanza shot the retired admiral a look, then said to Rozhenko, "What's your theory, Mr. Ambassador?"

"Being protectors of the Remans is something the Klingons take seriously for one reason: It gets the Romulans really mad."

Involuntarily, Esperanza laughed. So did Shostakova, Hostetler Richman, and Ross. "Great, so the Klingons are getting their jollies. Where does that leave us?"

Shostakova recovered from her brief fit of laughter at Rozhenko's bluntness. "With two options: turn over the refugees or abrogate the treaty. I do not believe that it is necessary to explain the consequences of the latter."

"Those are *not* our only options," Akaar said. "They are merely the most obvious."

Giving the Capellan a withering look, the secretary of defense said, "They are our only options under the law, Admiral."

Ross regarded Esperanza with a serious expression. "What do you think, Esperanza?"

"I think that precisely nobody in this room is qualified to make any of these decisions." She touched the intercom on the table in front of her. "Put me through to the clerk's office."

"Yes, ma'am," the Starfleet ensign who handled communications on this floor said.

Moments later, a voice said, *"This is Selk."*

"Bgdronik, it's Esperanza—can you tell whoever's clerking on the first floor today that the chief of staff requests that the president declare the current session sealed if it isn't already, and that we need to tie the Monet Room into the council chambers as soon as that sealing takes place."

"Of course."

"While we're at it," Esperanza said to Roshenz, "let's get Commander Bowles in on this. She's at the heart of the situation, and she'll be able to take the Remans' temperature."

Within a few minutes, the screen on the wall opposite the Monet painting was divided into three segments. On top, across the breadth of the screen, was the council chamber on the first floor. President Bacco was standing, facing the screen with her back to her podium. Behind her were the thirteen members of the security council, including Krim Aldos, the newest member, all in seats close to the front. On the bottom of the screen were two separate, smaller images, one of Spock and Rozhenko, the other of a human woman in a Starfleet uniform with a red collar holding three pips. Esperanza assumed the latter was Commander Heidi Bowles of Outpost 22.

Esperanza quickly brought everyone up to speed.

The president spoke first. *"So nice to see Ambassador K'mtok took me seriously. I told him we wouldn't look kindly on them being hardliners, that we wanted them to participate in the process of figuring this thing out."*

Spock said, *"The High Council was resolute in their decision, Madam President."*

Then Rozhenko asked, *"Ma'am, how did you phrase it to the ambassador?"*

Frowning, the president said, *"I told him that if they were gonna stick to their guns and insist on the most rigid stance without any negotiating, then I'd be inclined to go for an interpretation of Khitomer that served the Klingons poorly."*

Rozhenko sighed. *"That isn't how K'mtok expressed it to the High Council. Ma'am, it's my opinion that the hardliners on the council are pushing for a more hawkish stance."*

"That figures," Safranski said. "K'mtok was appointed as a message to President Zife after Tezwa. He has loyalties to Councillor Kopek, who's been the biggest thorn in Chancellor Martok's side over the last few years."

T'Latrek spoke up from behind the president. *"That is consistent with reports from both Ambassadors Worf and Rozhenko regarding the High Council."*

"There's more," Rozhenko said. *"Based on the reports from General Khegh, there's no basis to Jianuk's claims—that Shinzon's inner circle are revered among Remans, not reviled."* He hesitated. *"I also think I know why they're being so stubborn."*

The president chuckled. *"This oughtta be good. Go ahead, Mr. Ambassador."*

"I think—and Ambassador Spock agrees with me—that the Klingons like the relocation idea because it means that it'll be easier to protect the Remans. And also because—" Again, he hesitated.

Spock picked up the ball. *"The very quality that made the protectorate agreement palatable to the Federation makes it less so for the Klingons. They prefer a Romulan*

*government that does not have a focus for its ire. Chaos
suits the empire's purposes."*

Staring at Abrik, Esperanza said, "Funny—the Klingons're using the same argument you did, Jas."

Abrik just scowled at her. As manager of Fel Pagro's
presidential campaign against Nan Bacco, Abrik had en-
couraged a more hawkish attitude toward the Klingons.
Both Pagro and Abrik felt that the Federation shouldn't be
allied with such an imperialistic nation. Esperanza didn't
entirely disagree with the position, but she also knew that
the only alternative to being the Klingons' allies was to be
the Klingons' enemies. More long-term good would come
from being their allies, whereas being their enemies could
not possibly have a good end. An Organian magic trick had
been the only thing to stop an all-out war a hundred years
ago, and then Praxis had forced a détente. Neither was
something that was likely to happen twice.

"Madam President," Ross said, "I have to question the
wisdom of risking the Federation-Klingon alliance over
this."

"I agree," Abrik said. "I said this before and I'll say it
again—these are hostile Remans."

Councillor Mazibuko said, *"They are not hostile, Admiral."*

"Not yet," Bowles muttered.

Shaking his head, Abrik said, "They were allied with
Shinzon, Councillor. I think that makes them hostile by default."

"No one is hostile by default," Akaar said, "only by experience, and the Remans' experiences have not been
pleasant."

Shostakova added, "There is also the legal issue, and the
reports from the Klingons. This is not a simple situation."

The president rolled her eyes. *"Believe me, Raisa, the lot of us wouldn't all be banging our heads together if the situation weren't so damned complicated."*

Esperanza, however, was more interested in the commander's mutterered aside. "Commander Bowles, what's your impression of the situation?"

Bowles ran a hand through her short, dirty-blond hair. *"I've spoken with Jianuk and a few of the others about a dozen times now, and well—"* She let out a breath. *"They're all saying the right things."*

"But you're not buying it?" Esperanza asked.

"No, ma'am, I'm not. Every time we ask them why they're doing this, their answers are rehearsed, and they're the blandest reasons—freedom, liberty, and to avoid persecution from their fellow Remans. They've got something planned, I'm sure of it."

Councillor Bera chim Gleer said, *"While I'm sure the commander's instincts are well honed, we can't just turn these people away because she's sure of something."*

"Agreed," said Councillor Tomorok of Rigel in a tone that indicated his historic disdain for Starfleet. Esperanza had been on the receiving end of that disdain several times, even though her Starfleet career was almost four years behind her.

"It's not just that." Bowles sounded a little defensive. *"One of my officers is Betazoid, and he thinks they're hiding something. He can't get more than impressions—the Remans have pretty good telepathic shields—but they're definitely keeping secrets."*

"That's not conclusive evidence," Akaar said.

"No," Abrik said, "but combine it with the Klingon reports, and these people's history, and it doesn't look good." He turned to the screen. "Madam President, granting their asylum requests carries too many risks for insufficient gain."

Esperanza's arms spread wide in a gesture of frustration. "We're not in this for gain, Jas. The question is whether or not to let them in or turn them over, not what we win if we do the right thing."

"There is a third option." That was Spock.

"Good," President Bacco said, *"we could use one. What is it, Mr. Ambassador?"*

"Do neither. Deny their asylum request, but do not turn them over to the Klingons, either."

Akaar nodded. "The Federation and the Klingon Empire are hardly the only possible destination for Jianuk and his people. It might be wisest for the Remans to pursue other avenues."

"In what?" Bowles's expression was one of disbelief, her eyes squinting, her prominent cheekbones becoming even more so. *"The ship they came in is being held together with rusted stembolts and happy thoughts. It can't break warp three-point-five without falling apart. It'll take the* Ditagh *maybe three and a half seconds to track them down, and without our protection, they'll be sitting ducks."*

Ross said, "The *Intrepid*'s in the area. Can they get there before the *Ditagh* arrives?"

Bowles shrugged. *"Sure."*

Esperanza looked at Akaar. "I'm not up on the latest Klingon ships—can the *Ditagh* catch the *Intrepid?"*

"The *Ditagh* is one of the Chancellor-class vessels. It has a cruising speed of warp eight."

Eyes widening, Esperanza asked, "That's its *cruising* speed?" She knew the *Intrepid*'s cruising speed was warp six.

"Yes, but I have faith in Captain Emick's ability to avoid the Klingons."

"That raises a critical difficulty," Councillor Krim said. *"If the Klingons learn of our taking the Remans to neutral space, it will cause the same damage that granting them asylum would—with the added difficulty of leaving the Remans outside the protection of Starfleet."*

Esperanza couldn't help but smile at the look of irritation that Gleer shot at Krim. It was only a few days ago that the Tellarite had impugned Krim's ability to judge events on the galactic stage. Krim's quite cogent point belied Gleer's accusation rather handily.

Spock said, *"The* Intrepid *also has shuttlecraft and runabouts, all of which are capable of warp speeds far in excess of what the* Vkruk *can achieve. Such craft are notoriously difficult for some starships to hang on to."*

Esperanza squinted at the viewer. "You realize what you're suggesting, Mr. Ambassador?"

"Yes. I am suggesting a way to keep the Remans alive without damaging our relationship with the Klingon Empire."

The president put her hands on her hips. *"Mr. Ambassador, for the record, I have to say that I'm ashamed of you, and find your suggestion that we allow the Remans to steal from the* Intrepid *to be repugnant in the extreme, and unworthy of your position as a Federation ambassador. That's the sort of thing that would make us look like idiots."*

"Yes, Madam President." Spock spoke the words in his usual deadpan.

After a few moments' silence, the president then said, *"Commander Bowles, I assume you recorded everything that Ambassador Spock and I just said?"*

"Yes, ma'am, and I'd say I feel about the same way you do."

"Glad to hear that. I certainly wouldn't want to look like an idiot more than seven or eight more times in my administration."

Bowles smiled. *"Yes, ma'am."*

"All right, I want regular updates on the situation. Ambassador Spock, Ambassador Rozhenko—keep working on the High Council on the relocation notion. Since they do like that, we may as well keep their focus there."

"It may not matter," Shostakova said, "if they take umbrage to not getting the Remans."

"One step at a time, Raisa," the president said. *"I want hourly updates, people. Let's make this work."*

Zhres was running late for the afternoon meeting, but when he saw Krim, he had to stop to talk to him. "Excuse me, Councillor?"

Krim, who had been walking down one of the hallways on the second floor of the Palais, stopped at the Andorian's words. Zhres walked briskly down the hallway to catch up, admiring the complex earring that dangled from the councillor's right ear. *It's certainly more impressive than Jorel's.*

"What can I do for you—" Krim paused. "I'm sorry, but I've forgotten your name. You're Kant Jorel's assistant, yes?"

"Yes, sir—please, call me Zhres. Do you have a moment?"

"I was just heading for the transporter bay. I have a reception to attend."

"Right, the London Dinner."

Krim frowned. "Is that what you wanted me to talk about?"

"No." The London Dinner was an annual reception for selected members of the Federation Council. This year, Krim's name had come up for it for the first time since he'd joined the council three and a half years earlier. "We've gotten a request from FNS to do a feature on you."

At that, Krim smirked. Zhres had noted that the man rarely smiled. "Why would they wish to do that?"

"Well, Councillor, yours is an interesting story. You went from supporting a political movement on Bajor that favored breaking all ties with the Federation, and now you represent Bajor *to* the Federation. Not to mention your service both to the Resistance and the Bajoran Militia." Zhres then smiled at Krim's slightly irritated look. "That, at least, is how Alhara sold it to me."

"And Alhara is whom, exactly?"

"The producer at FNS who wishes to do the feature."

"Does Kant think this is a good idea?"

"Yes, Councillor."

Fixing Zhres with a stare that he had no doubt perfected as a Bajoran general, Krim asked, "Do you?"

"Absolutely," Zhres said. "FNS is the most comprehensive news source I've ever encountered, and the one with the most journalistic integrity. I firmly believe that it should be rewarded wherever possible, and this feature not only does that, but helps us."

"In what way?"

"I think it's good for people to see the real face of politicians."

Now the smirk came back. "I find that statement difficult to credit from someone who's met as many politicians as you have."

Zhres laughed.

"One thing confuses me, Zhres—why didn't Kant come to me with this himself?"

Zhres's antennae wiggled. "Well, he likes to delegate anything he considers unpleasant, and he numbers talking to you among those things."

That seemed to surprise Krim. "For what reason?"

"Well, Councillor—" Zhres hesitated. *How to put this delicately?* Then he thought, *What am I doing? Jorel wouldn't be delicate, why should I?* "Jorel's afraid of you, Councillor. Or, more to the point, he's afraid of your ex-wife."

"Many people are afraid of First Minister Asarem, Zhres, but former employees aren't usually among them."

"He thinks that she thinks he betrayed her by taking this job."

"Wadeen only has kind words to say about him."

Which makes her unique, Zhres thought. "Either way, I think it's best if you didn't disabuse him of that notion, Councillor. Anything that limits your contact with him is best for your mental health."

"Yes, I had gotten that impression both on Bajor and here in the Palais. In fact, you seem to have lasted considerably longer as his assistant than anyone else. Why is that?"

Again, Zhres's antennae wiggled. "I already knew before I took the job that he was an ass. But I also knew that he was good at his job, and that I'd be good at this."

Krim nodded. "Interesting. Very well, I shall do this show."

"Good. I'll have Farak set it up with Elos."

After Krim said his good-byes and continued toward the transporter bay, Zhres turned around and headed to Jorel's office. *That's one less thing to think about.*

He arrived as Jorel was finishing up a conversation with a Tellarite whom Zhres placed after a moment as being the political editor of the Tellarite News Service. "I'll do what I can, Phant, but you know how the Tzenkethi are. They'll probably deny that Brek was even on Kliradon."

"*I have proof,*" Phant said testily.

"And they'll say you manufactured it." Before Phant could object, Jorel said, "Look, I'll talk to Esperanza Piñiero, and we'll see what we can do, all right?"

"That's all I request, Jorel. Thank you."

As soon as Phant's face faded from the viewer, Zhres asked, "Did Brek get taken by the Tzenkethi?"

"I have no idea, but the evidence is pointing that way."

"He was warned not to go to Kliradon."

Jorel let out a long breath. *"Everyone* is warned not to go to Kliradon. But Brek doesn't view warnings as warnings, he views them as challenges. If he wasn't such a good reporter . . ." He trailed off.

Zhres said quietly, "If he wasn't such a good reporter, he'd probably be dead by now."

"How melodramatic. Why are you late?"

"I ran into Krim. He'll do the FNS piece. He also says you shouldn't be scared of First Minister Asarem."

"The man who divorced her thinks I shouldn't be afraid of her?" Jorel stood up from his desk. "That's advice I'm guaranteed to ignore."

Zhres smiled. "That should put it in good company with every other piece of advice you've ever received."

"At least I know not to go to Kliradon. All right, let's go over—"

"Excuse me."

Zhres turned around to see Esperanza Piñiero standing in the doorway. Zhres hadn't even noticed her approach.

"Esperanza, I'm glad you're here. We lost a reporter."

The chief of staff winced. "Where?"

"Kliradon."

"They're given warnings not to go to—"

"It was Brek."

"Ah." Piñiero scratched her ear. "I'll talk with Safranski, see what we can do. That's got to wait, though."

"It can't wait too long, Phant's breathing down my neck."

Zhres, however, felt the change in the air as soon as Esperanza walked in. *Something bad has happened.*

"We've got a situation on the Romulan border."

"The refugees?"

Piñiero gave a smirk that was frighteningly similar to Krim's. "Well, the Remans at Outpost 22 anyhow. About half an hour ago, shortly after their leader, Jianuk, had lengthy conversations with both Captain Emick of the *Intrepid* and Commander Bowles of the outpost—" Piñiero took a breath. "—the *Vkruk* made a suicide run at the outpost."

"In Thori's name," Zhres muttered.

Jorel's eyes went wider than Zhres had ever seen them. "How many people—?"

"Believe it or not, only three of our people died. Bowles was suspicious of the Remans from the start, so she beefed up the shields, stayed on yellow alert and at battle stations, and evacuated all the outer portions of the outpost for the duration of the *Vkruk*'s stay. As soon as they detected a warp buildup in the *Vkruk*, the *Intrepid* fired on them, which also reduced the damage to the outpost. The Remans are all dead, as are two engineers and one security guard who were part of the outpost's damage-control team."

"May they walk with the Prophets," Jorel muttered. "I assume you want me to brief."

Piñiero nodded.

"You sure that's a good idea? If they don't have the story, we can—"

"One of them's gonna have the story," Piñiero said. "You know that as well as I do. Besides, how's it going to look if Regia Maldonado or Edmund Atkinson or Sovan or somebody reveals it in the press room first? And what good reason do we have to keep it secret anyhow?" Piñiero chuckled mirthlessly. "In a lot of ways, this solves most of our problems, as ghoulish as that is." She shook her head. "Zachary's downloading the info to you now—the details, the names of the three dead people—"

Zhres asked, "Their families have been notified?"

Piñiero turned to Zhres. "The president's handling that right now." She turned back to Jorel. "One other thing— Jianuk sent a message out on all Federation frequencies right before the suicide run. It's why we're pretty sure somebody's gonna pick this up even if we do keep it quiet, which is all the more reason to let it out sooner rather than later."

"What'd they say?" Jorel asked.

"'Victory and freedom.'"

Jorel rolled his eyes. "How idiotic."

"Not entirely. That was Shinzon's battle cry." She sighed. "I'll talk to Safranski about Kliradon. Get this out ASAP, all right?" With that, Piñiero turned and left.

Zhres watched her walk down the hall toward the turbolifts. "Why does this make things easier?"

"Hm?" Jorel looked up.

"She said that the Remans' committing suicide—"

"I honestly have no idea, Zhres—and even if I did have an idea, I wouldn't waste precious moments of my life explaining them to you." He checked his workstation. "Get me everything there is to know about Outpost 22, the U.S.S. Intrepid, and—" He peered at the screen. "—Chief Avro Wraor, Technician Rulan Moody, and Ensign Jaron, all assigned to the outpost."

"They're the casualties?"

Jorel glared at him. "No, they're the dancing troupe I'm sending over to the London Dinner. *Yes*, they're the casualties, Zachary just sent 'em."

"I'll get right on it."

Zhres sat down at his desk and started a search through Starfleet records. He soon learned that Wroar had been in Starfleet security for fifty years, that Moody's enlistment period was going to be up in a month, and that Jaron was the first Evoran in Starfleet. *And now they're all dead.*

And thanks to his work, everyone in the Federation who read the news would know these things about them— know *who* they were, not just that they'd died. It might not have been grand work on the scale of what the president and Piñiero and Krim and the rest of the council and the cabinet and the president's staff did every day, but it was still, to Zhres's way of thinking, work worth doing.

MAY 2380

_____

"*There is no such thing as a perfect leader either in the past or present. . . . If there is one, he is only pretending, like a pig inserting scallions into its nose in an effort to look like an elephant.*"

—Liu Shaoqi

CHAPTER THIRTEEN

TIM LINCOLN WINCED as he watched the screen that took up the entire north wall of the Pioneer Pub. "They're bringing in Martinez."

Sitting on the bar stool next to Tim, Natalia Hatcher muttered, "Well, this game's over."

Tim held up a cautioning hand. "Now now, don't be so sure."

Natalia looked at her fiancé like he had grown a third limb. "Do you know when the last time Martinez gave up a run is?"

After thinking about it for a second, Tim said, "No."

"Me either. That's how long it's been since she's given up a run."

"It's not like we've followed the Seagulls all that closely. Maybe she gave up three runs her last time out and we don't know about it."

"You know, it's usually Prairieview fans who deny reality this much. Martinez coming in to pitch means the game's over."

Shrugging, Tim said, "We've got the two, three, and four guys up."

Natalia rolled her eyes. "Right—Farouk, who hasn't gotten on base all year, Addison, who hits against Martinez even worse than the rest of the world, and as for Yates— Yates is past it. Yates is so far past it he's on another planet.

In fact, he's about three star systems over, that's how far past it Yates is. I don't know why Diaz keeps batting him cleanup. He should retire and let Hayakawa get more playing time."

The Pioneer Pub had come into existence about five years earlier, and during baseball season, it was always one of Pike City's hot spots. The walls were covered in memorabilia from the Pike City Pioneers' decade-long history: The first home-run ball hit after the CBL was incorporated, slugged by the Pioneers' Aloysius McSweeney in the bottom of the ninth to win their first game against the Palombo Sehlats; the dirt-covered uniform worn by Illyana Petrova when she stole home to win the first Cestus Series for the Pioneers over the Prairieville Green Sox, the first of many disappointments for Green Sox fans; the shards of the bat broken when Hugues Baptiste blooped a single to center to win the Northern Division championship against the Port Shangri-La Seagulls; a chunk of Ruth Field that was blown off by Gorn weaponry when they attacked Pike City during the war; and the glove that Blaithin Lipinski wore when she threw her fifth career perfect game, this one against the Cestus Comets.

There were also three items from the various baseball leagues on Earth in the nineteenth through twenty-first centuries: the glove used by Josh Gibson when he played for the Homestead Grays in 1930, Babe Ruth's jersey from when he played for the minor-league Baltimore Orioles in 1914, and the ball hit into the center-field seats of Yankee Stadium by Buck Bokai to win the last World Series on Earth for the London Kings in 2042.

Tim and Natalia had entertained the notion of attending today's game, but that had been a forlorn hope. Games between the Pioneers and their toughest division rival, the

Seagulls, were always hot-ticket items, and so there had been no available seats at Ruth Field. So they'd come to the Pub to watch it with fellow fans.

Sadly, today's game wasn't much fun to watch. The Gulls had shut the Pioneers out, negating strong pitching performances by the Pioneers. As a result, it was 2-0 Gulls going into the bottom of the ninth, and the Gulls' best reliever, Faith Martinez, was in.

However, nobody told Yusuf Farouk that she was their best reliever—he drew a walk on six pitches. Then Nancy Addison fisted a single to left field, putting two on for Kornelius Yates. He'd been the Pioneers' cleanup hitter since the league had been incorporated ten years earlier, and Tim had to admit that Natalia was right when she said that his skills had deteriorated to the point where he probably wasn't a viable cleanup hitter anymore. Still, he wasn't ready to be put out to pasture yet—

—a point Yates himself made rather spectacularly by clubbing Martinez's first pitch over the center-field wall for a three-run home run to win the game.

The pub, which had been as silent as a tomb since the sixth inning, when the Gulls had scored their two runs, suddenly burst into life. People were shouting, hugging each other, yelling, banging their drinks glasses together, and generally acting the idiotic way people do when they celebrate.

From behind the bar, Gordon the bartender said the words everyone liked to hear: "Homebrews all around!" The Homebrew was the Pub's *spécialité de la maison*, and Gordon only served it when the Pioneers won.

Moments later, Tim was slugging down his Homebrew and asking Gordon if they could put FNS on.

"What for?" the bartender asked.

"They're gonna be talking about Governor Bacco on *ICL*."

Natalia almost sputtered her Homebrew. "They always talk about her on *ICL*, and it's *President* Bacco now, remember?"

"I'm trying not to. I can't believe she'd abandon us like that. Best governor this planet ever had, and she dumps us to go gallivant around the Federation."

"Hey, c'mon," Natalia said, punching him gently on the shoulder. "At least she came back to throw out the first pitch."

Gordon added, "Yeah, I heard she had to completely screw around her itinerary to make sure she was here on the right day." Moving over to the control for the big screen, he said, "Anyhow, I'll put it on if you want, but if we get complaints, down it comes." He entered some commands, which would provide the FNS feed from the beginning of tonight's *Illuminating the City of Light* installment.

"Fair enough." Tim raised his Homebrew glass in acknowledgment of Gordon's kindness.

Natalia stared at Tim. "You didn't use to care about Federation politics all that much."

"I don't—I care about Governor Bacco. Sorry, *President* Bacco. I want to know what she's doing that's so great that she had to abandon us."

"Oh, for crying out loud, Tim, she didn't 'abandon' anything."

The screen switched from the postgame highlights to an image of five people sitting around a desk. The host was the usual Kriosian woman, Velisa, and sitting on the far left was Fred MacDougan, who'd been part of Bacco's staff forever. Tim didn't recognize the other three—a human woman, a Gnalish man, and a Bolian man. Several people in the Pub muttered complaints, but nothing too loud, mostly relating to interrupting the highlight reel. One person pointed out that the game only had one highlight worth watching, and they just saw it two minutes ago.

"Good evening. This is *Illuminating the City of Light*. I'm your host, Velisa. Tomorrow is the state dinner at the Palais de la Concorde as President Bacco and the Federation Council welcome the delegation from Trinni/ek, on the heels of the president's highly successful goodwill tour of several Federation planets, incuding her homeworld of Cestus III."

That mention prompted a ragged cheer from the patrons of the Pioneer Pub.

"With me tonight to discuss these issues are Fred MacDougan, chief speechwriter for President Bacco; FNS's own Regia Maldonado; Councillor Gorus Gelemingar of Gnala; and author of *The Ripple Effect: Trials and Tribulations of First Contacts*, retired Starfleet Captain Rixx. Welcome, all of you. Fred, as one of the president's chief policy advisors, what is your take on the Trinni/ek state dinner?"

Fred, a bald-headed man with a hawk nose, laughed at that. "I wouldn't go so far as to call myself a chief policy advisor. At best, I occasionally have her ear, but she usually just yells at me and tells me to stop being an idiot."

Several of the panelists laughed at that. So did many of the Pub patrons—they knew of Bacco's occasionally scathing style.

"As for the state dinner, my take is that it's a great opportunity. Although it was a policy instituted under a previous administration, President Bacco has been a huge proponent of the *Luna*-class program, going back to when it was first floated almost ten years ago. Seeking out new life and new civilizations has always been the Federation's mantra."

"Yes," Gelemingar said, "and we all know that a planetary governor's support makes all the difference in a program initiated by Starfleet Command."

Fred frowned. "That wasn't my point, Councillor, I—"

"Of *course* it was your point. You were making a feeble attempt to attach the president to the tail of a program that she had absolutely nothing to do with. It was Captain T'Vrea and her crew who made the first contact, and the Diplomatic Corps who had the subsequent meetings that are leading to this state dinner. The president's contribution to this endeavor consists of making a toast that you will be writing for her."

The Gnalish's words led to booing from the Pub.

"None of which was the point of what I said, Councillor," Fred said with a sweet smile. "I was asked for my take on it, and what I said was that it was a great opportunity. Which it is. The Trinni/ek are a hardy civilization that survived the destruction of their homeworld's sun and forged a new life on a new world. They suffered the greatest catastrophe imaginable for a single-planet society, and they won."

"And I'm sure you and the rest of her staff are hoping that having her image on FNS alongside these hardy survivors will erase the memory of twenty-nine dead Remans and three dead Starfleet officers."

More boos. Tim couldn't believe this guy was actually trying to blame Bacco for what happened to those Remans. They'd committed suicide after Bacco had offered them asylum—how was that her fault? She'd done the right thing; it was the Remans who had spit in her eye.

Regia Maldonado, the woman from FNS, spoke up then. "Oh come on, Gorus, that's laying it on a little thick, don't you think? Those Remans killed themselves. President Bacco's not to blame for it."

"She refused to help them when they needed it."

Fred rolled his eyes. "She hadn't refused anything yet."

"Oh, and you were in those meetings, were you?" Gelemingar asked. "I was, since I'm actually *on* the security council, and I can assure you that the president had no intention of granting those Remans asylum, despite being implored to do so by myself, by Starfleet, and by her closest advisors."

Velisa pursed her lips. "That's a very strong accusation, Councillor."

The Gnalish folded his scaled hands on the desk. "I but speak the truth."

More boos at that, as well as cries of, "Get him outta there!" and the like.

Maldonado smiled and held up a padd that Tim hadn't noticed before. "It's interesting that you say that—yesterday parts of the security council session were unsealed."

Fred grinned. "You weren't at yesterday's council session, were you, Councillor?"

"I was in transit from Gnala." The tone in Gelemingar's voice sounded to Tim like someone had just told him his mother was sick.

Now reading the padd's display, Maldonado said, "Well, according to the transcript, President Bacco listened to *all* the options, it was a Starfleet officer who actually first proposed the notion that the Remans had ulterior motives, and you're completely silent. Councillors T'Latrek, Mazibuko, Gleer, Tomorok, and Krim all contributed to the discussion, but no record of any imploring by you. Were they made during the parts that have remained sealed for security reasons, perhaps?"

Now the Pub was filled with cheers. "If that woman's ever on Cestus," Gordon said, "she gets a Homebrew no matter who won that day."

Tim smiled. The only people who ever got Homebrew when it wasn't right after a Pioneers win were Nan Bacco and any Pioneers players or staffers who came by, so that promise indicated the depths of Gordon's happiness with the reporter's skewering of the Gnalish councillor.

"The president," Gelemingar said in that same mother's-sick voice, "is aware of my feelings on the matter."

"We've gotten a bit off the subject," Velisa said, prompting some jeers from the crowd, who wanted to see Gelemingar get some more of what was coming to him. "Captain Rixx, what can you tell us about the Trinni/ek, and do you think that an ongoing relationship with the Federation is in our future—possibly even membership?"

The old Bolian smiled. "We are getting *very* far ahead of ourselves, Velisa. First contacts come in many different shapes and sizes. The Trinni/ek are, based on the reports from the *Io,* a very friendly people—and they also have the capability of traveling faster than light. They had never encountered any other sentient species, but the galaxy is a big place."

"Do you feel optimistic about the future of relations between the Federation and the Trinni/ek?"

Rixx smiled, bunching up the ridge that ran down the center of his face. "Well, the *Io*'s captain is a Vulcan, and they are not known for exaggeration. If she says they're friendly, they probably are."

Maldonado, Cestus III's new hero, said, "It doesn't hurt that Trinni/ek has a lot of medicinal plants and minerals that are of use—*hovrat* grows there, as does *semtek*, and they've got uridium, some dilithium, topaline, and, best of all, kellinite."

Velisa smiled. "Are you saying that President Bacco's

motive for trading with the Trinni/ek is to make up for the loss of Aligar as a trading partner, Regia?"

Before Maldonado could respond, Fred spoke up. "That isn't the reason, Velisa, mainly because Aligar no longer being a trading partner is *not* a loss. That trade arrangement was long overdue for cessation. And as for Trinni/ek, that's just a fortuitous side effect."

"Yes," Gelemingar said, "but I'm sure this president will hammer that point home."

"It's what we do," Fred said with another sweet smile.

"You're certainly doing it now. What's next, declaring war on Aligar?"

Before Fred could reply, Velisa said, "Councillor, you have gone on record as opposing President Bacco's just-completed goodwill tour."

"Yes. It was an unconscionable waste of time, forcing her to be absent from several important council sessions. The president needs to be present *at* the seat of government, or she risks losing all touch with the process."

"I can't agree," Maldonado said. "President Bacco's tour is a continuation of something she did while she was governor of Cestus III."

The entire pub cheered, drowning out the rest of Maldonado's statement, but from what Tim could hear over the noise, she was just explaining about Bacco's town meetings.

"What possible use," Gelemingar asked, "could that be?"

Fred chuckled. "Call me crazy, but it seems to me that a government that doesn't listen to the people isn't much of a government."

"Very well then, I *shall* call you crazy," Gelemingar said, prompting more boos from the pub. "The people spoke when they elected me councillor. If they decide they dislike the job I'm doing, they can vote for someone else when my term expires. If they like it, they will reelect me. That is how the process works."

Leaning back in his chair and putting his hand to his chin, Fred said, "I find it interesting, Councillor, that you say that it's so unconscionable, considering that just five minutes ago you revealed that you missed an entire council session in which the vote to unseal the record of a session you participated in took place. The only person in this discussion that's lost all touch with the process is you."

"All right," Gordon said over the cheers that followed that statement. "He gets a Homebrew, too."

Tim said, "He's local, you know—been on Bacco's staff since she was a representative."

"Really?" Gordon sounded surprised.

Fred was still talking. "Meanwhile, President Bacco has talked with the people of Ventax II, of Lembatta Prime, of Taurus III, of New Paris, of Kessik IV, and, yes, of Cestus III about their concerns."

A few whoops at the mention of the homeworld.

"Did you know, Councillor, that the New Parisians have been trying to get a new medical treatment approved? It's a treatment for Irumodic Syndrome that they've had excellent results with. Unfortunately, they haven't been able to get the attention of anyone in the FMA." To Velisa, Fred added, "The president intends to talk with the head of the FMA and Starfleet Medical and see what—"

Gelemingar interrupted. "Incredible. Mr. MacDougan, neither the FMA nor Starfleet Medical nor the Federation government has time for such nonsense, and I'm amazed that the president would create an agenda based on a conversation in a large hall."

It was Maldonado who said, "Actually, that wasn't what she based it on. I was part of the press tour that accompanied the president, and she went after the meeting to a local hospital and saw the results. It's definitely worth pursuing if it means the possibility of a cure for all the humans over the age of eighty who suffer from the disease."

"*If* it works." Gelemingar now sounded sulky.

Rixx laughed again. "And how is that to be determined if it isn't tried, Councillor?"

At that, Gelemingar was finally silenced. "Take that!" one of the crowd cried. After a second, Tim realized that it was Natalia.

"Can we please turn this crap off?" someone else asked. "If I wanna be put to sleep, I'll watch a Cubs game."

Tim and Natalia and several others laughed. The New Chicago Cubs were the only franchise who, due to their city name, were allowed to use a team name from the city on Earth after which they were named. The Chicago Cubs were one of the longest-running franchises on Earth, having been one of the charter members of the National League in 1876, and remaining in that league until Major League Baseball died on Earth in 2042. That team had a history of perennial failure, leavened by occasional bursts of success; their namesakes on Cestus III had only managed the first part so far, as they had remained at the bottom of the Northern Division standings for a decade.

"All right, all right," Gordon said and turned FNS off.

Tim looked at Natalia. "Wanna go get some dinner?"

Natalia smiled. "Sure. How about we go to that new Bajoran restaurant. I hear that Kornelius Yates likes to eat there after games. Maybe we can catch him."

Smiling right back, Tim said, "Sure."

✦

CHAPTER FOURTEEN

✦   ✦

ESPERANZA STARED AT HERSELF in the floor-length mirror in her bedroom and tried to recognize the person looking back at her.

"You look great." Xeldara Trask's face was on the viewer on her bedroom desk.

She couldn't really deny Xeldara's words. The general Palais protocol for state dinners required attendees to wear whatever was considered formal wear on their home-worlds. For Esperanza, as well as Fred, Ashanté, several members of the speechwriting staff, and the president herself, that meant following the traditions of Cestus III—or, at least, Nan Bacco's interpretations of them. Her outfit, which hadn't been worn regularly on Cestus III since before the president was born, included a dark red high-necked jacket that was fastened all the way to the top—the top, in this case, being the ribbed neck of the jacket that went all the way up to her jawline, hugging her neck and impairing her ability to breathe. The main part of the jacket was made of velvet. At the bottom, the jacket flared outward to just below the pelvis. Under that, she wore dark blue conformer leggings that hewed to the shape of her legs down to the ankle. She also wore her hair loose, which marked the first occasion in ages when she was doing it where people could see it.

"Nobody's dressed like this since the *first* time the Gorn attacked Cestus III a hundred years ago."

"So why are you dressed like that now?"

"The president likes old-fashioned dress clothes for reasons passing understanding. At least mostly old-fashioned. From what I understand, this outfit is properly worn with heeled shoes, but I had to draw the line somewhere."

"Glad she's not insisting on that for everyone. I'm wearing a dress-wrap." Tiburonian custom called for a sarong-like outfit to be worn at formal occasions.

"Right now, I'd kill to be a Tiburonian. Or a Vulcan—they just have to wear nice big formless robes."

"You could've worn your Starfleet dress uniform. I'm sure the president would've understood."

Esperanza turned herself away from the peculiar reflection she was now casting and looked at her deputy. "There is no circumstance under which I will ever wear that white monstrosity in public again. I grinned and bore it while I was in Starfleet, but one of the joys of resigning my commission was that I could happily burn that thing."

"You burned your dress uniform?"

"Gleefully and with malice aforethought. I only wish I'd had marshmallows to roast over the flames."

"I know what those weaves smell like when they burn—the marshmallows would've tasted awful."

Shrugging, Esperanza said, "Good point. So everything's set, right?"

"For the ninth time, yes. We've run the entire menu by the Trinni/ek scientists, taken out anything they might not be able to process, and double-checked to make sure that they can eat what's left."

"And they approved—"

"Yes, Esperanza, they approved the itinerary. That hasn't changed since the last time you asked me three minutes ago, or when you asked me ten minutes ago, or when

*you asked me half an hour ago, or when you asked me nine
times yesterday, or—"*

"All right, all right," Esperanza said, "enough. I'm just
concerned."

Ashanté and Z4 had accompanied the president on her
goodwill tour. While Myk had been left to handle whatever
Palais business needed to be dealt with, Esperanza and
Xeldara, with help from Councillor Ra'ch B'ullhy's office,
had spent the month that the president had been gone
working with Ambassador Morrow and the Trinni/ek diplomats to make sure their trip to Earth went off without a
hitch. Morrow had a great deal of experience with first
contacts, though it was all as an aide—this was the first
time he was flying one solo, as it were—and Ra'ch's homeworld of Damiano was relatively close to Trinni/ek.

Tonight was the opening festivity: a state dinner, the first
of the Bacco administration. That would be followed over
the next several days by meetings with members of the
council, the cabinet, and the diplomatic corps, finally ending
with a joint press conference and a farewell party on Luna.

Esperanza turned all the way around one final time. "I
look like an idiot."

*"You look fantastic. I confidently predict that half the
men in the room will be trying to dance with you."*

Whirling back on the viewer, Esperanza gave Xeldara a
shocked look. "There's gonna be *dancing?*"

Xeldara seemed surprised at Esperanza's outrage. *"Of
course there's dancing. That was a specific request of
Speaker Ytri/ol."*

Frowning, Esperanza cast her mind back on the evening
plans, which had changed eight thousand times over the
course of the past four weeks. "You mean the *fleer/ic?* I
thought that was a kind of food."

"No, fleer/ok is food, and we had to take it off the menu because it's poisonous to humans, Vulcans, Bajorans, Trills, and Betazoids, and it gives Tellarites a rash."

"See if we can get a case sent to Gleer." She sighed. "So *fleer/ic* is a dance?"

"Yeah, a very simple one."

"Wait a minute, I thought we got rid of that—no, wait, that was the food. Right. Damn."

"Don't like to dance, Esperanza?"

"Don't know—never tried, and I don't plan to start tonight." *And if, for whatever reason, I do wind up making an ass of myself, I can be grateful that I was smart enough to avoid the damn heels.* "All right, I'm gonna make sure the president's ready. See you there."

After Xeldara signed off, Esperanza put a call through to the Château Thelian. Named after Thelianaresth th'Vorothishria, the early-twenty-fourth-century Andorian president who had had it built as his residence, the spacious château in the Loire Valley had been the residence of every president since then. Esperanza herself lived in a small chalet that was located nearby. She knew that the chiefs of staff usually had comparatively modest accommodations, though Min Zife's COS, Koll Azernal, had taken up residence in the Château de Saint Brisson, which was as large as the presidential château. Given what she knew of Azernal, that somehow didn't surprise her. Esperanza preferred the more modest chalet. *It's not like I spend any significant time here, anyhow—usually I'm here just long enough to not get enough sleep.*

The president appeared on the viewer. Esperanza braced herself for the inevitable criticism, probably related to her footwear.

"Wow. You look like crap."

"Good to see you too, ma'am," Esperanza smiled wryly.

President Bacco's outfit was similar to Esperanza's, but with three significant differences: Her jacket was ivory, which went nicely with her white hair; her leggings were black; and she looked fantastic. Esperanza sighed. She had gone for red and dark blue on the theory that they would work better with her olive skin, which they sort of did. The president's paler outfit, however, worked wonders with her own paler skin. She looked regal. *All right, so she isn't a monarch, but if there's one occasion where it doesn't hurt for the president to look like one, it's a state dinner.*

The president looked her over. *"I'm impressed that you let your hair down. I was starting to think that ponytail was just a fake stick-on."* She shook a finger at Esperanza. *"You know what your problem is?"*

Esperanza sighed. "No, ma'am, but I have every confidence in your ability to let me know what it is."

"Actually, using the singular was a mistake. You've got plenty of problems, plural, but we don't have time to go into all of them. On this particular occasion, your problem is the shoes. You're supposed to wear—"

"—high-heeled shoes with the outfit. I know, ma'am. However, it is my considered opinion—and I'm sure that the entire staff will back me up on this one—that it would be extremely embarrassing and detrimental to our attempts to form a relationship with the Trinni/ek if, during the state dinner welcoming them, the chief of staff fell on her face because she couldn't stand upright in those torture devices."

"Oh come on, they're not that bad."

"Ma'am, if we'd given a ship full of those shoes to the Jem'Hadar, we'd have won the war in two months."

"It still ruins the whole ensemble. Like designing a mansion and then building it on a swamp."

"They do that all the time on Ferenginar, ma'am."

"*This is who you want us to emulate?*"

"I bet they don't make women wear painful shoes at state dinners on Ferenginar."

"*Up until a few years ago, they didn't make women wear anything on Ferenginar.*"

"Good point."

"*Anyhow, I'm ready to go. Been practicing my* fleer/ic *steps.*"

"Sorry I missed that, ma'am."

"*Watch it, you, I'm a great dancer. You remember Annabella's wedding?*"

"Mostly what I remember from that wedding is Alberto's father hitting on me."

The president laughed. "*Yeah, Paolo's a pip.*"

"So's his wife," Esperanza said with a chuckle, remembering the wife in question dragging Paolo away by his beard.

Esperanza hesitated. At times like this, Nan Bacco wasn't the president, wasn't the most powerful person in the Federation—she was just Mom and Dad's eccentric old politician friend, Auntie Nan. Esperanza had always looked forward to her visits, filled as they had been with humor and stories and a genuine interest in what Esperanza had been concerned with, something small children rarely encountered among the adult population.

There were times when Esperanza missed that, so when they had the opportunity to be little Espy and Auntie Nan, even if only for a few moments, she treasured it.

But now the moment was past, and it was time to go to work. "We ready, ma'am?"

Nodding, the president said, "*Yeah.*"

Signing off, Esperanza went downstairs to the transporter station located in the chalet's basement. Touching the intercom to the Palais, she said, "Kirti, it's Esperanza. I'm ready to beam over."

Kirti Chandra, the Palais's head transporter operator, said, *"They're still getting the president ready, so I'll take you now."*

Esperanza nodded and stepped onto the small two-person platform. Traveling with a security detail, as the president did, always meant that using a transporter was a more complicated endeavor, so it didn't surprise Esperanza that she was ready first. Also, Esperanza benefited from her small chalet. It was a much longer walk from the bedroom to the transporter room in the spacious Château Thelian.

Moments later, she was in the second-floor Palais transporter bay, which was empty of all save three of the president's security detail, Kirti at the controls, and Esperanza. Moments after that, President Bacco and two more security guards coalesced into existence on the platform. The guards were also dressed in formal wear. The two human men were in tuxedoes, the Vulcan woman wore a skintight suit embroidered with Vulcan script (not the formal wear Palais tradition would have preferred, Esperanza suspected, but the woman did need to be able to do her job, and a loose robe would not have accomplished that), and the Trill woman wore a sky-blue one-piece dress that was sleeveless with a slit up the side of the knee-length skirt, which Esperanza suspected was there more for freedom of leg movement than fashion. The final member was a Saurian of indeterminate sex, who didn't wear clothes aside from a holster for a sidearm.

As the president and the security detail moved through the corridors toward the turbolift that would take them to the Roth Dining Room on the twelfth floor, Esperanza lingered behind as the comm in her ear beeped. Putting her hand to it, she said quietly, "Go ahead."

"Esperanza, it's Colton."

At the sound of Ambassador Morrow's voice, Esperanza smiled. *He's gonna love how I look in this outfit.*

That brought her up short. *Where the hell did that come from? I mean, he's nice and all, and we've certainly been talking a lot the last month, but—*

She shoved the thought to the back of her head. "What is it, Colton?"

"I'm not sure—I'm with Speaker Ytri/ol and his party. We're approaching the Palais now, and . . ."

When Colton refused to finish his sentence, Esperanza, who was now about to enter the turbolift, said, "What is it?"

"They've been acting—weird."

"Define 'weird.'"

"Cranky, irritable—not at all themselves. They didn't come over to the Venture *the entire time we escorted them here, except when we first made orbit and Captain Henderson had that small reception. But after we left their star system, they not only didn't come over, they barely ever returned messages. It may be nothing, but I'm concerned now that I'm with them."*

"Let's hope it's just jitters," she said as she entered the lift, crowding into it with the president and her entire detail. "See you there."

The president looked at her. "Problem?"

"Nothing you need to worry about." *I hope.*

"Why is it that whenever you say that, I get nervous?"

Esperanza smiled. "You're a crazed, paranoid old woman?"

"Yeah, that's probably it. Hey, did you hear about the game yesterday? Yates won it in the bottom of the ninth."

"I thought Yates was an infielder."

"He is."

"Okay, then how could he win it? I thought the pitchers got wins and losses."

"I swear, Esperanza, one of these days, I *will* have you shot, don't think I won't. Yates hit a home run in the bottom of the ninth with two on to win the game three to two. Sookdeo got the win, but Yates was the one who really won it. By the way, he hit it off Martinez."

"I'm gonna go out on a limb and say that Martinez isn't given to this sort of loss?"

The president glared at her. "Don't you *ever* pay attention when we watch games together?"

"Not if I can help it, ma'am."

"Hmp." The president looked ahead. "Shoulda worn the damn heels."

"Yes, ma'am."

The turbolift doors opened to the twelfth floor. A red-carpeted hallway greeted them. Two more guards—who were, like the president's detail, in formal wear appropriate to their species—stood at either side of the large wooden doors, which parted with a hiss at her approach.

On the other side of the door, another guard, a Tessenite male named Sxottlan—who'd gotten this duty because of his ability to project his voice—bellowed, "The president of the United Federation of Planets!"

Esperanza looked out over the room. Taking up all of the twelfth floor, the Roth Dining Room had hundreds of tables, all made of actual wood recycled from old sailing ships wrecked at sea on Earth, a project undertaken by the president for whom the room was named. A portrait of the man—a bald, smiling human—hung from the east wall. Throughout the room, people of hundreds of species intermingled, including most of the council, some of their staff, and a good portion of the presidential staff, as well as selected members of the press. Esperanza saw Regia Maldonado of FNS wearing a very nice, very practical outfit that actually conformed to modern trends. *Some people have all the luck.*

On the west wall was a raised platform with a fourteen-seat round table, at which the president traditionally sat during state dinners. The table would be half Trinni/ek and half Federation, comprising Esperanza, Colton, Xeldara, Xeldara's husband, Ashanté, Fred, and the president. Aside from Esparanza, the president, and Colton, they were all present at the table; Colton would, of course, be arriving with the Trinni/ek.

Everyone in the room who wasn't already standing rose from their seats. The Federation anthem—a tune that Esperanza had to admit to never liking, possibly because she was subjected to it at the beginning of every baseball game the president made her sit through—played over speakers.

The president proceeded to the table, where Ashanté, Fred, Xeldara, and her husband waited. *Dammit, what the hell is his name?*

On the way, several people complimented Esperanza on how good she looked, including Councillor Enaren. Being telepaths, Betazoids rarely paid attention to how humanoids looked, as they were more concerned with more thoughtful matters, so the fact that Cort Enaren took note of her outfit made Esperanza feel a little better about having to wear the outdated clothing.

When she arrived at the table, the president waited until the anthem ended before speaking. "Everyone please have a seat."

Esperanza sat at the seat to the president's right. She herself remained standing.

"Thank you all for coming. I have to admit, I've been

waiting for a decent excuse to have a state dinner, and I'm grateful to the Trinni/ek for providing me with one." Several people chuckled at that. "This room was named after President Hiram Roth. During his administration, a vicious probe attacked our planet, causing massive floods and weather changes and power outages all across our world. The recovery from that attack was long and hard, and President Roth was right in the thick of it. In fact, he worked so hard that he got sick, refusing to take better care of himself because, as he put it, 'There's still work to do.' He died in 2288, on the very day that he won another term in a landslide. Unfortunately, much as we'd wish it otherwise, when doctors tell you to take it easy, they often know what they're talking about." More chuckles. "I've always been a great admirer of Roth, who lived by the tenets of a human leader who lived in the pre-unification times named Theodore Roosevelt, who said, 'Far and away the best prize that life offers is the chance to work hard at work worth doing.' Hiram Roth lived by those words, and, sadly, he died by them. A special election had to be called for one month after his death, one of only two such special elections in Federation history. That election gave us Raghoratreii—the second one, of course, gave you me, thus giving me the opportunity to run off at the mouth right now."

Yet more chuckles. Esperanza noted that Fred was shaking his head and laughing. This was entirely off the cuff, filling time until the Trinni/ek arrived. The toast to the alien delegation had been written by Fred over the course of the previous week. Normally, a toast wouldn't take that long to write, but Fred wanted to make sure he got this one just right. Plus, he was using this toast as an excuse to procrastinate over the commencement address that the president was going to be giving to Starfleet Academy at the end of the month.

Esperanza also noticed Sxottlan giving her a nod. She nodded back and gently touched the president's leg.

"It also gives me the enviable job of welcoming a new species to what I hope will be a long and fruitful relationship with our United Federation of Planets—and that, my friends, is most definitely work that's worth doing. Please—if you'll all rise and welcome Speaker Ytri/ol and his party from Trinni/ek."

As Esperanza—and everyone else—got up from their chairs, they watched the doors slide open again, to reveal eight figures. One was human—that was the slim figure of Colton Morrow—and the others were most definitely not. They ambulated in a manner similar to some Earth primates: propelling themselves with their outsized arms as well as their legs. They never stood entirely upright, but rather at a forty-five-degree angle to the ground. Their bodies were covered with dark skin that ranged from an oak brown to obsidian, and absolutely no hair. Their clothes were bright and colorful, with sparkling beads on the shoulders, which differed from how they'd been dressed when Esperanza had spoken with them over subspace. *But then, I'm not dressed the same as I was for conversation. We all have our notions of formal wear. Just wish mine allowed me to breathe properly.*

Most everyone in the room applauded as the doors slid open. Although they were capable of moving quite fast, the Trinni/ek delegation moved slowly—one might say languidly—toward the table. As they got closer, Esperanza saw that Colton looked concerned.

As soon as they arrived, the leader of the delegation, Speaker Ytri/ol, went straight to his seat. "This chair is uncomfortable," he said in a voice that sounded strained.

Okay, this is bad, Esperanza thought. Over subspace, Ytri/ol had had a powerful, commanding voice. His eyes had been wide, his tone enthusiastic. Now he was squinting—and so were the rest of the delegates.

The president didn't miss a beat, despite the breach of protocol. She sat down so she and the speaker were on an equal plane. "Honored Speaker, it's a pleasure to finally meet you face-to-face. I'm President Nan Bacco. Welcome to Earth."

"Yes, of course," Ytri/ol said dismissively. "Why are there so many people here?"

"It's a state dinner," the president said slowly, "which in our culture generally means a big crowd. I'm sorry, Honored Speaker, but I was told you approved the—"

"Yes, I did, but I didn't realize it would be so tightly concentrated." He sat up straighter, though he was still hunched over. It put him at eye level with the president. "You are trying to intimidate us!"

"That is not our intention at all, Honored Speaker. We're simply all glad to have you with us. We're hoping for a prosperous relationship with the Trinn—"

"Lies!" That was another of the delegates. "You are trying to exploit us!"

Oh, this is getting very out of hand, Esperanza thought.

Colton stepped in. "Nothing could be further from the truth. As I told you on the *Venture* during the reception—"

Another delegate rose from the table. "That was where it happened! You poisoned us!"

Esperanza noticed the guards starting to move slowly toward the table, as well as the fact that there was unrest at the other tables.

"That's ridiculous." Colton laughed, but it was a shrill one. "We have been nothing but friendly."

The guards weren't the only ones advancing; the stewards were bringing the appetizer, which was supposed to come while everyone got settled. Trinni/ek tradition held that one always drank *frimk/ek* at the start of any meal, before any other business was conducted—including a toast. The president was going to give the address after the *frimk/ek* was through.

The delegate who accused them of lying turned to Ytri/ol. "Honored Speaker, we cannot countenance this—this—"

He doesn't look very good, Esperanza thought just as the delegate collapsed onto the floor.

Even as the guards now ran to the table, the standing delegate said, "We must quit this place at once, Honored Speaker, before they violate us further!"

"Do not *touch* him!" another delegate screamed at the guard who wanted to check on the delegate who'd collapsed.

Ever the voice of calm reason in a crisis, the president said, "Please, Honored Speaker, let our medical people take a look at—"

Now Ytri/ol rose from his chair. "No! I will not allow my people to be dissected by your physicians! We are not laboratory samples!"

"Honored Speaker, we have no intention of—"

"Take her!" Ytri/ol barked at the other standing delegate while pointing at the one who'd collapsed. "We will return to our ship immediately! If anyone stands in our way, they will learn what it means to cross the Trinni/ek."

"If that's what you want," the president, now also standing, said, "then the guards will escort you to the transporter bay, and you can be on your way. But I beg you to reconsider. After all our planning, we can't let this opportunity for both our worlds—"

"Be silent, woman, or we will beat you to death where you stand! Trinni/ek! Depart!"

With that, the speaker led the delegates—one being carried over the shoulder of another—out of the room. Esperanza activated her comm unit and called Sxottlan. "Escort them to the transporter, but stay at a discreet distance—don't talk to them, don't touch them, and tell Kirti to do whatever they say."

"Understood."

Moments later, they were gone, and the outraged buzz in the room started to build.

"I gotta say," the president said quietly to the remaining people at the table, "that wasn't really how I wanted my first state dinner to go, exactly."

Fred looked pained. "I spent *days* on that damn toast."

Patting him on the shoulder, Ashanté said, "Have another drink, sweetie."

A steward walked up to Esperanza. "Uh, ma'am, what're we supposed to do with the food?"

Esperanza rubbed her eyes for a moment. "Take the *frimk/ek* back—it's their tradition, not ours. Just bring out the main course as soon as it's ready. We came here to eat, we may as well eat."

"Yes, ma'am."

"Hang on," Colton said. "We can't just dump the *frimk/ek*. It's a sacred tradition of theirs."

Before Esperanza could say anything, President Bacco said tersely, "Right now, Mr. Ambassador, I could give a good goddamn about the Trinni/ek's sacred traditions." She finally sat back down and looked at Esperanza. "We'll have this dinner, and then we're having a meeting in the château—I want to know what the *hell* just happened."

"Absolutely, Madam President." Esperanza then looked at Colton.

He still looked pained—and scared.

◆

CHAPTER FIFTEEN

◆   ◆

WHAT OZLA GRANIV looked forward to most was eating good food.

She had been on Tezwa for four months now. Tezwans tended to make their food spicy to the point of being volcanic. At first it had been something of a relief when she'd started traveling to the areas that were being rebuilt in the wake of either the retaliatory Klingon strike or the terrorist attacks made by Kinchawn after his ouster. Food was hard to come by in those areas—as were water, proper shelter, and plumbing—so the people there were subsisting on Starfleet combat rations. Though initially a palliative to the gut-boiling Tezwan cuisine, after six days of the rations, Ozla had soon come to the same conclusion the Tezwans had when they'd first started eating them: They were appallingly bland.

Not that there weren't plenty of other reasons why departing Tezwa would be an enjoyable experience. On her first day, she'd visited the site of the makeshift hospital where a Starfleet runabout, the *Tsavo*, had been destroyed by one of Kinchawn's loyalist soldiers. Besides murdering Starfleet personnel, both security and medical, the attack had also killed dozens of civilians, including children. Some of the civilians had been injured while being evacuated; others had just been unfortunate enough to be nearby.

One of those had been Vara Tal, reporter for *Seeker*. Based on the padd that was somehow recovered from her remains, she'd been interviewing medics, having already spoken to several Tezwan, Starfleet, and Federation civilian physicians. Her last interview had been with Dr. Dennis Chimelis of the *U.S.S. Musashi*, who was also killed in the runabout explosion.

In the months since the crisis, new hospitals had been built to replace the ones that had been set up in buildings not originally intended for medical use. All that remained on the site now was a grave marker, which the locals called a memory stone, for the dozens who died in the explosion.

Ozla's mistake had been thinking that the overwhelming sadness she felt upon visiting the site of Vara's grave would be the worst it would get on Tezwa.

Over the last four months, she'd spoken to Tezwans of all stripes, including civilians and soldiers, rich and poor, well-fed and starving. She'd spoken to Starfleet personnel and the Federation ambassador, a harried but determined Bajoran woman named Lagan Serra.

She had come here hoping to continue Vara's work. Now, she was coming away with something far worse.

Tezwa was a defeated planet.

Kinchawn had seized power and brought the wrath of the Klingon Empire down on the Tezwans' heads. Then, when he'd been removed from power, he'd brought some wrath of his own. It had taken the Tezwans centuries to build up to being a minor spacefaring power. It had taken less than two months to reduce them to pre-spaceflight levels. Tezwa would be reliant on Federation assistance for at least the next two decades. Their infrastructure was decimated, their economy had collapsed, their government services were a shambles. Their most arable farming land had been blasted to mulch by the Klingons, and it would be at least another year before the planet's farming industry could even begin to perform its appointed task of feeding Tezwa.

Where once even the poorest Tezwans could at least be assured of a little shelter and enough food to survive, now over half the Tezwan population was homeless or living in temporary shelters that housed hundreds in a space that was a quarter the size of the Federation president's château.

There were many times in the past four months that Ozla had wanted to follow Baleeza Gral into retirement. But she'd persevered.

Just about the only good thing was the fact that Federation atmospheric scrubbers had been working overtime to eliminate the ash and smoke that had lingered in the air for some time after the attacks. When Ozla first arrived, she'd spent a quarter of each day having awful coughing fits, but now the air was as clean and as clear as it was on any Federation world.

Today was her last interview. Tawna Zelemka's name had come up during several discussions; she was doing a great deal for the orphans of the city of Alkam-Zar.

Ozla hitched a ride on a Starfleet shuttle that was bringing supplies to Alkam-Zar's food distribution center. The pilot was a gregarious young Benzite who seemed eager to talk to Ozla about what she'd experienced on Tezwa, but Ozla couldn't bring herself to record what she said. She'd had three dozen interviews with Starfleet personnel, and they'd all said the same thing—variations on "It's terrible, but we're doing what we can to help these people" and "I can't wait to get out of here."

Tawna's home was a good-sized dwelling that had apparently survived the orbital assault, which put it in exclusive company. Alkam-Zar had been one of the cities hit hardest when the Klingons had responded less than favorably to being attacked by nadion-pulse cannons. *Thankfully, those cannons were destroyed,* Ozla thought with a shudder. Apparently the weapons had been stolen from Starfleet, where they had been developed as a possible weapon to use against the Borg but abandoned; somehow the Orion Syndicate had gotten their hands on six of them and sold them to Tezwa. Ozla had taken notes on that, but the particulars of that part of the Tezwan tragedy had been covered during the crisis itself, including one rather nasty piece by Vara in *Seeker* taking Starfleet to task for not securing their failed weapons prototypes.

Ozla rang the doorbell, and shortly the door slid open to reveal a very small Tezwan. "Who're you?" the girl asked.

Putting on her best smile—which took some doing—Ozla said, "My name's Ozla Graniv. I'm here to see Ms. Zelemka."

From deep inside the house, a voice cried, "Be right there! Gyani, show Ms. Graniv in, please!"

"Okay, Tawna." The girl—Gyani—then turned back to Ozla. "You can come in now."

"Thank you."

Ozla entered the front door to find herself in a hallway. There were doorways in front of her and on either side. The sparse furniture was soft and worn, and she saw very little that was breakable in any of the three visible rooms. The reason for that was evident in the other thing she saw in all the rooms—many small Tezwans, running about with the boundless energy possessed only by the very young.

A tall, elegant Tezwan woman emerged from the entryway in front of her, which appeared to lead to the kitchen. "Ms. Graniv, I'm Tawna Zelemka. A pleasure."

"The pleasure's mine, and please call me Ozla. I'm glad you could see me."

"I'm Tawna, and please, come have something to eat. Though I'm afraid I only have Starfleet rations."

Ozla's stomach rumbled, but she nonetheless said, "Uh, thanks, I already ate." After this interview, she was going straight back to her hotel in Keelee-Kee, which was the only place on this misbegotten planet that had a proper replicator, donated by Starfleet as a gift to offworld visitors.

Leading Ozla to a small table in the kitchen, she said to the two children who were fighting over a toy, "Lenandro, Brelkel, stop it! You can share the toy, or I'll take it away from both of you."

"But Tawna, she said I could play with it!"

"I did *not!*"

Tawna stared down at them both. "What's the rule?"

Lenandro and Brelkel each exchanged a guilty glance. Together they said, "Everything is everyone's."

"That's right. So share it, or I'll take it away and give it to someone who understands the value of sharing. Now I need to talk to my friend here, so go upstairs and play, okay?"

"Okay."

"Sure."

The two kids ran out of the kitchen, Brelkel gripping the toy, Lenandro hot on her heels.

Opening a cabinet, Tawna took out a ration pack and tore it open. The smell made Ozla wince, even though the rations didn't really smell like much of anything. *Maybe that's the problem—food is supposed to have an odor, but this just smells like pure nothingness.*

"I've been trying to get some real food here, but it's tough. Luckily, these kids have duranium stomachs. They can eat wheat paste and they'll be happy, so the rations are doing the trick for now."

Ozla refrained from pointing out that wheat paste would be an improvement on the rations. Instead, she threw Tawna's phrase back at her. "'Everything is everyone's'?"

Tawna smiled as she chewed her food. "Over the past six months, I've taken in three dozen orphans. So many children in such an enclosed space, it's easy for resentments over possessions to build up. So I try to foster a sharing environment and make it clear that everything in this house belongs to everyone in this house."

Ozla nodded. "Mind if I record this?"

"Not at all."

Setting her padd to record, Ozla asked, "I guess the best question is why?"

Tawna chuckled. "Not how?"

"Well, how is obvious. You have this house."

"After a fashion." Tawna hesitated. "The house was a gift. I don't feel like it really belongs to me. And then, after the attacks and Kinchawn's trial, I started noticing the number of children who'd been left without parents. Nobody seemed to be in any hurry to take them in—and, to be fair, most didn't really have the capacity to do so. So I opened this house's doors."

"Who was it a gift from?"

Again, the hesitation. Ozla had been a reporter for all her adult life, so she knew that the real story wasn't in Tawna's kindness to the orphan community of Alkam-Zar. That was *a* story, of course, and she would report it, but *the* story was how she'd gotten this house. Every instinct she'd honed told her that the house had been a gift from some kind of illicit source. Of course, it could have been something simple, like an affair with a rich man, but Ozla had a feeling it might have been more than that.

"I'd really rather not—" Another hesitation, and then she said, "Oh, what does it matter? He's dead, anyhow, so what harm can it do?"

"Who's dead?"

"For the last few years, I was having an affair."

Okay, so maybe that's all it is. Trying not to sound deflated, Ozla remarked, "I didn't realize you were married."

"Well, I guess it's not fair to say that *I* was having the affair—*he* was. He was a military man and served as one of General Minza's adjutants." Yet another hesitation. "Major Olorun Meboras. That was his name. He has—he had a wife and three children, but he said he didn't love the wife and only stayed married for the sake of the children. He gave me the house a few months ago, and then the thing with the Klingons started, and Kinchawn was ousted, and then—" Tears started to roll down Tawna's feathered cheek. "Then he was killed during the trials. Executed." Wiping the tear away, she continued, "He was a good man, just doing his duty."

"I'm sorry." Ozla tried to sound sincere, but she couldn't bring herself to mean the words. She'd seen the damage done by Kinchawn's people—which was considerably more specific, and with much greater long-term damage, than the more random Klingon orbital assaults—and couldn't find it in her heart to be sorry that one of the people responsible for the devastation that she'd seen was dead.

I can't believe I just thought that. I have got to get off this planet. Just have to finish this one interview.

She then asked how Tawna's little halfway house got started.

"I worked at the hospital here as a clerk, but it was bombed out by the Klingons. When the new one was built, they didn't have any work for me. All I had was this house. One day, I was walking through the city, and I saw so many children. *Something* had to be done, and I had the space, thanks to Olorun, so here we are."

Ozla asked several more questions, including how she applied for government funding to run the place, which wasn't much, but it was enough to keep it going. "I'm not making much money for myself, but it enables me to do something good."

Tawna then talked a bit about Starfleet, and how helpful they'd been, ending with, "I always knew they'd be here to help us."

The phraseology struck Ozla as odd. "What do you mean, 'always'?"

"Well, the Federation's always been here to protect us. I mean, it became more overt after Kinchawn went crazy, but Olorun told me about how they gave us those cannons."

Ozla blinked. "I'm sorry, Tawna, but—" She shook her head. "Say that again, please."

"Say what again?"

"Major Meboras told you that the Federation supplied the cannons?"

Tawna nodded. "Of course. He told me one night while

we were in the bedroom." She smiled. "I have to say that Olorun was a spectacular lover. He treated me so well."

Having no interest in Meboras's sexual prowess, Ozla steered the topic back to the cannons. "You're sure he said that?"

"I don't see what the big deal is." Tawna shrugged. "Olorun told me that the Federation had brokered a deal with Kinchawn that guaranteed that Starfleet would always protect us, and that they'd taken steps to help us protect ourselves. He never said specifically how they did that, but after that Klingon fleet arrived, I just assumed it was those cannons. I saw on the news that they were Starfleet weapons, originally." She held up her arms. "And look around. Starfleet has been *so* helpful. I'm kind of sorry they gave us those cannons, to be honest, given what happened, but the Federation's definitely been making up for it."

Ozla's head was spinning. She asked a few more questions but barely paid attention to the answers.

It was possible, of course, that Meboras had been lying in an endeavor to impress his mistress. But that didn't make sense—what would creating a fictitious secret deal with the Federation get him?

Which meant there was a good chance this was true. Or, at least, that Meboras had had good reason to think it was true.

Rather, to think *something* was true. Meboras hadn't actually mentioned the cannons; Tawna had just made a leap in logic. Not an especially big leap, but a leap nonetheless.

I was right—there's a story here. And it looks like I'm going to be on Tezwa a little while longer. . . .

◆

CHAPTER SIXTEEN

◆   ◆

IT HAD BEEN NIGHTMARISH, getting through the state dinner without the guests of honor. Throughout the evening,
Nan had had to listen to Fred complaining about how his
brilliant toast would never be given and various and sundry
councillors complaining about the botched diplomatic mission. Everyone wanted to know what had happened, but
Nan had had no answers for them, nor had any been likely
to be forthcoming during an abortive state dinner.

She had been able to work the room a little, at least. It
had been good to talk to the councillors in an atmosphere
less formal than on the first floor. For the first time since taking the oath of office, she'd had a pleasant conversation with
Councillor Nerramibus of Alonis. They'd discussed the up-
coming vote on the Transporter Improvement Act, designed
to upgrade public transporters throughout the Federation,
of which Nerramibus had been an opponent. In the less
tense atmosphere, Nan had been able to make her case to
convince Nerramibus to reconsider his vote. Not a guarantee of anything, but a step in the right direction.

In addition, she had discussed the Pioneers' chances
this season with Cestus III's councillor, Altoun Djinian, as
well as Councillor Corices of Huanni, whom Nan had been
surprised to learn was a fan. She had talked about the relocation of the Remans with Councillors T'Latrek, Mazibuko, and Krim, as well as the reports of a fleet of
Romulan military ships led by an admiral named Mendak,

who had anywhere from three to seven warbirds under his command, and who had apparently gone rogue, making guerrilla attacks on both Klingon *and* Romulan targets. She had received a surprisingly gracious apology from Councillor Gelemingar, though Nan hadn't been sure what it had been for; given the Gnalish's performance on *ICL* the other night, she'd been more than happy to accept any apology from him. She had kibbitzed with Fred on the theme for the Starfleet Academy commencement speech. And, most surprising of all, she had actually shared a couple of jokes with Councillor Gleer.

Afterward, however, there had been business to do. She'd invited Esperanza, Xeldara, Ambassador Morrow, Secretary Safranski, and Councillor Ra'ch to the château for a meeting to discuss the Trinni/ek.

Nan generally liked meetings in the château, as they had a less formal atmosphere than the ones in the Palais. Although it was constructed less than a hundred years ago, Château Thelian had been built to the specifications of the other like structures in the Loire Valley. This meant, among other things, that the sitting room had beautiful wood-paneled walls, a large stone fireplace on the east wall, an elegant couch facing that fireplace, with comfortable chairs perpendicular to the couch. Nan sat in a chair that had been brought in from an adjoining room. Xeldara, Ra'ch, and Safranski were on the couch, leaving the two big chairs for Esperanza and Morrow. The fireplace itself was sealed and purely decorative despite the fact that there were times when Nan would have liked the comfort of a fire. However, Federation safety regulations frowned on open flames in government buildings, not entirely without reason, so Nan had to settle for the visual alone.

The west wall opposite the fireplace had portraits of all

the presidents since Thelian. For some reason, Nan's eyes fell on Min Zife's portrait. The Bolian looked so very small. She supposed it had something to do with how he looked next to his predecessor—Jaresh-Inyo had been a large bear of a man, and his portrait painter had emphasized that. Zife, by comparison, looked frail. Nan wondered when in his administration the portrait had been done. If it had been during the war, Nan understood how he might not have looked at his best: She'd been on the job less than a year, and she felt exhausted half the time in spite of the fact that she was running the Federation during a time of peace, the difficulties in Romulan space notwithstanding. Of course, it was also possible that Zife's portrait had been done near the end, when his presidency had started to get away from him, to the point where he'd been forced to resign.

Oddly, Zife was the only still-living president with whom she had yet to speak. Since taking on the job, she'd spoken regularly with Amitra, occasionally with Jaresh-Inyo—though less so the last two months, for some reason—and once or twice with Thelian, who was in poor physical shape. Indeed, Thelian was not expected to live out the year.

Turning to the group assembled before her, she asked the question that had been preying on her mind since Speaker Ytri/ol stormed out of the Roth Dining Room: "Somebody want to tell me what the *hell* happened tonight?"

"I don't understand it, Madam President." Xeldara, as always, tugged on her earlobe. "They've been nothing but enthusiastic about this for months. Honestly, they told us once or twice that they wished they could move the meeting *up*. If it wasn't for your goodwill trip, we might've considered it."

"I know all that, Xeldara, but that conveniently doesn't answer my damn question." She sighed. "Sorry, but it's been a long night."

Esperanza had her hand on her chin. "Colton said that they were acting funny the whole way over."

Colton? Nan hadn't realized that Esperanza and the ambassador were on a first-name basis. Then again, they *had* been working closely with the Trinni/ek. What was more, thinking back over the evening, the two of them had spent a lot of time talking during the dinner, including a great deal of smiling and chuckling—which meant they *hadn't* spent the whole night discussing the Trinni/ek.

Looking at Morrow, Nan prompted, "Well, Mr. Ambassador?"

Shifting in his chair, Morrow said, "I did say that, ma'am. They were escorted here by the *Venture,* and honestly, we almost needn't have bothered. Once we left their star system, they barely answered any comms and refused to beam over at all. It's like they were completely different people."

Ra'ch pursed her lips. "It was almost like they were all sick—one of them did faint, also. It might've been simple starship lag."

"They've traveled through space before," Xeldara said. "Hell, they're not even native to their world."

Safranski said, "Still, Councillor Ra'ch may be right. It could've been some kind of illness that hit all of them."

Xeldara tugged her ear again. "Illness doesn't account for that—even with the fainting. This was a whole personality shift."

Nan shook her head. "All right, how do we fix this?"

"I'm not sure that we do," Esperanza said. "They insulted us—publicly, definitively."

"It's not like the world is critical." Safranski shrugged. "Yes, they have plenty of resources we can use, but it's nothing we can't get elsewhere. Having them as a trading partner is more a luxury than a necessity."

Ra'ch nodded, an action that, thanks to the horn in the center of her forehead, made the teal-skinned councillor look like she was about to gore someone. "We can't force someone to be nice to us—the choice is completely theirs."

Morrow shook his head. "But they *chose* this. They were the ones who contacted the *Io*, not the other way around. They pushed for diplomatic relations, and they volunteered to come to Earth rather than having us go there. They were *eager* to make friends with us."

"Which brings us back," Esperanza said, "to the president's question of what the hell happened."

"I don't know, but I think it's worth trying to find out." Morrow sounded determined. Nan had the feeling that he viewed tonight's events as a personal failing on his part.

"How?" Ra'ch asked.

"The *Io*'s still in the same sector. Why not have them swing around there in a few weeks, see what they can find out?"

Nan turned to Esperanza. "What do you think?"

"It couldn't hurt. Worse comes to worse, Ytri/ol tells the *Io* to go away, and they go away. Best case, they apologize, and we can start again. We've certainly got nothing to lose by trying, and I trust Captain T'Vrea not to make things worse."

Nan nodded. "All right. Ra'ch, could you talk to Starfleet, see about diverting the *Io* in a couple weeks?"

"Of course."

"Okay, thanks everyone. Let's hope we can salvage this."

Everyone said, "Thank you, Madam President," except

for Xeldara. "Ma'am," the Tiburonian said meekly, "can I talk to you and Esperanza for a minute?"

Xeldara had never used a meek tone of voice in the entire time Nan had known her, so it got her attention. "Sure," Nan said and waited for Ra'ch, Safranski, and Morrow to leave.

Nan noticed a quick exchange of looks between Morrow and her chief of staff. After the door closed behind them, Nan looked at Esperanza. Nan's earlier snide remarks about her shoes notwithstanding, Esperanza looked fantastic tonight. She suspected that fact wasn't lost on Colton Morrow, either.

Making a mental note to tease Esperanza mercilessly about it at a more appropriate time, Nan turned to Xeldara with an expectant expression.

"Madam President, I—I'm afraid I have to resign."

Nan felt like she'd been punched in the gut. "What?"

Esperanza looked just as surprised. "What brought this on? If it's because—"

"It's not because of anything either of you have done, or anything I've done—exactly. Look, I know you both haven't always seen eye to eye with me, but you've never held that against me—which I appreciate. It's not that I don't love this job, but—" She sighed. "Tonight was the most time that my husband and I have spent together since I took this job. I've been working ninety hours a day, fifty days a week for nine months. I'm never home, and Arlon hates it here on Earth."

Nan cursed herself for not remembering Arlon's name until Xeldara said it.

Esperanza said, "He hasn't been—?"

Without hesitating, Xeldara said, "No! He doesn't even know I'm planning this, and he keeps insisting that he's fine and that he's proud of me. But we've been married a long time, and I can tell that he's miserable. I just can't keep doing this to him." She tugged on her earlobe again, and Nan found, to her surprise, that she was going to miss that irritating affectation. "I've been talking to Councillor Gnizbreg, and she's offered me a job as chief of staff in her office back on Tiburon."

Esperanza tensed. Before she could say anything, however, Xeldara quickly said, "She actually offered me the job three months ago. Apparently her last COS left the place a disaster. That was when I had first started thinking about resigning. Honestly, I'd finally decided to do it five weeks ago, but I didn't want to leave while we were in the middle of the Trinni/ek talks. But now that that's pretty much over, I just—"

Nan held up a hand. "It's all right, Xeldara. I'd rather have you than not have you, but I'd also rather you were happy."

Xeldara let out a huge breath, which Nan took for a sigh of relief. "Thank you for understanding, ma'am."

"It's all right."

Esperanza said, "We'll make the formal arrangements tomorrow. Be in my office at 0800?"

"Sure." Xeldara turned toward the door. "Thank you, Madam President."

When she left, there seemed to be a proverbial spring to her step. *This was definitely something she needed to do.*

Chuckling, Esperanza shook her head. "Honestly, I had pegged Myk as being the first to quit." Then her expression grew more serious. "I'm going to have Gnizbreg's head."

"Leave her alone, Esperanza, all she did was put the bug in her ear." Nan paused. "That expression takes on a whole new meaning with Tiburonians, doesn't it?"

"Yes, ma'am—and I won't do anything too horrible to the councillor. But poaching is an offense that definitely deserves some kind of retribution."

Nan sighed. "Fine, just keep me out of it." Another pause. "So, what's happening between you and the ambassador?"

"What do you—? I can't believe you're going to— Look, ma'am, what happens in— Oh, forget it."

Grinning, Nan said, "That's amazing—you ran the entire gamut from surprised to annoyed to pissed to resigned in about half a second."

"You bring out the best in me, ma'am."

"So does Ambassador Morrow—sorry, *Colton*. I bet you'd have done even better with him if you'd worn the heels."

"The ambassador is a nice person—"

"Fairly good looking, too."

"—with whom I've worked very closely these last few weeks."

"Months, actually."

Esperanza's voice grew tighter. "And we get along well, which has made the work easier."

"Right, of course."

Sighing, Esperanza said, "Ma'am, as we've just seen up close, romance and the Palais aren't entirely compatible."

Nan mentally conceded the point, but she wasn't anywhere near done teasing her chief of staff yet. "Fred and Ashanté manage."

"Fred and Ashanté have been in professional politics together for all their adult lives, and they work together. Colton's work takes him all over the Federation. I really don't think it'll work."

Before Nan could reply, the door opened to reveal one of the guards. "Excuse me, ma'am?"

"Yeah, Marta, what is it?"

"I'm sorry to interrupt, ma'am, but a message just arrived for you—the former president died."

Nan winced. "Ah, damn. Well, I suppose Thelian was bound to—"

"I'm sorry, ma'am," Marta interrupted, "but it wasn't President Thelian—it was President Jaresh-Inyo."

That took Nan aback. Her eyes immediately went back to his portrait, hanging between Amitra's and Zife's. Although he was fairly soft-spoken, Jaresh-Inyo had always had a commanding physical strength. As far as she knew, he was in good health.

Then again, I also haven't heard anything from him in a while. I'm guessing this was why.

"Thanks, Marta."

Marta nodded and went back to standing guard outside the door.

Esperanza said, "I'll find out what the arrangements are, then get your schedule rearranged. The funeral'll probably be on Grazer."

Still staring at the portrait, Nan said, "Yeah. I'll have to talk to his wife. And to Thelian and Amitra and Zife." She then turned back to Esperanza. "Do we know where Zife is?"

"I'll find out."

"Good." She sighed. "Damn."

Jaresh-Inyo had asked to have his death-watch not on Grazer but on Mars, where he had retired after losing the election to Min Zife. The former president was of the *semtir* tradition, which called for the body to be destroyed in front of a gathering of friends and family, after which any who wished to would provide a brief remembrance.

Esperanza stood in the back of the packed Squyres Amphitheater in Endurance on Mars. "Friends and family" was a tall order when you used to be president of the quadrant's largest political entity, and the amphitheater was standing-room-only. Besides the former president's wife, children, grandchildren, and siblings, people from Jaresh-Inyo's administration, dozens of councillors, prominent Grazerite politicians, and Presidents Amitra and Bacco were all present, as well as a Starfleet honor guard.

Conspicuous by their absence, even in the crowded space, were Presidents Thelian and Zife. The former had had to beg off due to illness—the old Andorian was sufficiently frail that his physicians feared a space voyage of any kind, much less from Andor to Mars, might necessitate a second state funeral.

As for Zife, he was nowhere to be found, though not for lack of trying on Esperanza's part. Though Admiral Ross had been the one to issue the ultimatum to Zife, forcing him to resign or have the arming of Tezwa exposed, he did not know where Zife had gone for his retirement. Neither of the two most prominent Bolians in the Palais—Councillor Nea and a reporter named Sovan—had any idea. Esperanza had contacted several members of Zife's staff and cabinet, most of whom hadn't been especially cordial to the person who, in essence, had taken their jobs away one year (or more, had Zife been reelected) sooner than expected.

Generally, all still-living presidents attended the death ritual of any president who died. Exceptions occurred when there were those who, like Thelian, had a good reason for not attending, or the recently deceased president's traditions did not have a death ritual with an attendance. *But if we can't find 'em, we can't get 'em here,* Esperanza thought with annoyance.

Jaresh-Inyo had been a living contradiction. A very large man with a ferocious mien, he had been in fact, one of the most levelheaded and calm people Esperanza had ever met. In many ways he had been the perfect peacetime president. Elected when the Federation had gone past conflicts with the Tzenkethi and Cardassians, when the Klingon alliance had been strong, when the only threats had come from the Romulans—only recently coming out of their fifty-year isolation—and the Borg—a distant and occasional threat at best—he'd been a compromiser, someone who hadn't worried or offended anyone. *He would never have spanked the council over Aligar the way the president did back in January, and he probably would've been a lot less proactive on the whole Reman thing.*

But then, two years into his term, contact had been made with the Dominion, and everything had changed. The Cardassian government had fallen, the Klingons had invaded and pulled out of the Khitomer Accords, changelings had begun infiltrating Alpha Quadrant governments, and Jaresh-Inyo had allowed himself to be manipulated by a Starfleet admiral into declaring martial law shortly after the attack on the Antwerp conference. The admiral had overreacted to the security situation, but only because the president had underreacted. Into that breach had stepped Min Zife, who—whatever his flaws—did put the Federation in a position to win a war that was by far the worst in Federation history.

For his part, the Grazerite had moved to Mars and lived a quiet retirement after a lifetime of service, first to Grazer as a councillor, then to the Federation as president, until he'd died in his sleep.

Still, he was a good man. He deserves the accolades— and to have a thousand people at his funeral.

The Starfleet honor guard—four security officers in their dress whites—walked in formation up to the podium, where the former president's body was shrouded with the Federation flag. They removed the flag, revealing the body, dressed in the traditional black hooded outfit that Grazerites considered formal wear.

The four officers neatly folded the flag into a triangle, then presented it to Jaresh-Inyo's widow. Esperanza knew that had its basis in some old Earth tradition; she personally found it a bit ostentatious, but she could see why it was still done. It had a certain dignity, a certain respect. *He lived his life in service to what that flag represents.*

Then a Grazerite *kelmek*—the word translated into "death-helper"—nodded to someone Esperanza couldn't see from her seat in the top row, and, moments later, Jaresh-Inyo's body dematerialized in a transporter beam. She smiled sadly. *Well, if it calls for destruction of the body, that's a pretty clean way of doing it.*

Jaresh-Inyo's brother, Jaresh-Uryad—about half the height of his brother—then moved to the center of the stage from the first row of the amphitheater. *If this follows the usual protocols, a couple of other family members will speak, then President Amitra, then President Bacco.*

Even as Jaresh-Uryad began to speak in a voice that was eerily similar to that of his late brother despite their differences in height and build, Esperanza's comm started to beep.

She sighed. One of the reasons why she had taken a seat in the top row was because it was near an exit. Zachary was fielding all her comms, and only he had the code to get through to her, and he was only to contact her if it was urgent. *I suppose going one hour without something urgent was asking too much.*

As soon as she was in the hallway outside the amphitheater—a thin ribbon of space that went around the top, but was dotted with support beams that Esperanza could stand behind so she would have at least a modicum of privacy— she said, "What is it, Zachary?"

"Abrik. He says there's a problem."

"What kind of problem?"

"Klingons, Remans, and Romulans."

Esperanza sighed. "Oh my."

"Yeah."

"Dammit." Things had finally started to quiet down once the Klingons had started moving the Remans to Klorgat IV. *So what's gone wrong* now? "Put him through."

"Madam President?"

It took all of Esperanza's willpower to keep from rolling her eyes. Then, remembering she was more or less alone, she did it anyhow. *I can't believe we're doing this again.* "It's Esperanza, Jas, what's the problem?"

"I need to talk to the presi—"

"The president is sitting in Squyres waiting for her turn to eulogize one of her predecessors. Unless the Dominion's reinvading—and I know that's not why you're calling—then I'm not disturbing her until the service is over."

"It's urgent, Esperanza, I—"

"Does this have to do with Klorgat?"

"Yes."

"Which is hundreds of light-years from here?"

A pause. *"Yes."*

"So will the president not finding out about this for another hour or so really matter in the grand scheme of things, especially since I'm here to deal with it in the interim?"

"You're not here, you're there."

Esperanza couldn't help it. "That's neither here nor there, Jas. What happened?"

Abrik let out a long breath before answering the question. *"One of Klorgat IV's moons blew up."*

"How?"

"We're not sure. Initial indications are that it was natural—but none of the surveys done of the Klorgat system indicated any kind of instability in the moon."

"How thorough were the Klingons' scans?"

"Of the fourth planet, very. Of the moons—we're not sure. Unfortunately, the ship that scanned it initially four years ago was the I.K.S. Azetbur. They had only transmitted basic sensor specs back to Qo'noS before they were called to Elabrej, where they were destroyed."

"So this could've been a natural disaster."

"Yeah, it could've."

Esperanza smiled. "You don't sound convinced."

"The Klingons are a lot of things, but they're not stupid. Their sensors are as good as ours, and any Starfleet vessel worth its salt would've picked up this kind of thing. Sure, maybe they missed something the first time, or maybe the Azetbur forgot to report it, but there's been dozens of ships in and out of Klorgat the last two months. They can't have missed this."

Seeing where this was going, Esperanza said, "You think it's Mendak."

"Yeah, I think it's Mendak. The Klingons also think it's Mendak."

Esperanza shook her head. "Of course they do, because the only alternative is that they royally screwed up." She sighed. "All right, keep on this. As soon as we're on the

T'Maran home, the president'll call you, and I'll make sure T'Latrek's in there with us. Round up Akaar, Shostakova, and Molmaan, too."

"They're already on their way, as is Ross, and we've got Rozhenko on standby. And we're trying to track Spock down."

"Good luck with that." Esperanza figured that was a lost hope. Spock had returned to Romulan space and had given every indication that he was going to complete his mission on his own terms, without interference from the Federation government. *Ninety years later, and he's still smarting because he feels responsible for Chancellor Gorkon's assassination. Must be something about mixing human and Vulcan genes that produces large amounts of guilt.* "We'll talk in an hour."

"Right." A pause. *"Look, Esperanza—I'm sorry. You're right, there is a chain of command. It's just—"* Another pause. *"I don't like the way any of this is going. The Klingons are pissed off, and they're only going to get more pissed off, and the lack of any kind of strong central authority on Romulus means they don't have a good target. Which means they may find another one."*

"Then we've gotta work to not give them one." She smiled. "Apology accepted, Jas. Let's get this done."

She signed off, then contacted Zachary again and told him that no matter what he had to do to accomplish it, he had to make sure that Ambassador K'mtok was on the fifteenth floor by the time the *T'Maran* touched down on the Palais roof.

Then she returned to the amphitheater, just as President Bacco was getting up to speak. *That was fast.* She wondered if Amitra let her go first or declined to speak.

For a moment, the president simply stood at center stage. By Grazerite tradition, the only ornamentation on the stage was the pallet for the body, and Esperanza feared Nan would be lost without a podium to stand behind. Then she thought that perhaps Fred's speech hadn't been put onto the holoprompt.

But then Nan started to speak.

"About a hundred and fifty years ago, the people of the Federation elected a wonderful Trill woman by the name of Madza Bral to be their president. She was the first person not from one of the five founding worlds to serve in that office. She served two terms and then declined to run for a third, citing exhaustion and old age. 'The presidency,' she said in what was, in essence, her retirement speech, 'is quite possibly the worst job in the Federation. The hours are long, the work is difficult, the decisions that have to be made are unimaginable to anyone who has never set foot in the Palais de la Concorde. Your successes are unappreciated, your failures are blown out of all proportion, and your life disintegrates before your very eyes. And having said all that, I would never, under any circumstance, trade the last eight years for anything.'

"I didn't know President Jaresh-Inyo very well. We met several times after I was elected governor, and I found him to be a good man, an honest man. It's easy now to criticize him as the president who failed to prevent the Dominion threat from escalating, or as the chief executive who let Earth be placed under martial law. And it's just as easy to ignore or minimize his achievements: expanding the rights of sentient beings under the Federation Charter; opening new diplomatic relations with the Children of Tamar; and normalizing our relationship with the Cardassian Union for the first time in fifty years. None of these were the stuff of news reports the way other aspects of his presidency were, but they should not—*cannot*—be ignored.

"This Federation is remarkable. We now have one hundred and fifty-four members, many of whom have more than one world under their purview. Think about it—that's hundreds of *planets*. And the president's job is to keep these worlds, populated as they are by the most diverse and, frankly, cantankerous collection of species you're likely to find in this universe, from flying apart. Any president who comes to the end of a term with the Federation still intact, well, that president has done the job. I've only been in office for nine months, but in that time I've learned that that's the only true test for success, and Jaresh-Inyo passed it.

"Jaresh-Inyo chose to run. He won. He served. And then he stepped aside for the next winner, leaving the Federation still intact four years later. For that, and for so much else, we honor him today. I am proud to be part of the same family as him, as President Amitra—" Here she nodded at the other former president. "—as Presidents Thelian and Zife, who couldn't be here, and as President Bral, and I close as I began, with her words: 'What matters, in the end, is that the Federation endures.' Because of Jaresh-Inyo, we've endured. Thank you."

Wow. Fred MacDougan wrote that speech on the *T'Maran* while flying here, a journey that only took three hours. *If there's time with the whole Reman mess, I am making sure he gets some of my single-barrel Jack Daniel's tonight.*

" 'Well'?"

Ashanté Phiri had to resist a strong urge to beat her husband about the head and shoulders as they walked to the spaceport where the *T'Maran* and the *al-Rashid* were docked.

"How could she just drop that in there? It's a rhetorically meaningless word, it threw off the rhythm of the sentence, *and* she sounded like an idiot."

Ashanté had known something was wrong when Fred had flinched during one part of the speech. Ashanté hadn't been sure when it was, exactly, as she'd been too caught up in her admiration for her husband's work. President Bacco had insisted on giving her own eulogy, so Fred hadn't thought about it, which was fine, as he'd had the Starfleet Academy commencement to worry about.

But then this morning, the president had announced that she hadn't been able to think of anything, and could Fred take a stab at it? Since he'd been, as he'd put it, "abso-damn-lutely nowhere" with the commencement talk, he'd leapt at the chance.

"What does 'well' *mean* there? It's a nonsense word."

"Fred, darling," Ashanté finally said as they were approaching the doors to the dock, "I didn't even notice it. I thought the speech was brilliant."

"The speech *was* brilliant—then she put that damn 'well' in there." He turned to glare at her. "And how could you *not* notice it? What I wrote was, 'Any president who comes to the end of a term with the Federation still intact has done the job.' It was a solid, declarative statement, giving the impression that she actually knows what she's talking about, what with being president and all. But no, she said, 'Any president who comes to the end of a term with the Federation still intact, well, that president has done the job.' Now it's not the authoritative declaration of an informed source, it's just some gosh-wow, off-the-cuff opinion that probably doesn't really mean anything."

"Sweetie, how long are you gonna go on about this?"

Fred let out a long breath, puffing his cheeks. "I figure at least another hour."

"Okay, then—just so you know, you're gonna need a new audience in a minute."

"Why?"

"Esperanza needs me on the *T'Maran.*"

Fred's look of righteous indignation modulated into a look of concern and husbandly understanding. He also knew better than to ask why, since if she could say why, she would, and if she didn't, it meant she couldn't, at least not yet. "All right. Which of the guards are going on the *al-Rashid?*" When the president traveled with two shuttles, the security detail was split evenly between them.

"Kenshikai, Trrrrei, and Lillius."

Fred smiled. "Perfect. I can bitch and moan at Hantra." Hantra Trrrrei was a very large, taciturn Coridani, who would likely respond to Fred's carrying on about the president ruining his great speech with complete indifference.

Smiling back, Ashanté said, "Just make sure that Una isn't anywhere nearby." Una Lillius was never one to shy away from an argument, even while on duty. "Anyhow, gotta go." She kissed her husband on the mouth, then made a beeline for the *T'Maran.*

Within a few minutes, she was ensconced in the aft section with the president, Esperanza, and Councillor T'Latrek, with Jas Abrik standing by on a secure channel in the Monet Room.

"Coop," Bacco said, "we're gonna need privacy back here."

"Okay, boss," the pilot said. He lowered the small bulkhead that separated the pilot's compartment, where Lan Cooper flew the ship, and the front part of the aft compartment, where Rydell, Aoki, and T'r'wo'li'i' stood guard, from the rest of the aft compartment.

Ashanté then took the call off standby. The screen lit up

with an image of the Monet Room, as well as an inset image of Ambassador Rozhenko from the embassy on Qo'noS. Present in the Monet Room besides Abrik were Secretary Shostakova, Councillor Molmaan, Admirals Ross and Akaar, and Captain Hostetler Richman.

"Have we figured out what happened?" Bacco asked without preamble.

"We don't really know much more than we knew already," Abrik said. *"Klorgat IV's largest moon exploded for no obvious reason."*

"How many people were killed?"

Akaar said, *"None."*

That surprised Ashanté, and she said, "Really?"

"The Remans that have settled there are on the largest continent on the world, and it was facing away from the moon when the explosion occurred. Most of the damage was done to an ocean halfway around the world."

Ross added, *"In addition, the Klingon and Reman ships that were handling the move were able to destroy some of the larger pieces of moon before they struck the planet."*

"Yeah," Ashanté said, "but that still can't be good news for the planet. If it's got oceans, the loss of a moon's gonna play merry hell with their tidal patterns."

Bacco nodded. "The dust will probably get into their atmosphere—we could be looking at an ice age." She looked at the screen. "Are we gonna have to evacuate them again?"

"Unlikely," Akaar said. *"Even with those changes, Klorgat IV is still several orders of magnitude more hospitable than Remus ever was."*

Rozhenko added, *"The Remans've already announced that they've got no intention of leaving, and the High Council's backing them up."*

"All right," Bacco said, "but I'm worried about that a lot less than why this happened."

"We still don't know that, ma'am," Abrik said.

"May one assume," T'Latrek asked, "that the Klingons claim the Romulans are responsible?"

Shostakova nodded. *"And the Romulans say it was a natural disaster. They also believe the irony is one the Klingons should be able to appreciate."*

"Actually," Esperanza said, "the similarity between this and Praxis is a lot of what leads me to think that this *isn't* an accident."

"But it happened when no Remans were in direct danger," Ashanté said. "If the object was to attack the Remans, why wait until the Remans are on the far side of the planet to blow it up?"

Hostetler Richman said, *"It depends on what the goal is—they may have been more interested in the long-term effects on Klorgat IV than doing short-term harm to the Remans. That'd be consistent with the usual Romulan MO."* She smiled. *"Besides, blowing up a moon, especially in secret, isn't exactly a precision maneuver. They may have intended it to go off sooner than it did—or later—but something went wrong."*

Ashanté looked over at the president, who sat with her left arm folded under her right elbow, her right hand on her chin. After sitting silently for a moment, the president said, "I think we need to investigate this."

Abrik started to say, *"Ma'am, the Klingons—"*

"No, Jas, I mean, *we* need to investigate this. There's a third reason why the Romulans might want to do damage to the Klingons and the Remans, and that's to start a war with the Klingons. Nothing unites a fractured people faster than getting them behind a war effort."

"It would be consistent with past Romulan behavior," T'Latrek pointed out. "Thirty-six years ago, Praetor Dralath ordered an attack on the Klingon world of Narendra III. It was an attempt to rally his people behind a war with the Klingons in order to stave off the economic depravations of his administration."

Shostakova said, *"That type of thinking is consistent with the reports we have been getting regarding Admiral Mendak."*

"The last report we have of Mendak's activities," Hostetler Richman said, *"from about a month ago has his fleet on a course that could take them to Klorgat. Of course, it could also take him to half a dozen other places that are actually in Romulan or neutral space, and he could easily change course."*

"I take it that Praetor Tal'Aura is still denying any responsibility for Mendak's actions?"

Nodding, Shostakova said, *"Our latest report from Ambassador Spock indicated that Mendak has officially been declared a criminal, and that any Romulan soldiers who see him are to shoot him on sight."*

Abrik rolled his eyes. *"That just means they want deniability. He hasn't done anything that's actually hurt Tal'Aura in any way—just the other factions."*

Bacco looked at T'Latrek. "What do you think?"

T'Latrek raised an eyebrow. "I believe that any attempt to speculate would be foolish without the benefit of an investigation."

"Me, too. I'm gonna talk to K'mtok when I get back. Meanwhile, I want an S.C.E. team going over that moon with a fine-tooth comb."

"The da Vinci is in the area. They'll be able to tell us exactly what happened."

Ashanté hoped that Ross's confidence was well placed. On the other hand, she had heard nothing but good things about the Starfleet Corps of Engineers and their ability to solve the insoluble, which this little mystery was shaping up to be.

"Good," Bacco said with another nod. "Ambassador Rozhenko, while I'm selling this to K'mtok, you sell it to the High Council. I don't want anyone going off half-cocked until we know for sure what happened."

"Of course, ma'am. As it turns out, I'm having dinner with Martok and several councillors tonight, so we can talk about it then."

Esperanza chuckled. "'As it turns out'?"

Rozhenko just smiled back.

Ashanté shook her head. She had been leery of the notion of appointing someone so young, with minimal diplomatic experience, to replace Worf as Federation ambassador, but Alexander Rozhenko of the House of Martok had proven as adept as his father at bridging the gap between the two cultures.

"Let's do this right, people," Bacco said.

Several of those in the Monet Room thanked her, and the screen went dark.

"Thanks everyone," Bacco then said to the other three, then she looked right at Esperanza. "Now then, you wanted to talk to me about Xeldara's replacement?"

"Yes, ma'am."

"Oh," Bacco said to Ashanté, "and tell that husband of yours that he did a fine job with the speech."

"Yes, ma'am," Ashanté said hesitantly.

Bacco smiled. "Let me guess, he spent the entire walk from Squyres to the spaceport whining about the way I changed some of the phraseology."

"Just one, ma'am. When you added in 'well.'"

"Well, you tell Fred that the holoprompter glitched for a moment, and I was just trying to cover it."

Ashanté blinked. "Really, ma'am? Because it didn't come across that way—you covered *very* well."

"Nah, it didn't glitch—I just changed the phrasing. But I want you to tell Fred that to shut him up."

"That's a battle I gave up three years before we got married, ma'am."

"Fair point. Now then, who've we got in mind for the new deputy?"

◆

CHAPTER SEVENTEEN

◆　　◆

CADET KARIN NOOSAR tried not to fidget in her seat. This year, as with most years, the Academy graduating class was having its commencement in Golden Gate Park. It was a cool, pleasant day in San Francisco, as it often was even without aid from the weather net, with the sun shining down on the grass and trees and the blindingly white dress uniform worn by Admiral Bernard McTigue, the Academy superintendent.

Normally, Karin didn't mind listening to Superintendent McTigue speak. Tall, elegant, and well spoken, he had a dry wit, friendly demeanor, and sharp mind.

But Karin had been listening to McTigue since his appointment three years ago. Today, in addition to throwing off the title of cadet in favor of ensign, she and the rest of the class of '80 were going to have their commencement address delivered by none other than President Nan Bacco herself.

Karin had grown up on several different Federation worlds, with most of her teen years being spent on Cestus III. While there, she had gone to one of then-Governor Bacco's town meetings as part of a class assignment. She had gone in there a bored thirteen-year-old hoping just to stay awake for the whole thing; she'd come out with a tremendous respect for Nan Bacco and a desire to grow up to be just like her.

That ambition had tempered as she'd gotten older and realized that it was Starfleet, rather than politics, that was her true calling, but her admiration for Bacco had never flagged, and Karin had actually done a little bit of campaigning for her—as much as had been possible, what with her studies—when she'd run against Fel Pagro for president. It had been difficult, since most of her classmates had actually been for Pagro, though some had changed their tune when Admiral Ross had come out for Bacco.

Now, Karin failed in her attempt not to fidget as she waited for McTigue to shut the hell up and let President Bacco talk.

At last, the superintendent said, "And now, cadets—who will not be cadets much longer—I am especially proud to present to you all your commencement speaker, President Nanietta Bacco."

Thunderous applause echoed off the surrounding trees of the park as the small-but-impressive-looking white-haired woman approached the podium. She shook Mc-

Tigue's hand, then turned to look out at the throng of Karin's class. Karin thought, oddly, that she looked smaller than she had nine years earlier, though that was probably due to her being farther away. The town hall used for her gubernatorial town meetings was much smaller than a San Francisco park, after all.

"'Ex astris, scientia.' Those words are on that flag over there." The president pointed at the Academy flag, which hung on a pole right next to the other pole that had the Federation flag. "It's from an old human language called Latin. Nobody's spoken it conversationally for several hundred years, mind you, but we like to trot it out every once in a while to make ourselves sound more interesting. It means, 'From the stars, knowledge.' Which makes it kind of a funny motto for a place that has you spending the bulk of your time right here on Earth."

Karin smiled. She remembered some of her friends from the class of '79, all of whom had been dreading the commencement speech, which had been given by the novelist H'jn Sowell, a great writer but an awful public speaker. The year before that, it had been some ship captain or other, who had been even more boring. *We lucked out in that department.*

"The thing about the stars is that they do provide knowledge—but that comes with a concomitant risk. Nothing underlines that risk more than the fact that you are the first Academy class in quite a while to have gone through your entire tenure at the Academy when the Federation *wasn't* at war. And that, my friends, is something to be celebrated, because the classes before yours either came as first-years when we were at war, or were cadets when the war was declared, or joined when they thought war was pretty damn likely. But you all are the first to come through without that particular Damoclean sword hanging over your collective heads."

Two of the cadets—neither of them human—gave each other confused looks, only to have the cadets on either side of them explain about the Sword of Damocles.

"There's an old human saying—not in Latin, you'll be happy to know—that says that knowledge is power, and another one that says that power corrupts. Since its founding two hundred and nineteen years ago, the Federation has tried to bring a message of hope and of knowledge to the galaxy. The galaxy, unfortunately, hasn't always been impressed. We may not be at war anymore, but the possibility always, tragically, exists. The people who sat in those seats seven years ago were embroiled in a war six months later when the Dominion took Deep Space 9.

"But the purpose of Starfleet isn't to fight the Federation's wars. That is their task—and that might be your task—when it's required, but it's important for all of you to remember that it is a last resort, not a first one. Starfleet was formed when the Federation was, but it grew out of Earth's space exploration arm, and they had a Latin motto too: *ad astra per aspera*. It means 'to the stars for hope.' And every time we go to the stars, we're filled with hope— no matter how many times it would be better to be filled with dread. Their job then, and your job now, is to seek out new life and new civilizations. Some of those will be like the Klingons or the Romulans or the Cardassians or the Tzenkethi or the Tholians, none of whom were kindly disposed to us at first, and some of whom still aren't. Some of those will be like Bajor or Evora or Cairn or Delta Sigma IV, all of whom joined the Federation in the last decade. Regardless of who you do meet out there, though, you will bring the hope of peace."

Bacco smiled then. "It sounds funny, doesn't it? You'll be flying around in ships that have sufficient weaponry to lay waste to a planet—not really much of a peaceful message, is it? When we've had to, we have fought, and we have bled, and we have suffered, but it's because with this Federation, we've found something that's worth fighting for, worth bleeding for, worth suffering for, and yes, worth dying for. And we've also found that the hope we come to the stars for must be tempered with a willingness to defend what we have, because if we don't, there are plenty of people all over the galaxy who'd be more than happy to take it away from us.

"Every day I go down to the first floor of the Palais de la Concorde, and there are over a hundred and fifty people in there. Each one is from a wholly different world than the person in the next chair, and both are from worlds wholly different from the person in the chair behind them. Yet they come together, they argue together, they discuss together, and they *work* together to make this Federation better than it already is. It would be easy to fall into old patterns. Before the Federation formed, Vulcan fought against Andorian, Tellarite fought against Klingon, human fought against Xindi, Romulan fought against pretty much everybody. But now, worlds stand together instead of apart.

"I've always had tremendous respect for Starfleet. My chief of staff and my security advisor are former officers. Some of our finest presidents are former Starfleet—Lorne McLaren, Thelian, T'Pragh. Still, I never really understood their importance until something that happened during the war."

Karin tensed a bit. She had moved off Cestus III by the time the war started, but she was pretty sure she knew what Bacco was about to talk about.

"When the war was getting particularly bad, Starfleet sent the *U.S.S. Enterprise* to talk to the Gorn, see if they could be convinced to ally with us against the Dominion. Turns out their timing was pretty spectacularly awful, since Starfleet arrived just in time for a coup d'état on the Gorn homeworld. The new regime sent ships to Cestus III and actually occupied the planet for a while. In the end, though, we were saved, because the *Enterprise* was able to stop the violence and convince the Gorn not to count us as their enemy. They didn't do it by force, they didn't do it by blowing Gorn ships out of the sky, though both things did occur out of necessity. But even with a war on, even with the powerful arsenal the *Enterprise* had at its disposal, their captain and crew were able to negotiate a settlement and bring the Gorn into the war. It was a show, not of force but of ideas that led to the Gorn signing a treaty with the Federation, which they signed in my office in Pike City.

"Starfleet is the glue that holds the Federation together. The responsibility you each have now is to maintain this little miracle that we've kept going for over two centuries, through tumult and strife, through feast and famine, through war and peace. It will be difficult. All of you will face hard choices in the years ahead, if history's any guide—and it usually is. But throughout it all, you must remember that it is from the stars that you find knowledge, it is from the stars that you find hope, and it is from the stars that you will find peace.

"I'd wish you luck, but I suspect you will not need it. Simply continue to do well. Thank you."

Karin wasn't sure if she was the first one to her feet when the president finished, but she liked to imagine she was—and that she was also the last one to sit down several minutes later when the applause finally died down.

She thought about what Bacco said about past presidents who were Starfleet officers first. Lorne McLaren, she knew, was a twenty-third-century president who'd run after the pressures of the Klingon conflict and the Organian Peace Treaty had led Kenneth Wescott not to seek another term; McLaren had negotiated the historic agreement with the Kelvans. Thelian had served during the early days of contact with the Cardassians, and T'Pragh had served during the Tzenkethi War.

Smiling, Cadet—soon to be Ensign—Karin Noosar thought, *Maybe I will go into politics some day after all.*

AUGUST 2380

---

*"It is better to discuss things, to argue and
engage in polemics than make perfidious plans
of mutual destruction."*
—Mikhail Gorbachev

CHAPTER EIGHTEEN

◆   ◆

"GOOD EVENING. This is *Illuminating the City of Light*, I'm your host, Velisa. Tomorrow night, the second attempt at welcoming the Trinni/ek to the Federation will be made. This time, rather than a state dinner, Speaker Ytri/ol of the Trinni/ek will be meeting with the Federation Council on the first floor of the Palais. Tonight on *ICL*, we'll be examining what led to this change of heart on the Trinni/ek's part, as well as other business on the council's agenda over the course of the remainder of the session.

"With me tonight to discuss these issues are Artrin na Yel, former councillor from Triex; Gora Yed, the new Palais correspondent from *Seeker;* Safranski, the secretary of the exterior; and, remotely from the *U.S.S. Io,* Commander Thérèse Su, first officer of that vessel. Welcome, all of you."

"Thank you."

"Thanks, Velisa."

"Thanks."

"Glad to be here."

"Commander Su, I'd like to start by asking you your impression of the Trinni/ek, both the first time you met them earlier this year, and your trip back a month ago."

"Honestly, the two impressions weren't any different. The Trinni/ek we spoke to on both trips were curious, friendly, and eager to open diplomatic relations."

"When they stormed out of the Palais three months ago, were you surprised?"

"To be honest, I watched the FNS footage, and I didn't recognize anybody from the Io's *trip to Trinni/ek—and neither did Captain T'Vrea or anyone else on the ship. It was like they were replaced with cranky duplicates."*

"What was the reaction when you returned?"

"The same as before, only very apologetic. Speaker Ytri/ol didn't know what happened and was sure that the Federation hated them. They were scared that when we came back we were there to attack them, and were very relieved to find out that we didn't hold a grudge."

"Safranski, do you think that this second trip will be more productive than the first?"

"It could hardly be less productive, Velisa. The Trinni/ek's reaction was what I would expect from a Chalnoth delegation, not a civilized race that Commander Su's CO referred to as 'friendly,' which isn't an adjective Vulcans use lightly. Assuming that what happened in May is an aberration, then I have every confidence in the ability of the president and the council to welcome them into the galactic community."

"And if it isn't an aberration?"

"Then you'll have a lot to talk about on your first show after the meeting."

"Fair enough. Speaking of the council, several items are on the agenda before the council goes into recess at the end of the month. One of those is a case for the judiciary council involving the Daystrom Institute, where one of the institute's scientists is petitioning to have an android under the institute's care dismantled. Others are insisting that the android, which is called B-4, has the same rights as any other living being. Artrin, you're no longer on the judiciary council, but surely you have some opinions on this?"

"I do, yes, Velisa. First of all, it should be pointed out that the jurisdictional issues are still being worked out. Daystrom is jointly operated by the Federation government and Starfleet. There has been some question about who should hear the dispute—Starfleet's Judge Advocate General or the judiciary council."

"But in the past, hasn't it been Starfleet?"

"It's not that simple, Velisa. The last legal issue surrounding Daystrom was a similar case to this one, but it was also a purely Starfleet matter, as both parties in the legal dispute were Starfleet officers—a Commander Bruce Maddox and an android officer, Lieutenant Commander Data, since deceased. In the end, Data's sentience was made into law."

"Excuse me, Artrin, but isn't B-4 a prototype of Data?"

"Yes, Gora. B-4 was also constructed by Noonien Soong."

"So if it's the same thing, why is there a jurisdictional issue?"

"It *isn't* the same thing. To begin with, in the previous case, all those involved were Starfleet, as I said. In this case, the complainant is a civilian, who is not under Starfleet's jurisdiction. Ironically, Maddox, who's a captain now, is now arguing the opposite side. Plus, B-4's status is as yet undetermined."

"Wouldn't this be where it was determined?"

"Yes, Gora, which is one of the reasons why it's taking so long."

"And people wonder why there are complaints about government not getting anything done."

"Turning to foreign policy for a moment, Secretary Safranski, can you tell us anything about the investigation into the destruction of Klorgat IV's moon?"

"Well, Velisa, the Starfleet Corps of Engineers' preliminary report was inconclusive, though the evidence seemed to point to it being an accident."

"Do you think this will finally be the straw that breaks the back of the peace between the Klingons and Romulans?"

"Actually, as someone who served on ships that patrolled both empires' borders over the years, I'd like to answer that, if I may."

"Of course, Commander."

"The Klingons live for conflict, but not for stupid conflict. One of the reasons why they haven't gone into all-out war with the Romulans is because there was no guarantee that they would win, and the entire Klingon population would fly into a supernova before they'd subject themselves to Romulan rule. Now, though, thanks to Shinzon's coup, the Romulan Empire isn't a quadrant superpower anymore. They're in almost as bad a shape as the Cardassians. So the Klingons may well be gearing up for a war that they've been itching for ever since Narendra III."

"Speaking of which, the aid to Cardassia is up for renewal this session. Despite the many setbacks they've had since Cardassia Prime was decimated at the end of the Dominion War, Federation aid has continued. Gora, what's your sense of how the council will go on this?"

"Well, you wouldn't think that it would be an issue, but there are rumblings around the Palais that helping Cardassia is putting good resources after bad, and that it's taking away from other postwar relief efforts, not to mention other efforts that were curtailed before the war and really do need to be gotten back to. Still, I'm sure the opposition will be token at best."

"Do you think that—"

Silence.

"Hey! I was watching that!"

Lagg rolled all six eyes at her husband's words. "You were asleep."

His tentacles flapping in denial, Rakos said, "I was not asleep, I was just resting my eyes. Put it back on."

Sitting down in the acid pool, Lagg said, "I could hear you snoring."

"I was just muttering about the weak commentary."

"You don't even know what they were talking about," Lagg said with a laugh.

Rakos's tongue slithered out of his mouth. "They were talking about that baseball team the president likes."

"Wrong. They were talking about aid to Cardassia. Some Trill reporter was babbling on."

Frowning with both mouths, Rakos said, "Really? Hm. I guess I did fall asleep."

"Come join me in the pool, dear, your skin is looking too smooth."

Rakos clambered out of the seating dish and slithered over to the acid pool. "Yes, dear."

✦

CHAPTER NINETEEN

✦   ✦

DOGAYN 418 WALKED OUT of hir fourteenth-floor office into the warp core, to see Eduardo de la Vega standing at the desk of hir assistant, Mikhail Okha.

Eduardo gave Dogayn a pleading expression. "Doh, will

you explain to this crazy man that I'm an old friend of yours, please?"

Mikhail turned and said, "Dogayn, this man claims to be a friend of yours."

"So I've heard." Dogayn smiled. "Do you have any proof of this, whoever you are?"

Rolling his eyes, Eduardo said, "Oh come *on*, Doh, will you just for once stop this crap?"

Laughing, Dogayn said, "It's all right, Mikhail—we used to be in the trenches together. Eddie here is an aide to Councillor Huang."

Turning a withering gaze, which Dogayn had already learned to fear, onto Eduardo, Mikhail said, "You could've said you worked for Councillor Huang in the first place."

"Sorry," Eduardo said in a small voice.

Mikhail turned back to Dogayn. "You have the transportation meeting in twenty minutes."

"I know. Are the latest stats on my padd?"

"How should I know, it's *your* padd."

"Of course." Dogayn resisted the urge to say something snide. Having once been an assistant hirself many moons ago, s/he knew better than most how important it was not to antagonize one's assistant, as one's life depended on that person more than most. Mikhail had not been Dogayn's choice—s/he'd inherited him from hir predecessor as deputy chief of staff, Xeldara Trask—but s/he wasn't about to complain. This was the opportunity of a lifetime, and the young Hermat wasn't about to make waves by complaining about hir assistant.

At least now I know why Trask didn't take this guy with her back to Tiburon, s/he thought with a grin as s/he invited Eduardo back into hir office.

"Actually," Eduardo said, "I was wondering if you wanted to have lunch."

Dogayn tried to remember the last time s/he had had time for a lunch that wasn't a lunch meeting. S/he failed. "Eddie, honest, I can't. You just heard, I have a meeting in half an hour—"

"Twenty minutes!" Mikhail cried with a long-suffering tone.

"Those things never start on time anyhow," s/he said to hir assistant, then turned back to Eduardo. "Anyhow, I've got a meeting with the arts commission after that, then I have to do prep for the Trinni/ek visit tomorrow, and then something on fifteen that I don't even remember what it is."

Without missing a beat, Mikhail said, "The president wishes to discuss tomorrow's council session with you and Ashanté."

"There you go. That's a late-afternoon meeting with the president, it's *guaranteed* to start at least half an hour late and go on two hours longer than scheduled. I'm sorry, man."

"That's a lot of meetings."

"It's normal, apparently. When Esperanza Piñiero sold me on this job, she didn't warn me about how many more meetings there'd be." Dogayn smiled. To hir surprise, Eduardo didn't. *Something's obviously on Eddie's mind.* Dogayn wondered what it was. They'd known each other since their early days in the world of politics, Eduardo as an aide to the councillor for Alpha Centauri, Dogayn in a like role for Councillor Saltroni 815 of Hermat. They'd both moved up to senior positions on the staffs of their respective councillors, Dogayn as Saltroni's chief of staff, Eduardo as Huang's primary legislator.

"Some other time?" s/he asked.

"I kinda need to talk to you about something right now."

Dogayn shrugged and moved back toward hir office. "Fine, let's talk here. I have a door that closes all by itself and everything."

"The thing is—"

As Dogayn approached it, the door to hir office opened three-quarters of the way, hesitated, then opened the rest of the way. "Of course, whether or not it ever opens again is, you'll pardon the pun, an open question. Mikhail, have you—?"

"Maintenance looked at the door this morning before you came in."

"And?"

"They said it was fine."

Dogayn rolled hir eyes. "It isn't 'fine.' Doors that are 'fine' don't open partway, take a coffee break, and then open the rest of the way."

"If you feel it's necessary, I'll call maintenance again."

"I feel it's necessary."

"Very well."

Turning back to Eduardo, s/he said, "Anyhow, I've got twenty minutes—"

"Fifteen now," Mikhail put in.

Ignoring him, Dogayn went on. "—so let's talk now."

Eduardo hesitated. "Thing is—"

"What?"

"I don't want to talk about this here. You and I have a closed-door meeting, people will notice."

Dogayn frowned. "Eddie, we're not having a closed-door meeting. We've known each other for ten years, we've worked together on a dozen pieces of legislation over the years, and you've just come up to see how I'm enjoying my cushy-tushy new job."

Eduardo just stared at hir.

"What?"

"'Cushy-tushy'? What does that *mean*?"

"It means my job is finally better than yours. Now will you *please* get in here?"

Letting out a very long breath, Eduardo finally said, "Fine, we'll talk here."

Dogayn entered hir cramped office. The office was a quarter of a circle in the center of the fourteenth floor of the Palais, matching those of the other three deputy chiefs of staff, with smaller offices and desks surrounding them, where their assistants and staff sat. It was smaller than hir previous office with the rest of Saltroni's staff on the eighth floor, but it was also better by virtue of hir not having to share it with anyone.

Offering Eduardo a seat on the only one of hir three guest chairs that wasn't piled with padds, s/he said, "So what's so urgent?"

"Cardassia."

Dogayn shrugged, assuming Eduardo was talking about the renewal of aid to Cardassia that was to be voted on the following day, and not the planet itself. "It'll pass in a walk, why?"

"It won't, Doh."

That got Dogayn's attention. "What?"

"It won't."

"How can it not pass?"

"Well," Eduardo said dryly, "the usual method is to not get enough votes."

"Very funny," Dogayn said, though that was the first sign s/he'd seen that Eduardo had regained his sense of humor. "Who's left the Neutral Zone?"

"I'm not sure."

Glaring at hir old friend, Dogayn said, "If you're not sure, then how—"

"All I know for sure is that Huang's voting against it."

That brought Dogayn up short. "What?"

"She's voting against it—and before you ask, I don't know why. All I know is that she told me not to bother drafting a decision on Cardassia."

"Which she wouldn't do unless she was voting against."

"Yup."

"Damn."

"This is why I didn't want to tell you this in a meeting in your office."

Dogayn still didn't get this. "Why the hell not?"

"Because I don't want Huang thinking I'm going behind her back to Bacco."

"Eddie, you *are* going behind her back to Bacco."

"Yeah, but I don't want it to *look* like that."

"Fine." Dogayn sighed. "If anyone asks, you just came here to set up lunch."

"I hope that works." Eduardo got up.

Dogayn did likewise. "Eddie?"

"Yeah?"

"Why *did* you go behind her back?"

Eduardo hesitated. "Remember that trip to Cardassia a few years back, after Ghemor was elected?"

Dogayn nodded. S/he hadn't taken that trip because Saltroni hadn't, but Huang had, and she'd taken her top aides, as part of a goodwill trip that several councillors had taken in order to help lend legitimacy to Alon Ghemor's rather fragile government.

"When I was out there, I met this reporter from FNS. She took me out to where they weren't letting the councillors go. We had to sneak through some checkpoints, and I swear to you, Doh, I thought for sure we were gonna get killed. And what she showed me . . ." Eduardo shivered.

In over a decade of working together, Dogayn had never seen Eduardo look like this.

"Children, Doh. Little children, who were skinnier than my finger. They were gathering stones from the rubble of bombed-out buildings in order to make some kind of shelter for themselves. The reporter told me about three kids who died when their shelter collapsed in a storm, crushing them to death and giving them their own grave, all in one shot. And things have gotten *worse* since then. We can't just stop helping them."

Dogayn didn't say anything for several seconds. Then, finally, in a weak whisper, s/he said, "Thanks, Eddie."

"Just do what you can, okay?"

With that, Eduardo got up and left.

Moments later, s/he activated hir intercom. "Mikhail, I need the next five minutes Esperanza has."

William Ross sat across from Esperanza Piñiero as the latter read over the report on the padd the admiral had given her.

"They're sure about this?" she finally said, after reading it for the fourth time.

"I know the S.C.E. crew on the *da Vinci*," Ross said. "If they say that Mendak did it, then Mendak did it."

Although Esperanza wasn't familiar with the folks on the *da Vinci* in particular, the S.C.E. in general had always impressed her with their ability to build anything that wasn't there, and figure out how to work anything that already was.

"All right, I'll bring this to the president. Thanks, Admiral."

Ross nodded but didn't smile. "You realize what this means, right, Esperanza?"

"Maybe." She let out a breath. "On the other hand, maybe Mendak *is* a rebel."

"That doesn't fit his profile."

Esperanza regarded Ross frankly. "Does *anything* on Romulus fit its profile anymore?"

"Good point. Still, I just don't see the hero of Brasîto as someone who'd be working without the express consent of the praetor."

"I don't see the hero of Brasîto as someone who'd be too thrilled with the woman who helped engineer Shinzon's coup as the praetor, either."

"Another good point." Now Ross did smile as he got up from the guest chair. "I need to head back to San Francisco."

Esperanza nodded.

After Ross left, she opened the intercom. "Zachary, is the president free?"

"I can check, but Dogayn wants to talk to you about something."

That surprised Esperanza. Dogayn 418 had proven to be a fine replacement for Xeldara, especially given hir knowledge of the first floor after working for Saltroni for so long. The Hermat also hadn't been one to ask for sudden meetings. In fact, that was one of hir qualities that Esperanza preferred over hir predecessor—Xeldara would ask to talk about the most ridiculous things at the most inconvenient times. Over the past three months, Dogayn had seemed happy to wait for the next scheduled opportunity.

Had it been Xeldara—or even Z4 or Myk—asking, Esperanza would have asked to put it off until after she could talk to the president about Klorgat IV, but the novelty of this type of request from Dogayn made her willing to take it. "Tell Mikhail I can give hir five minutes, no more—and check with Sivak about the president."

"Okay."

Two minutes later, Esperanza was told that she could see the president at noon—which was only fifteen minutes away—and that Dogayn was outside her office. "Send hir in."

Before the door had a chance to even close behind hir, Dogayn said, "We've got a big problem. Cardassia's not gonna pass."

Esperanza blinked. "What?"

"It's not gonna pass."

"Why the hell not?"

"Don't know, but Huang's voting against it."

Now Esperanza was confused. "Who else?"

"Not sure yet, but if Huang's voting against it, it's not gonna pass."

"That's ridiculous."

Dogayn shook hir head and took a seat in Esperanza's guest chair. "Unless the matter relates directly to Alpha Centauri, Huang has never, not once in twenty years in the council, voted against the majority on *anything*. She doesn't take stands, she doesn't go against the flow—again, unless it directly involved the homeworld. This doesn't, and if it looks like she's going against the tide, then that means the tide's shifted."

Esperanza got up from her chair and started pacing in front of the window that gave her a view of the Seine. "We can't just abandon aid to Cardassia now—they'll fall to pieces."

"My guess is the argument will be that they already have fallen to pieces, and why waste time picking those pieces up?"

Esperanza turned to stare at Dogayn. "What do you think happened?"

S/he rubbed hir chin. "Last year, during the Tezwa mess, Enaren wanted to introduce a bill that was cosponsored by Gleer and zh'Faila. It was to cut off aid to Tezwa and increase reconstruction on Betazed, Tellar, Andor, and a bunch of other worlds."

"What?" Esperanza didn't remember anything about this.

"The bill was pulled after Zife threatened to veto it," Dogayn added. "So it was never discussed on the first floor."

And therefore, Esperanza realized, *never in any official record.*

Dogayn continued. "But *everyone* was talking about it in here. It's possible that Enaren's looking to get back to that notion now, and Cardassia's aid renewal is the perfect time. If he's got Gleer and zh'Faila on his side again, then they can probably deliver all the votes they need. Gleer's been steaming ever since Krim's appointment, and he knows the aid's important to Bacco, so this will stick it to her. He's also got favors to call in because of the complete lack of support he got when he tried to block Krim—and even if he didn't, you know what Gleer's like when he gets on the warpath."

Esperanza snorted and walked over to the replicator. "Yeah. You want anything?"

S/he shook hir head.

"Tea, raspberry, iced."

The drink materialized in front of Esperanza with a quiet hum. "All right, get together with Ashanté and fix this."

That seemed to confuse Dogayn. "Huh?"

"Fix this," Esperanza repeated as she went back to her desk and grabbed the padd Ross had given her.

"I thought the president—"

"This never gets on the president's sensors." As she spoke, she entered some commands that downloaded the padd's data to her workstation. "Right now I've got to go upstairs and tell her we're gonna have to tap-dance on a supernova in order to keep the Klingons from invading Romulus, and that on top of risking a repeat of the biggest diplomatic disaster of her presidency tomorrow with the Trinni/ek. The last thing I want is her being distracted by this."

"Distracted? Esperanza, it's—"

"Very important to her, yes. That's why I want you and Ashanté to fix it before it even becomes a problem. Talk to whoever you need to talk to, but find out where the problem is and do what you can to fix it. If we can give some concessions, go for it—it took months to get the president and the council friendly, I don't want to reverse it over this."

Dogayn nodded and got up. "All right."

The two of them exited her office together. Dogayn moved toward the center of the floor, while Esperanza headed to the turbolift, saying, "I'm heading up there, Zachary."

"Right."

When Esperanza arrived on the fifteenth floor moments later, her thoughts turning to entertaining and painful ways of torturing Bera chim Gleer, Sivak gave her an odd look. "The president is busy."

And Sivak is just *what I need this morning.* "Zachary told me she was free at noon."

"It will not be 1200 for three more minutes. And even then, she only has ten minutes before—"

The door then slid open to reveal the secretaries of technology and transportation, as well as their assistants.

The former, a short Androsian woman named Forzrat, was saying, ". . . and that's not even taking power consumption into account. We just don't know if it's feasible."

Following them out the door, the president asked, "Isn't that kinda the point of a study, to give us the opportunity to stop living in ignorance about this sort of thing?"

"Yes, ma'am."

"Well, there you go. Take a look at it, that's all I'm saying."

"Thank you, Madam President."

Esperanza nodded to the four of them as they passed her and headed toward the turbolifts. The transportation secretary, a tall Berellian named Iliop, said to her, "We need to talk about Rigel later."

"Set it up with Zachary."

Looking inquisitively at Esperanza, President Bacco asked, "You need me?"

"I just finished with Ross about Klorgat."

Her face fell. "Great. C'mon in."

As the pair entered, Sivak said, "Madam President, you have only ten minutes before—"

"I beat you bloody with a large blunt object?"

"You are, of course, welcome to use Ms. Piñiero to hit me, ma'am, but that does not change the fact that you have the exterior secretary in ten minutes."

Smiling, the president said, "Fine." Looking at Esperanza, she said, "Can you believe what Diaz did?"

Esperanza knew that Taisha Diaz was the manager of the Pioneers, and she knew the Pioneers had played a game yesterday against the Salavar Stars, with whom they were in a dogfight for first place. Beyond that, of course, she knew nothing, but she had faith in the president's capacity for filling her in, so she played along. "I can't believe it, no."

"It's a tie game, you've got the heart of the order coming up, why the hell don't you put Sookdeo in?"

"It's a mystery to me, ma'am."

The president shook her head as she went to sit in one of the guest chairs. "I mean, really, what's to be gained by saving Sookdeo for the eighth or ninth? And even if you are, why bring in Gordimer? The Stars've been handing him his head all year, and sure enough, he gives up six runs before Diaz brings in Sookdeo to stop the bleeding, but by then it's too late. Now we're two games out instead of tied. Drives me nuts. What did Ross have to say?"

Taking this as a signal that the president was done with her daily harangue on the subject of the Pioneers' inability to hold onto first place this season, Esperanza handed her the padd, then took the seat opposite hers. "The S.C.E. is now definitively saying that it was Admiral Mendak."

Accepting the padd without looking at it, the president's eyes went wide. "It *was* the Romulans?"

"No, ma'am—it was Admiral Mendak."

President Bacco snorted. "So we're buying Tal'Aura's assurances now?"

"Not necessarily, but as that report indicates, we know that it's definitely Mendak himself, not anyone else."

After looking at the padd for half a second and frowning, the president then looked up at Esperanza with a slightly irritated expression. "Let's assume, just for the hell of it, that I know as much about engineering as you do about baseball."

Esperanza smiled. "What it boils down to is that Mendak's fleet put in for repairs during the Dominion War at Starbase 375. The engineers who worked on the ships noticed something different about the *Rhliailu*, which is Mendak's flagship: Its disruptors were tuned differently to get maximum power out of them."

"Why only Mendak's ship? I mean, if they could be re-tuned to be more powerful, especially in a war—"

"The engineer asked the same question. Turns out there was a design flaw in the *Rhliailu* when it came off the yard. The disruptor couplings are misaligned, to the point where they have to keep the temperature in the disruptor chamber down around a hundred degrees Kelvin because it overheats so badly. They tried it on a few other ships, and they all either had a complete power blowout or the whole system just shut down automatically. For whatever reason, they couldn't reproduce it. It was great for Mendak, though—it's why he was able to win at Brasîto—but it also means that the *Rhliailu*'s disruptors leave a distinct signature. That is to say, *if* you know where to look."

"And the S.C.E. knew where to look?"

Esperanza nodded. "If it had been a regular Romulan ship that did it, the evidence wouldn't have been conclusive, since regular Romulan disruptors leave a resonance pattern that's pretty similar to what you'd get with tectonic stresses. I'm willing to bet that the original plan counted on that."

The president leaned back in her chair. "Great. Well, this technobabble all sounds great, but you know what this means?"

"It means you need to talk to Tal'Aura right away—*before* you talk to the Klingons."

"No."

"Ma'am—"

"I'll talk to the Romulans, but I'm not going behind the Klingons' back with this. Set up a meeting for tomorrow after the council session with both K'mtok *and* the new Romulan ambassador. What's his name?"

"Kalavak."

"Right. This way the Klingons can't say we cut them out." She gave a half-smile, then she added, "And they'll be too busy yelling at each other to yell at me *and* I'm done talking about it in half the time." She sighed. "This is the last thing I need, with the Trinni/ek ready to attack me in my sleep."

Esperanza couldn't help but smile, though she was now even more grateful that she'd kept the Cardassia problem on fourteen. "They're not gonna attack you in your sleep, ma'am. You have bodyguards, remember?"

"That just reassures the crap out of me. You and your boyfriend are sure they'll be fine?"

Sighing, Esperanza said, "Ambassador Morrow is not my boyfriend, ma'am, and I talked to him this morning. He said they seemed a little tired, but eager to make up for their bad first impression."

"After this is all over, you should ask him out. You'd make a cute couple."

"Ma'am—"

"I know about these things, you know. Who do you think got Fred and Ashanté to finally tie the knot?"

"Yes, ma'am, when you're no longer president, you can spend your retirement years as a very successful *yenta.*"

The president laughed. "All right, I've got to talk to Safranski. I'll fill him in on this disaster, too. Mind if I keep this?" She held up the padd.

Esperanza nodded. "I've got a copy. Safranski did good on *ICL.*"

"I missed it. How was T'Vrea?"

"She wasn't—her first officer was on instead."

Again, the president frowned. "That's odd. It's not like T'Vrea's camera-shy."

"I wouldn't worry about it, ma'am. Something could have called the captain away, and she sent her XO."

"Yeah, I guess. All right, let me know when you set things up with Kalavak."

"Of course. Thank you, Madam President."

◆

CHAPTER TWENTY

◆   ◆

YOU KNOW, Ozla Graniv thought, *if I hadn't bothered interviewing Tawna, I'd be back in Paris by now, listening to Kant be snide, filing stories, and generally being happy.*

Instead, she was sitting naked on a crate, in a dank underground room on Deneva that smelled like *avro* dung, with two very large Balduks standing in front of her, aiming disruptor pistols at her head.

They'd been sitting there for about half an hour, ever since the two Balduks had shown up unannounced at her hotel room while she'd been showering. Showing no consideration for—or interest in—her nudity, they'd grabbed her and hauled her to a building on the outskirts of Downriver. Tellingly, no one had batted an eyelash at them.

But then, Ozla had done an exposé on the Orion Syndicate, so she knew that Ihazs, Deneva's local Syndicate boss, controlled dozens of interests on Deneva, and that everyone knew not to mess with his two Balduk bodyguards, even if—*especially* if—they were carrying a naked Trill reporter through a hotel lobby.

I guess I should be grateful that these two are just threatening me. They were content to stand facing her, brandishing their weapons, but never speaking. They didn't sit, either, though there were plenty of crates in the room besides the one she occupied. The room's illumination was dim, provided only by a weak overhead light, so her exact count of the number of crates was approximate at best, though she did try to count all of them by way of distracting herself.

Ozla's estimate of the passage of time was also approximate, but she was pretty sure they had gotten close to forty-five minutes by the time a door opened to reveal a slim Takaran. "Well, well, well," Ihazs said. "If it isn't the infamous Ozla Graniv. It's a pleasure to finally meet you in the flesh."

The Balduks laughed at the bad pun.

"And very nice flesh it is—for a Trill, my dear, you are *very* attractive. If not for those spots and your unfortunate skin tone, you'd make a delectable Takaran. I take it my guards have treated you well?"

"Depends on whether you define grabbing me from the shower as 'well.'"

"Yes, I do apologize for that," Ihazs said with an expansive gesture. "You needn't worry, though. These two have been genetically modified to have no sex drive. It's handy when they're asked to guard Orion women."

Ozla smiled. "I'd point out that it's illegal to perform genetic modifications on Federation citizens—but then, it's also illegal to kidnap people."

"Very true." Ihazs took a seat on another crate. "You've

been quite busy since you arrived on Deneva five weeks ago. Asking all sorts of questions. The last time you were asking questions about the Syndicate, of course, the end result was that lovely series of articles of yours. By the way, I wanted to thank you for those."

That took Ozla aback. *"Thank* me?"

"Yes. It provided a road map to several hull breaches on our ship, as it were." Ihazs waved his arms back and forth across his chest. "We were able to tighten up the organization and get rid of some people who were no longer of use to us—all the while providing the forces of law and order with some handy scapegoats whom we didn't want around anymore anyhow. There was a short-term falloff, of course, but that's to be expected. The price of doing business, and all that." He indicated her with his hand. "And besides all that, it was a most excellent piece of reporting."

Ozla said nothing, though she did contemplate whether or not Ihazs would be able to talk if someone tied his hands.

"And now you're looking into some merchandise that we moved to Tezwa."

"What makes you think that?" Ozla asked with a smile.

Ihazs's polite smile fell. "Do not play stupid with me, Ms. Graniv. It makes me angry, and when I get angry, my guards shoot things. You spoke with Yntral, you spoke with Fiske, you spoke with Tanaa—and brava for being able to hold your breath while being in the same room with *him*, by the way—you spoke with T'l'u'r'w'w'q'a, and you spoke with Argenziano."

Ozla had expected that one or two of her conversations would get back to Ihazs. She was distressed at the fact that all but one of them had.

Spreading his arms, Ihazs said, "I don't know what they

told you, and frankly, I don't care, because I'm about to give you something."

Blinking, Ozla said, "I beg your pardon?"

"Your presence on Deneva, Ms. Graniv, can only result in one of three things. One is that you continue your questioning, giving you the opportunity to expose more about the Syndicate. We've been dealt several severe blows of late, and I do not wish to add to them."

Ozla had heard rumors that the death of a boss named Malic four years earlier had resulted in some problems for the Syndicate, but nothing that she had been able to verify. She wondered if that was what Ihazs was referring to.

Gesticulating as much as ever, Ihazs continued. "The second is that I have you killed. That causes more problems for me, however, as you are a prominent reporter who has already written one exposé of the Syndicate, and who went on from there to being a reporter at the Palais de la Concorde on Earth. You're high-profile, and high-profile deaths tend to bring out law enforcement. Whatever we gain by your death we lose by the subsequent legal scrutiny." Pointing at her again, he said, "Which brings us to option number three. I will tell you what you want to know—or, perhaps, verify what you've already discovered—and then you go on your merry way. Yes, the Syndicate provided the nadion-pulse cannons to Tezwa."

"That much has been public record."

"Yes," Ihazs said with a smile, "but not where we got those cannons. You see, Ms. Graniv, the person who commissioned me to have those cannons delivered some eight years ago was a gentleman named Nelino Quafina, who, at the time the deal was consummated, had just been appointed the secretary of military intelligence by newly elected President Min Zife."

Ozla said nothing, refused to betray any emotion. Shortly after talking to Tawna, she had gone to Olorun Meboras's widow, Yalno. She had already known about her husband's infidelity but had said nothing, in part because she'd wanted to get on with her life, in part because of the good work Tawna was doing with the orphans of Alkam-Zar, who had enough problems without scandal falling down on their benefactor's head. However, Yalno had been more than happy to let Ozla read her husband's diaries, which verified his "pillow talk" with Tawna: As far as the major knew, the Federation had provided weaponry that would allow Tezwa to defend itself against exterior aggression, whether it be the Dominion or the Klingons.

From there, the trail had led her back to Deneva, mostly thanks to the information in Meboras's diaries, which Yalno had let her keep, combined with Ozla's own knowledge of the Orion Syndicate. Most of the sources of her exposé hadn't been mentioned in her articles, and Ihazs's earlier words confirmed that they hadn't found all her sources, since the people who'd been arrested had *not* been the ones who had given up information to Ozla.

"Now then, here is what I want in exchange for providing you with this information." Ihazs started counting off items on his thin fingers. "One, I will let you go free on the condition that you are off Deneva as fast as you can get dressed, pack, and secure a flight off-planet. Two, you do not reveal this particular piece of information unless you can confirm it from another source." Now his tone changed from one of false politeness to very real menace. "If you do so, I *will* have you killed, and damn the consequences."

Ozla swallowed, then cursed herself for betraying that kind of weakness. "Anything else?"

"Remember those setbacks I mentioned? One of them

was the resignation of President Zife. While I never dealt with the esteemed leader himself, of course, I did quite a bit of business with Secretary Quafina. He was one of my best clients, in fact. With Zife out of power—and, I might add, before I was able to receive the final payment for our last shipment to Tezwa—I no longer have that client. When that happened, I took steps to discover who, precisely, was responsible for the removal of President Zife from power."

"Nobody removed him, he resigned." Ozla was starting to see why Zife had taken so radical a step, if he had been involved with this. . . .

Now Ihazs laughed, which prompted the two bodyguards to do likewise. "No no no, my dear Ms. Graniv, it's not that simple. You see, there was no reason for the truth of our little arrangement to become public. If anyone in Zife's office talked, it would mean war between the Federation and the Klingons, plus a scandal on Zife's head, since he knew about the cannons and didn't tell Starfleet or the Klingon Defense Force. If anyone in my organization talked—well, I believe I already outlined the consequences of free talk inside the Syndicate."

Ozla tried not to shiver, which was hard while sitting naked in a dank room while two thugs aimed energy weapons at her. "So who did find out?"

"The only other party involved who had no hidden agenda: Starfleet. One of their admirals, a human named William Ross, forced Zife to resign at phaserpoint."

Now Ozla's head was spinning. "That's ridiculous."

Ihazs laughed. "Of *course* it's ridiculous. Just as ridiculous as the president of the Federation secretly arming an independent world with powerful weapons and sending his own troops, as well as troops from an allied nation, to that world without telling them that those weapons were in place *and* covering it up afterward." Opening his arms wide, he repeated, "Ridiculous."

The room was silent for a moment. Ozla's rear end was starting to ache from sitting exposed on the crate. She was sure she was going to catch something from being in this room.

Ihazs then stood up. "That is all. My guards will escort you back to your hotel. You have been given the terms. If you follow those terms, you will be able to write *quite* a story. If you don't follow those terms, you'll be dead less than twenty-four hours after you violate them." He walked toward the door, stopped, and turned around. "You really are *quite* lovely. A pity about all those spots."

Then he left.

If I didn't need a shower before, I do now, Ozla thought as the Balduks grabbed her by each arm and started to carry her forcibly up the stairs. This time she didn't resist, figuring it would just be easier this way.

I shouldn't have bothered interviewing Tawna. . . .

"Aleph, what's happening here?"

Smiling at Ashanté from across the table in the dining hall on the second floor of the Palais, the chief aide to Councillor Nea of Bolarus said, "I don't know what you're talking about, Ashanté."

Ashanté resisted the urge to throw her salami sandwich in Aleph's face. "Don't play games, I'm not in the mood."

The smile dropped. "Neither am I." Aleph took a bit of her *grakizh* salad. "How long are we supposed to keep pouring water into a sinking boat? Cardassia's a lost cause."

"So what, we should just let the Cardassian government fall apart?"

"One could make the argument that it already has."

Biting down on her sandwich, Ashanté paused to chew, swallow, and collect her thoughts. "Yeah, okay, you can make that argument. But you know how I'd argue back? With facts. Fact number one: The last time the Cardassian government fell apart, they had a big revolution, followed two seconds later by a Klingon invasion and over a year's worth of war against them. Fact number two: They were so demoralized by this that they jumped into the waiting arms of the Dominion. Fact number three: The only reason the war *happened* was because the Dominion had that foothold in the Alpha Quadrant. Do we *really* want to tempt the odds on history repeating itself?"

Aleph gnawed on one of the yellow leaves of her salad. After a moment, she said, "Look, Nea's never been hot on aid to Cardassia in the first place. It's a security risk. Pirates have been raiding the aid ships—if anything, that's gotten worse."

"What about the security risk of not helping them? I can guarantee that as soon as we stop helping, they'll close their borders. Then we won't know what's happening on Cardassia Prime until it's too late. Remember what happened the last time—"

Waving her arms back and forth, Aleph said, "Yes, I heard you the first time." She let out a breath.

Ashanté had saved the biggest for last. "The president's prepared to throw her support behind Nea's infrastructure bill."

Aleph shot Ashanté a suspicious look. "The president's come out against it."

"No, she hasn't."

"She hinted at it very strongly in the speech she gave to the Gatilili Society."

"Hints aren't commitments. What I'm giving you now is one. If Nea votes for aid, President Bacco will endorse infrastructure at next week's session."

"Why next week's?"

"Because this week is pretty crowded, don't you think?"

Aleph smiled again. "And you want to make sure she keeps her end—and to make sure that little promise can also bring in Sanaht, Corvix, Beltane, and Nerramibus."

"If that's possible, I think we'd all be very happy." Ashanté covered a large grin with a sip of her Altair water.

"What is it you want?"

Dogayn had sat in Je'er's office dozens of times as a fellow councillor aide. This was hir first time doing so when s/he was a deputy COS. S/he attributed hir new position to Je'er's reduced enthusiasm for having hir in the office today.

"Doh, I have a lot of work to do, and I—"

"Come *on*, Je'er, Nitram's never given a *targ's* ass about aid to Cardassia. Why's he got the urge to kill it now?"

"He doesn't."

That surprised Dogayn. "He doesn't?"

"No. But he does have the urge to grant the Falric—"

"Oh no," Dogayn said with a wince.

"To grant the Falric—"

"It's not gonna happen," Dogayn said, not letting Je'er finish her sentence.

Je'er was, however, determined. "To grant the Falric Institute's study on demiurgical phenomena."

"It's a crackpot study."

Frowning, Je'er said, "I don't know what that means."

"It's a human word, it means the notion's insane."

The folds of Je'er's skin tightened. "Why, Doh, I'm shocked that you would say such a thing about a Federation councillor."

Dogayn rolled hir eyes. "Don't even *try* that, Je'er, you and I have said worse in our day."

"In the *old* days, when we were equals. Now we're not, and you're not getting anything unless the president supports the Falric Institute grant."

"She's never gonna do that. She's come out against it."

Je'er looked down at her workstation and started studying whatever was on its screen with great interest. "Then I guess you don't want Cardassian aid that badly, do you?"

Dogayn sighed and got up from Je'er's guest chair. "You're no fun anymore, you know that?"

"You switched sides, Doh," Je'er said without looking up from her workstation.

Throwing up hir hands, Dogayn cried, "No, dammit, I didn't 'switch' anything. We're on the *same* side, I'm just on a different part of it. This isn't about 'sides,' anyhow— it's not a game, it's *government*. We're supposed to serve the people, not—"

Now Je'er looked up. "The people of Bre'el IV would be best served by allowing the Falric Institute to study demiurgical phenomena."

"I gotta tell you, Je'er—I don't even know what that means."

"Then you've got no business calling it insane. Now get out of my office, please, I have *real* work to do."

Dogayn stared at a woman s/he would have counted as a friend not a day earlier. *Hell, not an hour earlier.*

Shaking hir head, s/he departed the office without a word.

◆ ◆ ◆

"It's not gonna work."

At Dogayn's words, Esperanza looked up in annoyance at hir and Ashanté. "What's that supposed to mean?"

"We couldn't turn enough people," Ashanté said. "We've committed to Nea's infrastructure bill, but it wasn't enough."

Appalled, Esperanza said, "Tell me that wasn't all you offered?"

"That's all anyone took," Ashanté said. "A couple people bought a general plea of sanity without concessions."

"Nice to know common sense occasionally prevails." Esperanza got up and walked over to her replicator to get an iced tea. "You guys want anything?"

Ashanté shook her head, but Dogayn said, "A *frimlike*, if you could."

"Tea, raspberry, iced, and a *frimlike*, mildly heated."

Dogayn smiled as the replicator glowed, hummed, and provided the two drinks; the Hermat seemed suitably impressed that hir boss knew how s/he preferred hir *frimlike*. Then hir expression grew more serious. "We made plenty of offers, but several people wouldn't budge."

"Or they asked for crazy stuff," Ashanté added.

"Like what?" Esperanza asked as she handed Dogayn hir drink.

Shuddering slightly, Dogayn said, "You don't wanna know."

Esperanza closed her eyes and blew out a breath. "Nitram wanted the demiurgical study?"

Dogayn nodded.

"And Gleer's called in a *lot* of markers," Ashanté said. "He's made this even more his personal mission than Enaren has. I told Strovos we'd lift the tariffs on zenite, and he *still* wouldn't go for it."

Esperanza sat back down at her desk and sipped her iced tea. "That's been Strovos's pet cause since he got elected."

"It's been *every* Ardanan councillor's pet cause for the last hundred years," Ashanté said. "I don't know what Gleer has on Strovos, but it must be pretty good. And he's not the only one Gleer's got in a headlock."

"So where does that leave us?"

Ashanté folded her arms. "Assuming Ontail continues to not show up—and five'll get you ten they'd vote no anyhow—we've only got seventy."

Slamming a fist on her desk hard enough to almost spill her iced tea, Esperanza said, "Dammit! Where are we gonna get seven more votes?"

"Well, I've got a crazy idea," Ashanté said, now unfolding her arms.

Grasping at straws, Esperanza said, "Shoot."

"I was able to convince zh'Faila and C29 Green, and Dogayn was able to turn Govrin, just by the argument that voting no would be bad for the Federation."

Not sure where Ashanté was going with this, Esperanza said, "Right."

"So why not try that trick on Enaren? He's always been fairly reasonable. Maybe he can be convinced."

Esperanza considered the matter. "Yeah, okay, go talk to—"

"It shouldn't be either of us—or you," Ashanté said. "It has to be the president."

"No," Esperanza said emphatically. "It'll be me, but the president doesn't hear about this. Not with Trinni/ek and the Romulans and the Klingons and the Pioneers losing today."

Dogayn frowned. "What does baseball have to do with it?"

"In a perfect world, baseball's the president's safety valve—it's what she uses to distract herself when the nonsense threatens to overwhelm her."

"The problem," Ashanté said, "is that there's too much nonsense there, too. Her favorite team's screwing up."

Dogayn smirked. "Maybe she should find a different hobby."

"Be sure to suggest that," Esperanza said, "and then update your résumé." She hit the intercom. "Zachary, track down Councillor Enaren. Tell him the chief of staff needs to talk to him right away."

"Sure thing."

She looked up at two of her deputies. "You're sure you can't get the seven anywhere else?"

"We'll keep working it," Dogayn said, "but I don't think it'll work. Some people are throwing the argument right back at us."

"What do you mean?"

Dogayn frowned. "Cardassia's already proven they can't be trusted. So why should we even give them the chance?"

"Right," Ashanté said with a sigh, "because the kick-them-while-they're-down theory worked so well in Germany."

"Where's Germany?" Dogayn asked.

Before she could answer, Zachary said over the intercom, *"Esperanza, the councillor can talk to you now—he's en route from Betazed for tomorrow's session."*

Esperanza's eyes widened. "Uh, okay. Get him on standby—I'll let you know when we're ready."

"You want us to help out?" Ashanté asked.

About to say no, Esperanza held back. "Yeah—just you. Dogayn, keep working the councillors, in case this doesn't work."

Dogayn nodded again and left Esperanza's office.

Esperanza looked up at Ashanté. "Ready?"

After taking a very deep breath, Ashanté said, "Yeah. Let's do it." She walked around to stand just behind Esperanza and to her right.

Esperanza opened the intercom. "Put him through, Zachary."

A moment later, the screen on Esperanza's workstation lit up with the bland features of Cort Enaren. He had surprised her when they'd first met a few years earlier. She had heard stories of the member of Betazed's parliament who'd become the leader of the Betazoid resistance after the planet had fallen to the Dominion, and so she had expected someone more—well, impressive. *But then, with a telepathic species, physical characteristics are really the least important.*

"Councillor, thanks for talking to us. You remember my deputy, Ashanté Phiri?"

"Of course." Enaren nodded. *"It's good to see you both. I assume this is about Cardassia."*

Unable to contain a cheeky grin, Esperanza asked, "Your finely honed Betazoid senses tell you that, Councillor?"

Enaren did smile back, though the expression didn't reach his eyes. *"My transport is several light-years from Earth, Esperanza—my telepathy isn't that good. No, I simply heard from my aides. Your deputies aren't exactly being subtle."*

"We don't have time for subtle, Councillor," Ashanté said. "And this aid is too important to lose."

"Important to the Cardassians, perhaps, but I'm more concerned with the people of Betazed. What's left of us, anyhow."

"Sir," Esperanza said, leaning forward in her chair, "I'm aware of Betazed's losses during the war, but—"

"*Are you? Fifteen percent of our population died, Esperanza. They died when the planet was attacked, they died when we drove the Dominion offworld, and they died when they were taken by that Cardassian scientist for genetic experiments.*"

Esperanza winced. She had forgotten that part of the reason for the Dominion's interest in Betazed, as opposed to other Federation planets in that sector. It had been related to the native species' innate telepathy: A Cardassian scientist named Crell Moset had been performing experiments on the Betazoids in an attempt to engineer telepathic Jem'Hadar.

She was also starting to understand a bit of Enaren's motivation. "Councillor, I appreciate what your world went through, but—"

"*I don't think you do, Esperanza.*"

"And I don't think *you* appreciate what's happening on Cardassia right now, sir."

"*I know their government can't hold it together. I know that we've been propping them up for four years and that most of our relief doesn't even get where it's supposed to go.*"

Ashanté said, "The solution to that problem is to improve the delivery methods, not to cut it off altogether. That's like amputating an arm because the pinky finger is infected."

"*I disagree. And a majority of the council agrees with me.*"

Desperately, Esperanza wanted to answer that. *No, Gleer wants to help you give us a hard time, and he's got enough support to make it work.* But it wouldn't be politic to say so. "Councillor, I've been to Cardassia Prime. The ship I served on at the end of the war was part of Captain Sisko's task force that took the planet. Do you have any idea what the Dominion did to that world?"

"Yes—because I was in the capital city of Betazed when the Dominion invaded. I know all about the devastation, about the smoke in the air that chokes you, about people trapped in rubble, about—"

Esperanza could feel her temper starting to fray, so she was grateful when Ashanté interrupted, "Councillor, we can't let our outrage at recent history blind us to the lessons history teaches us."

"Ashanté, I don't need homilies." Enaren then turned back to Esperanza. "And I don't need to play a childish game of my-trauma-is-better-than-yours. What I know is this: Cardassia Prime had three cities rebuilt before one city on Betazed was back to full working operation. Off-world tourism has plummeted, offworld support has been all but nonexistent. My predecessor lost her last election because she had done nothing to get Betazed to become a priority with the Federation. The people have spoken to me, and I am doing their bidding, as is my duty as councillor for Betazed. This conversation is over."

"So what happens to Cardassia now?" Ashanté asked.

"Who knows? And who cares?"

"I can give you a clue. Here on Earth, before the planet was united, we had hundreds of nation-states. One of them, about four hundred and seventy-five years ago, was called Germany. They were at the forefront of one of the world's biggest wars. When they lost, their enemies hit them with massive reparations. They had already lost the war, but then they were considered third-class citizens of the world. A particularly charismatic leader was able to use that to rally the people. He rebuilt them into a superpower within a decade, and that led to an even bigger war. It was one that could've been avoided if the retribution against them hadn't been so harsh the first time."

This time Enaren's smile was genuine—and also one of amused irritation. *"Why is it that humans have the need to analogize someone they disagree with to the most extreme example from their own history? I don't appreciate being compared to Adolf Hitler."*

"I'm not doing that, sir," Ashanté said tightly, "I'm comparing you to David Lloyd George."

"Who?" Enaren asked, his confusion matching Esperanza's.

"He was the British prime minister at the end of that war and was one of those who imposed the reparations on Germany."

Esperanza nodded. "Councillor, this can't be about revenge."

"Why can't it? Do you know what they did, Esperanza? The Jem'Hadar were absolutely brutal, and ruthless, and brooked no resistance. But they were never cruel. They were soldiers, they were doing their duty, but it was never personal. Not so with the Cardassians. They beat people, they raped women, they tortured children—for the fun of it! I have sat by for the last year since I was elected to the council and said nothing, because the aid was already in place, but now—now, when I'm in a position to do something about it, I will not stand by and help those—"

"Children?" Esperanza spoke in a quiet voice. "Elderly? Sick, infirm people whose only crime was to be unlucky enough to be born at a time that would leave them alive during the worst period in Cardassian history? Those soldiers did horrible things to your world, yes—and they did it under orders from a government that *we drove away*. The ones paying the price aren't the soldiers who ravaged your world, Councillor, they're helpless people who need our help." Esperanza winced at the way that sentence sounded, but there was no taking it back now. "If we abandon them—"

"I swear to you, Esperanza, if you try to tell me that I become no better than they are, I will terminate this conversation."

Since Enaren had said this conversation was over several minutes ago, Esperanza chose to have some hope.

Ashanté said, "Sir, if you truly believe that you *are* better than them, then prove it. When the house next door to you is burning, you don't deny them an extinguisher. If we're to live up to what we stand for, then we have to help *everyone.* After Praxis exploded, it would've been easy to let the Klingon Empire fall to pieces. But we didn't, and we gained a strong ally where we used to have an implacable foe. One day, Cardassia could be strong again, only this time as a valuable ally. The galaxy's getting smaller every day. Between the Bajoran wormhole and Project *Voyager,* it's gotten even smaller the past decade. We have to—"

"Enough." But Esperanza noticed a different tone to Enaren's voice. *"I'll withdraw the resolution to deny aid."*

Esperanza blinked. *That was too easy.* "Councillor—"

"I know how to read people, Esperanza, even when I can't actually read their thoughts. And I can see how much this means to both of you, and you don't have any personal stake in this. It isn't even a matter of loyalty to the president—you both genuinely believe what you're saying." He smiled wryly. *"And you didn't make me any offers of concessions."*

Softly, Esperanza said, "We know how important this is to *you* as well, Councillor. We wouldn't insult you by trying to buy your vote."

"But you will buy Nea's."

Esperanza grinned. "We are still politicians, Councillor, much as we might wish it otherwise. And that means we have a responsibility—even to those who used to be our foes."

"I suppose we do." Enaren sighed. *"Thank you both for talking to me. I'll be on Earth in about three hours."*

With that, he signed off.

Esperanza looked up at Ashanté.

"What?" Ashanté asked.

"I don't know what impressed me more, that you had the name David Lloyd George at your beck and call, or that you actually used *implacable* in a sentence."

Ashanté laughed. "I always liked that word, what can I tell you? As for the first thing—I'm married to the speech-writer for one of the most trivia-obsessed politicians in the Federation. You pick stuff like that up."

"I guess so."

Moving toward the door, Ashanté said, "I'll call Dogayn off. Hey, we ready for tomorrow?"

"The Trinni/ek?"

Ashanté nodded.

Esperanza felt herself deflating. "How the hell should I know?"

✦

CHAPTER TWENTY-ONE

✦ ✦

AMBASSADOR COLTON MORROW had thought this new as-signment would be easy.

Previously, the Diplomatic Corps had sent him to Delta Sigma IV. On that world, two species, the Bader and the

Dorset, had managed to live in harmony, despite being at odds elsewhere in the galaxy. As a result, that world was part of the Federation, something neither the Bader nor the Dorset could say nor were likely to anytime soon.

Unfortunately, something had gone wrong. Both species had been suffering shortened lifespans, and an attempt to remedy that had wound up bringing out the worst impulses in Bader and Dorset alike. By the time a solution had been found by a Starfleet vessel assigned to the situation, the entire planet had practically been on fire.

Still, the day had been saved in the end, thanks in no small part to the efforts of Colton Morrow.

In light of that, he had thought the assignment to work out the details of establishing diplomatic relations with the Trinni/ek would be a comparative walk in the park—but also a major step forward in his career. This was a first contact with a new species, the gold standard for diplomatic work in the Federation. Morrow was in a position where he could make history. On top of that, Captain T'Vrea's reports all indicated a species that was the textbook example of the type of people the Federation liked to deal with, and who might eventually join up.

Until they'd gone insane in the Roth Dining Room.

This time, though, the signs were better. Speaker Ytri/ol had made an effort to be communicative during the journey here, though he had seemed much more tired.

Now Morrow was accompanying them into the council chamber on the first floor of the Palais after just beaming down from orbit. This time the Starfleet escort vessel had been the *Hood.* Captain DeSoto had been a fine host, and he was now walking alongside Morrow, Ytri/ol, and the delegation.

DeSoto leaned over and whispered to Morrow as they

approached the door to the huge chamber, "Don't worry, it'll be fine."

Morrow nodded. DeSoto's support had been very helpful. Morrow knew the man's war record—the *Hood* had suffered a great deal during the Dominion War—but De-Soto showed no signs of wear and tear. He was friendly and affable, and just the person to keep the Trinni/ek—who were apprehensive about their second trip to Earth—from worrying overmuch.

If only it worked on me.

As they entered, Morrow noticed that the room was packed. Most of the hundred and fifty-four councillors seemed to be present, seated on either side of the large pathway in the center of the room. President Bacco stood at her podium, smiling. In the back of the room, the gallery was packed with reporters, civilians, some government staffers—

—including Esperanza, who smiled at him as he entered.

Morrow hadn't expected to see her here, but he was glad for it. He was really growing to like the chief of staff.

"If you start drooling, it'll be *real* embarrassing," De-Soto whispered to him.

Trying to keep his dignity, Morrow whispered back, "I don't know what you're talking about."

"Right. Those diplomatic skills may need a little refining there, Colton."

Morrow said nothing, as Ytri/ol came to a stop at the center of the speaker's floor.

Bacco said, "The podium recognizes the delegation from Trinni/ek, as well as Federation Ambassador Colton Morrow and Starfleet Captain Robert DeSoto."

"Thank you, Madam President." Ytri/ol's voice sounded even weaker than it had on the *Hood.* "First, I must—I must offer the humblest apologies to the people of the Federation for the rather—embarrassing display that my staff and I put on in this—in this building three months ago."

I don't like the way he sounds. Morrow shot a look of concern at DeSoto, who returned it. They both started to inch closer to the speaker.

"We very—very much—" The speaker's breathing was becoming labored now. "—wish to—to open—"

Three of the delegates collapsed. A gasp shot through the room even as DeSoto ran to the one who fell first.

"I'm sor—" Ytri/ol wasn't able to get the word out before he, too, collapsed, as did the final aide.

Slapping his combadge, DeSoto said, "Medical emergency in the council chambers, five Trinni/ek have collapsed, repeat, five Trinni/ek have collapsed."

The guards at the door were also summoning people. Nobody would be beaming in, Morrow knew, as the chambers were shielded against transporters.

Moments later, six people in Starfleet uniforms ran in, and Morrow recognized one of them: Dr. Catherine Papadimitriou, the chief medical officer on the *Hood.* The other five were navigating gurneys into the chamber. Moments after that, two more people entered, both dressed in blue lab coats emblazoned with a caduceus, indicating that they were also medical personnel.

"Somebody talk to me," President Bacco said after a tense moment as two doctors examined the five Trinni/ek forms with medical tricorders while the others assisted.

The civilian, a Rhandaarite male, said, "I'm not sure what to make of this."

"I am." Papadimitriou had been kneeling by Ytri/ol, but now she stood and addressed the podium. "Something has shut down their peripheral nervous systems."

The other doctor sounded dubious as he asked, "How can you be sure?"

"I can't—but that's what the indicators are based on, from what I've studied of them on the way here from the *Hood.*" Papadimitriou turned back to the podium. "Madam President, the best nearby medical facility is on Starbase 1. Request permission to transport the patients there."

Bacco, to her credit, didn't hesitate. "Go."

Morrow and DeSoto helped the others load the five patients onto the gurneys, as did the guards. As they did so, the Rhandaarite said, "Are you sure they're safe for transport?"

"Transporting has no effect on the nervous system." Papadimitriou didn't look up from her tricorder as she spoke.

"Of most humanoid species," the Rhandaarite said. "They beamed down right before they collapsed. Maybe that is responsible for their condition."

Papadimitriou still didn't look up. "Maybe pigs'll fly out of my butt, but I'm not holding my breath. Right now, the best course of action is to get these people to Starbase 1." Now she looked up, even as the gurneys were being scooted down the hall to the turbolift to take them to the second-floor transporter bay. The guards had already cleared the way, and three empty 'lifts were waiting for them. "Unless you think the Hôpital V'gran is a better facility. Speak now, Doctor."

The Rhandaarite, who was apparently from the nearby hospital in question, shook his head, even as Papadimitriou got into the elevator with Ytri/ol. Morrow and DeSoto got into the second one with two of the delegates.

"What do you think happened?" DeSoto asked.

Morrow sighed. "My career coming to an end?"

DeSoto smiled. "I meant to the Trinni/ek."

"Do I look like a doctor?"

"You look like someone killed your pet."

Morrow sighed as the doors to the turbolift opened onto the second floor. The two medtechs navigated the gurneys out. "That's twice the Trinni/ek have done this—and *I* was the one who pushed the president to give them another shot. This isn't my finest hour as a diplomat." As they walked, the other gurneys came out of their 'lifts and moved to the transporter bay.

"Well, it could be worse," DeSoto said philosophically as they watched the five gurneys being transported to the large starbase in orbit of Earth.

As they stepped onto the platform for their own transport, Morrow asked, "How could it be worse?"

"They could be dead."

Morrow's reply was lost in the transporter effect.

It took all of Ambassador K'mtok's willpower to keep from wrecking the room in which he sat.

Not that it mattered, since if his willpower failed, he was sure that the four armed guards standing at the doors to the room would not hesitate to shoot him down where he stood if he tried that.

He turned in his chair to glower at Ambassador Kalavak. The Romulan man simply stared at the curtained window. K'mtok was grateful that the curtains were down, as he found human architecture to be intensely dull. He had specifically requested that his offices in the Klingon embassy have no exterior windows.

If he couldn't wreck the room, K'mtok would have been happy to kill the Romulan ambassador, just on general principles. He didn't know this new ambassador very well.

It had taken the Romulans six months to appoint a new ambassador to replace T'Kala after her cowardly suicide—*only a Romulan would find honor in taking one's own life,* he thought with disgust—so this one had only been on the job a few weeks. T'Kala had, at least, been as worthy a foe as a Romulan could be. He wondered if this one would prove as able. *I doubt it.*

Finally, the doors slid open to reveal the Federation president. "Sorry I'm late, but there was a bit of a problem with the Trinni/ek."

K'mtok had no interest in the doings of aliens. He rose from his chair; the Romulan did the same. "The High Council *demands* to know Starfleet's findings on Klorgat IV!"

Bacco walked over to her desk and said, "K'mtok, good to see you, too. I don't think you've met Ambassador Kalavak."

Kalavak spoke in a voice that K'mtok immediately classified as mewling. "The pleasure is, I'm sure, entirely the ambassador's."

"Unlikely," K'mtok said with a growl.

Now standing behind her desk, with her hands palmdown on its surface, Bacco said, "Gentlemen—and believe me, I'm using that term *very* loosely—please keep in mind that you're in *my* office and that I've got four armed guards in here who know five hundred different ways of killing people, and that's *before* you put phasers in their hands, and also that they work for me. Now both of you sit down."

"Madam President," K'mtok began.

"Do we have to go three rounds on who gives the orders in this room again, Mr. Ambassador? Sit *down.*"

K'mtok sat down, but not before he gave Kalavak another growl.

After they sat, Bacco did the same. "To answer your question, Mr. Ambassador, we have definitive proof that

Admiral Mendak—or, at the very least, the *Rhliailu*—destroyed Klorgat IV's moon."

Somehow, K'mtok resisted the urge to stand up again, as he knew it would be unwise. But he did bare his teeth at Kalavak. "All along, we knew that this was the work of a cowardly *petaQ*. We will—"

Kalavak interrupted, speaking to Bacco and ignoring K'mtok. "Admiral Mendak is a criminal whose actions are not sanctioned by the Romulan government."

Livid at the Romulan's words, as well as the fact that he'd both interrupted and ignored K'mtok, the Klingon bellowed, "You have been spinning those lies for some time now, Romulan!"

"They are not lies, Madam President, regardless of what *some* might believe." Kalavak was still ignoring K'mtok. "Praetor Tal'Aura has consistently condemned the admiral's actions, and had called for his execution."

"*'Had'* called?" Bacco said before K'mtok could rail against the Romulan again.

K'mtok reined in his temper. *This* toDSaH *is trying to provoke a response by ignoring me, and I will not play his childish games.*

"It is no longer necessary to call for Admiral Mendak's execution, because Admiral Mendak is dead." Kalavak picked a padd off the couch next to him, which K'mtok hadn't noticed before. "I have here a message that the admiral sent to Praetor Tal'Aura." He rose from the couch and handed the padd to Bacco.

To K'mtok's surprise, Bacco did not view it at first. Instead, she said to K'mtok, "Mr. Ambassador, would you like to look at this with me?"

K'mtok's instinct was to say that he had no interest in viewing Romulan propaganda, but he recognized that

Bacco was treating him as an equal and showing that the Federation and the empire were partners in this. So he got up and walked to the president's desk.

She activated the padd, and the smug face of Mendak appeared. In a deep, resonant voice, he said, *"My name is Lhian Mendak. For eighty-five years, I served as a loyal Romulan soldier. In recent times, however, I found that I could no longer pledge my loyalty to the Romulan government. The coup d'état by the Reman traitor Shinzon and the subsequent rise to power of his agent, Tal'Aura, exposed a corruption on Romulus that I could not tolerate. For the good of the empire, I refused to pledge my loyalty to a regime that would allow Klingons into our midst, and to grant concessions to Remans. To that end, I destroyed one of the moons that orbits Klorgat IV. For this, and for other actions, I have been condemned and branded a criminal. But I will not give Tal'Aura and her corrupt regime the satisfaction of arresting me, nor of executing me after a mockery of a trial. Instead, my crew and I choose to die as Romulans."*

K'mtok had to admit that it sounded very convincing. He also didn't believe a word of it.

Kalavak added, "The message was found on the *Rhliailu*, which was adrift in the Vorni system alongside the rest of Mendak's fleet. Everyone on all four ships was dead by their own honor blades." The ambassador then stood up and, for the first time, looked at K'mtok. "The praetor has asked me to convey the deepest apologies to the Klingon Empire for the actions of this madman. Our only regret is that he cannot be extradited to you to be tried on Qo'noS, and for that, we also apologize. You can rest assured that this Romulan government will do nothing to impede the relocation of the Remans to their new home."

With that, Kalavak turned on his heel and left the president's office.

Whirling on Bacco, K'mtok said, "Surely, Madam President, you do not believe these lies!"

"Of course not, K'mtok, don't be an idiot." Bacco got up. "Gotta give 'em credit, though—they played it *just* right. Let Mendak play the rebel for a few months, do some damage to Tal'Aura's enemies while she's condemning it the whole time, then, when he gets caught, sacrifice him to make yourself look good. Meanwhile, the actual goal of making a mess of Klorgat's been accomplished—and, best of all, there's not a damn thing we can do about it."

K'mtok had been about to compliment the president on her perspicacity, but the last phrase irritated him. "There are *many* things we can do about it, Madam President, starting with making war on the Romulans!"

"Based on what? The actions of someone the Romulan government's been condemning for six months? Sure, we *know* they're full of it, but we can't prove it. I can't take this to the Federation council and get them to approve this as a reason to go to war."

Now K'mtok smiled. "The High Council is not so strict in its need for motivation to do battle, Madam President."

"Yeah, but if you get into it, then we're obligated to either go along with you or pull out of the Accords, neither of which is an option I'm thrilled with. And let's just say we do manage to get everyone to agree—who are we fighting? Tal'Aura? What about the rest of the military? They're not all on her side, and not all the ones who are can be considered fanatically loyal. And what about the Romulan people who'll be caught in the middle of this? And then there's the question of fighting forces. We've finally got Starfleet back on an exploration footing, and the Defense Force isn't back up to full battle readiness, either."

K'mtok wanted to answer at least some of those questions, but the human refused to let him get a word in. He did, however, have to concede her last point. The end of the war hadn't meant the end of battle for the empire, and what with the coup against Martok right after the war, and battles at San-Tarah, Elabrej, Kinshaya Major, Tezwa, and others, the Defense Force was in no position to wage a prolonged conflict in a territory as large as the Romulan Empire.

Bacco wasn't finished. "Besides all that, the Romulan ambassador stood here in my office and *apologized* to you. When was the last time a Romulan official did that to a Klingon official?"

His teeth now grinding, K'mtok said, "I do not know."

"Me either, and the two of us are professional politicians whose job it is to know stuff like that, so I'd say the odds are pretty good on it being extremely rare." Bacco leaned back in her chair and let out a long breath. "Look, K'mtok, it's up to you guys. If you want to go to war on the basis of what all the evidence indicates is a rogue attack, the perpetrators of which have killed themselves, and for which the people you want to go to war with have apologized, then knock yourselves out. But you need to tell Martok and the High Council that there is absolutely no way you'll get support from the Federation. Even if I was inclined to argue for it—and, quite frankly, I'm not—I won't be able to convince the hundred and fifty people on the first floor of it, because I don't have a good argument to make. And if you do go to war without us, we *have* to pull out of the Accords, and that won't be good for anyone."

After a moment, K'mtok said, "I will convey this information to the High Council."

"Do me a favor?"

That request surprised K'mtok. "What?"

"Convey what I actually *said* this time." She stood up and came around to the other side of the desk. The human woman was half a head shorter than K'mtok, but somehow she managed to look him right in the eyes. "I didn't need to have you in here when I talked to Kalavak. In fact, my chief of staff said I shouldn't have. But you *are* our allies, and you were the ones who were attacked on Klorgat, so I wanted to make sure that you were included in all of this."

K'mtok sneered at her. "On what are you basing this ridiculous notion that I will not—"

"Cut the crap, K'mtok, I know that you didn't convey my precise words to the High Council when you and I did our little dance back in March. So right here, right now, I want your *word* that you will tell the High Council *exactly* what I told you."

"You insult me by implying that my word is necessary."

Bacco smiled. "Oh, I'm not implying a damn thing, I'm coming out and saying it. And you're insulting *me* by trying to convince me that it *isn't* necessary. Now then, please, may I have your word that you will pass on my message to the Great Hall? Not a version of what I told you that's been altered in order to provide a better political position for your allies on the High Council, but *exactly what I said.* Because if I can't trust you to do even that much, then I'm just gonna have to go over your head to Chancellor Martok. As I recall, it was my predecessor doing precisely that that led to *your* predecessor being replaced."

K'mtok stared at Bacco for several seconds. The human continued to stare right back at him.

Then he reared his head back and laughed. "Well played, Madam President, well played. You manipulate the pieces on the board like a master *zha* player."

Bacco frowned at that. "I don't know that game."

"Perhaps one day I will teach it to you." K'mtok wondered if the president knew the compliment he paid her by making the offer. Few non-Klingons were worthy of even knowing of *klin zha*, much less being taught how to play it.

Apparently she had some notion, for she inclined her head slightly and said, "I would be honored."

"As for the rest of it, I give you my word as a Klingon— the High Council will have your *precise* words."

"Thank you, K'mtok. That's all I ask."

Oh, that is not all *you ask*, K'mtok thought, but he did not say so aloud. This president was no fool.

However, she wasn't done. "One other thing, Mr. Ambassador."

That got K'mtok's attention—she hadn't called him that since the Romulan left the room. "Yes?"

"Please also tell Martok that I think it would be best for both the Federation and the empire if he and I met—perhaps on a neutral planet?—to discuss the future of both our nations."

Typical Federation, K'mtok thought with a sigh. *Their solution to everything is to* talk. *It grows wearisome.* However, he said, "I will pass that request along to the chancellor. Is there anything else?"

"No, that's it."

"Thank you, Madam President."

"*Ambassador Morrow, please report to the infirmary.*"

Colton Morrow sighed and drained the rest of his *allira* punch. Slamming the mug down on the table, he slowly departed the Starbase 1 lounge and meandered down the curved corridor toward the turbolift that would deliver him to the infirmary on the other side of the station.

It isn't going to be good news. I know it isn't going to be good news. It's been a week since Ytri/ol and his party collapsed in the council chambers, and there hasn't been any good news yet. If it was good news, they'd call me directly over the open channel instead of just paging me. If they need me in the room, it's because they need to consult with me about something they haven't figured out or to give me bad news. Neither of those options is palatable.

He arrived in the spacious starbase infirmary and went back to the office of Dr. Rebecca Emmanuelli, the chief medical officer of Starbase 1. Already waiting for him were Captain DeSoto and Dr. Papadimitriou from the *Hood;* Chirurgeon Ghee P'Trell, the head of Starfleet Medical; and Emmanuelli herself, sitting at her desk. On the screen behind her, he could see the lovely features of Esperanza Piñiero, obviously calling from her office in the Palais.

Under other circumstances, he'd be pleased to see the chief of staff's face, but this told him that it was a briefing for her, and he doubted there was any good news to tell her.

"Mr. Ambassador," Emmanuelli said, "thanks for joining us. I think you know everyone here."

Morrow nodded. "What's happening?"

"Any number of things," Esperanza said. *"But the reason why I called is that I just got a call from Second Speaker Rale/ar. She's accusing us of kidnapping Speaker Ytri/ol and his delegation."*

"That's ridiculous," DeSoto muttered.

However, Morrow could only sigh. "That's to be expected, honestly. I mean, think about it from their perspective. They weren't here, so they didn't see how Ytri/ol and the others behaved last time. Sure, they've heard reports, but trust me when I tell you that the way they were acting was *completely* out of character. I wouldn't be surprised if Rale/ar thinks we just made it all up."

"Why would they think we'd do that?" Papadimitriou asked.

"We're new to them," Esperanza said. *"Their only exposure to us was one ship and a couple of politicians."*

"So they leap straight to we're-deceiving-them?" Papadimitriou sounded incredulous.

"Not straight," Morrow said, "but it's a short jump from what happened last week to this."

"Regardless of the reasons, this has just become a major interstellar incident, if it wasn't already, and I need you guys to tell me you've made some progress."

"Not much," Emmanuelli said with a sigh. "We've stabilized them, but their nervous systems have practically gone inactive."

"Can we send them back to Trinni/ek?"

"I'm not entirely sure."

"Actually," DeSoto said, "we may have something."

"We do?" Morrow said with surprise.

P'Trell then spoke up. A Caitian, he nonetheless had an Andorian honorific for a physician. Morrow wondered what the story there was, but now wasn't the time to ask. P'Trell said, "This morning, I ran a second search to see if there were any similar cases. I was aware that Catherine had already run such a search last week, but I thought it should be tried again, with wider search parameters."

"And you found something?" Morrow asked, then realized it was unnecessary. *I'm letting this get to me.*

"Yes, although not because of my expanded parameters, but rather because a similar case has been entered into the records since Catherine's check last week."

Papadimitriou smirked. "I wasn't offended, Ghee. Honestly, I was hoping you'd find something I missed."

"Where was this case?" Esperanza asked, getting everyone back on track.

"That's the fun part," DeSoto said. "It was on the *Io*."

Morrow blinked. "Their nervous systems have shut down?"

"Not quite," Papadimitriou said. "Just the opposite."

Still confused, Morrow started, "I don't—"

Emmanuelli came to his rescue. "As far as we can tell, the peripheral nervous systems of the Trinni/ek are operating at a lower level than they should, not reacting to stimulus properly. The *Io* crew, including Captain T'Vrea, are suffering from the exact opposite problem: their peripheral nervous systems are overloaded, being stimulated all out of proportion to their surroundings."

Papadimitriou added, "They're losing control of their motor functions—arms flailing, legs buckling, joints turning, all for no good reason."

DeSoto said, "So we contacted the *Io* and their chief engineer—who is, by the way, the only senior officer on the ship who's not incapacitated, and she's still pretty sick—and they did a long-range scan of the one thing that both cases have in common."

"Trinni/ek."

Nodding to Esperanza, DeSoto said, "That's right."

Papadimitriou picked up the ball. "Based on the *Io*'s scans, their sun gives off some kind of magnetic field that plays merry hell with the peripheral nervous systems of most carbon-based life-forms. The *Io* chief engineer's a Nasat, and they're more resistant to that kind of tampering."

"I don't get it," Esperanza said, *"if it's so inimical—"*

P'Trell said, "The Trinni/ek developed an immunity to the magnetic field that eventually grew into a dependency. They were able to adjust to the field, to the point where

they can't live without it. Their PNSes have grown sufficiently accustomed to the extra stimulus that it's how it has
to function."

Morrow nodded, as several conversations with Ytri/ol and
other Trinni/ek came back to him. "That actually fits. Esperanza, remember that collection of folktales they sent us?"

Esperanza frowned a moment. *"Oh, right, the legends
about the landers."*

"Landers?" DeSoto asked.

"The Trinni/ek aren't from that solar system," Morrow
said. "Their ancestors left their homeworld when their sun
was about to go nova. They don't have a lot of records from
the time of the landers—the people who first colonized the
world—because the early days were so difficult, and they
were more concerned with surviving in their new home."

Emmanuelli whistled. "If they had to go through what
the *Io* crew's going through now, I can see why keeping
records wasn't high on their list of things to do."

P'Trell nodded. "The adjustment period would have
been lengthy and brutal."

*"All right then, someone please tell me that the solution
is as simple as letting them go home."*

Smiling, Papadimitriou said, "The solution is as simple as
letting them go home. In fact, the sooner we do it, the better. I'm worried their PNSes might stop working altogether."

*"Do it, please. I'll let the president and the second
speaker know that we're sending them back."*

"What about the *Io* crew?" Morrow asked.

"As long as they stay away from Trinni/ek," P'Trell said,
"the effects should reverse themselves in due time."

Papadimitriou asked, "Rebecca, can you prep them for
transport? I'll need to get the *Hood*'s sickbay ready."

"Of course." Emmanuelli got up and went out the door toward her biobeds.

"Papadimitriou to *Hood*," the doctor said with a tap of her combadge. "One to beam up."

As she dematerialized, DeSoto said to Esperanza, "We can ship out as soon as the Trinni/ek are on board."

"I'm going with them," Morrow said. "Now that we know what the problem is, we can try to work out some way of making this relationship work without subjecting anyone to the destruction of their nervous system."

"*Sounds like a plan.*" Esperanza smiled when she said that. Morrow really liked her smile.

"May I make a suggestion?" P'Trell said.

"*Shoot.*"

"Silicon-based life-forms would not be affected by the magnetic field of the Trinni/ek sun."

"That could work." Morrow recalled some recent reports from a sector not far from Trinni/ek. "We might be able to use the Strata as a go-between. They're a silicon-based species Starfleet discovered three years ago. It's been slow going—the Strata have a pretty weird notion of time—but we've got a good relationship with them, and we might be able to convince them to help us out here."

"*Definitely worth a shot. Try to get in touch with the Strata from the* Hood."

He grinned. "Will do. We'll keep you posted."

She grinned right back. "*You'd better. Do a job, Colton.*"

"I will."

Esperanza signed off.

DeSoto just stared at Morrow.

"What?" Morrow asked defensively.

"You're drooling again."

OCTOBER 2380

---

*"I have come to the conclusion that politics are
too serious a matter to be left to the politicians."*
—Charles de Gaulle

CHAPTER TWENTY-TWO

WHEN HIS ROOMMATE activated the viewscreen in the Academy dorm room they both shared, Cadet Casey Goodwin had to forcibly keep himself from throwing his padd at Cadet Jeremy McCall. The only thing that really stopped him was the surety that the padd would be damaged upon impact with McCall's thick head.

"What the hell're you doing?"

"*ICL*'s on."

Banging his head against the headboard of his bunk, Goodwin said, "Oh, for the love of kimchee, McCall. Do you *have* to watch that show every week?"

"I don't know, Goodwin, do you have to bitch and moan about it every time I do? And what does that *mean*, anyhow?"

"What does what mean?"

"'For the love of kimchee.' You do know that kimchee is—"

"Cole slaw, yes, I just—" He sighed. "It's something my mother says all the time, and I picked it up."

McCall shook his head. "You've got a weird family."

"I'm fully aware of that, McCall, having, y'know, grown up with them—and also having applied to Starfleet Academy and traveled across six solar systems to Earth from Alpha Proxima II for the express purpose of getting very far away from them."

"Unless you give me a very good reason not to, I'm watching *ICL* now."

"I don't suppose researching my final project for Professor Mlikk's first contact class constitutes a very good reason."

Smiling, McCall said, "Maybe they'll talk about Trinni/ek. That counts, right?"

Goodwin gave up even trying. "Just put the damn thing on, already."

McCall put the viewer on. Goodwin saw the Kriosian host, flanked on her left by an older human man in civilian clothes who looked eerily familiar, on her right by a Tellarite and a Betazoid (or a human with unnaturally black eyes). On a screen between the old human and the Kriosian was an elderly Andorian who looked a lot like President Thelian.

"Good evening. This is *Illuminating the City of Light,* I'm your host, Velisa. It's been one year since the election prompted by President Min Zife's surprise resignation was held, leaving Nan Bacco as winner and president of the United Federation of Planets, defeating Ktarian Special Emissary Fel Pagro in a hotly contested election. Tonight, we will look at the first year of the Bacco presidency, what's been done right, what's been done wrong, and what we can expect for the next three years.

"With me tonight to discuss these issues are Rina Tran, chief aide to Councillor Sanaht of Janus VI; Kav glasch Vokrak, the Palais correspondent from the Tellarite News Service; former Starfleet admiral and author of *Knowledge Isn't Always Power: My Life Among the Stars,* Gregory Quinn; and, remotely from his home on Andor, former President Thelianaresth th'Vorothishria. Welcome, all of you."

As the guests thanked Velisa, Goodwin's eyes went wide. "That *is* Thelian. Son of a bitch."

"I didn't think he was still alive."

Chuckling, Goodwin said, "Look at him—I'm not so sure he is."

"Thought Quinn looked familiar," McCall said. "His picture's in the big hall. He was superintendent here for a while before they moved him over to operations. Then that parasite mess hit and he retired."

"You read his book?"

"Please—like I care about some old admiral's war stories. I get enough of that just walking around here. 'Sides, it's got a stupid title."

"This from someone who willingly watches a show called *Illuminating the City of Light*."

Velisa moved on to her first question, which Goodwin missed, but he assumed it was directed at one of the panelists and that it was about Bacco's first year, since the Betazoid, Tran, spoke. Goodwin was now sure she was a Betazoid, since she was an aide to Councillor Sanaht. Though the Horta could speak through vocoders, it was more comfortable for them to communicate with telepaths; all of Sanaht's staff who weren't fellow Horta were Betazoids. Goodwin only knew this because he'd had to study the council for a government class last term.

"I have to say that I'm not all that impressed," Tran said. "I think President Bacco has proven herself incapable of dealing with the larger issues of the presidency after serving only one planet for so long. The Federation's a big place, and it takes a lot to run it."

Goodwin rolled his eyes. "Oooh, great wisdom there. 'The Federation's a big place.' For the love of kimchee . . ."

Velisa asked, "What, exactly, do you think she's done wrong?"

Tran smirked. "How long do you have?"

"Give us an example."

"Why do that?" Goodwin asked. "Much easier to take shots without giving specific examples."

McCall glowered at his roommate. "Will you shut up, please?"

After thinking about it for a moment, Tran finally said, "Well, just for one example, the Reman refugee situation. That was bungled from the outset and resulted in a ship full of dead Remans who should've been under Federation protection."

Kav made a snuffling noise. "That is *not* what happened."

"Oh, you were there, were you?" Tran said snidely.

"I did not need to be," the Tellarite said with a huff, which Goodwin had never seen anyone do in real life. "I read the reports, including the transcripts of the security council's discussions with various senior staff members and diplomats and Starfleet officers on the subject. The president did all that she could—the Remans chose to kill themselves instead."

"Fine, even if you give her that one," Tran said, "her appointments to the sub-councils have been a joke. First she appoints Artrin, then she calls for his resignation—and replaces him with Eleana, of all people? I have nothing but respect for the councillor from Delta, but she's got entirely the wrong temperament for judiciary. Tomorrow, the new session begins, and judiciary'll be listening to the B-4 case. That needs a rational legal mind, not Eleana and her bizarre interpretations of law. And I don't see how anyone can think it's a good idea to put so new a councillor as Krim on security. On top of that, she's done nothing to keep the peace on Romulus. She actually signed off on a plan that puts Klingon ships in the home star system of the Romulan Empire. It's a miracle that interstellar war hasn't broken out."

Before Velisa could follow up, Quinn said in a gentle voice, "But, Rina—war *hasn't* broken out. Don't you think it would have by now if it was going to? Besides, sending the Remans to Klorgat IV was an idea born in the Palais, and done in such a way as to keep the Klingon alliance intact."

"Actually," Tran said, "I question the wisdom of going to such trouble to do so. The Klingons have certainly done nothing to encourage keeping the alliance intact."

Kav snuffled again. "I would think that the people of the Federation made their feelings on that quite clear by electing President Bacco. Special Emissary Pagro had a much more aggressive strategy toward the Khitomer Accords and made it clear he would abrogate them if the empire did not change their way of doing things. If the people wanted to sunder the alliance, they would have voted for him, no?"

Tran waved her hand. "There were other issues besides the Klingons."

However, Kav wasn't finished. "And the Reman refugee situation at Outpost 22 could have been prevented if Starfleet had done its job properly. There was a starship at the outpost and a fully crewed base, yet they were almost destroyed by a handful of Remans in a ship that was one step away from flying apart?"

"Oh, *please*," McCall said. "Like that jackass has ever been out in space, facing the real dangers out there. I'd like to see *him* in the middle of nowhere with a cranky warp drive or facing a Romulan warbird with shields down—or be stuck on a shuttle in interstellar space with no communications and fading power—or—"

Goodwin had had enough. "If I recall, *Cadet*, the only time you set foot off Earth is when you went to Luna for training exercises, plus that one trip to Jupiter Station last year. Have you ever even been out of this solar system?"

In a small voice, McCall said, "That's not the point."

"Uh-huh."

"Shut up, I'm watching."

Tran was back to talking. "Look, I accept that she beat Pagro, but just because the people spoke a year ago doesn't mean they're right a year later. What about the Trinni/ek? They humiliate the Federation at a state dinner, and the president invites them *back*?"

"What a dip," Goodwin said even as Kav started defending the president. "Why are we watching this crap?"

"Shut up, I'm watching," McCall said again.

Goodwin pointed at Tran. "Come on, this idiot has it in for Bacco. The Trinni/ek were *sick*, it was all over everywhere. She's just got an agenda—or, at least, her boss does, and she's towing the party line."

Kav was finished saying whatever he wanted to say, then Quinn stepped over Tran's rebuttal. "The thing you have to understand about first contacts is that no two of them are alike. When you're dealing with an alien species, none of the rules apply, because the rules are being written as you go. Nobody knew about the effects of the Trinni/ek's sun's magnetic field. There was no way to know. It was a simple error, one that would've been made regardless of who was in the office on the fifteenth floor of the Palais de la Concorde."

Tran snorted, sounding frighteningly similar to Kav. "Well, if it doesn't matter who sits there, why bother even having a president?"

Velisa turned to the viewer behind her. "President Thelian, you've been quiet so far. Do you have an opinion on how President Bacco is doing?"

"Yes." Thelian's voice was barely audible. *"I spent very many years in Starfleet. When I retired, I decided to get*

*into politics. My reasons were very simple: I had met many
politicians in my time. I thought I could do better."*

"Yeah, well, that wouldn't take much," Goodwin muttered.

"Will you please for the love of cole slaw shut *up?*"
McCall asked.

This time Goodwin wound up to throw the padd at his
roommate, but again he declined to actually make the toss.

*"That thought proved to be baseless. As Ms. Tran said ear-
lier, the Federation is very large. It is proportionately difficult
to run. There have been days when I thought the job to be impossible. Most of those days were when I was president."*

Several people chuckled at that, and even Goodwin had
to admit that it was funny.

*"The point is that the job is difficult. The main reason for
that is not because of how one deals with the expected. President Zife was elected because everyone knew we would be
at war with the Dominion. Under his leadership, we were
ready. President Jaresh-Inyo was elected when no one knew
of the Dominion. He proved unable to handle that crisis.
That is why his presidency is remembered so poorly. When
President Bacco was elected, she was expected to be able to
keep the Klingon alliance intact. So far, she has done that.
But she also was not expected to have to deal with the fall of
the Romulan government. No one saw that coming. Such a
catastrophe could have sent the quadrant into chaos. But it
did not. For that, we have to give at least some of the credit
to the leadership of President Bacco."*

"So you'd say she's doing a good job?" Velisa asked.

"All right, that's it," Goodwin said.

"Goodwin—"

"No, I'm sorry, but this is ridiculous. He just spent half
an hour talking, and that host still can't figure out if he said

whether or not she's doing a good job? How can you *watch* this?"

"Look, Goodwin—"

He got up. "No, forget it, McCall, I'm leaving. I'll go to the lounge, the library, the commissary, *anything* so I don't have to listen to this garbage."

"Hey, if you're stopping at the commissary, will you pick me up something?"

Goodwin opened the handled door that led to the hallway. "Sure, what do you want?"

McCall smiled. "I'd *love* some kimchee."

This time, Goodwin did throw the padd at him.

◆

CHAPTER TWENTY-THREE

◆　　◆

KANT JOREL WAS ABOUT READY to poke his eyes out with hot pieces of metal when Zhres's voice came over the intercom. Jorel didn't understand it—he had done everything he could to alienate Zhres, same as he had every other assistant, yet the Andorian had now lasted a full year in the position, which shattered the previous record. Not only that, but Zhres even still had his will to live. It vexed Jorel no end.

"What could you *possibly* want right now?"

As unflapped as ever, Zhres said, *"Ozla Graniv is here to see you."*

Jorel's nasty retort died aborning on his tongue. "Ozla's back?"

"No, this is merely a convincing hologram of her. Yes, she is back and she says it's quite important that she speak to you."

"All right, send her in."

The doors parted to reveal a much slimmer Ozla Graniv. "It's about time you came back," Jorel said. "Gora's been driving me insane."

"Well, that's a short drive for you, isn't it, Jorel?"

Jorel couldn't help but laugh. "See? Gora's wit was never this caustic. So where've you been? I was considering sending search parties."

"I told you where I was," Ozla said as she sat down on the couch. "Tezwa."

Taking the seat on the other end of the couch, Jorel said, "No, you started off on Tezwa. You even filed some decent stories." They were, in fact, excellent stories, but Jorel was hardly about to say *that* out loud. "Then in June, you disappeared."

"It takes a while to get from Tezwa to Earth when you don't have Starfleet ships at your beck and call."

"It doesn't take four months."

"It does the way I went." Ozla took a deep breath. "Jorel, I need to tell you something very important: I know the *real* reason why Zife resigned."

"We all know the reason." Jorel said it with ease, even though he'd never been entirely sure of it. He knew that the notion that it had been planned for months was false, for all that he'd flogged that particular horse in the press room. The causes stated in Zife's resignation speech had certainly all been valid, and Zife's chances for reelection had dwindled with each new mishandled crisis in any case, but it was still a bit odd. However, he was hardly about to say so to a reporter.

"We all know the *stated* reason. But I know the *real* reason, and unless you give me a *good* reason not to print it, I'll be writing about it for all of *Seeker*'s subscribers to see."

Jorel didn't like the sound of this. "What're you *talking* about, Ozla?"

"I'm talking about Tezwa. I'm talking about six nadion-pulse cannons that the Zife administration put on Tezwa eight years ago."

Great, now she's subscribing to conspiracy theories. Jorel had seen several publications that had advanced this theory. Most were of the type that also said that transporters murdered you and replaced you with a soulless duplicate, that replicators were being used to disseminate mind-controlling drugs, that the universe was one big holodeck, and that the citizens of the galaxy were just pawns in a giant chess game among beings of pure energy. All had circulation figures that were at best in five digits. "Ozla, you can't possibly—"

"I have a source, Jorel. A reliable one who told me that Nelino Quafina, the former secretary of military intelligence under President Zife—and who, I might add, resigned when Zife did—brokered the delivery of those cannons to Tezwa via the Orion Syndicate."

Jorel laughed. "Ozla, come *on*. You're a legitimate reporter. In fact—and I'm not saying this lightly—you're one of the better reporters in the room." Jorel had to keep his eye from twitching as he said that; it went completely against his grain to compliment a reporter ever, much less twice in one conversation.

Testily, Ozla said, "You think I don't know how crazy

this sounds? Except it doesn't, really, once you take a look at it. I know the Syndicate, and I know what they charge for this sort of thing. Tezwa didn't have the money."

Jorel already saw the holes in her theory. "Tezwa had a bankrupt economy, they probably borrowed—"

"Their economy was trashed because they bought ships from the Danteri. *That's* what drove them to financial ruin. Even at their most economically stable, they couldn't afford both the cannons *and* the ships."

Not liking the turn this was taking, Jorel said, "Look, Ozla, that's all well and good, but you can't—"

"The cannons aren't why Zife resigned. Zife resigned because Starfleet Admiral William Ross forced him to or they would have removed him from power."

Now she was just getting silly. "And this is based on what, exactly?"

"I have a source who was part of the transaction. And I have the diary of one of the military leaders on Tezwa."

"A source."

Ozla regarded his dubious words with a nasty expression. "I have a lot of sources in the Syndicate, Jorel. Sources whose position in the Syndicate were improved by my exposé and who feel they owe me."

Witheringly, Jorel said, "How nice for you that you've helped criminals be upwardly mobile."

"Upwardly what?"

"Never mind." Jorel waved his hands back and forth. "This isn't—"

"I have this story, Jorel. But—" She hesitated. "You may have noticed I'm a bit thinner than I was the last time you saw me."

"Yes," Jorel said, seeing no reason to lie to spare her feelings at this point—nor, indeed, at any point.

"That's because I haven't been able to eat. This is killing me, because—" She closed her eyes and let out a slow, long breath. "I know what'll happen if I break this story. A Dominion War hero engineering a coup, a Federation president arming an independent planet—and the worst of all, the absolute worst, is that Zife knew about those cannons. You yourself said it in the press room when it happened, that the president himself ordered the *U.S.S. Enterprise* to escort the Klingon fleet to Tezwa to deal with Prime Minister Kinchawn's threat to the Qi'Vol colony. That means that Zife sent a Starfleet ship to Tezwa knowing they had these brutal weapons—and *didn't tell them*. That means Zife didn't inform the Klingons that the Tezwans had these brutal weapons that proceeded to kill thousands of Klingon soldiers." She clenched her fists. "Jorel, if I break this story—I don't know what will happen."

"There isn't a story," Jorel said forcefully. "Honestly, do you really think Zife or Ross is capable of such a thing?"

"Right now, Jorel, I don't know what to think. But the information I've been presented fits the notion that Zife armed the Tezwans and that Starfleet found out about it and forced him to resign. And I can't just carry that knowledge around with me and not *tell* anyone. I'm a reporter, this is my *job*."

Jorel shifted uncomfortably on the couch. "Ozla—" He tried to collect his thoughts, but he'd never had a conversation like this, either when he'd had a similar job on Bajor or since he'd moved to the Palais three years earlier.

He tugged on his earring and finally said, "What is it you want from me, Ozla?"

She stood up. "Like I told you before, I'm running this story unless you give me a good reason not to. You've got one day to find that reason."

With that, she turned on her heel and left Jorel's office.

Jorel sat on his couch for quite some time after that. He wasn't entirely sure how long it was, but two questions ran through his head the whole time. One was, What if she's right? The other was, What do we do then?

Finally he got up and walked out the door. Zhres was sitting at his desk, reading something on his workstation. "Jorel, FNS is reporting that—"

"Never mind that." Jorel meant to speak those words in anger, but they came out of his mouth weakly. "Call Zachary and give me the first *microsecond* that Esperanza has. Tell him it's crucial."

"What did Ozla—"

Now he did speak in anger. "When it becomes necessary for you to grow a brain, Zhres, I'll be sure to let you know."

Before Zhres could reply, Jorel stomped back into his office.

It can't possibly be true. I worked for Zife for two and a half years. He wasn't capable of—

Then he remembered what Ozla said about Quafina being the one to have brokered the deal—and that Quafina had resigned with Zife. That had always struck him as odd—that Quafina would resign when Zife's resignation would put him out of a job when the new election was held in a month's time anyhow. More to the point, he wasn't the only one who'd gone down with Zife.

Min Zife might not have been capable of what Ozla was accusing him of. But Koll Azernal? The Zakdorn chief of staff had once been jokingly referred to by an FNS reporter as "The Brains Behind the Bolian," but after working in the Palais for over two years, Jorel knew that it wasn't a joke. Azernal was a ruthless bastard who was more than capable of arming an independent planet on the Klingon border. *It was eight years ago. The Klingons had pulled out of the Khitomer Accords. War with the Dominion was only a matter of time. Paranoia about Founder infiltration of the Alpha Quadrant was at an all-time high.* Azernal, whose strategic mind was both amazing and frightening, was just the type to have hedged his bets by putting those cannons on Tezwa as a potential exit strategy.

And if Starfleet had found out about it, they would have been all over Zife. They wouldn't have been able to go public with it, because revealing it would indeed have angered the Klingons, thanks to the deaths those cannons had caused. *But is it out of the realm of possibility that they'd have forced Zife out of office?* Jorel had met William Ross several times and knew just how arrogant and self-righteous he could be, given the right provocation.

Jorel shook his head. *This is ridiculous.* As he'd said to Ozla, this was simply contorting reality to fit some scattershot information. They had no proof.

But will that matter? If Seeker—which isn't known for printing inaccurate information—runs this, and people start to look at all the things that don't make sense . . .

"Jorel?"

He tapped his intercom at the sound of Zhres's voice. "Yeah?"

"Esperanza's in San Francisco for most of the day. She's scheduled to be back at 1730, and Zachary says she can see you then—or, if it's important, she can comm with you at noon."

About to agree to that, Jorel then thought about it and realized that discussing this over an open channel—even as secure a one as that used within the Palais or in Starfleet

Headquarters, where Jorel assumed Esperanza to be—would be unwise. "Tell Zachary I'll see her at 1730."

"*All right.*"

The Articles of the Federation stated that the president was required to preside over meetings of the entire council, barring special circumstances. The precise nature of the circumstances were vague and generally varied to fit the times. These days, it mostly meant that the president was off-planet when the council was in session.

The same articles stated that the president had the option, but was not required, to preside over meetings of the various sub-councils. Most of the time, Nan Bacco was happy enough not to exercise that option and let the chair of the sub-council run the sessions.

In retrospect, today should not have been an exception.

After a great deal of legal wrangling, it had finally been determined that the Federation Judiciary Council, which was the highest legal authority in the Federation, would have final jurisdiction over the disposition of the android B-4 within the walls of the Daystrom Institute. Since the complainant was a civilian, it was deemed outside of the purview of the Starfleet judge advocate general's office to make law that would apply to the actions of a civilian.

That decision hadn't been reached until the recess, so it wasn't until the council was back in session that judiciary was hearing the case. The notion of sentience for artificial life had been a hot-button issue on several occasions, most recently a couple of years earlier during the so-called holostrike. Nan would have preferred to be watching the delayed feed of the Pioneers game right now—after falling to eight games behind the Salavar Stars in August, they had clawed their way back to a tie for first place, with the final four games of the season between the two of them to decide who would win the Northern Division—but this was too important an issue to have someone else preside over the session. Besides, leaving aside the politics, the notion of AI sentience was one that had interested her ever since the war, when she'd first met Data, the now-deceased android second officer of the *U.S.S. Enterprise,* during the Gorn crisis. So she wanted to see this particular case in action.

"Action" turned out to be the wrong word. The sessions had already gone on for two days, consisting solely of a civilian named Lars Patek arguing to dismantle B-4—one of Data's prototypes, discovered during the same mission on which Data died—for study and Captain Bruce Maddox arguing against it because that would constitute murder.

Patek was gesticulating wildly as he spoke. "B-4 is the only Soong-type android left in existence. We *have* to study it to see if the process can be replicated."

Maddox was much calmer as he answered. "There is a wealth of information available on all the other Soong androids, including Data, Lore, and Lal. We have the information recovered by the *Enterprise* from Graves World after Ira Graves's death, as well as information received from the studies of AIs over the past two centuries."

"All of which has proven useless!" Patek was yelling now, which only added to Nan's headache. "Data had all that information, yet Lal was a failure. We must study B-4 directly."

"Murder him, you mean, don't you, Lars?"

"Must we go down this road again, Bruce?" Patek asked.

Yes, must we? Nan managed to restrain herself from asking that question out loud. They'd only covered this subject several dozen times in two days.

Patek continued. "B-4 is not sentient. It's a prototype, an early copy."

At that, Councillor Gnizbreg spoke. Unlike full council sessions, in sub-council sessions, any member of the council could speak any time. The speaker's floor was for those outside the council who wished to speak, and they were the only ones who had to be recognized by the podium.

"On what are you basing the assumption that B-4 isn't sentient?" the Tiburonian councillor asked.

This perked Nan up. Nobody'd asked this yet.

"It barely has any cognitive functions. It cannot understand any but the most basic concepts. Before he was destroyed, Data downloaded his entire memory into B-4—which also included the memories of his twin, Lore, and the android he created, Lal, and the diaries of the colonists on Omicron Theta, where he was created. With all that knowledge, B-4 has shown an inability to perform any but the most menial tasks."

Councillor Ra'ch then asked, "Dr. Patek, are you saying that children born with lesser cognitive functions are not to be considered sentient? That they are to be killed so we can study how the human brain works?"

"Of course not!"

"Then why are you advocating it in this case?"

"Because we're not talking about a life here. We're talking about a machine that was built as a test run. Dr. Soong even named it in such a way as to make it clear that it was just a trial—it's the one that came before the final version. It's no more a sentient being than the first draft of a novel is a published book. Dr. Soong did not intend this being to live among people the way both Lore and Data did."

Maddox turned to look at Nan. "Madam President, I must protest my colleague's attempt to provide motives for a man whom he has never met and who's been dead for thirteen years."

"Protest noted."

Gnizbreg had another question. "Have you asked B-4 how he feels about being dismantled?"

Patek smiled, which Nan didn't like at all. "I can tell you B-4's exact words: 'I don't mind.'"

Maddox couldn't have looked more sour if he'd sucked down a lemon tree. "B-4 is not capable of understanding what that means."

"So you admit that he's not capable of cognitive thought?" Patek was gesticulating again. "When you challenged the notion of Data being sentient fifteen years ago, Bruce, you yourself said that one of the qualities for sentience was self-awareness. B-4 doesn't even meet that criterion."

"Then I bring you back to what Councillor Ra'ch said. If an organic life-form had cognitive difficulties, would you advocate killing it?"

Patek started to answer, but Nan cut him off. "Dr. Patek, Captain Maddox, much as I'd love to listen to you two hash out this argument over and over again, I think you've both made your positions clear. Councillor Gnizbreg, Councillor Ra'ch, do you have any further questions?" The Tiburonian and the Damiani councillors both shook their heads. "Does anyone else have a question?" She looked out over the remaining eleven councillors in the gallery. Nobody spoke. "Fine. Now, one of three things is gonna happen next. One is that you two call one of the witnesses you promised us yesterday. Two is that you both sit down and shut up and let the council deliberate. Three is that I rip this podium out of the floor and beat you both to death with it."

Archly, Patek said, "This council has already received copies of my research. I'd love to bring up witnesses, but the only ones available would repeat either my words or Captain Maddox's. The ideal witness would, of course, be a Soong android to compare to B-4, but Data was killed a year ago in the line of duty, Lore's positronic brain was destroyed about a year after he was deactivated in the Delta Quadrant, and Lal is nonfunctional—she's as dead as Data. There is no appropriate witness to bring."

Maddox's smirk came back. "Yes, there is. Madam President, I would like to call the Doctor to the stand as a witness."

Nan frowned. "The Doctor?"

"The *Voyager* Emergency Medical Hologram, ma'am," Maddox said.

Then Nan remembered. The EMH aboard that starship had been activated when *Voyager* had been lost in the Delta Quadrant and all its medical personnel had been killed. Along the way, the EMH had been outfitted with a mobile emitter and had become a valuable part of the crew by the time *Voyager* made it home seven years later. The Doctor was now part of a Federation think tank that had proven useful over the years. Nan had read several recommendations from that think tank over the past year and had always found them to be well researched, cogent, and valuable.

"The podium recognizes the Doctor as a witness."

One of the people in the gallery stood up. Looking for all the world like an unassuming, bald human, and dressed in a rather garish civilian suit, the Doctor stepped forward, walking past Maddox and Patek on the speaker's floor, taking the seat to the president's left.

Nan turned to the EMH. "Doctor, please be aware that

any testimony you give to this council has the weight of law, and any statement or statements you make that are proven to be false will make you subject to charges of perjury. Do you understand?"

"Of course I do, don't be ridiculous," the EMH said.

Frostily, Nan said, "Understand, Doctor, that I'm required by law to make that statement and ask that question, and also understand that you're in the Federation council chambers right now. Do you understand *that?*"

Again, the EMH said, "Of course," but his tone was—well, not conciliatory, but at least less aggressively snide.

Maddox smiled at his witness. "Doctor, thank you for coming. May I ask, for the record: What are you?"

"A sentient hologram."

"Are you a Federation citizen?"

"Yes. In fact, I voted in the last election." Casting a furtive glance at Nan, he added, "For you, of course, Madam President."

Smiling sweetly, Nan said, "Thanks."

"For how long have you been a citizen?"

"Since *Voyager*'s return at the beginning of 2378. Prior to that, I was, like the rest of the crew, in the Delta Quadrant."

"What was your status on the ship?"

"Chief medical officer."

"Prior to that?"

"I did not exist prior to that. Aside from the occasional test run prior to *Voyager*'s embarkation, I was first activated after *Voyager* was sent to the Delta Quadrant. I remained active for virtually the entire seven years of our sojourn toward the Alpha Quadrant."

"Who constructed you?"

"Dr. Lewis Zimmerman, one of the foremost authorities on artificial intelligence."

"Why were you created?"

"In order to provide a supplement to medical staffs on starships during emergencies. The EMH program was meant primarily for combat situations, given the threats from the Borg, and later the Dominion."

"You were built as the first generation of such holograms, yes?"

"I—and other EMHs like me—were the first, yes."

"Subsequent generations have been put to use since then?"

Up until now, the EMH had been answering Maddox's questions with all the aplomb of the rehearsed question-and-answer that Nan knew this was. At the mention of his successors, however, the snideness came back. "There have been newer EMH models, yes."

Before Maddox could ask his next question, Patek asked, "Madam President, I fail to see the relevance of this witness to the issue at hand."

Nan had lost all patience with both of them. "Dr. Patek, I could see the relevance of this witness if I was blindfolded, so don't think you're gonna impress the council by professing ignorance just at the moment." She turned to his fellow scientist. "As for you, Captain, move this along. The podium-beating option's looking better by the second."

"Of course, Madam President," Maddox said deferentially before turning back to his witness. "So you were a machine."

"A computer program, if one wishes to get technical, made photonic flesh." He smiled. "If one wishes to get poetic."

"And you were a prototype. Dr. Zimmerman even named you 'EMH Mark 1' by way of making it clear that you were the first of many."

The EMH folded his arms. "I suppose—if one must—one could look at it that way."

"So here you are—a machine built as a test run, named in such a way as to make it clear that you were just a trial. Yet here you sit as a Federation citizen. You've moved past your original programming."

Patek started waving his arms about again. "Madam President, while Captain Maddox has made a nice rhetorical point, it's—"

Nan pointed at him. "Don't knock nice rhetorical points. I happen to be rather fond of them, myself. And before either of you gets going, I think we get your point. The EMH here started out life pretty similar to B-4. He's done pretty good for himself, all told. We get it. Are there any other witnesses?"

Maddox looked disappointed, as if he had more to say, but as far as Nan was concerned, she'd let him go on too long. "No, ma'am."

"Dr. Patek?"

"No, ma'am."

She turned to the side seats. "Councillors?"

Eleana asked, "Where is B-4 now?"

It was Patek who answered the Deltan councillor's question. "At Daystrom, being cared for, as he has been for the past year."

"Has he asked to leave?"

"No," Patek said.

Maddox added, "He has said several times that he likes Daystrom more than the lab where he was born, the lab where Shinzon found him, or the *Enterprise.*"

"Do you believe that your institute is the best place for him to grow as the witness here has?"

At that, Councillor Nea of Bolarus said, "That doesn't fall within the purview of this case."

Rather snippily, Eleana said, "Perhaps it should."

You wanted her on judiciary, Nan thought as she said, "That can be discussed during deliberations, no?"

"It will be, Madam President," Eleana said.

Grateful that she wasn't obligated to be present for that, either, Nan said, "Good. Anything else?"

Silence. *Thank God.*

Looking to the witness, she said, "Thank you for your time, Doctor. You're excused."

Nodding, the EMH rose. "Thank you, Madam President."

"Dr. Patek, Captain Maddox, we are grateful for your testimonies, depositions, and statements. The council will contact you when the deliberations are complete and a decision has been reached."

Both of them said, "Thank you, Madam President," and left.

The guards then cleared the gallery—several reporters were observing the proceedings, for which Nan was grateful, as this was an important issue that needed to be covered, and she had faith in the reporters' ability to make the session considerably more interesting than it actually had been—so the council could deliberate.

"My friends, I have a security briefing, so I will leave you to it. I will say only that I think the Doctor's testimony might be worth reviewing."

With that, she left, hoping her own feelings on the case were made clear by her final statement. Right now, she wanted to find out what had happened on Cestus III. The Pioneers had lost the first two games, so they had to win today's and the last one tomorrow to stand a chance of at least tying for the division lead, which would force a one-game play-off.

✦

CHAPTER TWENTY-FOUR

✦   ✦

KANT JOREL HAD MEETINGS with both Myk Bunkrep and Z4 Blue during the day, but he couldn't bring himself to say anything about what Ozla Graniv had told him that morning. *This is something that needs to go right to Esperanza.*

After his meeting with Z4—the details of which he now honestly could not recall—he went back to his office. Zhres said, "Esperanza called—she said she'll be back in half an hour, right after your briefing. And, ah—" Zhres hesitated.

Not even a little bit in the mood for the Andorian's nonsense, Jorel asked, "What?"

Zhres simply handed Jorel a padd. Snatching it angrily, he read the display. It informed him that Brek chim Glamok, reporter for the Tellarite News Service, had been declared missing and was presumed dead. This was a change from his status over the seven months since he'd disappeared after going to Kliradon, when he'd simply been missing. "Wonderful."

"The rest of the briefing's loaded on there, too."

"Fine."

Zhres's antennae wriggled in an appalling manner. "Are you all right, Jorel?"

"Never ask that question in my presence again, Zhres." Jorel turned on his heel and walked toward the holocom to start his late-afternoon briefing.

He began with various bits of information, the president's itinerary, what some members of the cabinet and council were doing, and then, finally, the news about Brek.

The room was fairly silent after that.

"That's it," Jorel said, not in the mood to take questions.

Predictably, he got one anyhow from T'Nira before he could deactivate the holocom. "Will the judiciary council's decision on the B-4 matter be made today or will there be more discussion?"

For that, Jorel had to check his padd. "All the testimony's been taken, all the witnesses—*the* witness, actually—has been questioned, and now they're deliberating."

"Is an estimate available for when the deliberations will be complete?"

"Probably some time before the twenty-fifth century starts."

Sovan then asked, "Is there any truth to the rumor that the president wants a summit with Chancellor Martok?"

"I don't respond to rumors, Sovan, you *know* that, so kindly stop asking me to comment on them. That's it."

This time, he did deactivate the holocom before any more questions could come. He couldn't stand any more reporters probing just now.

What if she's right?

He had tried to convince himself that Ozla's source, whoever or whatever it was, was wrong. That the Tezwan soldier whose diary she'd read had been mistaken. But the more he thought about it, the less he liked it.

"Esperanza's ready for you," Zhres said as he got back to his office. "You were a trifle terse in there."

"I'm getting reviews from you now? Zhres, in the last year, have I ever shown even the slightest indication that I find your opinion in any way relevant or interesting?"

"No."

"Learn something from that, would you please?" He handed Zhres the briefing padd, then went to the turbolift.

Esperanza Piñiero was waiting for him in her office. She was studying something on her workstation intently. When he came in, she looked up and said, "Jorel, before I forget, next briefing, I need you to announce that we've come to an agreement with the Strata to act as intermediaries with the Trinni/ek. And if anyone asks about a summit again, don't deny it."

"I didn't deny it. I never comment on rumors, Esperanza, you know that."

Nodding, she said, "Yeah, I know, but the president's been trying to get the Klingons to agree to this ever since that Klorgat mess. Giving it a little bit of a higher profile might help things along a bit."

Jorel fixed her with an incredulous look. "You really think the Klingons are gonna give a damn about more attention in the Federation press?"

"I'm not talking about the Klingons, I'm talking about our people. Some of the Diplomatic Corps are dragging their feet—I'd like to stomp on those feet a little."

"I love your imagery sometimes."

"Thanks."

"I was being sarcastic."

Esperanza smiled. "I could tell—mainly because you were awake. Zhres said you needed to talk to me about something?"

Jorel nodded and took a seat in Esperanza's guest chair. "Ozla Graniv came to see me this morning."

"She's back?"

"No, Esperanza, it was a convincing hologram. Yes, she's back, and she has a story that she will run unless we give her a good reason not to."

"What possible reason would we have not to run it?"

Esperanza's face never changed expression the entire time that Jorel was telling her what Ozla had told him. He hoped, he wished, he fervently prayed to the Prophets that she would laugh at him, that she would tell him the whole idea was ridiculous, that she would reassure him that there was nothing to worry about, that Ozla's source was just out-and-out wrong.

She did none of those things.

Instead, she let Jorel tell the entire story. Then she leaned back in her chair.

"Hell."

"Esperanza, you can't tell me—"

"That she can't run the story? I wish I could. Dammit, this will—" She slammed a hand on the desk. *"Dammit!"*

"Esperanza—"

"I was hoping—I was so so *so* much hoping—that it wouldn't come to this. That that Zakdorn bastard actually covered his tracks well enough that this wouldn't come up." She laughed bitterly. "And that the Syndicate thing was a cover story. Guess not. God, I can't believe they actually *used* the Syndicate to funnel those weapons. I mean, how *stupid*—"

Jorel's stomach twisted in his gut. Bile started to rise, leaving a bitter taste in the back of his mouth. "Esperanza, you can't tell me that she's right?"

"I have to, Jorel. She is. Zife and Azernal and Quafina armed Tezwa behind the backs of the Federation Council and the Klingon Empire. When Kinchawn went nuts, Zife sent the *Enterprise* in to escort the Klingon fleet and didn't tell them about the cannons. And when Starfleet found out where the cannons came from, they forced the three of them to resign."

"They—" Jorel stood up. He tugged on his earring, the pain shooting through his lobe a reminder that he wasn't dreaming. "How could they do that?"

"I don't pretend to know what the previous—"

Jorel waved his hand back and forth. "No, not the president and Koll and that twerpy little Antedean, I'm talking about Starfleet. I'm talking about *Ross.* How could he—I mean, Starfleet's supposed to fight for what the Federation stands for, and they do *this?*"

"He didn't have a choice."

"Oh, come *off* it! Don't give me that military garbage, Esperanza, you're not *in* Starfleet anymore, you don't have to defend them."

"What else were they supposed to do?" she asked with a calm that just infuriated Jorel more. "Give me some alternatives."

"They didn't have to *do* anything!"

"So they should let a president who was directly responsible for the deaths of thousands of Starfleet officers, thousands more Klingon warriors, and *millions* of Tezwans just go right on with what he was doing?"

That brought Jorel up short. He knew that going public with the knowledge wouldn't have worked. The Klingons would have demanded retribution. At best, they would have had to turn Zife over to face trial in a Klingon court, which would have resulted in his execution. That was not something the Federation could have allowed to happen to one of their leaders, and it would have damaged Klingon-Federation relations at a time when the alliance had already been pretty frayed. "So Starfleet engages in a coup d'état, and they get away with it?"

"First of all, it wasn't a coup d'état—in order for that to

be the case, they'd have had to take over the government. They stopped a war, got a criminal off the fifteenth floor, and allowed the constitutional process to play out as spelled out in the Articles of the Federation. President Bacco was elected, not appointed."

Jorel sat back down. "What am I supposed to tell Ozla?"

Esperanza sighed. "Remind her of the consequences of her going public with this."

"She already knows that. She's going to run it anyway. And honestly, I don't blame her. Hell, right now, I'm tempted to encourage her to run it."

Speaking as if Jorel hadn't said anything, Esperanza said, "If that doesn't work, see what you can offer her in exchange. Reporters often have information they won't print because of its volatile nature. If she does understand the consequences like you said—maybe she'll trade it for something else."

"Like what?"

"Ask her."

Jorel knew Esperanza was right. Not all reporters were idiots, though it certainly seemed that way to Jorel half the time, and Ozla in particular wasn't. She wouldn't send the Federation into a war with the Klingons and tarnish the office of the president so readily, especially if she could use it to get something else.

However, there was one other concern. "What if there isn't anything she wants—or if it's something we can't give her?"

"Then she runs the story and we face the consequences. Freedom of the press means just that—they're free to do what they want. We can give them incentives not to say something in particular, but it's *their* choice to accept or decline them. We *cannot* get into the business of exerting undue influence, or we stop being the Federation and become—I don't know, something else, but not this." She looked Jorel right in the eye. "Not what so many people died for."

Jorel suddenly shivered.

Frowning, Esperanza asked, "What?"

"Nothing, I was just—" He shook his head. "About twenty years ago on Bajor, I helped run an underground newsfeed. We used to piggyback on the official Cardassian channels and send out bits of news about the resistance and messages of hope and prayer and citations of specific instances of gross oppression."

Esperanza chuckled mirthlessly. "Wasn't the entire occupation gross oppression?"

Rolling his eyes, Jorel said, "The more extreme examples. Can I tell my story please?"

"Sure." Esperanza made a "go-ahead" gesture.

"One time, we heard that the resistance was targeting a food storage unit, because the Cardassians were using it as a weapons depot as well. They probably figured that terrorists wouldn't target food. We ran one of our feeds and talked about how stupid the Cardassians were for thinking the resistance was so easy to manipulate and how those weapons weren't long for the world." Jorel closed his eyes. He hadn't thought about this in years, and he had no great desire to think about it now, but Ozla's demand, as well as Esperanza's confirmation of his worst fears, brought it slamming back to the front of his brain. "We thought we were just so damn brilliant, exposing the Cardassians' feeble attempt at subterfuge. Unfortunately, all we succeeded in doing was letting the Cardassians know that the depot would be attacked by the resistance."

Esperanza gave him a sympathetic look. "They were defeated?"

Snorting, Jorel said, "'Defeated' doesn't begin to cover it. They were massacred. And they wouldn't have been if we . . ." He trailed off.

"You should tell Ozla that story," Esperanza said in a softer voice than Jorel had ever heard her use.

Jorel nodded twice and got up. "All right. I'll talk to her and get back to you."

"Good. Oh, one other thing—I just got word when I got back, judiciary found in favor of B-4."

Smirking, Jorel said, "So the android gets the right to choose not to get taken apart. Lucky him."

"Yup. Let me know what Ozla says."

Jorel nodded again and left.

"You know, the colors in this room are just sooooooooooooo pretty."

"Ozla, what's the matter with you?"

Looking over at the viewer that hung on the wall of her apartment on Earth, Ozla Graniv saw the blurry face of her editor. "Sorry, Farik, wuzzat?"

"I said, what's the matter with you?"

"Oh." Somehow she had managed to sit up on her couch, but the effort was proving to be too much, and she fell back down into a supine position. "I'm drunk."

"Why are you drunk?"

"'Cause I've imbibed a substantial 'mount of alcohol."

"No, I mean, why've you been—"

"'Cause I *lied*, Farik! Lied like a lyin' stinkin' liar. 'M a reporter, 'm not s'posed t'lie, but there I was! Lyin' like a lyin' liar lyin' at Kant Jorel."

"Ozla—"

She rolled onto her side and picked up the Saurian brandy bottle, only to discover that it was empty. Next to it, so was the Orion whiskey—a going-away present from Ihazs, amazingly enough, that had been waiting for her when the Balduks had hauled her back to her hotel—and the Terran scotch. "See, it's this story I've got."

"The one you won't tell me about."

"Right, 'at's the one. See, I tol' Kant I had a source. Which was a big ol' lie, 'cause I ain't got a source. I mean, I got a source, but's a deep-background source." She had decided on her way from Deneva to Earth that she would not tell Farik that Ihazs had threatened to kill her if she revealed his info without a corroborating source. Editors tended to get overprotective and annoying when they thought their reporters' lives were in danger, so she decided that, as far as Farik was concerned, her source on the Zife/Tezwa story was deep background: could be used for background information, but not be quoted on the record. "So'f they don' confirm it, I ain't gotnee story. So I lied."

"To somebody who's lied to you dozens of times in the last two years alone."

"S'not the point!"

"Ozla, why did you call me, exactly?"

To her surprise—well, not total surprise, given how drunk she was—Ozla had no idea what the answer to that question was. "Don't 'member."

Then her house computer spoke. *"Incoming message from the Palais de la Concorde."*

"Oh, goody, Kant's gettin' back t'me."

For the first time since she lay back down, Ozla looked at Farik's face on the screen. It was heavily lined and etched with concern. Or maybe it was just the way his spots looked in this light. *"Be careful, Ozla, all right?"*

And then his face faded.

Ozla struggled to make her legs work, but she only succeeded in falling off the couch. At least that accomplished her goal, which was to move from the couch to the floor. She had been hoping to do it with her legs underneath her, but beggars couldn't be choosers. "Computer, hold call fr'm Palais."

"*Acknowledged.*"

Using a footrest to brace herself, Ozla somehow managed to clamber to her feet. She felt like she was wobbling, but at least she was upright. Then she had to convince her legs to not just support her weight—at which they were only barely succeeding—but also to walk.

Taking slow, easy steps, using whatever furniture she could to brace herself where possible, Ozla slowly made her way to the bathroom, which was where she kept her anti-intoxicants. She got them six years ago and had no idea if they were still any good or not, as she hadn't drunk this much—well, ever.

She had to touch the medicine chest control three times before it finally deigned to slide aside, and then she had to squint to make out the labels on the bottles inside. Finally she found the right one.

After pulling on the top for several seconds, she remembered that the bottle had a touch-sensitive control on the bottom that allowed ingress. She touched it four times before it finally opened. Then she swallowed three pills.

Seconds later, she was as sober as she had been when Ihazs had confronted her in that basement. And about as apprehensive.

Walking steadily, but nervously, back out to the living room, she said, "Computer, activate viewer."

Zhres's face appeared on the screen. "*Ozla, Jorel would like to see you as soon as possible.*"

Here it comes, she thought. *The moment of truth. Or the moment of lying.* "Tell him I'll be right there."

What Ozla didn't know was what answer she wanted more: that Ihazs was right, or that he was wrong. Because the thing that scared her the most, the thing that had driven her to drain her supply of Saurian brandy, Orion whiskey, and Terran scotch was the knowledge that this story would absolutely make her career. It would make the Orion exposé look like a university term paper.

And that scared the living hell out of her.

William Ross had first visited the presidential office as a child. His parents had taken him on the tour of the Palais, and this office had been the last stop. He hadn't gotten to meet President Thelian, of course, although he'd met several councillors during the tour. The seven-year-old Billy Ross had thought the room absolutely huge.

He'd been back many times in his Starfleet career, particularly under Presidents Jaresh-Inyo, Zife, and now Bacco. Each time he'd come in, the room had seemed smaller, never more so than when he'd stood and watched Min Zife give a resignation speech that had been hastily written, not by anyone on Zife's speechwriting staff but rather by a Vulcan woman named L'Haan. It had been right after that that L'Haan and her associates had taken Zife, Koll Azernal, and Nelino Quafina to their "retirement."

Ross had been surprised at being summoned to the fifteenth floor alone. Generally his visits with the president were in the company of other Starfleet officers, not to mention various members of the government—the chief of staff, various cabinet members, the security advisor, and so on. He was even more surprised when Bacco entered the office by herself, unaccompanied even by her right hand, Esperanza Piñiero.

"Can you imagine that I'm getting more trouble from the Diplomatic Corps than the Klingon High Council about this damn summit? Now they're concerned that we'll be insulting the Romulan Empire."

Allowing himself a small smile, Ross said, "It's been my experience, ma'am, that one should never underestimate the capacity of the Diplomatic Corps to give you more trouble."

At that, the president laughed. "Good point." She moved around to her desk and sat down.

"What can I do for you, Madam President?"

Bacco stared at him for a second. "Bill, it's been a bad day for me. The Pioneers lost three out of four to the Stars, which means they aren't Northern Division champions for the first time in four years. The Diplomatic Corps is giving me lots of reasons to order them all beheaded with guillotines on the ground floor of the building, just like the good old days six hundred years ago. And now I've had *this* dropped in my lap."

"What would 'this' be about, ma'am?" Ross asked, though the very fact that the president was calling him by his first name lent credence to several suspicions.

"The last person to have this office."

That confirmed the worst of those suspicions. "What about President Zife, ma'am?"

At once, all pretense of a friendly demeanor was gone, and Bacco angrily snapped, "Cut the *crap,* Admiral! You and I *both* know what happened. We *both* know that Zife armed Tezwa with those pulse cannons and didn't tell anyone—least of all the dozen or so ships that got torn to pieces *by* those cannons. And we *both* know that you served him, Azernal, and Quafina with an ultimatum."

Ross knew all this, of course, but he didn't know that Bacco did. "How long—?"

"Doesn't matter," Bacco said with a dismissive wave.

"Actually, ma'am, due respect—it does matter." Ross hesitated. Nan Bacco was a good woman, and he didn't want to make it sound as if he was accusing her of something, but he had to know the answer to this. "Did you know when I offered to consult for your campaign?"

"No. I found out later—the morning of the first debate, in fact. By then, the campaign was at full bore, and—" She shook her head. "I don't know, I didn't really think about it. We had eight billion other things on our minds at that point, and I was a lot more concerned with what Zife did than what you did. But what you did . . ." She got up and let out a long breath. "For the last year, I've been wondering what to do with you, Bill. I mean, you showed my predecessor the door, and there's a part of me that's been wondering, What happens if I do something to piss him off?"

"That's unlikely, ma'am. There were a lot of reasons why I chose to show such public support for your campaign, and one of the biggest was the fact that I had faith in your inability to put me in the position President Zife did."

Bacco, who had been staring out the window at the sunset over Paris, now whirled around at Ross. "God, do you know what you *sounded* like just then?"

"Ma'am?"

"It's not enough that you removed Min Zife from power, but then you took it upon yourself to use whatever influence you could to put the person *you* preferred in his place."

Ross shifted uncomfortably in his seat. "Ma'am, I think you overestimate my importance. You won that election without any help from me."

"Bull," Bacco said angrily. "I had plenty of help from you, and while I'm flattered that you think I could've managed without it, that doesn't change the fact that you did what you did. Now maybe I should've said something right after Esperanza found out, but I thought it was best to let it lie. We need to move past what Zife did to the Federation, and we couldn't do that if we rehashed Tezwa all over again."

Ross frowned. "I take the fact that we're having this meeting to indicate that something's changed."

Bacco nodded. "There's a reporter down on the second floor right now who just had a long conversation with Kant Jorel, who then had a long conversation with Esperanza, who just had a long conversation with me, during the middle of which I had Sivak call you over here." She walked back over to her desk and sat back down. "This reporter knows that Zife was responsible for the cannons on Tezwa, knows that Tezwa couldn't afford those cannons *and* the Danteri ships they bought, knows that Quafina used the Orion Syndicate to funnel the cannons to Tezwa, and knows that Starfleet found out and that they—that is to say, you—forced Zife to resign to pay for the rather vicious crimes he committed, since a public airing of them would be disastrous."

Appalled, Ross asked, "You're not going to let the story run, are you?" At that, Bacco tilted her head, and Ross realized he'd misspoken. "I mean, there must be some way to convince—I mean—"

"What do you suggest, Admiral?" Bacco asked tightly.

"We make this person disappear? That's not how we do things."

Ross had to almost physically restrain himself.

Then Bacco got a look of horror on her face. "Isn't it?"

"Ma'am?"

"Back in May when Jaresh-Inyo died, Esperanza tried to track Zife down to invite him to the funeral on Mars. She couldn't find him. She couldn't find any sign of him. Nobody on Bolarus, on Earth, anywhere knew where to find the most prominent person in the Federation for the last eight years. It shouldn't be that hard, if all he did was retire."

Ross said nothing. He worked for this woman, admired this woman, and because of that, because he knew how important she was to the Federation, how necessary it was that she keep doing the job she was doing, he could not under any circumstances afford to tell her the whole truth.

Because if she knew what he knew, she would disappear as completely as Min Zife, Koll Azernal, and Nelino Quafina had. And there would be nothing William Ross could do about it this time, either.

"You know, when I started this conversation," she said, "I was concerned about what I had to do, but the more I talk to you, Admiral, the less problem I have with it."

Now Ross was confused. "I don't know what you—"

"The reporter—and I think I'm going to refrain from giving you the person's name—has discussed the matter with the Palais press liaison and has informed him that there is a condition on which the story will not be run. If that condition is met, the story will in fact be buried where no one can find it."

Ross didn't hesitate. He stood up. "My resignation?"

Bacco regarded him. "Actually, the terms weren't that specific. All that was required was that you no longer have any influence over the running of the Federation or Starfleet. Resignation, retirement, ritual suicide, whatever, as long as you become just an ordinary Federation civilian who's no longer in a position to exert undue and illegal influence on the Federation government."

"Then I'll resign immediately, ma'am." Ross didn't hesitate. This was the only way to preserve the Federation, and Ross never hesitated when it was necessary to preserve the Federation. After he spoke, the thought occurred to him that he would no longer be the highest-ranking Starfleet officer who was answerable to the organization, which meant he'd no longer be able to control their actions. Then he laughed bitterly to himself, being careful to keep his poker face for President Bacco. *The control was always theirs, and I'm fooling myself if I ever thought otherwise.*

Then Bacco surprised Ross by saying, "No. Not resignation. Resigning sends up red flags. People resign in protest or resign because of disagreements or to avoid scandal. Retirement, though, that's normal—particularly for someone like you. You led our forces during a vicious war, and you've stayed at the forefront of the admiralty ever since. In fact, lots of people were surprised you *didn't* retire after the Founders surrendered."

Ross saw the wisdom in her words. "In that case, ma'am, I'll announce my retirement tomorrow morning."

She nodded.

"Thank you, Madam President." He turned to leave.

"Bill?"

He stopped and turned around. "Ma'am?"

Focusing a remarkable amount of anger and confusion into one word, Bacco asked, "Why? I can understand why you had to remove him from power, but why take the next step?"

Why kill them? Ross could understand why Bacco couldn't say the words out loud. He took a moment to compose his answer in such a way that it wouldn't even hint to Bacco the real reason. She had to be shielded from that— even though he knew that if there was ever a president who might be able to stand up to them, it was her—and so he said, "Because they killed millions of people—directly or indirectly. Every death caused by those cannons, every death caused by the Klingons' retaliation, every death caused by Kinchawn's guerillas after he was removed from power—all of those deaths were on their heads. And worse, they caused more death in order to keep themselves absolved of the crime, and they did it from a distance so they could create the illusion that their hands were clean." He took a breath. "And so for five minutes in the Monet Room last year, I became them. That reporter downstairs is absolutely right in that there should be consequences for that, and my only regret in all this is that I didn't take this action before it endangered your presidency, ma'am. For that, I am truly sorry."

Bacco said nothing. Ross hoped that she believed his words—which were certainly true, as far as they went.

Then, finally, she nodded her head.

"Thank you, Madam President."

As Ross turned back around, he wondered what the consequences for him would be. He suspected that they'd let him live out his life in solitude, as long as he didn't get on their sensor screen.

Whatever else he might have done, he had performed the paramount duty: Keep the organization a secret.

His cause for optimism lay in the knowledge that they acted only when they felt it was necessary, as well as in his faith in Nan Bacco's ability to steer the Federation onto a course that would keep them from finding that necessity.

The doors slid apart, and William Ross exited the presidential office for the last time.

DECEMBER 2380

*"Far and away the best prize that life offers is
the chance to work hard at work worth doing."*
—Theodore Roosevelt

CHAPTER TWENTY-FIVE

THE OBSERVER FOUND the limited beings to be most fascinating. His report to his superiors was almost finished. Over the course of his studies, he had noted that the limited beings would have public discussions about issues that were deemed relevant to their lives, which were disseminated throughout their nation. He had decided to witness one of these discussions, to see if it would provide any additional insight into the limited beings.

"Good evening. This is *Illuminating the City of Light*, I'm your host, Velisa. The Palais is gearing up for the summit, but there are still a lot of unanswered questions. Where will it be held? What will be on the agenda? Will the Romulans be involved?"

The person speaking was biologically of the fifth gender that he had catalogued, colloquial name *female*, and native of Planet AV9, colloquial name *Krios*. She seemed to be the leader of the discussion. To her left was another gender-five, a native of Planet AQ1, colloquial name *Vulcan*. To her right were a gender-seven *(male)* from Planet BT5 *(Earth)*, and a gender-two *(shen)* from Planet AC1 *(Andor)*. There was also a communication device between the AV9 and the AQ1, which displayed the face of another gender-seven, this one from Planet DO3 *(Delta)*.

"With me tonight to discuss the summit are retired Starfleet Captain Charles Reynolds, who has fought both against and alongside the Klingon Defense Force; former secretary of the exterior under Min Zife, Ythrilasifsa sh'Zathrosia; Councillor T'Latrek of Vulcan, the chair of the external affairs council; and, remotely from Qo'noS, FNS's Klingon Empire correspondent, Teneso. Welcome, all of you."

The observer amended his report to include the nomenclature and position, though they all had far too many syllables to suit him. Since what they did was more important than what they were called, he referred to them by position.

The discussion leader turned to the current councillor. "T'Latrek, can you tell us what the president and the council would like to get out of this summit?"

"To build on the cooperative efforts surrounding the investigation of the Klorgat IV disaster and the equally cooperative efforts to maintain peace in Romulan space."

"That is a forlorn hope," the former government official said.

The discussion leader turned to her. "Why do you say that, Ythril?"

"The Klingons don't cooperate. Neither do the Romulans."

"Short memory you've got there, Madam Secretary," the former Starfleet captain said. "You were in the cabinet during the war, weren't you—when all three governments cooperated?"

"That was a special case. That was an alliance of convenience. In their entire history, the Romulan Star Empire has never maintained an alliance with any outside power for more than a few years. Their entire culture is based on a belief in their manifest destiny to rule the galaxy."

The captain nodded his head up and down, which, the

observer had learned, was an indication of affirmation. "That may be—and I admit, I fought alongside some damn arrogant Romulans during the war—but it's not like there's a shortage of arrogance on our side of the Neutral Zone, either."

The councillor raised one of her eyebrows, an affectation common among her species. "Captain Reynolds's point is well taken, if a bit . . . colorful. But it is important to note that there has not been an all-out war among any of the three major powers since the Organian Peace Treaty was signed one hundred and thirteen years ago."

The former official's antennae made a peculiar motion that the observer did not know the significance of. "That isn't for a lack of trying on anyone's part."

The captain interjected a point. "I think that's only true if you don't count when the Klingons pulled outta Khitomer a couple years before the war, Councillor."

"That conflict was between the empire and the Cardassian Union," the councillor said. "There were skirmishes between Starfleet and Defense Force ships, it's true, but no formal conflict was declared by the council."

"A technicality," the former official said.

"Ythril's right," the captain said, "I was in charge of the *Centaur* then, and let me tell you, it sure felt like a war when those birds-of-prey hammered me to pieces."

Before any more could be said, the discussion leader turned to the person on the screen behind her, a journalist. "Teneso, what's your impression of the High Council's wishes for the summit?"

"Well, Velisa, there are plenty of people on the High Council who would be more than happy to declare war on the entire galaxy. But Chancellor Martok and his supporters on the council know how beneficial the Federation

alliance has been for the empire in the long term. Besides, it's not like the Klingons have been starved for battle in the years since the war. I think that Martok wants to strengthen the alliance, not weaken it, which is something that may cost him a little from some of the hardliners on the council, but which will ultimately work out for him. Martok has the advantage of being incredibly popular with the people of the empire, more than any chancellor since Kravokh, and probably even more than him. He's credited with winning the war and with continuing the work of Emperor Kahless."

"T'Latrek, do you think that President Bacco and Chancellor Martok will be able to work together?"

The councillor again raised her eyebrow. "Both the president and chancellor are reasonable. This is not a description that would apply to many Klingon chancellors— nor, indeed, to many Federation presidents."

The discussion leader's face changed into what the observer recognized as a smile, indicating agreement and/or pleasure. "What about the Romulans?"

Before the councillor could respond, the former official's antennae made that odd motion again, and she said, "They shouldn't be allowed anywhere near the summit. This is a meeting of superpowers, and that's not something the Romulan Star Empire can call themselves since their senate was rather literally dissolved."

"I wouldn't underestimate them," the captain said.

The former official turned toward the man next to her. "And I would not overestimate them, Captain. Nature favors the destructive process. It took that Reman all of a minute to destroy the senate, and it only took him another few days to get himself killed and ruin his own revolutionary government. That will take decades to rebuild."

Before the captain could say anything, the councillor said, "Your words are not false, Ythril, but just because it will not happen quickly does not mean it will not happen. Witness the Klingon Empire following Praxis."

"Yes, Councillor," the former official said in a voice that the observer thought indicated annoyance, "but this summit should not be concerned with what might happen fifty years from now but what *is* happening now."

The discussion leader asked the councillor, "T'Latrek, do you think Praetor Tal'Aura should be included in the summit?"

"There are benefits to including her—and to excluding her."

The former official's antennae went wild. "How equivocal of you, T'Latrek."

The journalist spoke up. *"I don't think the High Council will be too pleased with the idea of Tal'Aura being there, Velisa. There's no love lost between the Great Hall and Romulus, especially after the incident at Klorgat IV."*

The former official once again grew agitated. "Starfleet proved conclusively that Admiral Mendak was responsible for that, and he was a rogue element."

"Oh come *on*," the captain said, "you don't really believe that, do you, Ythril? Mendak's always been a loyalist. Hell, I met the man right after Brasîto. Patriotic to a fault."

The councillor said, "Even patriots will go against their government if they feel it necessary. Tal'Aura, remember, supported Shinzon's coup. Mendak has always been loyal to the Romulan government, yes, but he has also consistently spoken out in favor of continued Reman oppression. It is logical to deduce that it is at least possible, if not probable, that he refused to cooperate with the government as long as Tal'Aura was praetor and his status as a criminal was genuine."

"I don't buy it," the captain said. "Mendak didn't do anything that actually hurt Tal'Aura, and when the S.C.E. found him out on Klorgat, he conveniently commits suicide. I gotta go with Ythril here, that lady shouldn't be anywhere *near* the summit."

"The next question is about the issues under dis—"

Then the playback went dead. So did the observer's reporting equipment.

He let out a sigh. He supposed this was inevitable, since he had already gone over his allotted time to study this section of the universe several millennia ago. But they were so *fascinating!*

Sighing again, he collected himself and shifted the universe so that he would be back home to file his report.

◆

CHAPTER TWENTY-SIX

◆　　◆

"THE COUNCIL YESTERDAY RATIFIED the motion to allow Koa into the Federation. The Koas are now based in the Mu Arae system—though that's not where they're from."

Kav glasch Vokrak recorded Kant Jorel's words as he sat in the holocom—in truth, his small one-person office in Vancouver—waiting for him to finish babbling so he could ask his question. He'd heard that the summit was going to happen on Grisella, and he wanted confirmation from Kant. But he was still carrying on about these potential new members. *As if the Federation needs a one-hundred-and-fifty-fifth member. Was I the only one who wanted the Ontailians and the Trill to follow the Selelvians out the door? This government is too big for its own good.*

"When their sun was threatening to go nova about four years ago, they were able to make use of an ancient device to shrink their planet down and place it in a pyramid-shaped box. With some help from Starfleet, the box was brought to Mu Arae and the planet was deposited there, with the system actually rearranging itself to accommodate the new world. Talks began shortly after that, and now they're ready to join. The date for the signing ceremony still needs to be set." Kant looked around the holocom. "You all look sufficiently bored. It's pathetic, you know that? They put their planet in a *box*. Don't you think that's— Oh, never mind." He looked down at his padd. "One last thing."

Thank you, Kav thought toward every Tellarite deity who'd ever existed.

"The president's office would like to officially announce that the summit with Chancellor Martok, President Bacco, and Praetor Tal'Aura will be held on Grisella one week from today."

Kav blinked his sunken eyes. *He answered my question.* This relieved Kav, as it eliminated the need to try to get Kant's attention, which had always been problematic under the best of circumstances, and which had gotten worse the past seven weeks or so. It was right after judiciary's landmark decision in the B-4 case, the retirement of Admiral Ross, the passing of the new transportation bill, the birthday of three different councillors' chief aides, and Ozla Graniv's return to the Palais press room. *Knowing Kant, any one of those could have set him off. My bet would be on the birthdays—he never likes it when people are having fun.*

However, his announcement prompted more questions. It was Regia Maldonado who asked, "So the Romulans *will* be represented at the summit?"

Kant nodded. "Your powers of deduction remain ordinary, Regia. Yes, since the future of the Romulan Empire is one of the primary goals of the summit, it was felt that the Romulan government should have a voice."

Ozla asked, "Jorel, there are several indications that Tal'Aura's on her way out. Is including her in the summit the Federation's way of supporting her in light of her dwindling support on Romulus?"

"Including her in the summit is the Federation's way of including her in the summit," Kant said. "That's it."

Kav was suddenly back in his small office. Standing across from him in the small space between his desk and the door was a person he never thought he'd see again.

"Brek? Is that you?"

Brek chim Glamok nodded. Kav stood up and slammed his arm against Brek's. "I don't believe it! They declared you dead!"

"There were many times, my friend, that I wish I was."

"How did you get here? What're you *doing* here? You should be back on Tellar!"

"Kav, I'm only here—I'm only *alive*—because of Ambassador Emra and Zaarok."

At that, Kav almost swallowed his own tongue. "Zaarok? You mean the *Tzelnira* Zaarok?"

"That's who I mean, yes. He sent me because he needs our help."

"How would the Tellarite News Service help—?"

Brek spit at him. "No, you idiot, the *Federation's* help!"

"Spare me your anger, Brek!" Kav spit right back. "You disappeared months ago. You were declared *dead*. Phant almost ripped all his fur out."

"I know—and I apologize for that. It has been—difficult."

Kav nodded in understanding. "Of course. What is it you've been asked to do?"

"Zaarok has a son who is dying. He was diagnosed with *cal-tai* a year ago."

Frowning, Kav said, "I don't know what that is."

"It's something that only Tzenkethi get, apparently—some kind of growth in their spines. They had been hoping the diagnosis was wrong, but apparently all the best doctors in the coalition checked him over. The only cure that is known is a surgical procedure that removes the growth."

"So where does the Federation come in?"

Brek stared at Kav. "There's only one doctor who has ever successfully performed that surgery—a Starfleet doctor named Rebecca Emmanuelli, who was a prisoner during the Tzenkethi War."

"So let me see if I understand this," Nan said as she ran her hand through her paper-white hair, convinced that it was all going to fall out before her second year in office was halfway done. "The son of a *Tzelnira* is sick, the only doctor who can save him is in Starfleet, and the Tzenkethi are willing to ship the boy here for the operation?"

Sitting across from her were Esperanza, Secretary Safranski, Kant Jorel, Z4 Blue, Myk Bunkrep, Councillor Strovos of Ardana, Admiral Akaar, and Chirurgeon P'Trell, the head of Starfleet Medical. Nan had been surprised to see that P'Trell was Caitian, considering that he had an Andorian physician's title, but Esperanza had explained before he'd arrived that, although he was Caitian by species, he was born and raised on Andor and studied medicine there.

Esperanza said, "I wish it was that simple, ma'am. The Tzenkethi aren't willing to ship the boy anywhere. It's just this one *Tzelnira* that's trying to make it work."

"Ma'am," Z4 said, "I'm pretty sure this is what Emra was trying to see you about back in January."

"And how is this supposed to work?" Nan asked Jorel.

"Brek said a ship would be entering the Temecklia system in ten days carrying the patient."

Nan stared intently at the Bajoran. "You believe him?"

"In general, no. Brek's a sensationalist, and he takes ridiculous risks. But he's also spent nine months in a Tzenkethi prison on Kliradon, where they aren't known for treating Federation species with anything like kindness."

"All the more reason why he'd say anything to get out," Safranski said.

Nan looked at the Rigelian. "You think it's a setup?"

"No, ma'am, but I think we should proceed as if we're expecting it to be."

Z4 said, "I can't imagine it is a setup, ma'am. This was telegraphed almost a year ago. Yes, we should be careful, but the Tzenkethi don't strike me as being this sloppy."

"Reality tends to be a lot more sloppy than constructed plans," Esperanza added.

Nan smirked. "Occam's razor at its dullest. All right." She turned to Akaar. "Admiral, can we meet that ship?"

"The *Sugihara* is in the area. I trust Captain Demitrijian to be able to smell a trap."

"All right, get it over there, and let's see what happens."

She turned to P'Trell. "Assuming this is on the level, how soon can this doctor get here?"

P'Trell's ears flattened. "That may be a bit of a problem, Madam President."

"Why, where is she?"

"Her location is not the problem. She's stationed at Starbase 1, in orbit of Earth."

Nan frowned. "So what *is* the problem?"

"She refuses to perform the procedure."

That surprised Nan. Her eyes wide, her mouth constricting into a line under her nose, she said, "Say that again, please."

"She refuses—"

Slamming a hand on her desk, Nan said, "What the hell happened to 'First, do no harm'?"

Esperanza looked pained. "Ma'am, Dr. Emmanuelli was a prisoner of the Tzenkethi for four years. She was captured during the war, and they kept her alive because of her skill as a surgeon, and while a prisoner she saved fourteen Tzenkethi from *cal-tai*. They told the Federation that she'd died in prison so they could keep her out of the prisoner exchanges after the armistice. A civilian group called Liberation Watch obtained evidence that she was still alive, which they turned over to Starfleet. The *Saratoga* went to investigate further, and the Tzenkethi turned her over rather than risk another war."

Nan relented. "Yeah, okay, I can see why she'd be a little peevish." She sighed. "How old is this boy, anyhow?"

"Only two," Z4 said.

P'Trell added, "But Tzenkethi mature to full growth when they're five, so that's not as young as you might think."

"Chirurgeon—" She hesitated. "Ghee, can anyone else perform this operation?"

Again, the flat ears. "Tzenkethi biology is not common knowledge. Dr. Emmanuelli never published anything about her work on Tzenketh because she didn't wish to relive the experience."

"Can't blame her for that, either. So there's no one else?"

"It's a spinal operation, Madam President. A single wrong move, and the patient will die. Even Dr. Emmanuelli didn't have a one-hundred-percent success rate—although she saved fourteen, seven died under her care as well."

Softly, Esperanza said, "Sixty-seven-percent odds aren't bad."

"No." P'Trell fixed his gaze on Esperanza. "But those odds are reduced to less than ten percent with any other surgeon." Turning back to Nan, he said, "Madam President, I have tried to convince Dr. Emmanuelli that this is the right thing to do. I've done everything short of ordering her to, and I've not done that only because she's made it clear that she will resign before she followed that order, and I'm not about to lose a fine physician over this."

Nan drummed her fingers on the desk. "Admiral, what's the *Sugihara*'s travel time back to Earth from Temecklia?"

"Five days."

She nodded. "All right, then. We won't know a damn thing for ten days, and we've got two weeks to convince Dr. Emmanuelli of the error of her ways. Chirurgeon, keep talking to her."

"Yes, ma'am."

"Admiral, get the *Sugihara* out there. And—"

Jorel interrupted. "Excuse me, ma'am, but there is one other thing."

"What?"

"My staff has picked up some reports from some of the

Tzenkethi press. Until Brek showed up this morning, I didn't really think anything of it, but—"

"But what?"

Jorel tugged on his earring, a gesture that suddenly reminded Nan of Xeldara. "They're talking about how the Federation is attempting to kidnap *Tzelnira* Zaarok's son in an attempt to start another war—oh, and that the summit next week is so you and the Klingons can plan the invasion of Tzenketh that will follow your snatching of the boy."

Nan leaned back in her chair.

Esperanza said, "Now this seems a little more like a setup."

"No, it doesn't," Z4 said. "Zaarok's gone rogue, I'm sure of that. He couldn't get it done in January, so he pulled Emra back, but now he's desperate. He's high enough among the ministers to have the ability to do this quietly, but if someone else picked up on it, they'd be more than happy to use it as Federation propaganda."

"Honestly," Jorel said, "it's only different from what the Tzenkethi press says about the Federation insofar as it has some vague bearing on reality for a change."

Nan chuckled mirthlessly. "So we've got what is at worst a setup for an attack on the Federation, and at best an anti-Federation propaganda opportunity for the Tzenkethi."

Esperanza nodded. "That about sums it up."

Standing up, Nan said, "Well, I can't kill myself worrying about what the Tzenkethi press think of me—I have enough problems worrying about what the people in Jorel's room think. And ultimately, the only thing I really give a damn about is saving a two-year-old boy's life. Let's get this moving and see where it takes us."

"Thank you, Madam President," Esperanza said, and

everyone got up. However, while most folks headed for the exit to the turbolifts, Esperanza and Myk, who hadn't said anything the entire meeting, approached the president's desk.

"What's up?" Nan asked.

Myk said, "Ma'am, I've been looking into something for the last few weeks, and I think it's something you'll want to mention at the summit."

Nan shot Esperanza a look. "If we have to add something else—"

Esperanza held up a hand. "I know, I know, the Diplomatic Corps will put arsenic in your soup or whatever horrible retribution diplomats visit on sitting presidents when they annoy them, but I think this is worth it."

"Actually, they'll probably just talk me to death." Nan looked at Myk. "What is it?"

Myk handed her a padd. Nan read it over, then looked at the Zakdorn woman. "You sure about this?"

She nodded. "That's why this is so last-minute— Esperanza said she wouldn't bring it to you until I was absolutely sure, but I've spoken with about a dozen people who are involved in the project, including some of the Klingons. This is for real, but it's in danger of falling apart at the seams unless the governments step in."

Nan turned to Esperanza. "You think Martok'll go for it?"

"I know he won't if you don't ask him."

Smiling, Nan said, "Yeah. All right, I'll work this into the third meeting. I pull this out in either of the first two, I risk scuttling the whole thing." She looked at Myk. "Good work on this."

Favoring her with a rare smile, Myk said, "Thank you, Madam President."

◆ ◆ ◆

Martok, son of Urthog, head of the High Council, chancellor of the Klingon Empire, wasn't sure what to expect from Federation President Nan Bacco.

He had dealt directly with her predecessor, Min Zife, during the Tezwa crisis and had found him to be an irritating coward—about what one would expect from someone elected by the masses. Martok had always found democracy puzzling; power came from the judgment of one's peers, not the adulation of one's lessers.

Prior to this, his impressions of Bacco had come mostly from that *petaQ* K'mtok. Zife's going straight to Martok during Tezwa had given the hardliners on the High Council all the excuse they'd needed to call for replacing Ambassador Lantar with K'mtok, an ally of Martok's biggest enemy on the council, Kopek.

Tellingly, K'mtok's impressions of Bacco had changed as time had gone on. At first, K'mtok—whose reports had mostly gone to Kopek—had spoken of her dismissively and categorized her as weak. However, more recently he was reporting to the entire High Council that Bacco was a shrewd and worthy leader.

Over the past few days, they had sat in a dull, beige-colored room on Mount Dalwik, a high peak on Grisella. The room, like the planet itself, was a neutral party in galactic politics. The Grisella government had agreed to host the summit in the hopes of fostering peace, which was one of several reasons why the empire had had little use for the Grisella in general.

Each leader had been permitted two guards. Two of Martok's personal guards now stood at attention behind him, just as two Starfleet security officers stood behind Bacco, and two centurions stood behind Tal'Aura. Aside from that, they had remained undisturbed during the session, for which Martok was grateful. The presence of Federation journalists had annoyed Martok—Klingon news-gathering organizations were not permitted on such trips—but he recognized it as a necessary evil when dealing with the Federation, and he didn't mind as long as they stayed out of his way. Mostly they had, thanks to the chancellor's personal guard.

The summit had brought Martok around to the same conclusion about the Federation president that K'mtok had reached. Bacco understood the Klingon heart but was not willing to let that get in the way of serving her people.

About Tal'Aura, Martok had fewer kind words. She was quiet, uncommunicative, and spoke mostly in vague terms about her vision for the Romulan Empire, none of which seemed possible with the support she had. Martok hadn't realized how much of the Romulan economy depended on labor produced by Remans; with them removed from the equation, mostly to Klorgat IV, the Romulan people were suffering.

To make matters worse, Tal'Aura's voice reminded Martok for some reason of that of his late wife Sirella. To hear something even similar to his beloved's voice coming out of a Romulan just made his blood boil.

Martok thought the final session was over, allowing him to return to his people with something like a victory. Martok had agreed that the empire's expansionist policies would cease—not a difficult concession to give, as the empire's losses since the war were such that expansion was proving problematic—and in return the Federation renewed several trade agreements and opened a few new ones, including more extensive technology sharing, something that had been beneficial to both nations in the years since the Khitomer Accords. In addition, Martok reaffirmed that, even with the move to Klorgat IV, he intended to honor the agreement made regarding the Remans and that the empire would withdraw from its role as protector of the Remans at the agreed-upon date, which was three weeks from this summit.

Bacco then said, "There is one more thing I would like to discuss, Chancellor. It's not something that was on the agenda, and I'll understand if you don't want to, but I believe it's important."

Martok smiled. "The schedule for this meeting was due to the labors of the High Council and Ambassador K'mtok's office. I have no need to keep fidelity to their work, Madam President."

Bacco smiled right back. Martok noticed that she didn't consult with Tal'Aura. From what he'd been told, mostly by Alexander Rozhenko, including Tal'Aura had not been Bacco's idea any more than most of the Klingon side of the agenda had been Martok's, and had mostly come about due to the Romulan ambassador, Kalavak, lobbying several Federation councillors. *I wonder if Bacco's council vexes her as much as mine does me,* he thought with an internal laugh.

"Are you at all familiar, Chancellor," Bacco said, "with an organization known as the Matter of Everything? They're a civilian group, not affiliated with any government, and they include several Federation experts, as well as some prominent Cardassian and Klingon scientists, who are studying various space anomalies and trying to tie them together into a theory about the structure of the universe. I believe the Klingons in the group call it *HapHoch.*"

The first name was unfamiliar to Martok, but the second was, and his face soured. "Madam President, *HapHoch* was condemned by the Science Institute for—"

"I'm familiar with the condemnation, Chancellor—in fact, I've read it. It says that the *HapHoch* violates every tenet of scientific inquiry and is an obscene investigation into matters best left alone. There's only one problem: It's a project that the Science Institute actually pursued about five years ago. Then, suddenly, the project was shut down, and its head—a woman named B'Ekara—was fired from the institute. She's with MOE now, and the reason why all that happened was because she brought in the theories of someone else who's now part of MOE."

Martok felt a growl build in his throat. He knew some of this, of course, from when the institute's condemnation was reported to the High Council. He hadn't given it much thought at the time and had simply assumed that the institute's condemnation was for a good reason, and so he and the council had agreed to banning further research on the topic. Until Bacco spelled it out, he couldn't even remember exactly what it was they'd condemned, only that it had happened. "Madam President, I fail to see—"

Bacco, however, refused to be interrupted. "The scientist in question is named Kleissu—he's a Mizarian."

Now the growl was getting bigger. Mizarians were the vermin of the galaxy. Their world had been conquered dozens of times in the last hundred years alone, and the empire refused to have any dealings with that species.

"Chancellor, I read over these people's work on the way here. They might have something. If it keeps going on this track, they might be able to tell us about the way the universe works, how it's held together, what keeps it from flying apart. It'll probably take years, and may not even be done in either of our lifetimes—but honestly, is this the kind of thing you want to *ban* just because you don't like one of the people in the group?"

"You are asking me to accept scientific data provided by a *Mizarian?*" Martok found the entire notion repugnant.

"No, Chancellor, I'm not. I'm asking you to accept scientific data provided by some of the finest minds in the galaxy, one of whom happens to be a Mizarian. He doesn't even live on Mizar, for pity's sake. He's in no way representative of the Mizarian people, he doesn't speak for them, doesn't represent their pacifist ways, which I know disgust you—he's one person. One person who, along with a lot of other people who are, frankly, smarter than any of the three of us, might be able to tell us more about the place we live in. Isn't that worth putting aside a prejudice that doesn't do you any good anyhow in the hopes of a much greater goal?"

Laughing mirthlessly, Martok asked, "Is that all that is required of me?"

"It's nothing you haven't done before, Chancellor."

"That is ridiculous." Martok was losing patience. "This is a minor scientific curiosity that has no benefits in the short or long term. For that, you wish me to set aside the empire's policy regarding Mizar."

"This has nothing to do with Mizar. And how the hell do you know it has no benefits in any kind of term? You haven't even read MOE's research, and you don't know what they're going to turn up. Think about how many Defense Force vessels have come across spatial anomalies that they didn't know how to deal with—or that destroyed or damaged them. MOE might actually be able to figure out where they come from and how to survive them. And you're just gonna let all that potential fall by the wayside because you don't like the Mizarians."

"It is not a question of what I *like*, Madam President. You cannot ask me to reverse centuries of—"

Tal'Aura interrupted: "Klingon bigotry?"

It took all of Martok's willpower not to unsheathe his *d'k tahg* and kill Tal'Aura where she sat.

Bacco glanced at the Romulan woman. "There's a human cliché, Praetor, that people who live in glass houses shouldn't throw stones." At Tal'Aura's confused look, which matched Martok's own, she added, "It means that you don't have any basis to get superior toward Martok regarding bigotry toward other species—or should we go into the treatment of the Remans, the Miridians, the—"

Tal'Aura held up a hand. "Your point is noted, Madam President."

"Fine, then shut the hell up."

Martok couldn't help but smile at that.

Turning back to Martok, Bacco said, "About a year and a half ago, I met Benjamin Sisko for the first time."

The vicious smile directed at Tal'Aura changed into a warm one for the human Martok respected more than any other.

"He told me an interesting story from the war about how your flagship rendezvoused with the *U.S.S. Defiant* and you beamed aboard because you wanted to see the Starfleet doctor instead of the one in your own medical bay. I'm fully aware of the Klingon prejudice toward good medical practice, and I'm also aware that that's changed over the years, in part because of your own initiatives after becoming chancellor. That sounds a lot to me like reversing centuries of Klingon tradition for the sake of something better: healthier, longer-lived Klingons who have the opportunity to extend their record of battle and have a better chance of going to *Sto-Vo-Kor*."

Once again, Martok was reminded why K'mtok had so

changed his feelings about this human. Not only had she given an argument that a Klingon would understand but she had also done so in a manner that was eminently human. She could easily have made her point by accusing Martok of lying, citing his position on medicine as an example of his duplicity, an accusation that would have been sure to provoke a violent response in the chancellor. *Instead, she performs that irritating human task of appealing to my better nature.*

"What is it," he finally asked after a long pause, "that you are proposing?"

"That our governments jointly support MOE—or *HapHoch,* or whatever it winds up being called—and give them every chance to do what they want to do, and do it right. Let's give them support from Starfleet and the Defense Force. And let's show that we can work *together* on this and move *forward* on this and not let outmoded prejudices get in the way of doing the right thing."

Martok threw his head back and laughed. "It has been a long time, Madam President, since I was able to convince anyone on the High Council to admit their prejudices were outmoded—much less that they should do the right thing. However, I will bring this to them and make it clear that I wish it to be so."

Bacco smiled now, for the first time since she brought this up. "Thank you, Chancellor. I think the best thing for all our people is to work together as much as possible. The galaxy's gotten too small for us to keep hiding behind neutral zones and ethnocentric biases. And I think, my friends, that that's it."

Tal'Aura then spoke. "I'm afraid there is one more thing that I must discuss with you both."

Looking at Martok, Bacco said, "Well, I already went off the playbook, so I'm in no position to argue. Chancellor?"

Martok's instinct was not to care what the Romulan had to say, but she had also been very subdued throughout this entire summit, participating only as much as had been necessary. Given how hard her people had worked to get her here, it seemed odd to Martok that she would then have declined to involve herself in the goings-on of the summit itself. He suspected that the answer to his unspoken question would come from Tal'Aura now, so he nodded his affirmation.

Tal'Aura took a moment before she finally spoke. "Within a few days, an announcement will be made on Achernar Prime by Commander Donatra. She will be calling herself Empress Donatra, actually, and she will declare Achernar Prime, as well as all the worlds in that star system and three or four more besides—including Xanitla, Ralatak, and Virinat—to be the Imperial Romulan State under her rule."

"And how does this concern us?" Martok could have answered his own question—it was a cause for celebration. Tal'Aura had been holding the empire together with her teeth, and now two large morsels had slipped through.

"Those three worlds are our primary farming planets," Tal'aura snapped in a voice that sounded even more like Sirella.

"Does she have the support of the rest of the military?" Bacco asked.

"No—many are still loyal to me. However, the ships she has are guarding those three worlds."

Bacco nodded. "She's holding the empire's food supply hostage?"

Tal'Aura nodded. "I have managed, over the past year, to

unite at least some of the factions. The Tal Shiar, Durjik and his radical sect, and several admirals and commanders have all pledged their loyalty to me. But Donatra has fought me every step of the way. Now she has seceded from the empire."

"I'm afraid," Bacco said, "that I'm with Martok. What is it you want from us?"

"To not recognize the Imperial Romulan State. To refuse to trade with them, to impose sanctions upon them, and to aid us in retaking their worlds for the Romulan Empire."

Martok snarled at her. "You wish me to commit Klingon warriors to fight for a united Romulan Empire?"

"Donatra will reach out to you as an ally, or at least as a trading partner, offer you the resources she is now denying us in order to build her strength. And then, when she is powerful enough, she will try to succeed where Shinzon failed. Remember, Donatra was on Shinzon's side."

"So, Praetor, were you," Martok said in an even tone.

Bacco had been unusually quiet. In a soft voice, she said, "You're giving us a lot of hypotheticals here, Praetor, but none of this has even happened yet. Either way, though, I can tell you this: Like Chancellor Martok, I can assure you that there's no way in hell I'm committing any military resources to help you out."

"If you don't, our people will *starve.*"

"There, we'll be happy to help you. If your people need food, we'll provide it. But we're not gonna take sides in your little internecine conflicts."

Sneering, Tal'Aura said, "You are condemning the Romulan people to a slow and miserable death."

Bacco stared intently back at the praetor. Then, speaking with more iron than Martok would ever have expected from a frail-looking, elderly human woman, she said, "No,

Praetor, *you* did that when you left a thalaron bomb in the senate chamber on Shinzon's behalf. *That* is what put you on this course, and if you find now that you can't turn around, then I will pity you, and I will help you in whatever way I can, but I will be *damned* if I will let you try to foist the blame on me. You got into bed with a lunatic, Praetor, and now the people you claim to lead are paying the price for your stupidity. If the Imperial Romulan State does indeed declare itself a sovereign entity, then the Federation will carefully consider whether or not to recognize it as a legitimate government. I can tell you this for damn sure: Our decision will take a lot of factors into account, but what makes *your* life easier will be extremely low on that list."

Tal'Aura turned her gaze to Martok. "I assume that the Klingon Empire, as usual, trails behind the Federation like a pet eager for approval?"

"No." Martok smiled. "The Federation may require time to make that decision, but the empire's is already made. We will recognize any political entity that fractures the Romulans further."

That obviously did not please Tal'Aura, which only pleased Martok more. After a brief silence, she rose from her chair and left the meeting room, the two centurions trailing behind her.

Bacco looked at Martok. "Can't say as that was much of a shock. Honestly, I'm amazed the empire's held together as long as it has. I figured they'd start falling to pieces once you guys took the Remans to Klorgat IV."

Martok nodded. "That was, in fact, our hope."

Chuckling, Bacco said, "Yeah, we kinda figured that." Growing serious again, she said, "I meant what I said,

Chancellor. We won't get involved in the Romulans' internal politics, but we're not just gonna stand around and let their people die."

"I would not expect you to do anything other than what you have always done, Madam President," Martok said.

Bacco rose from her chair. "I'd say this summit is concluded, Chancellor."

"Indeed, Madam President." Martok also got up.

"I think we've done some good work here today, Chancellor. I hope this isn't the last time we do this."

"I can promise nothing, Madam President. If I have learned nothing else in my five years as chancellor, it is that predicting the future is unwise."

"Wasn't asking for a promise, Chancellor—was just asking for hope."

"My only hope, Madam President, is to die in battle and cross the River of Blood to *Sto-Vo-Kor*. Whatever happens on that journey happens, and we can do little else but fight it to the end."

"Well, I'm a little more concerned with getting the most I can out of this life." She smiled. "But I think we've done a pretty good job on both ends."

She held out her hand. Recognizing the human gesture, Martok accepted the handshake.

As they shook hands, Bacco said, *"Qapla'*, Martok, son of Urthog."

"Qapla', Nan Bacco."

✦

CHAPTER TWENTY-SEVEN

✦   ✦

DR. REBECCA EMMANUELLI had been to many dangerous places in her seventy years of life: the brutally hot sands of Vulcan's Forge, the treacherous fire caves of Bajor, the uncertain mists of Berengaria, the toxic Mayak swamp on Ferenginar, and the hideously dense petrified forests of Selmak. Plus, of course, there were the four years she'd spent on Tzenketh, but she tried not to think about that.

None of those places made her as nervous as she was right now as she sat outside the president's office in the Palais de la Concorde.

An elderly Vulcan sat at a workstation, giving her the occasional disdainful look. She wondered if that disdain was a direct result of what she had been refusing to do for the past two weeks and would continue to steadfastly refuse to do, no matter what it was that President Bacco said to her when she went into her office.

She knew what was going on, of course; given the fact that the patient in question was in Starbase 1's infirmary, it would be impossible for her, as the head of that infirmary, not to know. The son of one of the *Tzelnira*—the people who'd ordered the attack on Starbase 55, during which Emmanuelli had been captured; the people who'd ordered her to be declared dead so she could remain on Tzenketh and treat their sick and wounded—was now in one of her biobeds, awaiting an operation that only she could perform and that she swore she would never perform again as long as she lived.

The door to the office slid open, and Rebecca saw the face of the president herself. Under any other circumstances this would be a thrill. It had been a big enough deal, talking with the chief of staff back in August during that mess with the Trinni/ek, but now . . .

"Dr. Emmanuelli, please come in."

The Vulcan looked at the president. "Is the intercom no longer working, ma'am?" he asked in an arch voice that made Rebecca realize that the disdain was more general and not directed necessarily at her. For some reason, that relieved her.

"It's a personal touch, Sivak."

"Whatever excuse you feel compelled to give to cover your inability to remember how to use the intercom from day to day is—"

Gesturing to the inside of her office, the president interrupted her assistant. "Come in, please, Doctor, we've got a lot to talk about."

Emmanuelli got up and followed the president in. Seated on the couch was the very same chief of staff she'd spoken to before, Esperanza Piñiero, as well as Chirurgeon P'Trell. *I guess I should've expected Ghee to be here,* Emmanuelli thought with a sigh. They weren't going to make it easy on her.

Well, I'm not gonna make it easy on them, either.

"Have a seat," the president said as she herself sat in one of the chairs perpendicular to the couch.

Rebecca took the chair facing the president, grateful that Bacco had given her the opportunity to sit face-to-face. The president could just as easily have chosen to preside at her desk, with all the power that conveyed. Instead, she was treating this as a conversation among equals, even though it most assuredly wasn't. Rebecca truly appreciated the gesture.

"My head speechwriter has this thing for old, dead languages. He likes to put references to them in my speeches. Half the time I take 'em out, since I don't think it's such a hot idea to try to convey something to people by using words they're not gonna understand. But thanks to him, I know all kinds of odd bits and pieces in Latin and ancient Greek and the like. So I know a certain phrase that goes, *primum non nocere.* It's the start of an oath you—"

Rebecca had intended to interrupt much sooner, but it had taken her this long to screw up the courage to do so. "Madam President, with all due respect, I think throwing the Hippocratic oath in my face is cheap."

"Maybe it is, Doctor, but so's what you're doing."

Aghast, Rebecca asked, "I beg your pardon?"

"You're not the only one who took an oath, Doctor. I took one a little over a year ago, and it said that I would lead the Federation and do what was best for its people."

"And how does my operating on a Tzenkethi fulfill that oath, ma'am?" Rebecca asked in a tight voice.

"First of all, it's not 'a Tzenkethi.' It's a two-year-old boy named Zormonk. Secondly, the Tzenkethi have been at loggerheads with us for decades. We fought more than one war against them, and they still view us as some kind of evil empire that has to be stamped out of the galaxy. Not a day goes by without our press liaison coming across some piece of anti-Federation propaganda from the *Tzelnira.*"

"Ma'am, I'm aware of what the *Tzelnira* are capable of. In fact, I think I know better than anyone in the Federation, to say nothing of anyone in this room."

"True. I know what you went through was horrible, but—"

"Horrible? Ma'am, it would have to improve by several thousand orders of magnitude before it got as good as horrible!" Realizing that she was yelling at the president, Rebecca took a breath and said in a softer voice, "I'm sorry, ma'am, but you have to understand what they did. It wasn't just that they held me prisoner, and it wasn't just that they forced me to treat their sick and injured. They only let me treat certain people—certain *important* people, who were worthy of it. I had to let two women, one man, and three children die because they weren't of the right social caste while I wasted my time operating on the cousin of one of the *Tzelnira* who had no hope of recovery, no matter what I did, which I told them over and over, but they forced me to do it anyhow, and he *still* died. And then, when the armistice happened, they told the Federation I was *dead* and *kept* me there. My husband remarried, my children grieved for me—and then when I came back, it destroyed my husband's new marriage, and my children blamed *me* for lying to them. So ma'am, please, don't presume to tell me that you know *anything* about what I went through."

Somehow, Rebecca managed to keep her composure. It helped that she had been rehearsing this very confrontation for the past two weeks. She felt like her chest was about to explode, but outwardly she remained calm.

The president sat and listened to everything she said. Then she picked up a padd from the table in front of her. "For the last five days, we've been getting more reports from Tzenketh—things about the son of one of the *Tzelnira* being kidnapped by the Federation and being experimented on."

Unable to contain a snort of derisive laughter, Rebecca

said, "Ma'am, if you're trying to convince me to perform the operation—"

"I'm not finished."

In a small voice, Rebecca said, "I'm sorry, ma'am." She suspected she had tested the president's patience as much as she was going to get away with.

"There've been statements from almost every member of the *Tzelnira*. The one exception is Zaarok. His son's the one who's supposedly been kidnapped, yet there's nothing from him." She set that down and picked up another padd. "Technically you're not cleared to know this next part, but I'm invoking executive privilege. This is a Starfleet Intelligence report that indicates that Zaarok has been secretly put in prison for sending Zormonk to the enemy." She put that padd down. "You yourself just said you know better than anyone else in this room what a Tzenkethi prison is like. This is a member of the most privileged class in Tzenkethi society, and he's cooperated with his people's greatest enemy and allowed himself to be imprisoned because he wants his son to live."

The president stood up. *So much for being on equal footing,* Rebecca thought.

President Bacco started pacing back and forth. "I can very easily order you to do this, Doctor. So could Chirurgeon P'Trell, and you'd be obligated to follow it or face severe consequences. But I'm not going to do that, because that would defeat the whole point. If you performed this operation under duress, or went to prison because of it, then it would be just like what the Tzenkethi did to you. And there's no way I'm going to allow something like that. Instead, I'm asking you—I'm *begging* you—to look at what Zaarok did. He made a choice. He put aside his own people's prejudices, went against every principle that the government he represents lives by in order to save a two-year-old boy who never did anything to anyone."

Stopping at her desk, the president leaned against it. Rebecca noticed that she was leaning right next to a rotating holo of a young girl who resembled the president but definitely wasn't her. There were other pictures too: an adult with the same face as the girl, whom Rebecca realized was the president's daughter, along with three children; another of just the children; and finally a wedding photo of two people who were neither the president nor her daughter. Rebecca suspected that the president stood by reminders of family on purpose.

"We have such a great opportunity here, Doctor. For the first time ever, we have a chance to bridge the gap between the Federation and the Tzenkethi, to show that our people *can* work together for the greater good instead of perpetuating the evils of being opposed. But the *only* way that's going to happen is if you go back to Starbase 1 and save Zormonk's life. If you don't, then we've got someone else unjustly placed in a Tzenkethi prison, a dead child, and an enemy that will be more vicious than before, because they'll have the corpse of the son of a member of the *Tzelnira* who died under Federation care."

The president walked back over to the chair and sat down. "Understand something else, Doctor—if you still refuse, then that'll be the end of it. There'll be no reprimands, no censure, no blackballing. Chirurgeon P'Trell and I have agreed that you have every reason to hate the Tzenkethi and what they did to you. You can go right back to Starbase 1 and continue your career without any repercussions."

Rebecca found that impossible to credit. Even if there were no official repercussions, she knew that lines would be drawn. Some would view her as the one who'd refused to save a child's life. Others—those who'd fought the Tzenkethi or knew those who had—would support her, telling her she'd done the right thing.

This one decision would define the rest of her life.

She thought back to the look of anguish on Raphael's face when he'd introduced her to the woman he'd married two years after she'd been declared dead. The overwhelming feeling of joy she'd felt when she'd materialized in the *Saratoga* transporter room. The knife-twist of Daniel and Gustavo's anger, projecting the bile that only a teenager could muster at a mother who they thought had abandoned them. The horror of watching those six people die so she could perform a pointless operation. The bone-sore agony of her cell, a cold, windowless room where she'd lived between treatments, with only a flat piece of cloth and two buckets for furniture.

Then she thought about Zaarok, whom she'd met more than once in her time as prisoner, who'd referred to her as the "pet doctor," sitting in a cell just like that one.

The thought gave her immense pleasure.

However, Zaarok, she suspected, would remain in that cell no matter what happened. He had violated Tzenkethi law, and he had consorted with their worst enemy. No, his suffering would be long and hard—and it would be made worse by the knowledge that he'd failed, that his son had died.

And then she thought about Daniel and Gustavo, who hadn't spoken to her in fifteen years. Yet if she found out they were sick and that only a Tzenkethi doctor could save them, what would she do?

Just what Zaarok had done.

She realized something else as well: If she refused to do

this, she was finished as a physician. The president's assurances notwithstanding, if she let a patient die due to her own negligence, she would have violated the very oath the president tried to guilt her with, and she would no longer be worthy of her medical degree—in her own mind, if in no one else's.

"All right," she said in a small voice.

"I'm sorry?" the president said.

Louder, Rebecca said, "I'll do it. God help me, I'll—I'll do it."

Esperanza felt like a black hole had opened up in her stomach. She got off the turbolift on fifteen and walked slowly toward the president's office door.

Sivak gave her one of his looks. "The meeting has already commenced. President Bacco has expressed surprise at your tardiness, and also instructed me to—"

Ignoring him, Esperanza went into the president's office. Ashanté, Myk, Dogayn, and Z4 were all present, as were Fred, Admiral Akaar, Safranski, and Raisa Shostakova.

"About time you got here, Esperanza," said the president, who was leaning against the front of her desk. "We—"

"Ma'am, I just got a message from Starbase 1. Zormonk is—is dead."

The president's face fell. "What?"

"According to Dr. Emmanuelli's report, the *cal-tai* was too advanced. If she had been able to get to him sooner—even as little as a month sooner—she might have had a chance to save him."

"Damn."

"There's more, ma'am. According to Chirurgeon P'Trell's report, Dr. Emmanuelli went to extraordinary lengths to try to save him, long past the point where most doctors would have given up, and he's put her in for a commendation." She took a breath, then added, "She accepted the commendation right before she resigned her commission, effective immediately."

The president's office grew very quiet. It stayed that way for some time.

✦

CHAPTER TWENTY-EIGHT

✦   ✦

NAN BACCO ADMIRED THE VIEW through the shuttlecraft window of the verdant field where the signing ceremony would be taking place. Thousands of Koas—large arachnoids with octopus-like heads—were already gathered to watch the event, which would end with Koa's official entry into the United Federation of Planets.

The shuttle belonged to the *U.S.S. Venture*, which had escorted the president to the Mu Arae system for the ceremony. That vessel was in orbit, alongside the *U.S.S. da Vinci*, which was formally representing Starfleet at the signing ceremony. Normally a tiny *Saber*-class vessel attached to the Starfleet Corps of Engineers wouldn't be assigned to represent Starfleet at a signing—indeed, that was the type of duty that the *Galaxy*-class *Venture* generally had—but it had been the *da Vinci* crew who'd aided the Koas when they'd moved their planet to its new home, including deciphering the controls on the box into which the planet had been placed and opening it to let the planet out. The *da Vinci* crew were heroes in the Koas' eyes.

When the shuttle touched down, Nan started walking slowly to the rear. Esperanza was next to her, and she said, "You've been awfully quiet, ma'am."

Chuckling, Nan said, "I'd think you'd have been relieved."

"Well, going an entire shuttle trip without a lecture on the physics of traveling in a box, or the history of the S.C.E., or more gnashing of teeth about the Pioneers not making the Series was something of a relief, ma'am, but it's pretty out of character."

"Yeah, I guess." Nan sighed as she disembarked. They had landed about thirty meters from the backstage area, where Caliph Sicarios, as well as Councillors Mazibuko and Jix and several members of the *da Vinci* crew, were waiting to greet her. As they traversed that distance, Kenshikai, Aoki, Rydell, and T'r'wo'li'i' walking alongside them, she said, "I've just been thinking about all the crap that's come down. The Tzenkethi are hopping mad about Zormonk, the Imperial Romulan State is making things even worse in Romulan space, which I wouldn't have thought possible, it's looking increasingly likely that Gelemingar's bill is going to pass, which is gonna be an absolute nightmare, and the Tholians are acting up again. Plus, of course, there's the Pioneers, which I'd managed to put out of my head until you kindly reminded me, thank you *so* much."

Esperanza smirked. "My pleasure, ma'am." Then her face grew more serious. "Ma'am, do you remember when you visited my parents one time when I was about nine—it was right after I had a fight with one of my friends in school?"

Nan frowned. "No." She chuckled. "Honestly, Esperanza, there was no way in hell I could keep track of what you were carrying on about at that age—I just nodded a lot and let you babble on incoherently."

"That explains why I find the tactic so useful against you, ma'am—knew there was karmic justice in the galaxy. In any case," she said quickly to overlay another snide remark, "there was one time where I'd gotten into a fight with my best friend, Irina. All our other friends took her side, and I felt like I was all alone. I told you that I hated all my friends and I was never gonna speak to them again. You told me that I shouldn't say things like that, because friends are too important. I said they were all awful and weren't my friends anymore, and you said for me to think back to all the nice things they'd done for me."

Nan smiled. "You're saying I should pay attention to the good stuff I've done?"

"Well, I could mention that you kept the Reman situation from getting out of hand, or that you opened up trade talks with a new species that was ready to break off with us because their people got sick. I could say that you strengthened our relationship with the Klingons to the best it's been since the war, which is impressive, since the alliance was on the brink of falling apart when you took office. I could talk about all the legislation you got passed or the good decisions you made or that you got the Deltans and the Carreon to talk to each other." She smiled. "But I think I'll just stick with this: The Federation's still intact. So nice job, so far."

Nan couldn't help but laugh. "Yeah, I guess. Of course, you left off one thing." They were now coming to the backstage.

"What's that?"

"I get to be the one to welcome a new world into the Federation."

"Yeah, ma'am—fun job, isn't it?"

Again, Nan laughed. "It has its moments." She approached the leader of the Koas. "Caliph Sicarios, I'm President Nan Bacco. It's truly an honor to meet you, sir."

"Thank you, Madam President, for honoring us in this way—and for all that your Federation has done for us."

Nan shook her head. "Don't be ridiculous—we should be the ones to thank you."

"I do not understand. We have done nothing."

"Nothing?" Nan's eyes widened. "Caliph, I've read the reports, not to mention your planet's history. You heard tales of a great federation, one that accepted anyone and everyone. So you shrunk your planet down and put it into a pyramid in the vague hope that those tales might possibly be true. You are a brave and noble people, and it is the Federation who should be thanking you for letting us enjoy the fruits of your bravery and your nobility."

An odd excretion appeared near Sicarios's head, which Nan supposed was probably their equivalent of tears. "You do us honor, Madam President. This is the beginning of a new age for Koa."

"For the Federation, too, Caliph. I understand you'll be representing your world to the Federation Council?"

"Yes, ma'am, I will."

"Then I look forward to a lot more conversations with you when you report to Earth for the next session." She indicated the staircase that led to the stage. "Now, then—let's get you people joined up."

"Thank you, Madam President."

APPENDIX

KNOWN PRESIDENTS OF THE UNITED FEDERATION OF PLANETS

What follows is an incomplete and partly conjectural list of people who have served in the office of Federation president since the nation's founding in 2161. If the president in question appeared or was mentioned in a movie, episode, or work of fiction other than this volume, it is cited.

Haroun al-Rashid. Human male. One of the first presidents of the Federation, serving in the twenty-second century.

T'Maran. Vulcan female. One of the first presidents of the Federation, serving in the twenty-second century.

Avaranthi sh'Rothress. Andorian *shen*. One of the first presidents of the Federation, serving in the twenty-second century. Former Andorian councillor.

Madza Bral. Trill female. Served in the early twenty-third century. First person not from one of the five founding worlds of the Federation to be elected president.

Kenneth Wescott. Human male. President during the Klingon conflict and subsequent signing of the Organian Peace Treaty, in 2267. Declined to run for reelection in 2268. One of the fifteenth-floor meeting rooms in the Palais de la Concorde is named for him. (*Star Trek: Errand of Fury* Book 1: *Seeds of Rage* by Kevin Ryan.)

Lorne McLaren. Human male. Former Starfleet officer. Elected president in 2268. (*Star Trek Core Games Book* by Last Unicorn Games.)

Hiram Roth. Human male. President during the so-called Genesis incident, as well as the attack on Earth of a probe seeking out humpback whales and the subsequent rebuilding, all in 2285–2286. Died in 2288 on the day that he won another term in a landslide victory. (*Star Trek IV: The Voyage Home.*)

Ra-ghoratreii. Efrosian male. Elected during the first special election in Federation history after the death of President Roth. Served during the assassination of Chancellor Gorkon and subsequent signing of the Khitomer Accords in 2293. Served three terms. One of the fifteenth-floor meeting rooms is named after him. (*Star Trek VI: The Undiscovered Country*)

Thelianaresth th'Vorothishria. Andorian *than*. President during initial talks with Cardassian Union in 2327. Former Starfleet officer. Had a château built to serve as his residence, which is now the permanent home of the president, named the Château Thelian in his honor. (*Star Trek: Enter the Wolves* by A.C. Crispin & Howard Weinstein.)

T'Pragh. Vulcan female. Served during the Tzenkethi War in the mid-twenty-fourth century.

Amitra. Pandrilite female. Was a cabinet member under three prior presidents. Moved presidential office to the smaller Ra-ghoratreii Room. Her sole term ended in 2368.

Jaresh-Inyo. Grazerite male. President during both the quadrant-wide paranoia regarding Founder infiltration prior to the Dominion War and the Klingon withdrawal from the Khitomer Accords in 2372. Former Grazer councillor. Lost reelection bid after Starfleet tricked him into declaring martial law in 2372. ("Homefront," "Paradise Lost," "Extreme Measures" [DS9]: *Star Trek: A Time for War, a Time for Peace* by Keith R.A. DeCandido.)

Min Zife. Bolian male. President during the Dominion War and its aftermath, after being elected in 2372. Moved presidential office back to the larger space, returning the Ra-ghoratreii Room to its original purpose as a meeting room. Resigned three years into his second term in 2379 to avoid public disclosure of Tezwa scandal. (*Star Trek: A Time to Kill* by David Mack, *Star Trek: A Time to Heal* by David Mack, *Star Trek: A Time for War, a Time for Peace* by Keith R.A. DeCandido, *Trill: Unjoined* by Michael A. Martin & Andy Mangels.)

Nanietta Bacco. Human female. Elected in second special election, held after Zife's resignation. Former governor of Cestus III. (*Star Trek: A Time for War, a Time for Peace* by Keith R.A. DeCandido.)

ACKNOWLEDGMENTS

As always, the biggest thanks have to go to my editors, Marco Palmieri and John J. Ordover. John was the one who first came to me with the notion of doing a *Star Trek* version of *The West Wing*. Marco was the one who saw the book through, and, as ever, he made it far better than it was when I started. I also have to give kudos to Ed Schlesinger, the editor on my novel *A Time for War, a Time for Peace*, which set this book up, and John Van Citters at Paramount, whose brilliant feedback was invaluable.

Secondary thanks go to David Mack *(A Time to Kill* and *A Time to Heal)*, Michael A. Martin & Andy Mangels *(Taking Wing)*, Michael Jan Friedman *(Death in Winter)*, and the team of John Logan, Brent Spiner, and Rick Berman *(Star Trek Nemesis)*, whose work also set much of this novel up. In addition, one cannot forget all the folks who wrote the many episodes of *Star Trek* (both live-action and animated), *Star Trek: The Next Generation*, *Star Trek: Deep Space Nine*, *Star Trek: Voyager*, and *Star Trek: Enterprise* and the other *Star Trek* feature films referenced in this novel, all far too numerous to list here.

Some of the characters who are mentioned and/or appear in this book were brought to life on the screen originally, and those actors deserve thanks for providing form and substance to their roles: Fran Bennett (Admiral Taela

Shanthi), Michael Berryman (Captain Rixx), Brian Brophy (Captain Bruce Maddox), Michael Cavanaugh (Captain Robert DeSoto), Shannon Cochran (Praetor Tal'Aura), Ward Costello (Admiral Gregory Quinn), Robert Ellenstein (President Hiram Roth), Jonathan Frakes (Captain William T. Riker), J.G. Hertzler (Chancellor Martok), Barry Jenner (Admiral William Ross), Stephen Macht (Councillor Krim Aldos), Kate Mulgrew (Admiral Kathryn Janeway), Leonard Nimoy (Ambassador Spock), Brock Peters (Joseph Sisko), Robert Picardo (the Doctor), Alan Scarfe (Admiral Lhian Mendak), Kurtwood Smith (President Ra-ghoratreii), Herschel Sparber (President Jaresh-Inyo), Brent Spiner (B-4), and Marc Worden (Ambassador Alexander Rozhenko).

More thanks go to the following writers for various bits of inspiration and/or guidance: Kevin J. Anderson & Rebecca Moesta *(The Gorn Crisis)*, Diane Carey *(The Dominion War* Book 2), Bill Clinton *(My Life)*, A.C. Crispin & Howard Weinstein *(Enter the Wolves)*, Peter David *(Stone and Anvil, After the Fall)*, J.M. Dillard *(Resistance*, the novelizations of *Star Trek VI: The Undiscovered Country* and *Star Trek Nemesis)*, Charlotte Douglas & Susan Kearny *(The Battle of Betazed)*, John M. Ford *(The Final Reflection)*, David R. George III *(Mission: Gamma* Book 1: *Twilight,* "Iron and Sacrifice"), Christie Golden *(Homecoming, The Farther Shore)*, Robert Greenberger *(Doors Into Chaos, A Time to Love, A Time to Hate)*, J.G. Hertzler & Jeffrey Lang *(The Left Hand of Destiny* Books 1 & 2), Heather Jarman *(Balance of Nature, Andor: Paradigm)*, J. Noah Kym *(Bajor: Fragments and Omens)*, David Mack ("Twilight's Wrath," *Small World)*, Michael A. Martin & Andy Mangels *(Trill: Unjoined)*, Terri Osborne ("Three Sides to Every Story"), Kevin Ryan *(Errand of Fury* Book 1:

Seeds of Rage), Josepha Sherman & Susan Shwartz (*Vulcan's Heart*, the *Vulcan's Soul* trilogy), Robert Simpson (*Lesser Evil*), Aaron Sorkin (*The West Wing*), John Vornholt (*Gemworld*), and J. Steven York & Christina F. York (*Spin*). Thanks also to GraceAnne Andreassi DeCandido, Jennifer Heddle, Steve Mollman, and Man Fai Wan for various and sundry bits of assistance. And I suppose I should thank myself, since I pilfered rather liberally from my own past *Star Trek* work.

The usual suspects: the Geek Patrol, the Malibu Gang, the Forebearance (who were especially useful kibbitzers on this one), and all the folks on the online bulletin boards (www.psiphi.org, www.trekbbs.com, www.startrekbooks.com, www.booktrek.tk, www.startreknow.com, www.trekweb.com, and the various *Star Trek* novel-related boards on groups.yahoo.com). Plus, one cannot forget the many *Star Trek* reference books floating around, in particular *The Star Trek Encyclopedia* by Mike & Denise Okuda, with Debbie Mirek, and *Star Charts* by Geoffrey Mandel.

And finally, thanks to Aoki, the new kitten who came home with us right around the time I started this book, and whose enthusiasm, affection, and all-around cuteness kept me going during those long days and nights of writing.

ABOUT THE AUTHOR

KEITH R.A. DeCANDIDO wrote his first *Star Trek* novel in high school. Proving this is a just universe, that piece of immature work never saw the light of day. Fifteen years later, WildStorm published his *Star Trek: The Next Generation* comic book miniseries *Perchance to Dream*, which was a much better piece of writing. Since then, Keith has written and edited a wide variety of *Star Trek* material in an equally wide variety of media. His most recent *Treks* include the *USA Today* best-selling *A Time for War, a Time for Peace*, the novel that introduced President Nan Bacco; Book 3 in the *I.K.S. Gorkon* series, *Enemy Territory;* the novella *Ferenginar: Satisfaction Is Not Guaranteed* in *Worlds of Star Trek: Deep Space Nine*, Volume 3; the eBook *Security*, #54 in the monthly *Star Trek: S.C.E.* series; the short story "Letting Go" in the *Star Trek: Voyager* anthology *Distant Shores;* and editing the anthology *Tales from the Captain's Table*, for which he also wrote the story *"IoDnI'pu' vavpu' je."* Outside of *Star Trek*, Keith has written the acclaimed fantasy novel *Dragon Precinct;* the first novels in the series of books based on *Farscape* and *Gene Roddenberry's Andromeda;* the novelizations of *Serenity* and both *Resident Evil* films; *Doctor Who* and *Xena* short stories; two Spider-Man novels, one with José R. Nieto in 1998 *(Venom's Wrath)*, one solo in 2005 *(Down These*

Mean Streets); and much more. Keith—whose work has been praised by *Entertainment Weekly, Booklist, TV Zone, Cinescape, Dreamwatch, Library Journal, Starlog,* and *Publishers Weekly*—is also a musician and an avid New York Yankees fan. He lives in the Bronx with his girlfriend and the world's two goofiest cats. Learn too much about Keith at his official Web site at DeCandido.net, or just send him silly emails at keith@decandido.net.

As many as 1 in 3 Americans
have HIV and don't know it.

TAKE CONTROL.
KNOW YOUR STATUS.
GET TESTED.

To learn more about HIV testing,
or get a free guide to HIV and
other sexually transmitted diseases.

www.knowhivaids.org
1-866-344-KNOW

It all began in the *New York Times* bestselling book *Ashes of Eden*.

James T. Kirk gave up his life and his wife for Starfleet, now he faces a threat that could bring down the entire Federation... his son.

STAR TREK®
CAPTAIN'S GLORY

William Shatner

with

Judith & Garfield Reeves-Stevens

This Summer from Pocket Books

STAR TREK
STRANGE NEW WORLDS
8

**Edited by Dean Wesley Smith
with Elisa J. Kassin
and Paula M. Block**

All-new *Star Trek* adventures——by Fans, For
Fans!

Enter the *Strange New Worlds* short-story
contest!
No Purchase Necessary.

Strange New Worlds 9 entries accepted
between June 1, 2005 and October 1, 2005.

To see the Contest Rules please visit
www.simonsays.com/st